ALYS CLARE

Heart of Ice

HODDER &
STOUGHTON

First published in Great Britain in 2006 by Hodder & Stoughton
A division of Hodder Headline

A Hodder & Stoughton Book

1

A CIP catalogue record for this title
is available from the British Library

ISBN 0 340 83115 4

Typeset in Plantin Light by Hewer Text UK Ltd, Edinburgh
Printed and bound by Mackays of Chatham Ltd, Chatham, Kent

Hodder Headline's policy is to use papers that are natural, renewable
and recyclable products and made from wood grown in sustainable
forests. The logging and manufacturing processes are expected to
conform to the environmental regulations of the country of origin.

Hodder & Stoughton Ltd
A division of Hodder Headline
338 Euston Road
London NW1 3BH

For my brother Tim Harris
with much love
(and in the faint hope of replacing
the *Autocar* on his bedside table)

Tua pulchra facies
me fay planszer milies,
pectus habet glacies;
a remender
statim vivus fierem
per un baser.

Your lovely face
makes me weep a thousand tears;
your heart is of ice;
in the semblance of a cure
a kiss
would give me back my life.

From *Carmina Burana: cantiones profanae*
(Author's translation)

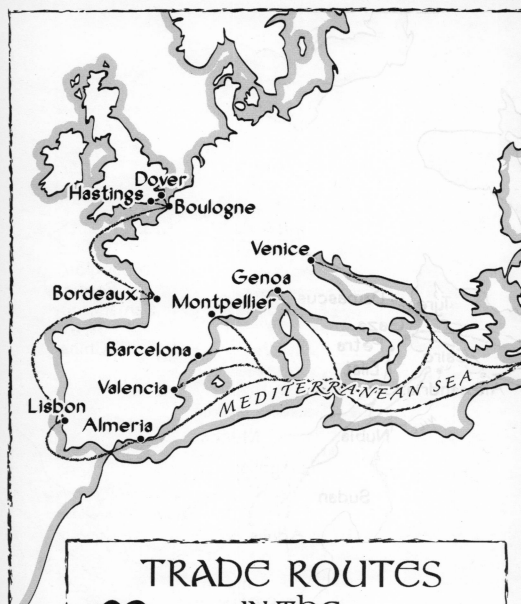

Hastings
Dover
Boulogne
Venice
Genoa
Bordeaux
Montpellier
Barcelona
Valencia
MEDITERRANEAN SEA
Lisbon
Almeria

TRADE ROUTES
IN THE
MEDITERRANEAN
c.1200

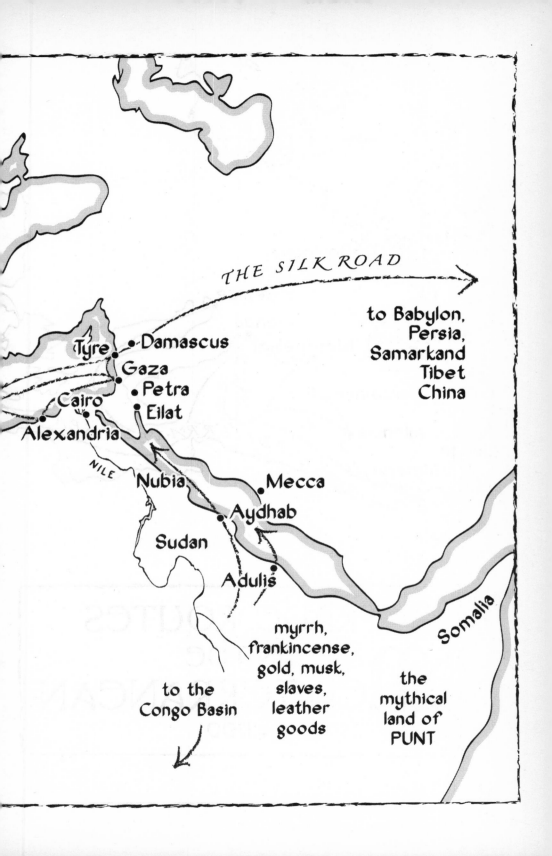

PROLOGUE

In the port of Boulogne, the enemy lay hidden. The journey –
by land and by sea over thousands of miles – was almost at an
end; all that remained was the narrow band of water that
separated continental Europe from England.

And that would be crossed tonight . . .

The epic voyage had begun in an obscure land far to the south,
in the dark heart of a steamy river basin whose few inhabitants
were utterly ignorant of the races and the civilisations of
Western Europe; as, indeed, most people in those temperate
latitudes were ignorant of them, few even knowing that the vast
and secretive continent of Africa existed. The enemy was born
there in the heat and the humidity and its first hiding place was
not with humans but with a troupe of monkeys. Unwittingly
carrying the foe with them, the monkeys travelled slowly north-
eastwards until one of their number, weakened and falling
behind the rest, was caught in a hunter's trap. The hunter
butchered the little creature and smoked its flesh, later enjoying
it as a rare delicacy and savouring each slow mouthful.

The hunter went on his way. At first all was well, although
he was increasingly troubled by a wound on his hand. He had
nicked the flesh of his left forefinger as he stripped the
monkey's flesh from its bones and now the cut was weeping
and pus-filled; its painful throbbing kept the hunter awake at
night. But such inconveniences were quite normal in his hard
life and the handicap did not prevent him from proceeding on

his way. He had a small cargo of slaves to trade with one of his usual contacts but he was one short: as he approached the coast and entered more populous regions, he kept his eyes and ears open and soon came across what he was looking for.

She was young – perhaps thirteen or fourteen – and exquisitely lovely. Tall, lithe, well-muscled but slender, she had put on a clean robe in a bright pattern of red and yellow and wound her hair into an intricate braid; she had to fetch water from the spring and there was a fair chance that the young man she liked might be there too. Sadly for the girl, he was not; instead the slave trader lay in wait for her and, as she bent to fill her calabash, he leapt on her, threw a heavy piece of sacking over her head and had her bound, gagged and helpless before she could even draw breath.

When at long last the sack was removed, she found herself in a small and stinking hut chained to four other women. Dazed and in deep shock – the slave trader had raped her twice on the journey and she was bleeding from the wounds he had inflicted – she sat slumped in a corner with no will left to care about what might happen to her next.

Soon afterwards – perhaps four or five days, she did not know – the girl and her companions were sold to a Muslim spice trader for shipment up the Red Sea to Eilat. Despite the girl's filthy and bloodstained appearance and her catatonic state, she was still beautiful; the merchant had her hosed down and he took her to his narrow cabin where he too raped her.

By now she was very sick. As the merchant's lust was sated his sense returned and suddenly he was very afraid. Observing the girl, he listened to her moans and noted the shivering, the bright flush of high fever, the vomiting, the passage of bloody and watery faeces. He made an attempt to rouse her and demand to know what ailed her but she was too far gone to respond. She was deeply unconscious but not quite dead; the merchant hastened the inevitable by throwing her over the side.

The Muslim merchant fell sick as he sailed into Eilat. He made haste to unload and sell his cargo; the remaining slaves were bound for Egypt and the spices were to be traded with a regular contact of the Muslim, a Levantine whose caravans trudged the overland route from the Red Sea to Petra and Gaza. The Levantine cared for his Muslim associate, taking the sick man into his own home and tending him, trying to spoon cool lemon water into his parched mouth and washing him when he soiled himself. When the Muslim died, the Levantine was careful to have him buried according to the rites of the man's own faith.

The Levantine set off for Petra and the coast, where he had an appointment to meet a Venetian who would buy his myrrh and ship it to Europe. The Venetian put in to Gaza having sailed from Tyre, where he had just picked up a cargo of silk. He and the Levantine celebrated the satisfactory completion of their business by eating a meal together, in the course of which the Levantine handed the Venetian a piece of bread. Neither man noticed the strange little blister on the Levantine's hand, which had just burst and which weeped two or three minute droplets of clear fluid on to the bread.

In the cramped quarters of his ship, the Venetian's sickness took hold swiftly and raced through his system. He had been at sea for months and his diet had been typically poor throughout that time; his resistance was low. By the time the ship put in at Genoa, the Venetian and several of the crew were dead and more were sick. But his associates hushed up the deaths; such things were terrible for business and, God knew, times were hard enough, what with so many ships now muscling in on the highly lucrative spice trade between the East and Europe. The death ship was unloaded with all haste and the various consignments of its cargo were hurried on their way. Among the items were crates of spices bound for Montpellier, Barcelona, Almeria, Lisbon, Bordeaux; there was also a crate of ivory and a large wooden box of frankincense, musk and myrrh that were destined for Boulogne for onward shipment to England. The Genoese captain, unaware of what had happened on the voyage from Gaza, sailed out of the port and set a course for Montpellier.

Two of the Genoese captain's sailors had come up from Gaza on the death ship. It had not been a deliberate act to infect the Genoese ship: they had seen their former shipmates fall sick and die but, still healthy themselves (or, at least, as healthy as any other sailor of the age), they believed themselves to have been spared.

They were wrong.

As the Genoese ship left Barcelona, one of the two became ill. Fearing the worst, his shipmate from the death ship fell into a panic and was quickly brought before the captain. An enlightened man, the Genoese captain had the good sense to isolate the sick man and, within his limited powers, he did his best to have the wretch cared for.

Days passed. The dreaded rapid progression of the disease failed to happen; perhaps because the weather was stormy and cooler now as the ship sailed towards the Pillars of Hercules; perhaps because the Genoese captain was a stickler for cleanliness. It was his habit to insist that his crew and their quarters were regularly doused in sea water and in addition he used some of the spices that made up the majority of his cargo to burn as purifying incense and to scent the water with which he made his companions wash their hands and faces before eating.

Nevertheless, the disease continued to spread.

The captain and his senior crew remained well but below, in the crowded conditions where the crew lived, ate, urinated, defecated and slept so close together, men continued to fall sick. The captain was a devout man as well as a clean and enlightened one; he made up his mind that, whatever the cost to himself and his crew, they must keep themselves apart from other men while the sickness lasted. He decided to drop the last of his cargo at the final destination – Boulogne – and then sail back to Genoa in ballast and hope that the disease would have burned itself out by the time he reached home. It was a sound and conscientious plan and it ought to have worked; unfortunately, despite the captain's best efforts, one of the men slipped ashore at Boulogne.

The captain faced a dilemma. Did he send other men to hunt for the fugitive and bring him back on board into the captain's self-imposed quarantine? Or did he sail off and, praying that the man was not infected, leave him behind? After much agonised thought, the captain decided that to send more men ashore to search for the missing man would only increase the risk of infection. With a heavy heart and a guilty conscience, he ordered the ship to be prepared for sea and set sail for home.

The fugitive watched his ship disappear into the misty night. Silently rejoicing – wasn't he the clever one, getting away from both the ship and the awful secret it carried? – but his happiness was short lived. Soon he began to feel ill, and the faint symptoms escalated so quickly that he was unable to fool himself that it was merely a matter of his body adjusting to dry land after so long at sea. He tried to find help, knocking on door after door, but the people of Boulogne were used to importunate sailors begging for their help and they firmly turned him away.

The sick man crawled off to die.

He was found by a kindly Hastings merchant staying in the port while he waited to take ship back home to England with the large consignment of myrrh and frankincense which he had just bought. For a day or two the merchant tended the sick sailor as best he could, in his anxiety biting his nails and tearing at his cuticles until they bled, but any help he offered came far too late and the sailor died. The merchant, aware that the ship that would take him across the Channel had just docked and that he needed to make haste to see her captain, gave a local lad a few coins and ordered him to dispose of the sailor's corpse. Then he hurried away. (The lad pocketed the coins and, as soon as the Hastings merchant had gone, tipped the body into the harbour.)

The merchant made his way to an inn where he washed his hands (the sailor had been steeped in his own filth) and ordered food and drink for a swiftly consumed meal before joining his ship. Then he walked down to the quay, where, boarding the ship, he met up with a young man who was also returning to England. This man was the assistant and apprentice of a rich Newenden apothecary and he was on his way home with a parcel of rare ingredients that his master had ordered from the great fair at Troyes, in the Champagne country south of Paris. Believing themselves to be the only passengers, the two men settled down together to pass the voyage as comfortably as they could. It seemed to the Hastings merchant that the young man was scared out of his wits; kind-hearted soul that he was, he made up his mind to encourage his companion to unburden himself in the hope that he might be able to offer the younger man his help.

Unseen by either man, nor by the captain or the crew of the small vessel, someone else crept aboard just as the ship slipped her moorings.

Elsewhere, the disease was already beginning to die out. The inhabitants of Eilat and Gaza, accustomed to plague and possessing the knowledge of how to restrict its spread, had quickly taken the necessary measures. In Genoa too, they had managed to contain the disease and only a handful had sickened and died; a lucky half dozen had fallen ill and later recovered. On board the Genoese ship, now sailing across the Bay of Biscay, there had been no new cases. The sailor who had jumped ship in Boulogne was dead and his body was at the bottom of the sea.

But the well-meaning Hastings merchant had touched the sailor's sores and blisters in his vain attempts to help the man's pain; both the blood and the bodily fluids of the dying man had entered the merchant's body through the small cut that he had made with his own teeth in the cuticle of his forefinger. Unbeknownst to the merchant, the deadly virus was even now multiplying in his system and soon it would make its presence felt.

The terrible enemy was on its way to England.

Back in his comfortable home in Hastings, the merchant developed a high fever and a raging headache. His nervous and reclusive spinster sister took fright and locked herself away, ordering the household's overworked maidservant to take care of the merchant as best she could. What care she was able to provide did the poor man no good whatsoever and he died within a matter of days.

The apothecary's assistant sickened four days after returning to Newenden, suffering from excruciating pains in the joints and a fluctuating fever. His master offered one or two remedies but soon came to the alarming realisation that this ailment, whatever it might be, was beyond his considerable skill. Lending the assistant his horse, he ordered the young man to get himself over to Hawkenlye and see what the good sisters and brothers made of him; the apothecary had a scientist's scepticism about the benefits of the famous holy water spring at Hawkenlye Abbey but considered it was probably worth a try.

And, he reassured himself, if his assistant went to Hawkenlye, the sickness would leave with him.

The apothecary's assistant knew all about Hawkenlye. He had heard the tale of the dying merchant who saw a vision of the Blessed Virgin and, drinking from the spring that she indicated, promptly regained his health. As he rode, slipping in and out of consciousness, his head aching as if a fiend were hammering inside it with a red-hot hammer and his back so painful that he moaned at any variation in his horse's gait, the young man prayed fervently that the Virgin would help him too. The weather was deadly cold; he had wrapped himself in his warmest cloak but sometimes, despite its thickness, found himself shivering so violently that it was all he could do to remain in the saddle. Then suddenly he would be hot, sweating, gasping for air that, when it entered his lungs, seemed to burn like fire.

He rode down into Hawkenlye Vale as the short January light was failing. The path wound along beside what seemed to be a lake or a pond, presently covered with a thin layer of ice that he thought he could hear creaking, as if complaining about the steady increase in its own weight. His sight was fading but he could just make out what seemed to be a huddle of low buildings some distance off. One of them, he fancied, had a cross on its roof.

He slipped off the horse's back and tried to run towards the little chapel. Stumbling, he cried out in what he thought was a loud voice to the Blessed Virgin to come out and find him, take him in her loving arms, give him her healing waters.

His prayers were answered.

Ahead of him a figure stepped out on to the path. His fever-filled mind made his eyes see what he wanted to see and he thought the figure was a woman in a blue robe with a kindly smile on her beautiful face. Lurching towards her, he said the words of her special prayer, eager, hands held out to her, confident that she would help him, heal him.

But the dark figure was not smiling. Was not, indeed, a woman and as far away from being the mother of God as it was possible to be.

The apothecary's assistant had no time to be afraid. A blissful expression on his face, he knelt with open arms before the figure in expectation of a cool hand descending on his hot forehead in blessing.

It was not a cool hand. It was a club, wielded with such force and such skill that one swift blow was all that was necessary to end the young man's life.

After checking to make sure he was dead, the dark figure quickly went through the contents of the pouch attached to the young man's belt, then rolled him across the path and over the frosty grass that edged the pond. Breaking the ice with the heel of his boot, he slid the corpse into the black water. Then he mounted the apothecary's horse and rode away.

The temperature plummeted that night. By morning, the pond and its deadly secret were covered in a thick sheet of ice.

PART ONE

The Enemy

I

The mood at Hawkenlye Abbey was festive. A short spell of very cold weather had covered the pond in the Vale with almost a hand's breadth of ice and, in the spirit of turning an affliction into a gift, the monks and lay brothers were trying to teach themselves to slide across the ice on their sandalled feet without falling over. Brother Augustus recalled having once been told that tying deer-bone blades to the feet increased the speed at which it was possible to glide across the ice and he was busy experimenting; so far he had only a sore thumb and a large bruise on his backside to show for his troubles.

Word spread quickly that there was fun to be had in Hawkenlye Vale and soon others, at first children but then their older sisters and brothers and their parents as well, began to arrive and clamoured to be allowed to join in. The local people were in the middle of a cold, miserable and desperately poor winter, there was never enough to eat and Christmas was a dim memory; nobody needed any encouragement to stop what they were doing and remember what it was to be playful and carefree. Old Brother Firmin, who felt it was one thing for the brethren to risk life, limb and death by drowning but quite another for outsiders to do so, cast suspicious looks at the ice and shook his head dubiously. Brother Saul, observing the disappointed faces of the onlookers, said he would test the ice by walking the Abbey's hefty cob across it once or twice. With the eyes of the growing crowd upon him, he did so; once, twice across the pond and two or three times along its length, he led the patient horse and listened somewhat nervously for the first sound of cracking ice.

No such sound came. With a grin, Saul called out, 'The ice is strong. Come and try your skills!'

Catching the air of celebration, Brother Erse asked permission to make a fire and, using birch shavings and some seasoned odds and ends of wood from his carpentry bench to get it started, soon had a good blaze going. Brother Augustus abandoned his experiments with the bone skates and, with Brother Adrian, set about preparing a large pot of thin but nourishing broth whose chief ingredients were the carcases of three or four fowl scrounged from the Abbey's kitchen, some onions, some garlic, several large handfuls of barley and a big bunch of dried herbs. They suspended the pot over Brother Erse's fire and soon an appetising smell was wafting out over the pond; very quickly a line of hungry children (and not a few of their parents) formed beside Erse's fire. More monks came to help and the broth was ladled into the rough earthenware mugs that the brethren kept for the use of pilgrims coming to the shrine in the Vale. The monks imposed order on the queue and started handing out the broth to the visitors. Sounds of laughter and merriment floated up to the Abbey; before long, some of the nuns came down to the Vale to find out what was going on.

Among them was Sister Caliste, who worked in the infirmary under Sister Euphemia, one of the most senior of the nuns. Sister Caliste reported back to the infirmarer, who in turn told the Abbess Helewise. Just as the sun was setting, the Abbess went to see for herself.

Brother Firmin, watching her face as her grey eyes looked slowly from one end of the pond to the other, taking in the cheerful, red-cheeked people struggling to keep their balance and laughing loudly when inevitably they failed, waited apprehensively for her to speak. 'I am sorry, my lady Abbess, not to have asked for your permission,' he began, 'but in truth—'

She held up a hand and, with a smile, interrupted him. 'No need to apologise, Brother Firmin,' she said. 'I do not think any permission was necessary; there is nothing wrong with making people happy on a cold winter's day.' Her glance lighted on the remains of the broth in its blackened pot. 'And, in charity, how could the sternest heart object to the provision of hot broth to hungry people?'

Brother Firmin decided her question was rhetorical and kept his peace.

The Abbess put a light hand on his arm. 'Sister Euphemia will not thank us if there are too many broken limbs to be treated,' she said, 'but, otherwise, you and the brethren have done splendidly. Carry on, Brother Firmin.' With another smile, she gave him a quick nod of approval and, turning, set out along the path that led back up to the Abbey.

Brother Firmin could not be sure – his eyesight was not what it had been – but he saw his dignified superior stop and turn as she left the pond's shore and he was pretty sure she gave the frozen water and the happy revellers a very wistful look.

There were two more days of fun and games on the ice. Then overnight a thaw set in and the next morning the ice had begun to melt. The pond was declared strictly out of bounds and everyone went back to work.

In the middle of the afternoon, Brothers Adrian and Micah were sent off along the path that ran alongside the pond to repair a large hole that had been opened up by the frost and which Brother Firmin had declared might be dangerous; 'Some poor innocent soul,' he suggested, 'might come a-hopping and a-skipping along the track, all unsuspecting, and catch their foot in that great crack and, what with the water being so near, it could be very dangerous.'

Adrian forbore to point out that even if this poor unsuspecting person did fall in the pond, then the mishap would be unlikely to prove fatal, the pond being only as deep as the length of a man's forearm just there where the crack in the path snaked its way across the packed earth. Micah was about to remark that it was rare for visitors to the Vale to hop or skip but, catching sight of Brother Firmin's careworn and concerned face, he changed his mind. 'Of course, Brother,' he said gently, 'Adrian and I will see to it straight away. Don't you worry; there won't be any nasty accidents.'

The two monks collected some tools and set off along the track, remarking to each other – softly, since they did not want to hurt his feelings – on Brother Firmin's engaging little ways and his general resemblance to a fussy old mother hen. They found the crack in the path and were just rolling up their sleeves and spitting on their palms in preparation for beginning their excavating, digging and filling work when something in the water a few paces along the bank caught Micah's eye.

He hurried off to have a closer look. Then, as soon as he saw what it was, he paled and, in a voice that sounded as if there was a strong hand at his throat, said in a hoarse whisper, 'Adrian, run for help. God help us all, but it looks as though Brother Firmin was right – there's some poor soul face-down in our pond and I reckon he's drowned!'

Two brothers raced back along the track with Brother Adrian, carrying a hurdle between them. With gentle hands, the four monks pulled and dragged at the sodden clothing until they managed to get a good enough grip to haul the body out of the pond. Even this short immersion turned their hands blue with cold; the waters of the pond had, after all, only lately thawed. The body was laid on the hurdle and, with one monk at each corner, they bore the dripping burden back to the settlement by the chapel. Brother Firmin was deeply distressed – 'If only I had noticed that crack sooner! Oh, but it is all my fault!' – and it was left to Brother Saul to take charge. 'You four, take the corpse up to the infirmary,' he said quietly, very aware of the dead body so close by, 'and I'll go on ahead and warn Sister Euphemia.'

Shortly afterwards, Sister Euphemia was standing in a curtained recess at one end of the long infirmary, watching while two of her nursing nuns began carefully to remove the clothing from the corpse in preparation for washing it. Not a pauper, the infirmarer mused to herself, nor yet a rich man, if these garments are a guide; the cloak, tunic and hose are quite new but of poor quality. A young man, she thought, looking at the dead face, not yet twenty, I would guess, and no doubt just beginning to make his way in the world. God bless him, he'll advance no further in *this* world.

She was silently praying for the young man's soul when Sister Caliste said softly, 'He is ready for you, Sister.'

The infirmarer stepped forward and, carefully turning back the spotlessly clean linen sheet with which the nursing nuns had covered the corpse, began her inspection. She worked quickly and thoroughly, barely speaking, and when she was finished she said, 'Sister Caliste, be good enough to hurry and tell Brother Firmin that he can stop beating his breast; this death has come about through no fault of his, since it was not through tripping on any crack in the path that this young man fell in the pond.' Sister Caliste bowed and hastened away. Then, turning to Sister Anne, the infirmarer added, 'And you, Sister, must go and find the Abbess and ask her if she could spare me a moment.' Sister Anne's mouth had dropped open. 'Quickly now!'

With a bob of the head and a muttered 'Yes, Sister,' Anne too scurried off.

Sister Euphemia stood alone by the dead man's body.

Perhaps I am mistaken and have been too hasty to remove the blame from Brother Firmin's cracked path, she thought. Gently she pushed back the wet hair from the corpse's forehead and looked again, studying the front of the head intently for some moments. No, she decided eventually, I am not mistaken.

When, not long afterwards, the Abbess entered the infirmary and, escorted by Sister Caliste, made her way to the curtained recess, Sister Euphemia was quite ready for her. She made her reverence and then said with admirable brevity, 'My lady, this young man has been slain by a blow to the top of his head, after which he either fell or was pushed into the pond. The death must be investigated and we must therefore seek help.'

The Abbess stood quite still, listening to the infirmarer and studying her with expressionless eyes. As soon as Sister Euphemia finished speaking, the Abbess turned to look at the young man lying on the cot. Tenderly she put up a hand and touched her fingertips to the terrible blow on the top of his head. She said calmly, 'Yes, Sister, indeed we must send for help.'

Sister Euphemia opened her mouth to reply but then, as if the Abbess could no longer maintain her air of efficient indifference, she muttered passionately, 'This was done with great force. See, Sister, how the bones of the skull have been crushed! What can he possibly have done to bring down such hatred upon himself? He is but young, and—'

She did not complete her remark. Achieving detachment once more, she straightened up, lifted her head and said, 'I shall send word to Gervase de Gifford down in Tonbridge.'

'And—' the infirmarer began. She stopped herself.

But her superior had already read her mind. 'Yes, Sister,' she said with a faint smile. 'I shall also send word to Sir Josse and ask, if he is not too busy, if he will kindly pay us a visit.'

★

Gervase de Gifford sent a message back to the Abbess that he would be at Hawkenlye first thing in the morning. The monk who had ridden off to New Winnowlands to find Sir Josse d'Acquin did not return that evening, which was no cause for alarm since he would undoubtedly have been pressed to come in, warm himself by Sir Josse's fireside, refresh himself with a good, hot meal and a jug of ale and stay overnight. Expecting just such a turn of events, the Abbess had given the brother – it was young Augustus – permission not to return until morning. She only hoped, as she left the Abbey church after the final office of the day, that he would bring Sir Josse with him . . .

Sister Euphemia was still in the infirmary. She had dismissed the other nuns who earlier had worked on the body with her and now she and the dead man were alone in the privacy of the recess. Beyond the curtains she could hear the sounds of the long infirmary ward settling for the night: there was one of the nuns helping an old man suffering from a hacking cough to pass water before he slept; there was the soft voice of Sister Caliste soothing a fractious child with griping pains in his belly. That sudden shrill cry, swiftly curtailed, was the new-born baby at the far end of the infirmary demanding to be fed and having her demand met. These were the normal sounds that were part of Sister Euphemia's everyday life; she heard them, registered them and dismissed them.

There was something far more alarming right under her eyes.

She went over the body again. It was too soon to share her anxiety for, if she were wrong, then she would have caused a worrying stir all for nothing. And she must be wrong, surely she must! Sister Euphemia found she was praying in quiet desperation, the same words over and over again: *Dear merciful Lord, please let it not be so!*

Think again, she told herself firmly. Reconsider. Go over every inch again.

There was the wound on the top of the head; it looked to Sister Euphemia as if the young man had been struck from directly in front and above. Either his attacker had been a very tall man or else the victim had been on his knees when he was hit. That was the more likely, she decided, for the young man himself was not particularly short and so, to inflict a wound in such a place, the attacker would have had to be a giant of a man. She put her hand to the wound in the skull. Its position was what had prompted her to send the message to Brother Firmin: it was just not possible for someone to trip and fall in such a way that they struck the *top* of their head on the hard ground, unless perhaps they were a professional tumbler. Sister Euphemia smiled wryly at the unlikelihood of this poor young man having been *that*.

And in any case she could almost trace the outline of the weapon that had made that fearful hollow in the young man's skull – she was no longer smiling – and the shape was almost certainly that of a club, or perhaps a stout stick or staff with a bulbous, rounded end. No; she had been right to inform Brother Firmin that he was not to blame. At least he, she reflected, with his conscience eased, is probably having a good night's sleep . . .

She continued her examination of the body. The condition of the skin suggested that the man had been in the water for a few days, although the flesh was still quite firm and there was no sign of decay yet. This, Euphemia reasoned, was no doubt because the water had been so cold; indeed, so cold that it had been ice until this morning. She had observed before that cold temperatures seemed to arrest the decay of both plant and animal matter – including human flesh – and it occurred to her that, until this poor dead body warmed up, it would remain virtually in the same condition in which it first went into the water.

The dead man's eyes had been closed – presumably by one of the monks who pulled him out of the pond – and now Sister Euphemia gently raised one of the eyelids. He'd had light eyes, this young lad; soft blue-grey. Now in death they were blood-shot and the surrounding tissues were red and inflamed. The infirmarer closed the eye again and, putting a hand on the jaw, pressed down firmly and opened the mouth. The roof of the mouth appeared to be covered in small transparent blisters . . .

Then there was nothing else but to look again at what had so alarmed her.

Sister Euphemia closed the mouth and picked up the tallow lamp that stood on a small shelf above the cot where the body lay. Holding it just above the bare shoulders, she bent down for a closer look. Was she seeing things? Was it a product of her tired eyes and the dim light, or were there really spots on the young man's face, chest and abdomen?

Instinctively the infirmarer put her hand over her mouth although, since she had been in close proximity to the body for some time, the gesture was futile; she would long ago have breathed in whatever noxious humours it might be emitting and it was far too late to worry about that now. But her nursing instincts were automatic and, she was very afraid, she had good reason to be wary of this particular body.

She stared at the spots. They were flat and did not appear to contain fluid. In some places they had flared up and joined together into large blotches. On the shoulders there was a sort of – Sister Euphemia searched for the word – a sort of *scaly* look to the skin. She touched one of the roughened patches with a fingernail and a tiny piece of skin flaked off. Swiftly she wiped her hand with a piece of linen soaked in lavender oil, carefully cleaning under the nail with which she had scraped the skin, and the familiar smell of the oil – so clean, so heartening and refreshing – calmed her.

After a moment she returned to her inspection. Placing her

hands on the body's right hip, she tensed the muscles in her strong arms and pushed the corpse away from her until it was lying on its side. For all that the nuns had thoroughly washed the dead man, there was still a faint reminder of the stench; undressing him, they had found a nasty surprise when it came to pulling off his hose and the long under chemise, for he had soiled himself. Copiously; his poor stomach, Sister Euphemia thought compassionately, must have been in a frightful turmoil. She studied the buttocks and the area around the anus, as if the dead man were a baby and she was checking for the rash that comes when an infant is left too long unwashed. The man's skin was red and sore-looking; whatever had caused the flux in his bowels, the condition had been present for some time.

The infirmarer wiped her hands again and then gently laid the body flat once more, drawing up the sheet and covering the dead man from his head to his toes. She felt, despite herself and her professionalism, an attachment to this young man, unreasonable since she had no idea who he was and had no reason to mourn him. Except, she said to herself, the fact that he was young, quite handsome and just starting out in adult life, and someone has chosen to halt him in his tracks with that savage blow.

Sister Euphemia put her hand on the tangled brown hair – it was still damp – and, closing her eyes, asked God to see His way to admitting this poor soul to Paradise.

Then, worn out, very anxious and with aching feet and back, she left the recess, put the bar across its entrance that was the accepted signal for *do not enter* and, with dragging steps, made her way slowly to the dormitory and her bed.

2

Josse had been both surprised and pleased to see Brother Augustus ride into his courtyard. More than pleased: he had found himself hurrying down the steps into the courtyard to embrace the young man as if he were a long-lost son, an action which, when Josse stopped to consider it some time later, suggested to him that he might just possibly be lonely.

Darkness had fallen by the time Augustus arrived and the temperature had dropped. Before the lad could say much more than 'Good evening, Sir Josse', Josse had yelled for Will to come and see to the Abbey's cob, to Ella to get something hot to eat as fast as she could and to Augustus himself to hurry on inside and warm himself by the fire.

Augustus was wearing his customary sandals and his feet were so white that it looked as if they could not be part of a living human body.

Josse tutted as he fussed round the young man. 'Could the Abbey not have found you a pair of boots?' he muttered. And, noticing the thin black fabric over the boy's shivering back, 'Would a winter cloak be too much to ask?'

Ella brought a mug of hot, spiced, watered wine and thrust it into Augustus's hands. He said a polite 'Thank you', to which the taciturn Ella responded with a sound that might equally well have been a reply or a brief attack of wind. Augustus looked up at Josse, an irrepressible grin spreading across his face, and Josse hurriedly despatched Ella back to her kitchen.

'She's rather shy,' he whispered to Augustus.

Augustus nodded knowingly, as if gauche serving women were his daily lot. 'The wine's wonderful,' he said. His nose was in the mug and he seemed to be breathing in the spicy fumes. 'It's going straight to my toes.'

'Ella will bring you food soon,' Josse said confidently. 'I'll ask her to make a bed up for you, lad – it's far too late to ride back to the Abbey tonight.' Then belatedly he said, 'What can I do for you?'

Augustus grinned again. 'Sorry, Sir Josse, I should have said straight away. The Abbess sends her compliments and asks if you could possibly come to Hawkenlye because there's a young man been hit on the head and thrown in the lake in the Vale. It was frozen, you see,' he added, 'and the *cadaver* only came to the surface when the ice melted today.'

Cadaver, Josse thought. The careful way in which young Gussie had pronounced the word suggested it did not form part of his day-to-day vocabulary and Josse decided he must have been listening to the infirmarer.

'The dead man was hit on the head,' he repeated. 'He could not have tripped on a patch of ice on the path, perhaps, and done the damage accidentally?'

'No.' Augustus spoke firmly. 'To hit himself where the wound is, he'd have had to be walking on his hands.'

'I see.' It did not seem very likely. 'A young man, you said?'

'Aye.'

'What sort of a person?'

Augustus shrugged. 'I can't say, Sir Josse. I helped get him out of the water and carry him up to the infirmary but you can't accurately judge a man's station in life when he's soaking wet and dead.'

'No, I suppose not.' Josse was thinking. 'Nobody knows who he is?'

'No. I don't think so.'

'Hm.'

'The Abbess has sent for Gervase de Gifford,' Augustus offered. 'Maybe he'll recognise the body.'

'Aye.' Again, Josse hardly heard. He was busy with his conscience because, for quite a few moments, he had been so pleased at this summons back to Hawkenlye that he had quite forgotten to be sorry about its cause.

Josse and Brother Augustus rode through the Abbey gates in the middle of the following morning. Augustus offered to take Josse's horse off to the stables and Josse made his way straight to the Abbess's little room at the far end of the cloister.

She got up to greet him, advancing towards him and holding out her hands to take his. 'Thank you for coming,' she said. 'Dear Sir Josse – what a friend you are.'

Embarrassed, he dropped her hands as quickly as he could and waved away her gratitude. 'Young Gussie said that Gervase de Gifford had been summoned,' he said. 'Is he here?'

The Abbess frowned. 'He intended to come up first thing this morning,' she said. 'However, he has sent word that another matter has called him away. Knowing you were to arrive, I believe he must have thought that this other matter took precedence.'

Josse could not tell from her carefully neutral tone what the Abbess thought about this, so wisely he made no comment. 'Gus told me about the dead man in the pond,' he said instead. 'Shall we go to see him?'

'Of course.'

He stepped back to let her precede him and she led the way around the cloister and across to the infirmary, where she turned to her left and, removing a bar that had been put across its narrow entrance, went into a small curtained recess. Wondering about the barrier – and why, indeed, they had just ignored it – he moved to stand beside her in front of the narrow cot.

The body lying on the cot was covered with a sheet.

Sister Euphemia must have seen the Abbess and Josse walk along to the recess; she appeared almost immediately and, with a brief bow to Josse and a deeper one for the Abbess, said quietly, 'I'll show you the wound, Sir Josse.'

He watched as she folded back the sheet to expose the head; he noticed how careful she was that the rest of the body remained covered. He looked at the blow that had killed the man and he saw straight away what Augustus had meant. 'Aye, the man was murdered,' he muttered, half to himself. Glancing up at the infirmarer, he asked, 'Any more marks on him, Sister?'

The infirmarer exchanged a look with the Abbess. Neither spoke for a moment; then the Abbess said, 'Come with me, please, Sir Josse. I will show you the dead man's clothing and his pouch. They are back in my room.'

Increasingly mystified, Josse followed her out of the infirmary.

'Here,' she said, picking up a dark bundle from the floor and depositing it on her table, 'are his garments. Sister Euphemia has been drying them by the fire but they are still a little damp.'

Josse inspected the hose, the tunic, the undershirt and the cloak. The items were cheap; the linen shirt was of poor quality and the underarm seams had split. Its hem, he noticed, was stained. Both the hose and the shirt smelled unpleasant.

'He suffered a flux of the bowels,' the Abbess said. 'Despite his immersion in the lake, the odour is still detectable.'

Josse nodded. He was looking at the cloak – it was of heavy wool and, he thought, would have dragged the body down as it soaked up water – and unpleasant images were filling his mind of dark water and a sheen of ice forming. But, he reassured himself, the poor lad would have known nothing about all that, not with such a frightful wound. He'd have been dead before he hit the ground.

'There is also this.' Josse looked up to see that the Abbess was holding out a leather pouch. 'It was attached to his belt and it, too, we have dried as best we could.'

Josse took it from her. 'Is there anything inside it?'

'See for yourself.' She sounded unlike herself, Josse thought; she was distant, almost aloof . . .

He turned his attention to the pouch. There was a small pocket sewn inside and it looked as if someone had searched it with a rough hand, for the stitching had been torn. Had robbery been the motive for this death, then? Josse put his hand right down inside the pocket and his fingers touched something hard, cold and round. More than one thing; extracting what he had found, Josse looked down on five heavy coins.

'If he was killed for the contents of his pouch, then the assailant did not make a very thorough search,' he said. 'See, my lady? These coins were tucked away right at the bottom of the pouch's pocket.'

She looked. 'I see.'

Josse put his hand back inside the pouch. There was something else . . . it was cold and slightly damp and felt like a little bag made of waxed cloth. Carefully drawing it out, he put it down on the Abbess's table.

'What's this?' he asked, not really expecting an answer; the Abbess's strange mood was worrying him.

She leaned close to him, studying the bag. She sniffed then, bending down so that her nose was right over the bag, sniffed again. 'I believe,' she said slowly, 'it may be a potion. A remedy.' Eyes on Josse's – and for the first time she began to look like herself – she added, 'I've smelt this stuff, whatever it is, before; I'm sure I have.' She frowned. 'It's used for . . .' Giving up, she shrugged, smiling at him. 'I don't know. Come on!'

He turned to watch her as she scooped up the little bag and strode out of the room. 'Where are we going?'

The Abbess did not answer but then she didn't really need to because Josse had guessed. Pacing along behind her – she was almost running – he followed her along the path that led round in front of the Abbey church and along inside the wall to the herb garden where, cosy in her small and fragrant little hut, the herbalist was sitting peacefully tying bunches of dried rosemary.

The herbalist got to her feet and bowed to the Abbess, giving Josse a quick smile and what could have been a wink. Barely pausing to acknowledge the greeting, the Abbess thrust the small bag at Sister Tiphaine and said, 'Can you tell us what this is?'

Sister Tiphaine took the bag in careful hands and went to stand outside the hut, so that the full daylight fell on to it. She did as the Abbess had done and sniffed at it several times. Then she pinched one corner of the bag between finger and thumb and sniffed again.

'Smells of lemon balm and vervain,' she observed. 'That's interesting . . .' Glancing up at the Abbess, she said, 'May I open it?'

'Yes.'

The herbalist spread a clean piece of linen on her work bench and then took up a small knife and sliced through the string that held the neck of the bag closed; the string, Josse had noticed, was suffering from its time under water and appeared to have shrunk, making the knot quite impossible to untie. Then Sister Tiphaine gently shook the bag's contents on to the piece of linen, picking them over and inspecting each item.

After quite a long time – Josse could sense the Abbess restraining her impatience – Sister Tiphaine spoke. 'This is a remedy,' she announced.

'That much we have already surmised. What is it for?' demanded the Abbess.

'There is a mixture of herbs here,' Sister Tiphaine replied. 'They are used to treat a variety of symptoms.'

'Well?'

If Sister Tiphaine had also noted the Abbess's unusual asperity, she gave no sign. Calmly she began to list the ingredients in the bag and to describe the sickness that they treated.

'Lemon balm, that calms and helps soothe a headache. There's yarrow, that's for flux of the bowels.'

'Yes, yes, we know full well he suffered from that.'

With a quick glance at the Abbess, the herbalist continued. 'There's wormwood; now that's good for treating gripes in the belly and they do say it brings down a fever, although me, I find the bitter taste puts folks off swallowing it down. Rue, now, that'll help calm a headache, as will this' – she held up a tiny stem of some withered plant – 'which is wild marjoram. And here's a piece of mandrake; expensive, that is, and it's hardly surprising given how folks fear it and don't dare handle it.'

'So this remedy is for the flux, fever and headache?' The Abbess, Josse thought, was trying to hurry the herbalist along.

But Sister Tiphaine would not be hurried. 'Hmm,' she murmured, still picking over the bag's contents. 'Here's water mint and peppermint – both for the bowels – and quince; now that's normally saved for when the bowel leaks blood. And here's henbane; that's a strong remedy and few use it.'

'What does it do?' Josse asked.

'It eases pain, although take too much and you'll never feel pain again.'

As she spoke the herbalist was deftly dividing the little sack's contents into two piles, one containing those items that she had already identified and described, one containing nothing except some small, shrivelled flower heads, some withered leaves and some coarse grains of a bronze-coloured substance.

'What are those?' the Abbess asked.

'The granules are ground resin of myrrh. It relieves pain, especially in the muscles and in the stomach. These flowers are marigolds and these' – she pointed to the cracked, crumbling leaves – 'are vervain. The vervain is unusual because it's a magical remedy and I am surprised to find it included in this potion.'

'Magical?' the Abbess and Josse said together.

'Aye. Folks say it has the power to protect a fighting man. Also lads and lassies put it in love potions.'

'What is it doing here?'

'I cannot say, my lady, other than to tell you that it is said to have another purpose. As do the marigolds.' Sister Tiphaine frowned, almost as if she was reluctant to go on.

'What purpose?' the Abbess's voice was barely above a whisper.

The herbalist looked up, first at the Abbess and then at Josse. Then she said, 'Both are said to ward off the foreign pestilence that folks call the plague.'

'*Plague?*' Josse's horrified cry seemed to echo in the small room. Turning to the Abbess, he said, 'My lady, there is no time to waste, we must—'

But she was not looking shocked or frightened; she was staring at him with kindness and compassion in her eyes. He thought about how strange she had seemed, how detached. And then he thought about the body on the cot, covered carefully right up to the forehead. And about the barrier that had been erected across the entrance to the recess where the dead man lay.

'This was no surprise,' he said wonderingly. 'You already knew the dead man was suffering from the pestilence. Didn't you?'

And yet you brought me here, he wanted to shout, led me right up to where the victim lay and deliberately kept me in ignorance as to what killed him!

But he kept the flare of anger under control. And he thought, no, that is not right; the pestilence did not kill him, for the man was murdered.

The Abbess seemed to be waiting until his train of thought ran its course. When at last she spoke, it was to say, 'Sir Josse, it is true that I suspected. Sister Euphemia told me today that when she studied the dead man's body last night there were signs of a rash, although when she looked again first thing this morning, it had faded. Now we cannot say for sure what the sickness was, for, as Sister Euphemia points out, many diseases bring spots and not all are fatal.'

Josse tried to cheer himself up by trying to think of a few non-fatal rash-producing diseases but the attempt was a dismal failure. 'Were there—' He started again. 'Did the infirmarer observe any other marks on the body to suggest the pestilence?'

The Abbess shook her head. 'Not those that I suspect you have in mind. The eyes were bloodshot and inflamed; there were strange spots inside the mouth.' She put out her hand and briefly touched Josse's arm. 'No black swellings,' she said softly. 'Thank the Lord.'

'Amen,' Josse said fervently.

For some time there was silence in the herbalist's hut. Then Sister Tiphaine spoke. 'I would suggest,' she said slowly, 'that a dead man with the pestilence in his body is less of a danger than a living one. Unless you're planning on eating him,' she added, quite mystifying Josse, who could not see the relevance of the remark.

Neither, it seemed, could the Abbess. With a look of faint distaste at Sister Tiphaine – who noticed and, observed by Josse but not by the Abbess, gave a quick grin – she pointed at the contents of the little bag and said, 'Where, Sister, do you think the victim could have acquired this remedy?'

Sister Tiphaine began gathering the ingredients together,

pushing them carefully back into the bag. 'Not from some village wise woman, that's for sure,' she said, 'for there are things here that even Hawkenlye Abbey doesn't keep.'

'But we have to be careful to—' the Abbess began, apparently sensing a criticism. Then she stopped. 'Please, Sister,' she said majestically, 'go on.'

'My lady, the things I refer to are not necessarily the costly items,' the infirmarer said gently, 'although for sure I would hesitate to use as much myrrh as this in any remedy unless I could be sure of getting my hands on some more. Wasteful, I call it,' she added in a mutter. 'I was thinking of the vervain.' With a swift look at Josse – which he failed to understand just as thoroughly as he had done the Sister's remark about eating bodies – she said, 'I could understand the vervain if this were a potion produced by the Forest Folk, but it isn't. I can be quite certain of that because they don't use mandrake.'

'Ah, I see,' the Abbess said. 'You mean that vervain is not used at Hawkenlye because of its magical associations?'

'Aye. Which I reckon suggests our dead man wasn't given his remedy in any convent or monastery.'

'Where, then?' asked Josse.

'I would say that this' – Sister Tiphaine held up the little bag, whose neck she had tied up with a length of string – 'was purchased from an apothecary. A good one, I'd say, and probably an expensive one. No man would put so much mandrake and myrrh in a potion and then give it away.'

Asking the question more in hope than expectation, Josse said, 'Do you know of such an apothecary hereabouts, Sister?' The infirmarer shook her head. 'And what of you, my lady?'

'No,' the Abbess said reluctantly. 'I have never consulted an apothecary and I would not even know how to go about finding one. What shall we do, Sir Josse?'

Feeling at that moment quite bereft of any sensible suggestions, Josse held his peace. Then gradually an image began to form itself in his mind: a dead body on a narrow cot, a vicious, crushing blow in its skull.

The man carried nothing with which we might identify him, Josse thought, except for this little remedy in its cloth bag. Sister Tiphaine, bless her for her skill, has told us far more about it that I for one could have hoped for, including the very useful fact that it was put together by a master in the apothecary's art. None out of the three of us knows of such a man, but this man, whoever he is, must be located because, once shown the remedy, he will be able to tell us for whom it was prescribed.

Or at least let us hope that he will . . .

'My lady,' Josse said, with more confidence that he felt, 'we must, I believe, await the arrival of Gervase de Gifford. We shall ask him whether there is a skilled apothecary in Tonbridge or anywhere else in the vicinity, and if such a man exists and cannot help us, then we must broaden our search until the right man is found. Then we will . . .'

'. . . ask the identity of the man for whom he prescribed this potion so that, provided the purchaser did not give the potion to someone else, we shall then be able to put a name to our dead man,' the Abbess finished for him. 'Yes, Sir Josse, I fully understand your reasoning.'

Of course she did. 'Aye, my lady.'

But, as they thanked Sister Tiphaine and left her to her bunches of rosemary, Josse wondered if the Abbess had extended that reasoning as far as he had. What he was thinking was that being given the dead man's name and circumstances was a very good start in discovering who had killed him.

And why.

Gervase de Gifford arrived shortly after Josse and Helewise had returned to her room. Helewise experienced a moment's regret; she had hoped for a few moments alone with Josse in which to apologise for having summoned him into danger. She also had the feeling that she had been distracted when he knocked on her door and wanted to explain that it had not been through any lack of pleasure at seeing him again; quite the contrary.

It had been simple fear.

She asked Josse to describe to de Gifford what had happened, which he did. There was a brief pause while de Gifford assimilated the information, then he said, 'My lady, it would seem that if there is even a remote possibility that the dead man carries the pestilence, then the sooner he is buried, the better.'

'I agree,' she said. 'Do you wish to view the body, Sheriff de Gifford?'

De Gifford looked at Josse. 'Is there anything that I should see?'

'There is but the one wound, to the top of the head. Done, I would suggest, with a club or something of the type. Other than that . . .'

'My lady, I take it that your infirmarer has examined the corpse?' De Gifford asked.

'She has.'

'Then I bow to her medical skill and Sir Josse's knowledge of killing blows. I will not view the body' – Helewise had to admire his judgement – 'and, if I may make a suggestion, it is that the dead man be buried by those who have already come into contact with the body.'

'You make sound sense,' Josse said.

'Indeed,' Helewise agreed. 'We cannot say whether or not there is a risk of infection, but let us assume that there is and take what measures we may to contain its spread.' She got to her feet. 'I shall send word to Father Gilbert. The dead man will be buried today.'

Josse gave her a nod of acknowledgement. 'That is wise, my lady.' He glanced at de Gifford. 'If Gervase and I might be excused from attending the interment, then I propose that we set off straight away and begin trying to locate the apothecary who sold the potion to the dead man.'

'There is no reason for either of you to witness the burial,' she said. 'By all means, set off on your search – the sooner we can make some progress in identifying our poor victim, the better for all of us.'

She watched as the two men bowed and took their leave. Only when the door had closed behind them did she allow her shoulders to slump. She sat down heavily in her chair, buried her face in her hands and, for the first time, made herself face what would be the probable consequences if it proved to be true that the pestilence had come to Hawkenlye.

These consequences were so awful that, after a very short time, she made herself stop. Then she left her room, slipped quietly across the cloister to the Abbey church and, falling on to her knees, began to pray as hard as she could that Sister Euphemia was wrong.

3

As Josse and de Gifford rode down to Tonbridge, the sheriff racked his brains to think of anybody in the area who could have sold the victim a sophisticated and costly remedy that included an element commonly regarded as magical. Thinking out loud, he narrowed the possible Tonbridge candidates down to one, 'and I'm almost sure we'll be wasting our time with *him*.'

In the absence of any other place to start, de Gifford led the way to the business premises of the town's one reasonably renowned apothecary. As soon as Josse understood that the shabby-looking dwelling tucked away between two others – in slightly better repair – was actually the residence of their quarry, he silently began to agree with de Gifford.

The apothecary's house was towards the end of a narrow, muddy and rubbish-strewn street that led away from the river and the wealthier parts of the town and off south-eastwards in the direction of the boggy, marshy, ague-ridden areas where nobody lived unless poverty and desperation drove them there. The stench was appalling; human waste mixed with melted frost ran in a gully in the middle of the road and rats scrabbled among the rotting heaps of rubbish that had collected at regular intervals. The dwellings were of poor construction and their timbers had warped; here and there walls looked on the point of collapse and several of the roofs had gaping holes. Hoping that he was not about to breathe his last and suffocate beneath a mixture of wattle, daub, rotten vegetables and shit, Josse drew rein behind de Gifford's horse and watched as de Gifford dismounted and – with an expression of disgust and stepping carefully in his highly polished boots – approached a low door over which had been hung, in touching optimism, a bunch of very ancient lavender to advertise the herbalist's presence.

While they waited to see if there would be any answer to de Gifford's knock, the sheriff looked up at Josse and said, 'He does most of his business at a market stall. I would imagine he'll not expect callers at his door and he may well not—'

At that moment there came the sound of bolts being drawn back. There were several of these, and Josse suppressed a smile at the thought of anyone bothering to fit so many when the flimsy fabric of the door would surely yield to one determined kick from a booted foot. A gap appeared between the door and the lintel and, with the air of a tortoise poking out its head, an old, creased and unshaven face peered out.

'Whadyewant?'

De Gifford eased the door open a little more. 'I am Gervase de Gifford, sheriff of Tonbridge, and this is Sir Josse d'Acquin.'

The old man appeared singularly unimpressed by the titles. 'Aye?' The word came out as a sort of bark. Deep-set eyes under prickly eyebrows stared out warily at the visitors.

With a snort of exasperation, de Gifford said, 'You're not in any trouble, man; we've come to ask for your help.'

'My *help*?' The old man made it sound as if it were the most unlikely request he had ever had, which was strange, considering his profession.

De Gifford was reaching inside his tunic for the bag of herbs. 'Did you prepare this remedy?' he asked, holding it out to the old man.

The apothecary took the little bag gingerly, as if expecting it might burn his fingers. 'What's in it?' he demanded, scowling ferociously up at de Gifford.

The sheriff glanced at Josse, who began to enumerate the ingredients. 'Er – rue, rosemary, myrrh—'

'I don't do myrrh!' the old man objected. 'Can't afford myrrh, it's far too expensive. They charge you a king's ransom, y'know.'

'. . . vervain—'

'Don't do vervain neither!' protested the old man. 'That's magical, that is, and the church don't hold with magic.' He nodded self-righteously, then opened the neck of the bag and peered suspiciously inside. 'Here's a bit of mandrake root!' he cried. 'Now that's a tricky one, is mandrake, you mustn't touch it with iron, y'know, you has to delve for it with an ivory staff and it flees from an unclean man. It—'

Cutting short the discourse on mandrake, de Gifford said, 'You did not prepare this potion, then?'

The apothecary thrust it back at de Gifford, shaking his head so violently that he dislodged the tight-fitting black cap that covered his head, ears and most of his neck. 'No! No! No, I never!'

Josse grinned. One *no* would have sufficed, he thought, and, given the way in which the old man's clear gesture of renunciation had spoken, even that was superfluous.

'Can you think,' de Gifford said, with what Josse thought was remarkable patience, 'of anyone hereabouts who might have prepared it?'

The old man thought. He screwed up his face, scratched his head under the black cap, sniffed, frowned. Then he said, 'No.'

De Gifford thanked him and, remounting, turned his horse. Josse did the same; it was not an easy manoeuvre, given the meagre width of the street. They set off back into the town, Josse leading the way.

'I always thought it was a waste of time,' de Gifford said. 'But then—'

Something occurred to Josse. Pulling Horace sharply to a halt – he heard de Gifford give a muttered curse as his own horse threw up its head – he turned and said, 'Gervase, where does that old boy obtain his supplies?'

'He goes out and picks his plants by moonlight with the dew on them, Mars in the mid-heaven and a south-west wind blowing, I expect, like any other herbalist. Why?'

'He said' – Josse could barely contain his excitement – 'that myrrh was too expensive. Well, how would he know what it cost unless he'd tried to buy some? He wouldn't gather it locally himself, would he? It comes from . . .' Josse tried to think, but to no avail. 'Well, it's foreign, anyway. It must be imported and I was just thinking that the old apothecary back there might well know of a supplier somewhere near here who brings myrrh and other exotic plant drugs into England . . .'

De Gifford was off his horse and running back towards the apothecary's house. Josse watched as once again he knocked on the door. It was answered more quickly this time and there was a brief conversation between de Gifford and the old man. Then de Gifford called out his thanks, sprinted back along the alley and, vaulting on to his horse – whatever he had just found out seemed to have put a spring in his step – said, 'He prepares most of his simples and his remedies himself from locally grown plants, but the few things he uses and can't gather or grow he buys from a lad who does the rounds three times a year.'

'A lad?'

'Yes. The boy's apprenticed to an apothecary in New-enden.'

'And this apothecary imports foreign ingredients?'

'Yes. It sounds as if he's both a practitioner and a merchant.'

'And therefore could very well have prepared a remedy

containing myrrh,' Josse concluded. 'Newenden,' he said slowly. Then, looking at de Gifford, he said eagerly, 'We could be there in a few hours. New Winnowlands is close by and we could put up there overnight and ride back to Hawkenlye in the morning. What do you say?'

De Gifford grinned. 'I say yes! Ride on, Josse, I'm right behind you.'

At Hawkenlye Abbey, two travellers arrived in the Vale dragging a dilapidated hand cart on which lay a middle-aged man, a boy of about ten years old and twin babies of perhaps eight or ten months. The men – one of them was little more than a boy – said they had come up from north of Hastings. Both of them were exhausted and the lad was near to tears. The older man collapsed on the ground, head in his hands, temporarily speechless; the lad was too distressed to relax.

Brother Firmin took the boy's arm and gently invited him to go into the pilgrim's shelter and warm himself, but he shook off the old monk's solicitous hand and cried, 'Me mam's dead! Me dad too, *and* me gran and me auntie's ma! He' – he indicated with a thumb the older man who had arrived with him – 'he's me mam's brother, and them on the cart, they're me brother, me dad's brother and his two little 'uns.' Turning beseeching eyes on to Brother Firmin, he said, 'Can you save them, Brother? We've come all this way to find you and we're desperate.'

Brother Firmin looked horrified – he had been a healer for long enough to know what four deaths and four sick people all at once probably meant – but swiftly he disguised his fear and set about trying to help the stricken family. Summoning Brother Saul and Brother Adrian, he sent the former to seek out the infirmarer and the latter to organise a working party and prepare accommodation there in the Vale for the lad and his uncle.

While he waited for Sister Euphemia, Brother Firmin approached the cart. He saw immediately that the middle-aged man was in a bad way; he was shivering and trying to clutch the thin blanket closer to him, yet he was soaked in his own sweat and his face felt hot to the touch. His shirt was open at the neck and Brother Firmin could see that the great blotches of dark pink extended down from the face over the chest. Brother Firmin got a phial of holy water out of the pouch at his belt – he always carried some of the precious water about him – and said gently, 'Will you take a sip of our precious water, friend? It is powerful strong and it will aid you.'

The man's eyes flickered open for an instant – Brother Firmin noticed that the flesh inside the lids was severely inflamed – but then, with a groan, shut his eyes again and tried to turn away.

Brother Firmin looked at the others on the cart. The young boy was stirring and, when the old monk offered water to him, he accepted it and drank it down as fast as Brother Firmin could tip it into his parched mouth. 'There,' the old man said with a kindly smile, 'that will put you right. You'll see!'

Then he uncovered the two babies. To his distress he noticed that one was already stiff; the infant's bowels seemed to have ejected more than such a tiny body could possibly have held and its faeces were watery and streaked with blood and mucus. Brother Firmin looked at the other baby, which was crying weakly and pitifully; with a practised hand he let a couple of drops of holy water fall on the infant's lips, at which it instantly put out its tongue and licked them off. Brother Firmin smiled and repeated the process once, twice, three times, each time encouraging the infant to accept a little more. Then he said softly, 'That's enough for now, my little one.'

Taking care to leave the living child wrapped up, he extracted its dead twin. Then, covering the tiny face with a fold of the baby's thin shawl, he began to pray.

Brother Firmin knew what the church had to say about unbaptised infants not being permitted into the presence of God. It was perfectly possible that the dead child in his arms had been baptised already but it did not do to take any chances; putting his heart into his prayer, Brother Firmin stood on the cold ground and said the words that brought both the dead baby and its twin into the blessed family of God. He put a couple of drops of holy water on to his thumb and drew the sign of the cross on both tiny foreheads.

There, he thought. Now they'll be all right.

Then he found a quiet corner in which to place the dead baby and went back to see what he could do for the living.

Josse and de Gifford reached Newenden as the light was beginning to fade. The cold weather was keeping most people indoors but de Gifford spotted a man hastening off along the main street with a puppy under his arm and called out to him, asking if he knew where the apothecary might be found.

'You're wanting Adam Pinchsniff?' the man replied, shifting the wriggling puppy to the other arm and, when it snapped playfully at his fingers, giving it a smart tap on the nose.

'If that is the name of the apothecary, then yes, I am,' de Gifford said.

The man eyed both de Gifford and Josse. 'Hope you've brought full purses with you,' he said with a grin. 'Follow this road down till you see the river appear in the valley before you, then turn sharp left past the church and it's the third house on the left. The one with the fresh plaster,' he added, his grin widening. 'He's no pauper, old Adam.'

De Gifford thanked him and set off in the direction the man had indicated, Josse close behind. The house with the fresh plaster stood out clearly from its shabbier neighbours and the men would have known it even without the traditional apothecary's sign hanging above the door. The front wall of the house extended into a lower wall and Josse, curious, went to have a look. The wall enclosed what was apparently the apothecary's garden, a neat quarter-acre of carefully tended ground which, although winter-bare, showed clear signs that every inch was put to good use. Low box hedges divided the beds, in most of which the soil had been recently dug over. Trees and shrubs formed a dense barrier at the bottom of the garden and Josse was quite sure that every last one of them grew or produced some lucrative plant drug that could be used alone or blended into some popular remedy.

De Gifford had dismounted and was knocking on the door which, Josse observed, was considerably more substantial than that of the Tonbridge herbalist and made of oak studded with iron. Well, if the man were wealthy, then it made good sense to lock himself up carefully at night . . .

Josse slid off Horace's back, wincing a little; he and de Gifford had ridden hard and Josse's lower back was complaining. He was just wondering how much this Adam Pinchsniff might charge him for some soothing liniment when abruptly the oak door was flung open, revealing a man perhaps in his sixties wearing a luxurious black velvet robe lined with fur. His long hair was white, as was his beard, and smoothly combed; on his head he wore a cap of similar design to his Tonbridge fellow-practitioner, except that Adam Pinchsniff's was made of deep maroon silk and, as far as Josse could see, spotlessly clean.

'Yes?' he demanded, eyeing de Gifford up and down.

For the second time that day the sheriff introduced Josse and himself. Then – for Adam Pinchsniff was clearly a man of a very different quality from the Tonbridge herbalist – he proceeded swiftly and without prevarication to the reason for the visit.

'We have come from Hawkenlye Abbey on an urgent matter concerning a death,' he began. 'You are Adam Pinchsniff?'

The apothecary flushed. 'No I am *not*,' he said crossly. 'My name is Adam Morton. The people have given me the eke name of Pinchsniff, although I really cannot imagine why.' He gave a short snort of disapproval, the action appearing to draw in his nostrils so that his already thin nose became positively beak-like. Observing, Josse could see exactly how the name had come about.

'I apologise,' de Gifford was saying smoothly. 'I meant no offence; it is merely that I asked a man in the town where I might find the apothecary and that was the name by which he called you.'

The apothecary sniffed again. 'Very well. A matter to do with a death, you say? Then you and your friend – what's his name? – had better come in. You there, Sir Joseph, tie those horses to the hitching ring; they'll be safe enough out here, nobody would dare to steal so much as the smallest coin from a guest of *my* house.'

Thinking that the welcome would have been warmer had Adam Pinchsniff offered to have the horses attended to, for both mounts were displaying the signs of a hard ride, Josse did as he was commanded. Then he followed de Gifford into the apothecary's house.

It was a timber framed building with walls of plaster-coated mud brick. The stone floor of the interior had been recently swept and was covered in a scattering of fresh, clean-smelling rushes. There were few articles of furniture – a large chest, some shelves on which there were several wooden boxes of various sizes, a long, narrow table and a large chair – but what there were appeared to be of excellent quality and obviously costly. A fire burned in a hearth, the aroma of the burning wood – apple, Josse thought – mingling with that given off by the spirals of blue and golden smoke rising up from several small dishes of fragrant, smouldering incense.

'So he's dead, then,' the apothecary said.

'To whom do you refer?' De Gifford's tone was wary.

'Why, to young Nicol, naturally. Nicol Romley, my apprentice. He took sick and I lent him my horse so that he might ride over to see what the good nuns and monks of Hawkenlye could do for him, since whatever ailed him failed to respond to my potions.' Again the sniff, disdainful now, as if the young man had been to blame for throwing out an illness that Adam Pinchsniff could not treat. 'I presume, from your tidings, that the sisters and brothers could do no better than I.'

Josse did not trust himself to speak. That poor young man – Nicol; at least he could now be called by his given name – had died, alone and sick. And here was the lad's former master, reacting with the sort of indifference a man might display on being told he'd trodden on an ant.

De Gifford seemed to be having a similar interior struggle. After a moment he said, in almost his usual voice, 'Nicol Romley, if indeed that is the man who lies dead at Hawkenlye, was sick, just as you say. The Abbey infirmarer examined his body and observed . . . certain signs.' The apothecary made as if to speak but de Gifford held up a hand. 'With your permission, sir, I would finish what I have to say. The young man may well have been dying of whatever it was that ailed him, but he was not given the chance. He was struck down by a blow to the head and thrown in a pond.'

Adam Pinchsniff had settled himself in an immense throne-like oak chair whose back and front legs were elaborately carved. He rested his elbows on the chair's wide arms, pressing his hands together, the slender, broad-ended thumbs and each long finger pressed lightly against its equivalent on the opposite hand. He stared at de Gifford, apparently thinking. Eventually he said, 'Struck down. And so close to a great abbey! Dear me. These vagabonds and thieves grow bold. And no doubt the assailant made off with my horse, fool that I was to allow Nicol to borrow him.' He sighed, shaking his head, and neither Josse nor, he imagined, Gervase was in any doubt that he regretted the loss of the animal over that of the man.

De Gifford, displaying what Josse considered admirable self-control, extracted the bag of herbs from inside his tunic. He walked across the hall and held it out to the apothecary who, after a suspicious look, took it and held it up close in front of his eyes.

'This was found in the dead man's purse,' the sheriff said.

'Then the dead man is indeed Niçol Romley,' the apothecary said, 'because this potion is my work and I gave it to him not a week ago.' He untied the string around the neck of the bag and stared inside. 'It has been opened!' he said accusingly, raising angry eyes to meet de Gifford's.

De Gifford made a visible effort to control himself. Then: 'It was necessary. This bag was the only item found on the body that yielded any possible means of identification. The contents were examined by the herbalist at Hawkenlye Abbey and from them she deduced that the potion had been prepared by a skilled and sophisticated apothecary.'

Slightly mollified by the flattery – perhaps, Josse thought, that had been de Gifford's intention – Adam Pinchsniff gave a self-deprecating shrug. 'I suppose I can understand the line of reasoning,' he admitted grudgingly.

'We went first to a herbalist in Tonbridge,' de Gifford pressed on, 'and he too looked at the ingredients of the potion. He told us of a certain apothecary who imported and sold rare foreign plant herbs and extracts and whose apprentice was wont to call on him a few times every year, and he revealed that the apprentice's master lived in Newenden. That is how we found you, Master Morton.' He gave the apothecary a long stare. 'Now that we have what we came for, we shall leave you in peace.'

The sheriff was turning to go when the apothecary spoke.

'Wait!' he commanded. De Gifford stopped but he did not turn round. 'What do you mean, you have what you came for?'

Now de Gifford faced him again. 'We have a name for the dead man at Hawkenlye,' he said coolly. 'Now Nicol Romley may be buried in a marked grave.'

'Don't you want to ask me what ailed him? What it was that I – *I!* – was not able to treat, and for which I sent him to Hawkenlye?'

Now de Gifford began to smile. It was a chilly smile, but a smile all the same. 'That we have already surmised,' he said courteously. 'For all that the cause of poor Nicol's death was clear, nevertheless his body was examined by the Hawkenlye infirmarer. She deduced from certain symptoms that he had been suffering from a serious illness and she feared that it might be the pestilence.'

He paused but the apothecary did not speak. There was some new expression in his eyes, Josse observed. Was it fear? Guilt? Or perhaps a mixture of both?

'We guessed,' de Gifford went on, 'that you prescribed as best you could to treat Nicol's symptoms. He suffered from headache, fever, flux of the bowels and severe pains through-out his body. You also included two of the sovereign remedies against plague: vervain and marigold. We concluded that when your remedy failed to make him better, you washed your hands of him and sent him to Hawkenlye.'

'I do wonder what became of my horse,' the apothecary muttered, apparently following a train of thought of his own. 'You will be sure to bring him back should he turn up, won't you?'

Shooting him a look of such savage dislike that Josse fancied he saw it score a mark across the apothecary's pale cheeks, de Gifford ignored the remark and instead said, 'Did you fear infection, Master Morton? Did you shut the poor lad away the moment the first symptom appeared? I smell incense; have you been fumigating your house?'

The apothecary gave his careless shrug again. 'For what good it may do me, yes.' Then, glaring at de Gifford with matching venom, he said, 'Would you not have done the same?'

'I might,' de Gifford owned evenly. For a moment Josse thought that the seething atmosphere in the room was about to ease – he hoped it would; there were several questions that he wanted to put to the apothecary – but then, in the same reasonable tone, the sheriff went on, 'I'll tell you what else I might have done, Master Morton. I might have gone with my young apprentice to ensure that he reached his destination and stayed by his side praying for him while the Hawkenlye nuns fought for his life. If their help came too late, I might have sat in vigil over Nicol and arranged for his burial. When finally I left him, I might have paid for masses to be said for his soul. That's what *I* might have done.'

Oh dear, Josse thought. Observing the apothecary's cold mask of fury, he realised that the slim chance he had had of posing his questions had now irrevocably vanished. De Gifford was on his way out of the room; Josse caught the heavy oak door just as the sheriff was forcefully swinging it shut and, wincing, he followed him out.

On the doorstep, Josse turned.

'Thank you for your time, Master Morton,' he said politely, 'you have been most helpful.'

Then, with a low bow, he gently closed the door.

'Why did you do that?' de Gifford demanded as they rode away. 'Did you have to touch your forelock to the man? He's a monster, Josse, he worked that young man like an animal and he couldn't have been less concerned to hear that the poor lad's dead!'

'Aye, I know,' Josse said soothingly. 'It's just that . . .' He hesitated, because what he was about to say would sound very like criticism – well, it *was* criticism – and in de Gifford's present mood, and given that the two men were about to put up at New Winnowlands together overnight, Josse wasn't sure that antagonising the sheriff was a very good idea.

'Oh, go on, Josse, out with it.' There was a smile in de Gifford's voice. 'It's not you I'm angry with.'

'Very well. I tried to wish the wretched man a courteous farewell because there may be more to be gained from him.'

'About Nicol Romley?'

'Aye. God forbid it, but if there should be more cases of this pestilence, then it will be important to find out all we can of Nicol's recent movements. Will it not?'

De Gifford was nodding slowly. 'Yes. Oh, yes, you're right, Josse, and I thank you for your foresight.'

They rode in contemplative silence for a while. Then de Gifford laughed shortly. 'I propose, Josse, that if the acquisition of that knowledge ever becomes necessary, you go on your own to see Master Pinchsniff.'

In Hawkenlye Vale, the middle-aged man died late in the afternoon. Sister Euphemia had taken the difficult decision not to move him up to the infirmary: for one thing, he was very weak and movement seemed to hurt him; for another, he was clearly close to death and there was little the infirmary could do for him that the monks in the Vale could not. And if this was indeed the pestilence, then the fewer cases of the sickness introduced into the Abbey infirmary, the better it would be for all.

Sister Euphemia stood in the Vale watching over the surviving infant and the young boy for the rest of that day. She encouraged Brother Firmin in his efforts to make both patients drink and soon they were sufficiently revived to ingest quite large draughts of liquid. The infant opened its eyes and began to cry; a good sign, the infirmarer decided. The young boy regained consciousness and began to moan that his head ached (his brother said this had been the lad's chief complaint from the start) and Sister Tiphaine brought him a measure of her strongest pain-relieving potion. She slipped a sleeping draught into the mixture and very soon the boy had fallen asleep.

The two nuns studied both patients. Neither had the frightening dark pink spots, nor the inflammation around the eyes. After some time, Sister Euphemia said, 'I reckon the sickness is on the wane in these two. I will take them to the infirmary, where I'm sure we'll be able to hasten their recovery. With God's help,' she added.

Sister Tiphaine muttered something that might have been *Amen*. 'You'd best check with the Abbess,' she suggested.

Sister Euphemia sighed. 'Aye. That I will, for I must have her permission.' She sighed again. 'But you know as well as I do,' she whispered to Tiphaine, 'that obtaining her permission in no way absolves me of the blame and the guilt if I'm wrong and . . .'

No. She wouldn't think of that.

Sister Tiphaine gave her an encouraging nudge. 'You may be wrong and you may be right,' she said. 'The Abbess will realise that. She wouldn't want folks left out here in the cold any more than you do, especially young 'uns like these two here.' She nodded at the baby and the boy. 'For charity's sake, we must make them as comfortable as we can, and that means moving them to the infirmary.' She set off along the path back towards the Abbey.

'Where are you off to?' Sister Euphemia called after her.

'I'm off to summon the Abbess,' the herbalist answered.

Late that night, all four of the surviving visitors were sound asleep. Two were on the mend; the ten-year-old boy and the surviving twin baby who, on closer inspection, turned out to be a girl child. The older boy who had struggled so bravely to drag his ailing relations to Hawkenlye would be rewarded by not sickening with whatever frightening disease had wiped out half his family; his uncle was not so lucky. Even as the older man slept, tucked up beside his nephew in a corner of the pilgrims' shelter in the Vale, the elements of the deadly pestilence were multiplying, spreading stealthily through his blood like an invading and secretive army.

And, unbeknownst to anyone, it had already sent out its advance troops into the Hawkenlye population.

4

Helewise was awake early. She rose and dressed quietly and then made her way in the pre-dawn February darkness across to the infirmary. Sister Beata was on duty and she rose to greet her Abbess.

Moving close to speak quietly right into her ear, Helewise said, 'How are they?'

Sister Beata smiled. 'They are sleeping, my lady, and in both the infant girl and the lad, the fever is down.'

'I see.' Oh, thank God!

'The baby girl woke up a while ago and drank some more water. I did as Sister Euphemia ordered and heated the water, melting a little honey in it. The lad was restless earlier in the night but now that the fever's turned, he's sleeping natural-wise.'

Helewise was still silently praying her thanks. She said quietly, 'Good tidings, Sister. Where is Sister Euphemia?'

Sister Beata nodded towards a cubicle at the far end of the infirmary. 'She's sleeping,' she whispered. 'She was exhausted, my lady; dead on her feet.'

'I am glad, Sister Beata, that you managed to persuade her of the need to rest,' Helewise said, and Beata blushed with pleasure.

'Oh, my lady, I don't know as how I had anything to do with it,' she said modestly.

'You have a kind heart, Sister,' Helewise said. 'I am quite sure that Sister Euphemia would not have given in to her fatigue had you not gently and lovingly insisted.'

'Oh!' Sister Beata blushed.

'Please tell Sister Euphemia when she wakes that I shall return later,' Helewise said. Then she left the infirmary and went across to the Abbey church. It was almost the hour for Prime but there was just time for some moments of private prayer before the rest of the community arrived.

After the first office of the day Helewise set off down to the Vale to check on the man and the youth. Both were still sleeping; observing this, the monks had left them alone. Nodding her approval of this, Helewise went back up to the Abbey, leaving instructions that word be sent to her when one or other of the men stirred. 'You might tell them when they wake,' she added, 'that their kinfolk up in the infirmary have passed a good night and this morning they are better.'

Word came later in the morning, as Helewise was returning to her room after Tierce. She accompanied Brother Augustus, who had brought the message, back to the Vale.

'It's the young man who's awake,' Augustus told her. 'He's well, my lady, as far as we can tell. He's slept, he's eaten, and he says he feels fine and that there was naught wrong with him but exhaustion.'

'I am relieved to hear it,' she replied. 'What of the older man?'

Augustus frowned. 'He's not so good. He's restless and hot.'

Helewise felt dread flood through her. Then, rallying, she made herself say with false cheer, 'Perhaps he too is merely worn out with anxiety and a hard road?' Despite herself, she could not help turning her remark into a question.

Augustus gave her a quick look. 'We're praying that is so, my lady.'

She noticed that he did not very sound confident of having those prayers answered.

In the Vale the monks had had the good sense to move the

older man to the far corner of an empty area of the shelter. Brother Firmin was sitting beside him holding a cloth to the man's forehead. As Helewise watched, he removed the cloth, wrung it out in a basin of water and reapplied it. Helewise gave the old monk a smile, which he returned. Then, turning back to Augustus, she said, 'Where is the young man?'

'Follow me, my lady.'

Augustus led her into the area where the monks and the pilgrims ate their meals. Sitting at one of the long tables in front of a large bowl of broth sat the young man. Seeing the Abbess, he hastily swallowed his mouthful and stood up to give her an awkward bow.

'My lady Abbess,' he said, 'with all my heart I thank you for taking us in.'

He must have been schooled in the correct form of address, she thought; all credit to him for remembering it amid his many worries.

She moved nearer and sat down on the bench beside him, indicating that he should sit too.

'You need not thank us,' she said gently, 'for it is what we are here for. What is your name?'

'Waldo,' he said.

'Waldo,' she repeated. She studied him; he was about fifteen or sixteen, with a broad face in which the bones were already strengthening and enlarging into their adult shape. On his cheeks were the beginnings of a beard. His eyes were light brown and, she fancied, had an open, honest expression. His hair, as far as she could tell, was dark, but as it was sorely in need of a wash, she could not be sure. He wore a long-sleeved brown woollen tunic that had been mended several times – very neatly – and, over it, a sleeveless leather jerkin. He smelt of sweat and cabbage.

He waited to see if she would speak again and when she did not, he said tentatively, 'They tell me that my brother and my baby niece do well, my lady. May I – is it possible for me to see them? They're only young and it's likely they may be a-feared, waking in a strange place with unfamiliar faces. Oh!' Flushing brick-red, he added, 'That is, I'm sure they're kindly nuns up in the sick folk's place. I meant no offence, my lady.'

'Of course you didn't, Waldo,' she reassured him. 'And you are quite right; it will do your little brother a lot of good to see you, I'm sure, and the baby girl too.'

Waldo made as if to leap up and run off up to the infirmary there and then. She put out a detaining hand.

'Finish your broth first,' she suggested. He looked at her and then down at the bowl of broth, obviously wondering if it would breach some rule of Abbey etiquette to eat in front of an abbess. 'Go on,' she said softly, 'don't let it get cold!'

Gratefully he dipped in his spoon and slurped up the rest of the broth. When he had almost finished and was mopping the bowl with a piece of bread, she said, 'Waldo, before I take you to see your kinfolk, may I ask you one or two questions?'

'Questions?' Alarm filled his face. 'Have we done wrong, my lady? We thought it was the right thing to do, to bring our family here. My mother died, you know, and my father, and my grandmother and the old aunt.' Controlling himself with an obvious effort, he muttered, 'Uncle and Mariah and me, we were beside ourselves. Uncle was wailing and taking on so and it were all I could do to calm him. When the others took sick, we feared to lose them all.'

'It's all right,' Helewise said. 'You have done nothing wrong and we shall do all that we can for you. But, Waldo, it seems that this disease spreads fast. What I have to discover is where it might have come from. The more we find out about it, the better are our chances of restricting how many other people catch it. Do you see what I mean?'

He had already been nodding as she spoke; thank God, she thought, he is quick to understand. 'Aye,' he said. He screwed up his face for an instant as if in pain, then said, 'It was my mam. She's maidservant in the household of a Hastings merchant, Master Kelsey, and she'd been looking after him. He came home from a trip away off in foreign places and took to his bed straight away with a fever and that. He has a sister' – Waldo's grimace spoke his feelings for the sister – 'but she's a *lady*, wouldn't soil her hands with anything dirty like caring for a sick man, even if that man was her own brother. Anyway, Mam was with him when he died, then she cleared up after him and left him neat and tidy like, all ready for his burial. That sister of his would have had Mam do that and all if it was possible, *and* she'd never have paid her for her trouble.' He turned to spit, then blushed violently again and muttered an apology.

'It's all right, Waldo. Please, go on.'

'Well, Mam comes home and tells us all about what's been happening.'

'She came home to her family – to all of you – straight from tending the merchant?'

'Aye. She were sick, my lady. She had these dreadful pains in her head – she thought it were demons poking around inside with red-hot pitchforks and she were sore afraid they'd come for her to take her down to the fires. We got Father Christian to come to her and he managed to comfort her a bit, although he couldn't do nothing for her pain.' He swallowed and then said starkly, 'She died. Me dad had taken sick by then and he died too. Then me gran and me uncle's wife's mother died and all.'

Lost in the complexities of this apparently endless family, Helewise said, 'You all live close together?'

'Oh, aye,' Waldo said resignedly. 'Me dad and his brother, they built our house in the first place out of the old cottage and barn that their own parents left them. They both married, although Dad's brother, he only found a wife a couple of years back, and their wives brought their mothers to live with them. Mam's brother, too' – he jerked his head in the direction of the Vale's sleeping quarters – 'that's him in there; his name's Jabez. He's never been quite right in the head. Then Mam and Dad had me, me sister and me brother, and Dad's brother's wife had the twins. See?' he concluded hopefully.

'Er – yes. Quite a household,' Helewise remarked. 'Let me see . . . twelve of you.'

'Not so many now,' Waldo said sadly. 'Four dead at home and one of the twins gone yesterday.' Then, eyes on Helewise's, he said, 'We're all on top of each other at home, see. Mam did her best to keep everything clean and tidy but she were away in Hastings more often than not, slaving away with all the worst of the chores for Master Kelsey and that bitch of a sister of his. Sorry, my lady.'

'Never mind, Waldo.' Perhaps, Helewise thought, she should pull the lad up for speaking in such a way of his mother's employer, but then that mother had just died. It was surely charitable to make a few allowances for the poor boy. 'Did – er – did none of the other women of the household try to help?'

Waldo gave a snort of disgust. 'Not if they could think up a good excuse not to. Me auntie – that's me dad's brother's wife – she still says she can't do no heavy work, what with her just having had the twins, but they're eight months old now so it's not as if . . .' He trailed off. Probably, Helewise decided, he was recalling that one of those twins was dead.

'And what about the older women?' she pressed, more with the intention of taking his mind off his grief than for any real desire to know.

'The old auntie was no use to anybody, not unless you had a need for a spiteful and demanding crone who moaned all the hours she was awake and snored loud enough to wake the dead whenever she fell asleep. Me gran weren't too bad. She'd try to do what Mam asked her to do, only she had the twisting pains in her hands and she never seemed to manage much.' Waldo gave a sigh. 'It's mainly Mariah and me does the work when Mam's in Hastings. Tam helps us when he has a mind to, but seeing as he's only ten, he's easily distracted.'

'And what work did your father and your uncle do?'

'Dad's brother did a bit of this and a bit of that. Dad, he worked for a master mason.' There was sudden warmth in Waldo's voice. 'He were a stone cutter. He didn't do the fancy work; he cut the big stones into the rough shapes and sizes as were required.'

Trying to come up with something kind to say to this poor lad who had just lost both parents – of whom, to judge from the way he spoke about them, he had been both proud and fond – Helewise said after a moment, 'Then your father, Waldo, has left a memorial to his life's work.'

Waldo's eyes widened. 'I hadn't thought of that, my lady.' Turning to give her a shy smile, he said, 'That's nice, that is. I'll tell Tam when I see him and save it up to pass on to Mariah when we go home.'

'Your sister remains in the house alone?' And the girl could not be much over fourteen, if Helewise had guessed Waldo's age correctly.

'Don't you fret, my lady.' Waldo had clearly followed her reasoning. 'She may be only twelve but our Mariah can take care of herself.'

'How old are you, Waldo?' Helewise interrupted.

'Fourteen last birthday,' he said. There was a faint suggestion of a youthful chest being thrown out. 'I'll be fifteen this summer and then I'll be 'prenticed to Dad's stone yard. I'm big enough now, but Master, he doesn't want me till the summer.'

He was, Helewise reflected, mature for his years . . .

'And anyway she's got me auntie there,' Waldo was saying, 'me dad's brother's wife. She's looking after her.'

'Your aunt did not fall sick?'

'Aye, she did, but she's better. I meant Mariah's looking after Auntie, not t'other way round.'

'I see.' It was a silly thing to say, Helewise thought, because, until she could slowly go through it all again with Waldo, preferably with her stylus and a piece of parchment so that she could take notes, she was very far from seeing anything very much.

But making sure that she had committed every last detail to memory was not the priority: taking Waldo to see his remaining kin was. Standing up, she said, 'Come along, young Waldo. Let's go and find Tam and your little niece.'

In a day full of anxiety and looming threat, Helewise found a rare moment of happiness when she ushered Waldo into the infirmary and took him to the adjacent cots where his brother and his little niece lay. The young boy – Tam – was sitting up in bed and his face lit up at the sight of Waldo striding along the ward towards him.

'Waldo! Waldo! I'm mended!' Tam cried out, and one or two of the nuns smiled. 'They've given me 'orrible stuff to drink but the one what does the herbs and that says it's to make me strong again and she made me hold me nose so's I di'nt taste it! Coo, Wal, it were like sheep's piss and I don' know what were in it!'

'Hush, Tam!' Waldo hastened to take his brother's out-stretched hands, then, perching on the cot, enveloped Tam in his arms. Helewise heard him say something in an urgent whisper – something to do with not likening the Abbey's remedies to sheep's piss, she guessed – but the irrepressible Tam was too happy at being free of pain and reunited with his brother to take any notice.

'They're not cross here, they're nice, Wal,' he said earnestly. 'They gave me a wash – all over! – and the nun with the big round smily face said oh, look, I'd got a brand-new white skin just a-waiting to be discovered!'

That, thought Helewise, must have been Sister Beata.

Waldo gave Tam another hug, then turned to look at the small cot where the baby girl lay. She was awake, her large dark eyes wide open and a nervous little smile on her lips, staring at Waldo as if she was hoping against hope that it was really him. He leaned down over her cot and said very gently, 'Hello, Jenna. Where's your spots gone then, eh?' Then he tickled her under her firm little chin and she squirmed and chuckled with delight.

When, a few moments later, Waldo stood up and faced Helewise, she saw the glint of tears in his eyes. And, with the dignity of a much older man, the lad said, 'Thank you, my lady; your nuns have given me back two of the people I really care about. Please may I go to the church? I'd like to thank God and all.'

Josse and de Gifford reached Hawkenlye Abbey late in the morning. They learned about the sick family from Sister Ursel, who informed them that the Abbess had been visiting the lad down in the Vale and had brought him up to see his kinfolk in the infirmary.

'How are they all?' Josse asked.

Sister Ursel gave a grimace. 'The little lad and the girl child do well. The older lad is fine but the man is now feverish.'

'You mean to imply that he has sickened since the family arrived here?' de Gifford said.

Sister Ursel nodded glumly. 'Looks that way.'

Josse and de Gifford exchanged a glance. This was not news they had wanted to hear.

They went across to the Abbess's room to wait for her. It

was not long before they heard her quick footsteps coming along the cloister and, after the most perfunctory of greetings, she told them all that she had learned from the lad Waldo – who, Josse soon decided, sounded a sensible and a courageous boy – concerning how the disease had come to the stricken family.

'The mother tended a Hastings merchant?' Josse said when the Abbess finally finished her account. Looking at de Gifford, he went on, 'And Gervase and I have just met an apothecary who imports plant herbs and extracts from overseas. Can there be a connection?'

'This is the apothecary who sold the potion to the youth who died here at Hawkenlye?' demanded the Abbess.

'Aye, my lady.' Josse turned back to her. 'Gervase and I located him; he lives in Newenden.' Briefly he told her how they had found Adam Pinchsniff and what he had had to say on the subject of his apprentice. 'The youth's name was Nicol Romley,' he concluded. 'God rest his soul.'

'Amen,' the Abbess said.

There was a moment's silence as all three of them thought about the apprentice and his lonely, violent death. Then, as if aware that there was little time for such delicacy, de Gifford said, 'So, we have two initial victims of this pestilence: the Hastings merchant—'

'His name was Master Kelsey and he lived with a spinster sister,' the Abbess put in.

'Thank you, my lady. Master Kelsey, then, returns from abroad and falls sick. Nicol Romley, whose master sends him about the land selling the apothecary's wares, also succumbs. Let us assume that there is a link between the two men; perhaps Nicol was sent to Hastings to collect goods from the merchant. Master Kelsey is nursed by his maidservant but he dies. Adam Pinchsniff fails to cure his apprentice and sends poor Nicol off to Hawkenlye but he is slain before he reaches the Abbey. Meanwhile Master Kelsey's maid has fallen sick and she returns home to this extensive household, where she passes on the pestilence to – how many was it, my lady?'

'Eight, to begin with,' the Abbess replied tonelessly. 'Four of them, including the maid, died. Two more died here yesterday and now the simple-minded uncle has a fever.'

'Dear God,' de Gifford muttered. Eyes on the Abbess's, he said, 'My lady, we have all the evidence that we need of the speed with which this terrible sickness spreads. We should close the gates to new arrivals and concentrate on doing what we can for the victims already here.'

He did not say that closing the gates and shutting themselves inside would also keep any of the Hawkenlye community who had already been infected away from the healthy; but then, Josse thought grimly, he did not need to.

After quite a long time the Abbess said, 'I understand your reasoning, Gervase, but I will not close the gates.' Her eyes wide with distress, she said, 'If there are to be more victims of this sickness, then it is to Hawkenlye that they will come. Our whole purpose here is to tend the sick, to allow them to avail themselves of the precious healing water and of the skill of our infirmarer and her nursing nuns.'

'But—' de Gifford began.

'I know what you would say,' the Abbess interrupted, 'and of course I appreciate that you speak good sense. Nevertheless, sense is not the only factor in this matter; there is duty, charity, love of our fellow man and, above all, love of God. Do you think, Gervase, that our master Jesus would have me close the gates? He who went among the sick and the dying with no thought for his own safety?'

De Gifford stared at her for some moments. Then, with a sigh, he said, 'No. Of course not.'

'We shall take what measures we can to keep the sick apart from the healthy,' the Abbess said. She was speaking quickly, setting out her arrangements with such fluency that Josse guessed she had thought them all out beforehand. 'The boy and the baby girl were already on the mend when they were taken up to the infirmary, so I would venture to suggest that, thankfully, no dangerous element has been introduced up here. The man Jabez – Waldo's uncle – is being cared for apart from the community, in a corner of the sleeping quarters in the Vale.'

'Who is looking after him?' Josse asked.

'Brother Firmin.' She looked up and met Josse's eyes.

She has the same thought as I, he realised. *She fears that this – thing – is too hungry to be content with its present tally of victims. And Brother Firmin is an old man, and not strong . . .*

I must not dwell on that, he told himself firmly. *There is work to do and I will offer to help where best I can.* 'My lady,' he said, 'and Gervase, I suggest that the next step is to return to Adam Pinchsniff in Newenden to ask him if he knows of any connection between Nicol Romley and Master Kelsey in Hastings. Such a connection will be reassuring because it will tell us that these cases of the sickness all stem from the one source.' It was, he thought, unthinkable that there should be two separate outbreaks of this deadly disease. 'And, in addition, the more we find out about Nicol's recent movements, the sooner we will be able to discover why he had to be killed and who killed him.'

'Fine optimism, Josse,' de Gifford said with a smile.

Josse gave a quick grin. 'Aye, I know. But optimism and a plan of action are preferable to standing here wringing our hands and waiting for catastrophe to overwhelm us.'

'Indeed,' de Gifford murmured.

'I will go back to Newenden,' Josse said, with another grin in de Gifford's direction, 'for it is likely that the apothecary will be more willing to discuss the matter of his apprentice with me than – er – than with the sheriff here.'

'Why—?' the Abbess began.

But that, Josse decided, was too long a tale to tell now and anyway it was irrelevant. With a bow, he interrupted her. 'With your leave, my lady, I should set out as soon as possible,' he said. 'Horace is none too lively, given that we have only just arrived here from New Winnowlands, and—'

'Take the cob,' the Abbess suggested. 'He has not been ridden for some time and you will go faster on a fresh horse.'

'Thank you, my lady. I will return as soon as I can.'

He hurried out of the room, only just catching the 'God's speed' that she called after him.

5

The Abbey cob was hard-mouthed and not in the first flush of youth, and Josse was pleasantly surprised to find that the horse had a good turn of speed. But then Sister Martha knew how to look after an animal and the cob did her credit.

He reached Newenden late in the afternoon and rode straight to the apothecary's house. 'Master Morton,' he muttered to himself as he dismounted and tied the cob to the hitching ring. It would not be the best of beginnings to antagonise the man by calling him by his village nickname, appropriate though it was.

Adam Morton opened the door and said, 'Oh, it's you again. What is it now?'

'Good day, Master Morton. There have been more cases of the sickness,' Josse said without preamble. 'A family from near Hastings has arrived at Hawkenlye. I am told that six people are already dead and now another has developed a high fever. The sickness was—'

His opening words had earned him the apothecary's full attention. Grabbing hold of Josse's sleeve, Adam Morton pulled him inside and closed the door. 'Fool!' he hissed. 'Do you want the whole town to hear you? Such things spread terror and panic!'

Making himself ignore the insult, Josse said evenly, 'No, Master Morton; panic is the last thing I want, since it might have the effect of sending half of Newenden scurrying to Hawkenlye.'

The apothecary waved a hand. 'I apologise,' he muttered. 'But you frighten me, sir knight.'

'We are all frightened,' Josse agreed. 'I am here to discover your late apprentice's recent movements, if you will tell me them. It seems there must be some connection between Nicol and the family from Hastings, since both he and they appear to have been suffering from the same sickness. I guess that this contact may be through a merchant named Master Kelsey.'

'Martin Kelsey, aye, I know of the man,' Adam Morton said. 'I've sometimes purchased my supplies from him.'

'And your apothecary has been recently in Master Kelsey's presence?' Josse said eagerly.

'Aye. They sailed home to England together not a fortnight ago, although they were not known to one another and I doubt that they were aware that they had a common associate in me. I had sent Nicol over to Troyes for the fair; there were items I needed – foreign herbs and drugs; musk and myrrh and the like – that cannot be obtained in our land other than at an exorbitant rate from some importer. Nicol met Martin Kelsey in Boulogne; the man had been on some venture over there, although I cannot tell you what it was.'

Boulogne, Josse thought; Troyes. Hardly able to contain his excitement, he pictured a huge fair swarming with people from all over Europe and even further afield. Then he thought about a large sea port where ships put in from the oceans of the world. Nicol Romley had been to Troyes; Martin Kelsey might well have gone there too. The two men met up in Boulogne to take ship for England and one of them, already carrying the pestilence, infected the other.

It appears, he told himself, that we have found our link . . .

I must visit the home of this Martin Kelsey, Josse decided, and find out, if there is anybody there who can tell me, where he went and whom he met, particularly after his return home.

'Thank you, Master Morton,' he began, already impatient to be off, 'I shall—'

But the apothecary was frowning and did not seem to hear. 'There was something odd about young Nicol when he returned from France,' he said slowly.

'Odd?' Josse was instantly on the alert. 'But he was sickening with the disease. Would that not make a man seem odd?'

'No, it wasn't that.' Adam Morton rubbed a hand across his jaw. 'I'd say it was more that the lad was afraid. And it wasn't the threat of the sickness that scared him, sir – er, sir knight, for he was acting in a strange way before he fell ill.'

'What was he doing?'

'He seemed to think that somebody was after him,' Adam Morton said slowly. 'He kept opening the door and peering out and one evening when I told him to deliver a basketful of simples to some of my customers, it was all I could do to get him out of the house. Then he came scurrying back in double-quick time, bolted the door behind him and raced up to his room where he shut himself in and wouldn't come out till morning.'

'To what did you ascribe this peculiar behaviour?' Josse asked.

The apothecary smiled thinly. 'I thought perhaps he'd involved himself with some young lass and that her father was after him with a horse whip.'

'Was that likely?'

'Oh, yes. Nicol was a well-favoured lad and he had the girls queuing up.'

The apothecary bowed his head, but not before Josse had caught the expression on his face. Gervase, I wish you could witness this, he thought; for, at long last, Adam Morton was acting like a human being and grieving for the young man whose life had been so suddenly and so violently ended.

'You have been very helpful, Master Morton,' Josse said

gently. 'I do not think it was any enraged father who was looking for Nicol; I think it was the man who killed him. And I shall do my best to track him down and bring him to justice.'

Adam Morton raised his head. 'Do that, sir knight,' he said. 'I shall dance at his hanging.'

Such was his fervour to follow this new and promising lead that for a moment Josse considered setting out for Hastings there and then. But he soon changed his mind; for many reasons, only a fool willingly rode through the night and Josse was not a fool, even if Adam Pinchsniff had called him one.

He rode instead to New Winnowlands, where he was fed by Ella and brought up to date by Will with the few noteworthy things that had happened in his absence. Will took the cob away to restore the animal as best he could for the next day and, quite soon, Josse retired to bed and slept dreamlessly until the early morning. Soon after the sun had risen, he was on his way to Hastings.

He made good time, for the tracks and roads were hard with frost and the cob was frisky. Reaching Hastings around mid-day, he made his way through steep and narrow streets to the port, where he found a tavern, took a mug of beer and enquired after Master Martin Kelsey. He managed to feign surprise on being told that the merchant had died a week ago and, explaining that he would like to pay his respects to Kelsey's family, asked for directions to the merchant's house.

A burly, dark-haired man standing beside him gave a snort. 'If you're expecting victuals and a mug of good wine in exchange for your sympathy, you'll be disappointed,' he said. 'Majorane Kelsey keeps her larder locked up tight as a cat's arse.'

The tavern keeper shook his head at the irreverence but Josse noticed that he was grinning. 'Martin's widow is not popular?' Josse said, keeping his voice down.

'Majorane's his sister; she ain't nobody's widow,' the dark man said. 'No man with eyes and wits in his head would have her, not unless he were intent on increasing his sufferings here on earth.'

'I see.' Josse stored the remark for future reference. Finishing his ale – which was very good – he thanked the two men for the information, bid them good day and set off to find the merchant's house.

Martin Kelsey had done well, Josse thought as he approached the place. His house was soundly constructed and well maintained, the roof in good repair and the doorstep swept. The wooden shutters over the windows looked quite new. He tethered the cob to a hitching-ring and, straightening his tunic and brushing a stray lock of hair off his face, he knocked at the door.

It was opened by a long, thin woman whose face wore the expression of one who was constantly on the look-out for misdemeanours and usually found them. Her eyes were pale blue and her hair was forced back so tightly under the stiff white headdress that it seemed to lift her eyebrows and open up her eyes, giving the impression that she was wide-eyed with horror at the unpleasant surprises that the world constantly threw at her. The mouth was small and the lips were barely perceptible, pursed up into a tight circle of disapproval.

Summoning his most courteous manner, Josse said, 'Have I the honour to address Mistress Kelsey?'

'If you're after settlement, you'll get the same as everybody else who comes knocking,' she snapped. 'Go and consult my brother's lawyer!'

She was about to slam the door, very forcefully, but Josse put his foot in the gap. 'It is not on a matter of business that I wish to speak to you, Mistress,' he said, suppressing a gasp as the heavy door closed on his foot. 'I am Josse d'Acquin and I have come from Hawkenlye Abbey. The matter is – well, in fact it is somewhat delicate. Might I . . .?' He jerked his head towards the interior of the house, putting on his most winning smile.

Majorane Kelsey glared at him for a few moments. Then she grunted and said, 'Oh, very well. You had better come in; there's far too much interest being taken in my affairs already and I don't want to set my neighbours' big ears flapping again.'

With a scowl up and down the street that would have frozen most of the curious in their tracks, she opened the door just enough for Josse to pass through the gap and led the way into a pleasant but chilly room with shining stone flags on the floor, two stout wooden chests against one wall, a table, two chairs and a bench. There was a fire of sorts in the hearth but the wood was damp and it was giving out more smoke than heat.

Majorane settled herself on one of the chairs but she did not invite Josse to be seated. 'I advise you not to remove your cloak,' she said, 'I've no maidservant at present and the idiot boy who does the outside work cannot tell seasoned wood from green.' She, Josse observed, wore a man's heavy fur-lined over-tunic on top of her woollen robe.

No maidservant, Josse was thinking. Aye, I know, Mistress, what became of *her*.

'I have heard of the death of your brother,' he said, 'and I am sorry for your loss.'

'You knew Martin?' she asked sharply.

'No.'

'Then why should you be sorry?'

'I am sorry for *you*, Mistress. To lose a close relative is always painful.'

She considered this for a while and then said, 'Perhaps, perhaps.' Eyes raised to meet Josse's, she went on, 'I am angry, Sir Josse, as well as aggrieved. Do you know' – the pale eyes were suddenly bright with passion – 'even as poor Martin lay dead in his bed and before I found him there, somebody had broken in and ransacked the house! Today is the first time that all this' – she indicated the tidy room and the spotless floor – 'has looked as it should since he died! Muddy footprints all over the place, a broken panel in the door, everything taken out of the chests and strewn on the floor!'

Josse could appreciate her fury. For a thief to take advantage of a man's death and break in to rob him was despicable. 'Were many things taken?' he asked sympathetically.

The pale eyes roamed the room. 'That, sir, is the odd thing. As far as I can tell, apart from some pretty but inexpensive silver trinkets, nothing is missing at all.'

'And – forgive me, but you and your late brother possess – er – easily portable treasures?'

She gave a grunt of laughter. 'You're asking if a thief would have found anything here worth the taking? Oh, yes, sir knight. My brother was a successful merchant and we did not lack for life's luxuries.'

'Forgive me, lady, I meant no offence.'

'Hmm.' She continued to frown at him but then, her high brow clearing, she said, 'What is this delicate matter, then?'

Deciding that his best bet was the direct approach, Josse said, 'A young man arrived at Hawkenlye Abbey and has died there. It appears he was suffering from the foreign pestilence. I understand that your brother died of a similar disease and I am told by Master Morton, an apothecary at Newenden to whom the dead youth was apprenticed, that your brother and the apprentice travelled home from Boulogne together. I am commanded by the Abbess of Hawkenlye to discover whatever I can concerning these two men known to have had the sickness, with the aim of finding out who else might have been infected so that, if possible, we can take measures to restrict the spread of the disease.'

It sounded reasonable to his own ears and, with relief, he saw that Mistress Kelsey obviously thought so too. 'Laudable,' she commented. 'Martin indeed died of some disease with which neither I nor our maidservant were familiar. There was little that could be done for him; we summoned the local apothecary and he mixed up some foul herbal concoction, but Martin brought it straight up again. I found him dead when I went into him at dawn the next day. He was already cold and I would say that he must have passed on in the small hours.'

'I see.' Josse held back from expressing sympathy; Majorane's demeanour just did not seem to invite it. 'Your maidservant . . .' he began.

'Gone,' Majorane said abruptly. 'Took sick a few days after she began nursing Martin and I packed her off back to her own family. She had another thing coming if she thought *I* was going to look after her.'

So you sent her home, where she infected eight other people, Josse thought bitterly, not counting the simple-minded brother who has subsequently fallen sick at Hawkenlye. Waiting until he was sure his voice would not reveal his emotion – there was no point in antagonising her – he said, 'The disease is virulent, lady. Your brother and young Nicol the apprentice dead, the maid sick and now—'

'Yet I remain well.' Majorane gave him an ironic look. 'I kept myself away from my brother, sir knight. It was the maid's job to nurse him and I saw no reason to put myself at risk.'

Josse decided that, unless he changed the subject, he might very well hit her. Still speaking politely, he said, 'Your brother crossed from Boulogne, I know that. Had he been anywhere else, Mistress Kelsey?'

'He visited Paris,' she replied, with a touch of pride in her tone. 'Martin made good friends among the merchants of southern England and northern France and it was his custom to combine business with pleasure. This last visit was typical in that he concluded his commercial affairs in the city and then spent some days enjoying the hospitality of two fellow merchants who have a residence on an island in the middle of the river. My brother deals in many costly and exotic items that can only be obtained from far away; silk, naturally; spices, incense and plant drugs; bronze, gold and precious stones, sapphires, emeralds, rubies. Leather and ivory goods from the dark country that lies far to the south, as well as tortoiseshell and glassware. Why, we have a warehouse full to the roof with such exquisite things not half a mile from where we sit!' She gave a small, smug smile. Then, apparently recalling Josse's question, concluded, 'When he left Paris, he travelled north to Boulogne and took ship for home.'

'With Nicol Romley,' Josse added, half to himself. Who had perhaps mentioned to Martin Kelsey of his grave fears that he was being followed . . . 'Mistress Kelsey, did your late brother mention anything unusual about his trip?'

'No,' she said instantly. 'He was very pleased with the outcome of his meeting with the Paris merchants and in good spirits on his return; that is, he was until he began to feel ill.'

'Did he mention travelling with Nicol Romley?'

She shrugged. 'Perhaps. Yes, I believe he did.'

'And—'

But there was something she wanted to say. Raising her chin, she said, 'I will tell you, sir knight, how my brother became sick. Would you like that?'

Like it? God's boots, it was too good to be true, if indeed she knew. 'I – aye, I would.'

The disdainful, scornful expression deepening, she said, 'He found a dying man in Boulogne. He tried to help the wretch but, of course, could do nothing for him. The man was lying in his own filth, bleeding all over and his forehead was hot enough to fry an egg. My brother's exact words,' she explained. 'Martin was with him when he breathed his last and he gave a street child a few coins to ensure the body was buried. Not that the foul little urchin would have done anything of the kind,' she added, 'not without Martin standing over him to make sure he did. But that was typical of my brother; too kind and far too soft hearted for his own good.'

'He has paid the price,' Josse said quietly.

'So have I!' cried Majorane. 'I have lost my brother! I kept house for him and he supported me. What do you suggest I do now, sir knight, all alone in the world?'

You have a home and you have your health, Josse wanted to reply, not to mention that warehouse full of exotic cargo. Few of those things can be said of many people. Instead he murmured, 'I am sorry for your plight, Mistress Kelsey.'

'Sorry, yes, sorry's all very well! Sorry does not put food on the table.'

Silence fell, although it seemed to Josse that the room rang with the echoes of her last furious words. There was just one more thing that Josse needed to know; hoping that she would be able to answer, he said, 'Mistress, do you know the name of the ship that brought your brother home?'

She stared up at him. 'Yes. The *Angel of Mercy*, out of Hastings here. Ironic, isn't it?'

The quay was quiet and Josse guessed that most people were sitting down to their meal. He found the *Angel of Mercy*, a small ship in good order, and, calling out, attracted the attention of a sailor sitting on a coil of rope and apparently doing nothing but gaze out to sea. Josse explained that he wished to speak to the captain and the sailor invited him to step aboard.

The captain was also doing nothing, but he was enjoying his moments of idleness in the comfort of a narrow bunk. He waved a hand to Josse to sit down on top of a seaman's chest, then asked what he could do for him.

'You sailed here from Boulogne, I believe, about a fortnight ago?'

'Not quite a fortnight, but near enough,' the captain agreed cheerfully; he had been drinking and Josse could smell alcohol on his breath from three paces away.

'You had two passengers, a merchant named Kelsey and a young apprentice from Newenden?'

'Never found out the details but that sounds about right. As long as they pay, that's fine by me!' The throaty laugh sent more second-hand alcohol Josse's way.

'You have been informed that the merchant took sick and died?'

'Aye. He was healthy when he went ashore from the *Angel*, that I can tell you.'

'Aye, I know,' Josse said reassuringly. 'The young apprentice became ill as well and he also died.'

'God rest them both,' the captain said.

'Amen,' Josse muttered. Then: 'Have there been any more cases of sickness among your crew, Captain?'

'Thank God, no,' the captain replied. He looked sideways at Josse, who guessed that both were sharing the same thought: no more sickness *yet*.

'This pestilence spreads quickly,' Josse said. 'If you all remain well then soon, Captain, you may start to be optimistic that you and your crew have been spared.'

'Can't think what we've done to deserve that blessing,' the captain observed. Then, lifting the jar of whatever he had been consuming and waving it at Josse, he said, 'Here's my remedy.'

Despite himself, Josse laughed. He stood up and, with a grin, said, 'I wish you luck. Thank you for your help, Captain.'

As he approached the head of the gangplank in preparation for descending to the quay, the sailor hurried up to him. 'I were listening,' he said disarmingly. 'It weren't two men we brought back from Boulogne, it were three. Leastways, I'm pretty sure of it.'

'Three?'

'Aye. We was just slipping our moorings when this dark shadow comes creeping along the quayside, all shifty-like as if he didn't want to be seen. I saw him, though. Well, I *think* it was a him.'

'And he came on board the ship?'

The sailor shrugged. 'Reckon he must have done. He weren't on the quay no longer and weren't nobody in the water, so wasn't no place else he could have gone.'

'But nobody actually discovered him aboard?'

The sailor laughed. 'No, but there's a hundred places a man could hide on the old *Angel*. And,' he added reasonably, 'nobody was looking for him, was they?'

'No,' Josse agreed, 'I suppose not.'

An image was forming in his mind. A dark figure following the merchant and the apothecary on board the *Angel of Mercy*, trailing Nicol home to Newenden. Not quite carefully enough, for Nicol had suspected his presence and was afraid. With good reason, it seemed.

But why? Why should anyone go to the trouble of stowing away on a ship and following the poor lad all the way to England; first to Newenden, then to Hawkenlye, where, if Josse's instinct was right, this someone waylaid Nicol and killed him?

Oh, but he was so far from getting at the truth of it!

He reached inside his pouch and, extracting a coin, flipped it at the sailor, who deftly caught it. 'I'm grateful to you,' Josse said. 'Have a drink on me.'

Then, with a great deal to think about and one or two possibilities already forming in his mind, he made his way back to the inn where he had left the cob and set off for Hawkenlye.

★

In the day and a half that Josse had been absent, Hawkenlye Abbey seemed to have filled up with fear, pain and sorrow.

The simple-minded man called Jabez, young Waldo's dead mother's brother, had died early that morning. Two merchants had arrived a little later, both complaining of terrible pains in their heads and their joints; one of them, the weaker of the two, was showing a rash of dark pink spots on his face, throat and chest. They were being cared for in the far part of the shelter where Jabez had died. The less unwell of the two was able to take in fluids and, as Brother Augustus remarked, the liquid consumption really appeared to help, for all that it seemed that the poor man was losing it out of his rear end as fast as they poured it into his mouth. The older merchant was deep in delirium by midday and too far gone to drink; his fever was steadily increasing and the monks did not think he would last the night.

A little over a week ago, the merchants had put up overnight in Newenden, where, according to the younger man, they had delivered a consignment of frankincense to a certain apothecary's apprentice.

In the afternoon a woman came in with a dead child. The little girl had only just died and the rash still stood out in ugly, vivid blotches all over her small face.

Sister Euphemia, standing in the Vale with Helewise, was setting out her orders for what must be done. So preoccupied and worried was she that she had been talking for some time before she recalled whom she was addressing: 'Forgive me, my lady; hark at how unsuitably I'm speaking, telling my Abbess what she should and should not do!'

'Please, Sister Euphemia, do not stop to consider such a thing,' Helewise replied swiftly. 'I thank God that, at this dreadful time, he has seen fit to supply us with someone like you. Go on with your instructions and, if you can, think of me simply as another pair of hands.'

The infirmarer's dubious expression suggested that she was going to find this difficult. Nevertheless, she went back to her ordering and soon, as her clear-sightedness took over, she forgot all about what was suitable and what wasn't.

Her instructions were based upon trying to keep the sick well away from the healthy and to this end she decreed that, since there were sick people there already, the sleeping shelter in the Vale be converted into an emergency infirmary. Braziers would be installed and the monks would do what they could to make the roof and walls more substantial; 'Patients with fever,' said the infirmarer, 'feel the cold something wicked.' She would send nursing nuns down to tend the patients as required.

Nobody who did not have to mingle with the sick in the Vale for the purposes of taking care of them would go anywhere near them. Those monks who had already tended the sick would bear the brunt of the nursing; 'It's nothing that requires special skill,' Sister Euphemia said, 'and I'll be here if anybody's unsure what to do.'

'You can't carry everybody all by yourself,' Helewise said gently. 'Let me help you; I'm not skilled but I'm willing.'

'Aye, I know, my lady. But we need you to go on performing the role you were chosen for. Besides' – she gave Helewise a swift and preoccupied smile, possibly in apology for having so summarily dismissed the offer of help – 'I've already accepted the first two volunteers.' She gave a nod back up the track that led to the Abbey and Helewise, looking in that direction, saw two black-clad figures hurrying towards her.

Soon they were close enough for their identities to be distinguished. Helewise felt a lump in her throat. As she might have expected, Sister Beata and Sister Caliste had been the nuns who had stepped forward when volunteers were called for. And Helewise, who valued both women not just for their loving, generous hearts and nursing skill but also for themselves, did not know whether to be glad or sorry.

That evening, Brother Firmin complained that his head hurt.

Up at the Abbey, Helewise knelt in the church and prayed that there would be no more cases of the terrifying sickness, that those who were sick now would get better – oh, especially Brother Firmin! Oh, dear Lord, please spare Brother Firmin! – and, perhaps most urgently of all, that Josse would come back.

As the first panicky outpouring of her appeal spent itself, she began to speak the words of the familiar prayers and, as always, felt comfort fall on her like a soft shawl around her shoulders.

And then – perhaps it was the juxtaposition of thinking of Josse and about Brother Firmin, that staunch believer in the benefits of holy water – something slipped into Helewise's mind. At first it was faint and elusive . . . a snatch of memory, nothing more, from, what, a year and a half ago? But then the dreamy images began to clarify and she knew what it was that something – someone – had prompted her to remember.

In the autumn of 1192, a stranger had presented Josse with an ancient treasure that had rightfully belonged to his father. Josse's father was dead and so, as the eldest son, the treasure had come to Josse; it came from Outremer and they said it had the power to detect poison and that, dipped in water, it made a powerful febrifuge. But Josse, fearing not only its magical power but, even more so, the awesome prediction that accompanied it, had given it to Helewise and begged her to hide it away. 'It would be best to keep it here,' he had said, 'because it is only safe in the hands of the very strong, the very wise and the very good, and you and your nuns here at Hawkenlye are all of those.' Deeply touched, she had agreed, although she had firmly told Josse that if ever the day came that he wanted his treasure back again, he had only to ask. 'I won't want it back,' he had assured her, 'I'll be delighted to see the back of it!'

Helewise had taken the treasure and prayed for guidance as to what she should do with it. There were associations of violence in its long and complex history and, to cleanse it, she had decided it should be placed near the altar. Pleading with God that he would make the treasure fit for the healing work that might one day be performed with it, she had left it in its little silver box tucked away on a hidden ledge beneath the altar, where a wooden support was concealed by the linen cloth that covered the altar. Where for the past fifteen months, other than a brief excursion for a first tentative testing of its powers, the treasure had quietly remained . . .

Helewise debated with herself. Magic jewels are a relic of heathen, pagan times, she thought, and we should have no use for them, trusting only in the merciful, healing love of God and his precious son.

But here you are, another part of her instantly replied, kneeling before God's altar, and what happens? A memory of that jewel of Josse's pops into your head, for all the world as if God himself were prompting you! And did you not see fit to let Sister Euphemia try it out – successfully – when there was that outbreak of fever a year ago last autumn?

To and fro the argument went until Helewise felt quite distraught. Then, as if a cool hand were smoothing her brow, she had the sudden thought: I'll ask Josse. It is his jewel, so that will only be right. And if, as I'm sure that he will, he gives his permission, the thought went on – it seemed to have a life and a purpose all of its own – then I shall authorise that the treasure be used.

And we shall see, she concluded as, stiffly and with aching knees, she got to her feet, whether Josse's Eye of Jerusalem is really as powerful as we have been led to believe.

6

Helewise did not know, when she awoke in the morning, that part of her desperate prayer had already been answered: Josse had arrived back in the Vale the previous evening, soon after the monks had settled for the night.

He presented himself in her room in the usually quiet time between Prime and Tierce and she had rarely been as glad to see anybody.

'What news?' she demanded, forgetting in her haste to greet him.

'Some; not much,' he replied, 'although I believe that I begin to see a pattern in what was hitherto a mystery. My lady, unless there are matters about which you wish to speak with me, then, with your leave, I would set out what I see as a possible version of events.'

'Yes, yes, do!' she urged. Then, reminding herself that the poor man had been in the saddle for much of the past two days, she restrained her impatience and added more gently, 'If you would, please, Sir Josse.'

His swift grin, there and gone in a flash, suggested he wasn't convinced by her belated show of good manners. Then he said, 'The foreign pestilence came to England with the Hastings merchant, Martin Kelsey, who had been on business in Paris and caught the sickness when he tended a dying beggar in Boulogne. Kelsey travelled back to Hastings on a ship called the *Angel of Mercy* in the company of the apothecary's apprentice, Nicol Romley, who had been to the great market at

Troyes buying supplies for his master. Someone followed the men on board the *Angel*, although employing such secrecy that nobody except an observant sailor spotted him. Kelsey went home and shortly afterwards fell sick; his spinster sister baulked at nursing him and delegated the task to her maidservant. Kelsey died and, with a cruel opportunism, that same night someone broke into the house and stole a few trinkets. The maidservant fell ill and went home to her family, whose surviving members are even now recovering here at Hawkenlye. Or so I pray?' He looked at her with raised eyebrows.

'The boy and the baby girl are better,' she confirmed. 'The simple uncle died yesterday.'

'Ah.' He muttered something under his breath; probably, she thought, a blessing on the poor man's soul.

'Go on,' she said when she could no longer endure the wait; a matter of all of four heartbeats.

'Nicol Romley fell ill soon after returning to Newenden,' Josse said, 'but there's something else: the lad was mortally afraid that somebody was following him.'

'You mean—' she began, but stopped herself; Josse would tell his tale more succinctly and swiftly if she refrained from interrupting him.

With a quick nod, as if he understood her thought, Josse went on, 'Nicol's master tried to treat him but failed and instead sent the lad off to Hawkenlye. He got as far as the Vale, but then someone attacked and killed him. It's unlikely that this was a simple case of robbery because, although it appeared that Nicol's purse had been searched, the coins hidden at the bottom of it were still there when he was found.'

He waited to see if she wanted to comment but she shook her head.

'So, my lady,' he concluded, 'a virulent and deadly pestilence has come by evil chance to our land. At the same time, some unknown assailant whose purpose we cannot begin to

guess follows a young man home from France and kills him.'
With a helpless shrug, he said, 'Would you care to propose a
likely explanation?'

'Not yet,' she replied with a small smile. 'Although one or
two things occur to me . . .'

'Let's hear them!'

'Well, I am thinking about those coins that were overlooked
in the apothecary's purse. It seems that there is a similarity
between this and the few trinkets stolen from the merchant's
house.'

'Aye, that had crossed my mind too. In addition, the
merchant's sister's best guess was that he died in the small
hours, and she claimed that the ransacking of the house took
place between the time that her brother died and when she
found his body soon after daybreak.'

'The house was ransacked?' Helewise asked. 'Did the sister
not hear any sound?'

'Apparently not, but I have an idea that she may have
exaggerated the offence; my guess is that the intruder broke in,
quietly looked into one or two rooms and, finding a dead man
in one of them, took advantage of his good fortune and made a
quick search, taking anything that caught his fancy and was
small enough to carry away.'

'Supposing,' she said slowly, 'good fortune had nothing to
do with it?'

'You mean—' He stopped, had a think and then, as he
realised exactly what she meant, said, 'My lady, I had got as
far as wondering if our mystery assailant had been watching
Martin Kelsey's house and, guessing that it would be an easy
matter to search the house of a dying man, took his chance and
by coincidence chose for his intrusion the very night that Kelsey
died. But you, if I hear you aright, would go one step further?'

'I am thinking,' she said, 'that, for some reason, the man
who slipped aboard the *Angel of Mercy* has need of total

secrecy for his mission in England, whatever it is. Therefore he had to make sure that the two men who might have seen him – the merchant and the apothecary's apprentice – could not live to give testimony to the fact of his having made the crossing from France to England. So he broke into the merchant's house, put a pillow over his face and then, to make his crime look like theft and not murder, he picked up one or two items and made off with them.' Leaning forward, she said eagerly, 'It was to his advantage that the merchant was so ill! Why, the killer may not even have known that Martin Kelsey *had* the sickness! If he was still in the vicinity in the morning, he would have been amazed at his good luck when it was assumed that the merchant had died of the pestilence and not by another's hand.'

'Martin Kelsey died first,' Josse said. 'It is possible, my lady, that, having smothered the poor man, the assailant then hurried off to Newenden to hunt down the other passenger from the *Angel*.'

'And Nicol Romley, already perhaps feeling the first symptoms of the sickness, also realised that somebody was haunting his footsteps. Then he set off for Hawkenlye, the assailant picked up his trail and followed him . . .'

'And slayed him right here in our Vale!' Josse finished triumphantly.

For a moment they stared at each other, sharing the pleasure at having come up with a possible explanation.

But then Josse began to shake his head. 'Oh, no. It won't do, my lady.'

'Why not?' she demanded; she was not ready to see the tidy theory dismissed out of hand, even if he was.

'Because we're forgetting the captain and crew of the *Angel of Mercy*,' he said dolefully. 'If our hypothetical killer took such trouble to eliminate Martin Kelsey and Nicol Romley, why did he allow the seamen to live?'

She frowned, chewing her lip. 'Unless he was quite con-vinced that none of them had seen him, then because . . .' she began. But it was no use: she could not think of a reason. Undaunted, however, she said, 'Sir Josse, I am sure that we have stumbled on the truth behind this matter, albeit not the complete truth. Do not let us abandon the entire picture for want of one or two small details!'

'Very well,' he agreed. 'Ignoring the small detail of the crew' – he laid a slight ironic emphasis on the word *small* – 'then perhaps we should proceed to speculate on what this killer's mission in England might be and why he is driven to take such pains to conceal his presence here.'

'Oh!' she exclaimed, aghast at the magnitude of the task. Then, with a rueful grimace, 'Where do we start?'

Both Helewise and Josse concluded quite soon that trying to guess what an assailant's purpose might be in coming in such secrecy to England was about as likely as guessing the number of grains of sand on a beach; with relief, they abandoned their speculation.

Helewise, who had been uneasily awaiting an opportunity, said tentatively, 'Sir Josse, there is another matter about which I must speak to you.'

'Please do, my lady.'

She looked down at her hands and then, after a pause, said, 'Two sick men arrived yesterday, one of whom is close to death. Later a young woman arrived with her little girl, who was already dead. Now the mother sickens and' – she con-trolled the urge to sob – 'Brother Firmin has a fever.'

'Old Brother Firmin? Oh,' Josse cried, 'but I spent the night in the Vale! Why did they not tell me? I must go to him!' He made a move towards the door, abruptly curtailed. 'Or perhaps not?' He turned back to face her.

'Sir Josse, we all wish to tend those whom we love who fall

sick,' she said softly. 'But Sister Euphemia has ordered that we must not do so.'

'For fear of spreading the affliction,' he murmured.

'Yes,' she agreed. 'Two of the nursing sisters have already volunteered to work with Sister Euphemia in the temporary infirmary that she has set up in the Vale. She has undertaken to ask when she needs more help.'

I said *when*, she realised. Not *if*.

Josse must have noticed too. 'There will be more sick and dying making their way to us, my lady?' he asked gruffly.

'I fear so.' Rather than allow either of them to dwell on that terrifying prospect, she hurried on. 'That is why I must make this request of you, my friend. May we have your permission to remove the Eye of Jerusalem from its hiding place and use it?'

His expression would have made her laugh had the circumstances been less deadly. 'The Eye?' he echoed. 'Oh, no, my lady Abbess! I gave it to you in the earnest hope of never having to catch sight of it again, for I fear it and would have no dealings with it!'

'People are dying, Josse,' she said quietly. 'May we not even try to use this – this thing that has found its way to us?'

'*You* may!' he shouted, driven to discourtesy by the strong emotion. 'You and your nuns may do whatever you like with it, only do not ask *me* to use it!'

'I do not do so,' she said, in the same soft tone. 'I propose to give it to Sister Euphemia and see what she can make of it, and then to Sister Tiphaine, to see if she might be able to use it to make a febrifuge.'

Josse was already contrite. 'My lady, I apologise for my rudeness,' he said, 'but you may recall why it is that I fear the Eye?'

'Oh, yes I do,' she agreed. 'You shun it because you were told that it would be used by one of your female descendants, someome who would possess strange power, and you would not put this burden upon the girl children of your brothers.'

'The progeny of my brothers are the only descendants that I have!' Josse said. 'The little girls are but children, my lady; I cannot make them take on this dreadful burden!'

'No, of course not.' She tried to soothe him, but it was difficult to sound adequately sincere when her mind was so preoccupied with another thought . . . Pulling her mind away from that thought – not without effort, for it was something that had nagged at her and intrigued her for eighteen months or more – she said, 'Sir Josse, what I ask is simply that you allow my nuns the opportunity to work with the Eye and see whether it can come to our aid in our desperate need. You told me that the Eye will only put out its powers for its rightful owner' – oh, how can I speak in this way, she cried silently, I who have put my trust and my life into God's hands and have no use for superstition! – 'and my hope is that, if you lend it to us willingly and in good faith, then perhaps the question of rightful ownership may be overcome.'

'You can have the wretched stone!' Josse cried.

No, we can't, Helewise said silently, for it is an heirloom of your family, my friend; it belongs to the women of your blood. But she did not speak her thought to him; for the moment at least, it remained a matter for her alone.

Instead she said, 'Thank you, Sir Josse. I will take the Eye to Sister Euphemia and we shall see what happens.'

The infirmarer had been summoned from her patients inside the temporary infirmary and now she stood in the Vale with Helewise and Josse. In a brief, late-morning burst of February sun, she took the jewel from Helewise's hand and held it up to the light.

The Eye was a large, round sapphire about the size of a man's thumbnail. At some time in its past it had been set in a thick gold coin, whose centre had been softened in order that it could be moulded so as to hold the jewel securely. The coin and its precious stone hung on a heavy gold chain.

The Eye, or so they said, had the power to protect and defend its rightful owner. Dipped in a mug offered by a stranger, it could detect the presence of poison. Dipped in a draught of clear, cool water, its force entered the liquid and produced a medicine that stemmed bleeding and lowered fever.

And, according to its own history, it was a thousand years old . . .

'Aye, I remember this pretty thing,' Sister Euphemia said after a moment. 'I have seen it before and indeed I have used it before.' She looked at Helewise. 'We had some success, my lady, did we not?'

Helewise had never managed to make up her mind whether those particular patients had recovered because of the jewel or because of the infirmarer's nursing skill and God's help. But now, she thought, was not the time to say so. 'Indeed we did,' she agreed readily.

'I'd give much to have a remedy that lowered fevers and brought a halt to bleeding,' Sister Euphemia murmured, half to herself, 'for most of our patients are delirious and burn as if with hell fire and not a few have begun to show ruptures and cracks in their skin, so that a constant and painful seepage of blood is added to their woes.'

'How many lie sick at present, Sister?' Helewise made herself ask, conquering her revulsion and trying to replace it with pity.

'There's the two merchants – one, the elder man, is close to death and will not last the day, but the other begins to recover. There's the woman who brought in the dead child; she takes a little water and all may be well with her. There's dear old Firmin, bravely trying not to complain but beside himself with fever most of the time.' Glancing at Helewise, she added quietly, 'And there's the five who arrived just before you came down here, plus their three relatives who are making their way to us.'

'Are all the victims from Newenden?' Josse asked quietly.

Sister Euphemia turned to him. 'The merchants had called in at the town,' she said. 'They sold a bunch of basil leaves to the woman with the dead baby. Today's arrivals come from a village to the east of Tonbridge.'

'It lies between Newenden and Hawkenlye?' Josse asked in a pressing whisper.

'Aye, it does,' the infirmarer agreed.

Josse let out a gusty sigh of relief. 'Then let us hope and pray that our two merchants came straight from that village to Hawkenlye,' he said. 'If they paid a visit to Tonbridge first, then . . .'

He did not finish his sentence, for which Helewise was very grateful; she did not even want to think about what would happen if the pestilence broke out in the narrow, dirty and crowded streets of the town.

She sensed Josse's sudden restlessness. 'I shall ride down to see Gervase de Gifford,' he announced abruptly. 'I must report to him of my discoveries concerning the young man who died here,' he added, explaining himself to the infirmarer, 'and in addition I shall be able to gain up-to-date news as to whether – well, I'll see how things are down there,' he finished lamely.

Helewise caught at his sleeve as he made to leave. 'Be careful,' she said, although she could not have said quite why.

'I will,' he promised. Then, with a smile, he hurried away.

Sister Euphemia sent for the herbalist, and for most of the afternoon they busied themselves preparing what they hoped would be a miracle cure for the sickness. Sister Tiphaine fetched several flasks of the precious healing water from the natural spring that bubbled up out of the sandstone rocks in the Vale; the very water whose discovery had led to the foundation of the Abbey. Sister Euphemia carefully washed the sapphire in its coin in a pot of warmed water, scrubbing off as best she could the grime of centuries. Then she and the infirmarer, heads together as they muttered quietly to each other, set about dipping the Eye into the flasks of spring water.

'How long should we give it, d'you think?' Sister Euphemia asked.

The herbalist shrugged. 'I couldn't say. If it's magic, then a brief moment ought to suffice. If there's some element in the stone that's leaching out into the water, then we ought to leave it for quite a lot longer.'

When they thought and hoped that the jewel had had enough time to do its work, Sister Euphemia tucked it away inside her scapular and took the first flask of water into the shelter. Sister Tiphaine went with her but the infirmarer stopped her at the door. 'Best not,' she said shortly. The herbalist nodded her understanding.

Of the nine people who were given the new medicine – the group who were making their way to the Abbey had yet to arrive – five were very sick. The dying merchant was beyond making any attempt at swallowing and so Sister Beata, who was nursing him, contented herself with using the water to bathe the suffering and delirious man's hot face. The woman who had brought in her dead child – and who had appeared to be recovering – had taken a sudden turn for the worse; the rash on her skin had begun to take on the appearance of fine scales, which were falling off to leave a weeping, bloody mess. She too was no longer sufficiently aware to take in fluid and instead Sister Caliste gently bathed the lesions in her skin.

Two of the five who had arrived that morning – an elderly

man and his middle-aged son – were also close to death and neither of them managed more than a mouthful of water.

Brother Firmin was slipping in and out of consciousness. On being told by Sister Euphemia that she had brought him some of the holy water and would he like a drink, he had given her a beautiful smile and said he'd try a sip, but that he'd really prefer to leave the blessed remedy for others.

His sip was minuscule. Then he slumped back on to his pillow.

Down in Tonbridge, Josse sought out Gervase de Gifford and told him what he had found out in Newenden and in Hastings. De Gifford's interest was aroused at the idea of a man making his way in secret into England for some unknown and clandestine purpose and, with the air of someone thinking out loud, he expounded on the subject.

'They say the King was to be freed early this month,' he mused, 'and I reckon someone, somewhere, will know the truth of that. But, sooner or later, we'll have our Richard back home again. He'll have some sort of a new crowning ceremony, no doubt about that, if only to take away the taint of captivity.'

'Such a ceremony would also serve to remind anyone who might be tempted to forget that Richard is still God's anointed and our king,' Josse put in.

'Yes indeed,' de Gifford agreed.

'How will the King's party travel home, think you?' Josse asked.

'They will be coming from Mainz,' de Gifford replied, 'so they'll probably come by boat up the Rhine into the Scheldt estuary and take ship for England at Antwerp. If I were the King,' he added, 'I wouldn't set sail without a strongly armed escort fleet.'

'You fear the French?'

'I do. King Philip and John Lackland are as thick as thieves and Philip would not be above sending his ships to intercept our King's passage back to England. Should the King fall into Philip's hands, I fear that it would not be a question of merely a year or two spent in captivity.'

'You think it would come to that?' Josse asked, although in his heart he knew that de Gifford's comment was no exaggeration. 'King Philip and our Richard's own brother in league to keep him prisoner?'

'I have heard tell,' de Gifford said quietly, 'that the negotiations for the King's release were brought to a standstill last month because John and Philip outbid his mother's offer.'

'I heard that too,' Josse said glumly. He did not add that his first reaction had not been a prayer for the King's safe release but a sudden and very urgent hope that England would not be in for yet another tax demand to augment the ransom. 'My guess,' he continued, turning from that thought, 'is that John and Philip would give much to have Richard remain a prisoner until they can consolidate the gains they've made together in Richard's French territories.'

'Yes, that would make sense,' de Gifford agreed. Then, as if suddenly recalling what had begun the discussion, he went on, 'But what any of that has to do with the matter in hand, I cannot begin to guess.'

'If, indeed, it has anything to do with it,' Josse added.

'And yet,' de Gifford said softly, 'I wonder . . . A spy sent by John or Philip to discover how the land lies here in England? To set about rallying opposition to Richard with a view to setting John on the throne in his place?'

'One man, to do all that?' Josse asked wryly. 'Gervase, I think that is more a task for an army.'

'Armies do not make good spies,' de Gifford murmured. Then, with a small frown as if he were working something out which, at present, he chose not to share with Josse, he fell silent.

But there were, Josse realised, more urgent things to speak about. With apprehension making his heart beat faster, he asked de Gifford if anyone in Tonbridge had fallen sick of a strange illness.

By the time all those in the community not engaged in vital and life-saving work assembled for Vespers, the sicker of the two merchants, the elderly man and the woman were dead. The three reported as being on their way had arrived; one of their number, a strong young woman, had pushed a handcart on which lay her father, who had apparently been lucid when he was carried out of his home but was now very sick. The father had been clutching a crippled boy who was almost at death's door.

Each of the sick had, in one form or another, been given some of the water that had been treated with the Eye of Jerusalem; not one was showing any improvement.

Helewise sat in her room late into the night. Compline was long over and, down in the Vale, Josse had returned from Tonbridge and, presumably, had settled down for the night. One bright spot in the day had been the welcome news, relayed to her by Brother Augustus soon after Josse had got back, that nobody in Tonbridge was sick of a mysterious foreign pestilence.

Josse, Helewise thought. Oh, Josse. What shall I do for the best?

She knew what she ought to do, for her first – indeed, her only – duty was to fulfil her role as Abbess of Hawkenlye and care as best she could for those who came to her in need. That meant doing all she could to cure the sick, which, in turn, meant using each and every tool put into her hands for that purpose.

She had resigned herself to ordering the employment of the Eye of Jerusalem and, she had to admit, she had been bitterly disappointed when it had not worked. Not only for the poor victims and for Sisters Euphemia and Tiphaine, but also for herself; because she knew that, if the first attempt failed, then there was something else that, dislike it as she may, she was duty-bound to try.

Even if in so doing she was forced into an action that would have a potentially devastating effect upon someone who was very dear to her . . .

Now, in the night-time quiet of the Abbey, she made herself face up to what she knew she had to do.

PART TWO
The Secret Weapon

7

The iron-hard cold of February was not the best time to resume the exacting life of a forest dweller. As she trod the long road back to the hut in the Great Wealden Forest, strong legs tirelessly pacing out the miles, Joanna was filled with a mixture of excited pleasure at the prospect of her return to the place where she had made her home and dread of what she might find there.

Dread, too, of how she would cope with being on her own again when, for the best part of a year, she had lived in the powerful embrace of her adopted people. They had taught her, tested her, taught her some more and made her face up to who and what she was; even now, far away in both distance and time from those experiences, they still had a strange force that reached out to her, so that an echoing shiver of atavistic terror ran down her spine.

Her people had also given her their love and that gift, in a life that had largely been loveless, was what had empowered Joanna and endowed her with the strength to achieve almost all that had been demanded of her. She had a long way to go – it had been impressed upon her with belittling regularity just how little she knew and how much there was still to learn – but, as the day dawned whose evening would, with the Great Ones' blessing, see her back in her forest hut, she reflected back over the extraordinary twelve months that she had been away and knew in her heart that she had at least made a good start.

★

She had left the Hawkenlye Forest the previous March, almost a year ago, setting out on the road alone but for the baby Meggie, secure in the snug sling that Joanna wore across her chest. Joanna had been initiated into the life of her people in the February prior to her departure on her travels but the Great Ones had known – even as she had known herself – that there remained a barrier to full acceptance. She had killed two people and, although both acts were done in defence of innocents who would otherwise themselves have been slain and had therefore been no crime in the eyes of her people, nevertheless death had resulted. 'You have taken life,' she had been told, 'and these acts must be assimilated into the great web that is the life of the tribe.' It was as if, these violent acts having happened, somehow accommodation must be made for them. After an initial month of contemplation and meditation in a cave hidden away deep within the forest, Joanna had been sent on her way, off along the ancient and secret tracks that led into the north-west.

To Mona's Isle.

Her fear and apprehension at what awaited her there might, had she been alone, have slowed her pace to a crawl; might even have made her turn round and run away to hide in some lonely place where they would never find her. But she had not been alone. She had endured solitude during the month in the cave; the main reason that she could find the optimism and courage to keep going on the road to Mona's Isle was because the small person whose absence then had all but beaten her to her knees was with her again. Meggie, four months old, brown-eyed and with the first silky curls forming on her round little head, sat in the sling that Joanna carried across her chest and beamed up at her mother with a tooth-less smile that never lost its power to go straight to Joanna's heart.

Those smiles, Joanna well knew, were probably more often

the product of wind than any conscious response to mother love, but it made no difference whatsoever.

So they had covered the miles together and Joanna sang aloud as she marched. She had never doubted that she would find her way; although she had not known it at the time, there were long periods of her childhood that had been preparing her for this new life. The lessons that she had unconsciously absorbed from Mag Hobson, the beloved woman who had cared for her, now provided the necessary knowledge to get her safely to her destination. She found that she knew how to locate the tracks that were hidden from the casual eye but quite obvious to those who knew where – or perhaps *how* – to look. She knew how to maintain direction when there was no sun by day and no stars by night to guide her and it became second nature to keep a part of her awareness concentrated on making sure that the wind stayed on the appropriate side of her face. The prevailing wind that February of her long march north-westwards had been in the east: as long as it blew on her right ear, she knew she was moving roughly north. She had memorised the markers that would confirm that she was on the right track and, confidence growing, she had hastened on her way.

She had taken the road with her people once and they had taught her the forest arts of making a snug camp, with a shelter made out of discarded branches and dead bracken and a small, careful fire that usually escaped the notice of the curious. Most important of all, she had been taught the methods by which the temporary camp could be abandoned in the morning with no sign, except a narrow circle of burned ground, to show that she had ever been there. Her people did not abuse the earth for the Earth was their mother; their love and respect were too great to risk doing anything that might cause her harm.

Eventually she had reached the channel that cut off Mona's

Isle from the mainland. Not that she could see the island, for all that it was not much more than a mile away, because a thick white mist hung like a heavy curtain over the water.

She waited – a day, two days; she could not be sure – and, just as her faith was starting to slip, a round boat with a willow and wicker frame covered in heavily tarred leather appeared out of the mist in the shallows before her. It was being propelled along swiftly with a single oar by a dark-haired man with a gold ring in his right ear. He wore a leather tunic that was made of the colours of the earth and his arms were bare. As were his feet, Joanna noticed when he skilfully brought the small craft up on to the shore and leapt out.

'Aren't you cold?' she asked, half laughing; he was smiling broadly, apparently taking delight in the day, although the wind was icy and Joanna was clutching Meggie under her cloak and close to her breasts.

'No!' he cried. 'The Sun is always there and always warms us; we have only to remind ourselves of that to feel his heat!'

Even if I could make myself believe that, Joanna thought cynically, it will not avail poor shivering Meggie.

As if the man had read her mind, his expression grew serious. 'You have had a long wait and the little girl is cold,' he said. 'I am sorry for the delay but I could not come for you until Moon was past her full.'

'Oh.' Joanna did not immediately understand; it was the cold, she told herself later, numbing her brain.

The man must have noticed her vacant expression. 'The tides run dangerous high at full Moon,' he explained gently.

'Of course,' Joanna muttered. Then the man picked up her pack from where it lay beside her feet and stowed it under the little boat's central thwart. She took his outstretched hand and, clutching Meggie so tightly that the infant let out a protesting squawk, climbed aboard. The man pushed the craft off the beach, leapt in, picked up his oar and within the blink of an eye they were out in the open water and racing towards the distant shore of Mona's Isle.

Joanna wondered afterwards if her people always made the crossing to and from the island under cover of mist or darkness, both of which conditions ensured that no inquisitive eyes observed the comings and goings. Certainly, on that day the concealing mist did its work well and she was aware of no other living being except the man with the gold earring. He ferried her safely to the island, where he beached his craft, hiding it away in the hollowed-out heart of a thorn brake, then, shouldering her pack as if it contained nothing heavier than feathers, led the way up a short, steep track that gave on to open ground covered in tussock grass and heather. The mist was still swirling thickly around them, silently covering them in drops of moisture, and Joanna could not tell how the man kept to whatever track he was following; perhaps that too, she thought, was intentional.

They walked for what seemed a long time. He stopped for one brief rest, during which Joanna fed Meggie and accepted sips from the man's flask of some sweet, spicy liquid that brought a comforting heat to her mouth and warmed her throat and stomach. Then, all three renewed, they went on their way.

Eventually they reached their goal. They climbed up a long grassy slope strewn with boulders, as if giants had once had a battle and their missiles still lay there abandoned. Then, scaling a sort of lip that seemed to be a part of the natural landscape, they descended into a wide glade guarded by a circle of huge trees. Just at that moment the mists began to clear and Joanna saw that – *of course* – the trees were oaks.

★

So began her time on Mona's Isle. The sense of timelessness that she had already fleetingly experienced became a permanent state and she could never afterwards say exactly how long, in days and weeks, that first stay was. She knew only that, in terms of acquisition of knowledge, it seemed to go on for ever.

She and Meggie were housed in what was clearly one of her people's temporary dwellings, but this had been carefully constructed and was warm and snug. They lived with the other young mothers and their infants, whose company – in that time of learning so much that was strange, frightening, intense – was, at the end of each day, a wonderful reminder that she was still human, still a new mother whose prime concern was to put her child to the breast and watch her grow strong. The women welcomed her but asked no questions concerning who she was and where she came from; they did not even ask her name, although they did enquire as to Meggie's.

Joanna was given a day or two to settle in. Then they sent for her and her instruction began.

She learned so much.

On a night of dark Moon a fortnight after her arrival, her people enacted the ancient tales of Mona's Isle. She wondered at first if this was for her benefit – part of the teaching – but she soon realised that this was a regular event, the means by which the tribe ensured that the story did not die and that the people remembered their own past, and she chided herself for her presumption.

The ceremony took place on a mild night. Joanna and the other mothers were ordered to take their babies with them and, well wrapped in a fur cloak, Joanna settled on the ground and waited in expectation.

The tale unfolded with men in hide cloaks and animal masks creeping through the encircling oak trees and into the clearing. Their first act in the dark, sacred grove was to give praise, in a sudden screaming shout to the night sky that made Joanna's heart leap into her mouth and set Meggie wailing. The woman beside her gave her a grin and told her to put the babe to the breast: 'That'll give her something else to think about!' As Meggie suckled, Joanna gave herself up to the performance.

She watched as the men in masks were joined by others – women and children – and a society was formed. She watched the people divide themselves into small groups, some hunters, some berry gatherers, some the guardians of the people's stock animals. She watched as some of the men and the women stood up tall and put on robes of pure white, miming the action of cutting something obviously precious from the oak trees with small golden sickles. She watched as the lore of the people was passed from the old to the young, always by word of mouth, always muttered softly so that only the designated ear should hear.

Then came the attack.

She thought it was real and would have shot terrified to her feet, ready to flee for the cover of the trees and the undergrowth, but for her neighbour's firm restraining hand on her arm. 'Be still,' the woman hissed, 'there is no danger now!'

Men came pushing and shoving into the grove; men dressed in leather boiled until it was hard and stained red with the bruised fruit of the mulberry. They carried long wooden poles and short stabbing swords that, at a distance, looked like iron. They went among the people and cut them down and then they began on the trees. The people put up a fierce resistance, with women in black robes and wild hair waving torches and hurling themselves, spitting and screaming, on the invaders, while the men raised their hands to the black sky and called down curses on their enemy. But spittle, screams and curses could make no immediate impact against swords and javelins; soon it was all over.

Joanna thought that they had actually cut the trees down for, as the soldiers departed and left the grove to the dead, she saw great felled oak trunks lying across the grass. She had tears in her eyes, weeping not just for the people but for those glorious trees . . .

A voice was chanting. Softly at first – Joanna could not tell if it issued from a woman or from a man – it seemed to be recounting the list of the dead. Then the voice grew louder and the cursing began, shouting aloud the name of the enemy and begging the Great One to keep the commander and his army in perpetual torment in retribution for their sacrilege and their pitiless slaughter.

'They thought they had killed us all, tribe and tree, people and practice,' cried the voice, soaring now up out of the grove and into the night sky. *'They were wrong, for the people of the oak do not die and we are still here!'*

As the echoes of that great cry died, a vast shout came from the people, a shout that had no words but was a simple opening of throats as, their pent-up energy at last flowing from them, the people screamed their defiance and their pride.

And Joanna, with them, one of them, joined in.

In the course of her subsequent instruction, Joanna was taught the cruel reality that lay behind the tale. Her people were the indigenous race of the islands of Britain, old in their ways long before the invader from the hot south arrived. Driven progressively westwards, they had thought to be left in peace, for they had yielded the prime lands to the relentless newcomers and it seemed for a time that, having gained military dominance, the invader would be satisfied with that and allow the people to live and to worship as they saw fit. But the people had a strong and enduring power that the invader perceived to be a threat; as systematically as they did everything, the leather-clad, sword-wielding armies from the south began the annihilation of their rivals. The Great Ones of the people fled before them, making their way in the end to the holy groves and the sanctuary of Mona's Isle, but this sanctuary was but illusion.

The leader of the invaders drew up his men on the far shore and commanded them over the water and on to the attack. The men were afraid, for rumour of the people and their strange powers had spread like sickness through the southerners' ranks, but their commander was not a man to abandon a mission. He ordered the most vociferous of the reluctant ones to be brought forward and he ordered savage punishment. Having thus made an example of the cowards, once again he gave the order to proceed across the water. This time there was no hesitation.

'They killed everyone that they found,' sighed the old man who was Joanna's teacher in this vital part of her instruction. 'Men, women, children; mercy was shown to none. Then they cut down the trees, for Suetonius was a wily man and he knew that destroying our sacred groves would be a blow from which we would not recover.'

There was an extended silence. Finally, when she could bear it no longer, Joanna said, 'But you *did* recover!'

The old man smiled. 'Oh, yes.' Then, after a pause, he went on, 'Have you ever seen a tree in a dry summer? Hm?'

'Er . . .' She thought frantically what he meant. Then suddenly she knew, or believed she did. 'We had a birch tree in the place where I grew up,' she said softly. 'One year there was a prolonged drought and the birch put out a myriad small seeds. They went everywhere and we were finding them in the house for months afterwards. Later we noticed that there were dozens of little birch saplings.'

'Well done.' The old man was nodding his approval. 'Your

Lady Birch perceived the threat and she put forth her strength and ensured her survival; even had she herself perished, she would live on through her daughters.' Leaning forward, he said, 'In this same way did the sacred oaks of Mona make sure that they would endure.'

Joanna frowned, trying to absorb this. 'But they – that is, the trees' – she was finding it difficult to speak as naturally as her teacher did of trees as sentient beings – 'they could not have known in advance that they would be destroyed, so how could they have had the time to produce a particularly generous crop of acorns?'

The old man was watching her. 'They knew,' he said simply. 'That is a fact for, even as the armies went marching away back to the conquered lands, already the acorns were putting down their tap roots. By the time Boudicca died those roots were strong and, the next spring, the first leaves appeared. Four hundred years later the invader went away, as do all invaders in the end, and here in the sacred grove, it was as if he had never been.'

'And what of the people?' Joanna whispered, although she felt she already knew what the old man would say.

The old man smiled gently. 'If a tree can survive, so can men and women,' he said. 'Child, from what you already know of us your people, can you believe that, unlike the oaks, we had no forewarning?'

Something about what he said snagged in her mind but she was preoccupied with discovering how they knew and did not pause to look at what it might have been. 'Do you mean that the people saw the enemy on the far shore?' she asked. 'Or that they had sent out spies to see what the soldiers were doing?'

'Both of those things, naturally, for they are common-sense actions. But think beyond such things. Think how it is that you, even you, young and green as you are like a slim birch sapling, *know* when your child needs you, even when she is out of range of your eyes and your ears.'

'Well, I suppose that's a mother's instinct,' Joanna said without pausing to think.

'Instinct,' the old man repeated. 'The use not of eyes, ears or touch, but of something far more fundamental and subtle. Ponder that, child, and come back to me when you have done so.'

It was the old man who bestowed her new name. He must have likened her to a birch sapling knowingly for he named her Beith. The birch, she learned, was the first tree to grow after the retreat of the ice and so was sacred to the Mother Goddess. Among her people Joanna was so called for ever more.

There was no warning of what came next. She was shaken awake very early one morning soon after the spring equinox – and when, indeed, she and the rest of the community were still catching up on their sleep following the extraordinary night of celebration – and told to pack up, feed Meggie and get herself ready. She had learned that it would do no good at all to say, 'Ready for what?' and she did not, instead meekly doing as she was ordered and then sitting down patiently to wait.

It was the man with the gold earring who came for her and the fact of its being him straight away gave her a clue. Sure enough, and without allowing the time for goodbyes, he led the way out of the settlement by the grove and back across the grassy moor land to the shore, where once again he helped her into his little boat to ferry her across the narrow channel. On the mainland shore he gave her a nod, wished her good speed and the Great Mother's protection, then nimbly turned his boat and paddled swiftly away.

She had no idea where she was to go. Back home to the hut in the forest? Surely not, for there had been hints in plenty that something was being planned for her that had nothing to do with quietly returning to where she had come from.

She waited for much of that day. At sunset, a small, neat ship entered the channel from the north-east and, its sails furled, slipped quietly along until, offshore from where she stood, it lowered an anchor. As she watched, a small boat was lowered and rowed across the water towards her. A man with weather-roughened skin called out to her and, picking up her pack, she ran down the beach and jumped into the boat, Meggie in her sling bouncing up and down with the violence of the action. The man gave a nod and in silence rowed her out to the ship, where he helped her climb up a rope ladder hanging down from the wooden deck. A group of sailors stood watching her; a couple of them gave her friendly smiles.

Then a tall man in black stepped forward from the shelter of a companionway. 'I am called Nuinn,' he said in a rich, deep voice. 'I am to take you south across the sea to Armorica, which is the Land Beside the Sea. It is a long way. Come with me' – he stepped back inside the entrance – 'and I will show you to your quarters.'

The cabin was tiny but at least she and Meggie had it to themselves. There was room on the floor – which was spotlessly clean – for her pack but for little more, and the rest of the space was taken up by a narrow bed with several thick woollen blankets and a small pillow. Under the bed were a bucket and a jug, both at present empty.

'The bucket is for your personal use,' the captain said tactfully; 'come up on deck and empty it to leeward before it's full, else you'll spill what's in it and have to mop it up.' He gave her a swift grin. 'Jug's for washing water; you'll be told when it's available.'

'Thank you,' Joanna managed.

He grinned again. 'It'll be rough once we're out of the

shelter of the island,' he said. 'You may be sick or you may not; people are different. If you're sick, remember to eat whenever you can; better by far to be sick when you have something to be sick with.'

As he spoke those disconcerting words, there came the sound of voices from above and she felt the ship give a sort of bounce. Then there was a definite sensation of movement, quickly accelerating. She sat down heavily on the bed and Meggie gave a small cry.

The captain was already half out of the cabin. 'Come up on deck if you wish,' he said, 'but do not get in anybody's way.'

Over the next three days Joanna experienced so may new sensations — some of them wonderful, some unspeakably awful — that, by the end of the crossing, she felt as if it had lasted half a lifetime. She was very seasick at first, heaving up her stomach's contents into the bucket, then, when she felt the instant relief that comes just after being sick, hurrying up aloft to empty the vomit over the side and to eat some dry bread and drink a mug of watery beer before the nausea began again.

But the sickness subsided and soon Joanna began to congratulate herself on being as good a sailor as Meggie, who had watched her mother's convulsions and listened to her moans with a polite look of puzzlement on her little face, as if asking what all the fuss was about; Meggie had suffered no ill at all. Then it was heavenly to stand up on deck, warmly wrapped and with Meggie held against her body inside her cloak, feeling the bite of the wind and the sea spray in her face and watching the endlessly changing waters race by.

In time she thought she saw land; there was a line of reddish-brown on the horizon which gradually resolved itself into low cliffs. As the ship neared shore, the water seemed to change from grey-blue to a sparkling, vivid green that looked like emeralds.

And, not long after that, the ship furled her sails and slid into a narrow, secretive bay. As before, a boat was lowered; Joanna and Meggie were helped down into it and rowed the short distance to the shore. The fearsome red rocks at the mouth of the bay surprisingly hid a small area of sandy beach, where two men appeared to help Joanna on to dry land. She was so busy trying to keep her footing in the deep, soft sand that she forgot to turn round until it was too late and the ship that had carried her south was already moving off towards the mouth of the bay.

The men took her to a small cottage deep in woodland and left her in the care of a woman and a younger girl, who looked after her for a couple of days. She was offered a bath and the women took every single garment she and Meggie possessed, washing them and hanging them out to dry on the holly and hazel bushes that grew in abundance around the cottage. While her clothes dried, Joanna moved about wrapped in a soft length of woollen cloth; such was her instant familiarity with the two women that, had the late March weather been a little warmer, she might have even done away with the wrap.

The women spoke a version of the language that Joanna had been speaking on Mona's Isle; which, indeed, she had always used with her own people and which she dimly recalled having spoken with Mag Hobson. The ordering of the women's days was familiar too; the pattern of life was very well known to her . . .

When Joanna, her child and her limited wardrobe had been fully restored, the women took her off on yet another journey. This time they travelled south into the heart of Brittany, and were soon deep in a vast forest that seemed to go on for ever. They made two, perhaps three, overnight camps – again, Joanna was experiencing a disorienting sense of timelessness – and then one morning they entered an area where the rocky granite outcrops rising up among the trees and the grassland were as red as the cliffs that had called out a welcome up on the coast.

They followed a narrow track that wound under trees, the beaten earth beneath their feet as red as garnets. Then they came to a small settlement: some of the typical temporary dwellings but, this time, also some low and sturdy little cottages made of the local pink granite. From one side of the settlement a path marked with stones along either side wound away up into a particularly dense area of forest, where pine, birch and holly gradually supplanted the broom and the gorse; both women gave a bow of reverence in that direction, as if something precious lay hidden there.

Then they approached the largest of the stone dwellings and the elder woman tapped softly on the door. It was opened by a man of perhaps sixty, vigorous even in age, with a tanned and weather-beaten face and long white hair and beard. He wore a deep blue robe which, as it caught the light, sometimes looked silver. He nodded to the two women and said something to the elder one, waving a hand back inside the house to where a jug of ale and a loaf of bread had been set out, together with a pat of butter and a round cheese with a particularly piquant smell; Joanna thought it might be goat. Her stomach gave a growl of hunger.

The white-haired man turned, gave her a wide smile and then, opening his arms, said, 'You are Beith. I am Huathe. You and your girl child are expected and all is ready for you.'

Joanna moved into the circle of his arms and was given a powerful hug which, because Meggie was still in here sling, included her too; Joanna heard the infant give a soft gurgle of happiness and she was just thinking that it was odd for Meggie to respond so positively to such a robust greeting from a complete stranger when the man spoke again, inviting her inside to eat and drink her fill.

Loosening the hug but keeping hold of Joanna's hand, he led her into the house. 'This place,' he said, 'is called Folle-Pensée. Here we heal those who are sick in body and in mind, and here too we teach those healing skills.' There was a pause and then he added, 'Welcome to your new home.'

8

Quite soon after her arrival in the secret place at the heart of the forest of Broceliande, Joanna discovered why the location was so precious to her people.

The revelation came about on a bright April morning of sudden warm sunshine after several days of rain. There was peaty standing water in the low-lying areas of sallow and dogwood around the settlement, which gave off a pungent, invigorating scent that was the very distillation of growth. The trees were putting on their spring green raiment, the tender, unfurling leaves brilliant with raindrops, and the air smelt heady and sweet, like a potent drug. Joanna and the younger of the two women who had escorted her to Folle-Pensée – the older woman had returned to her cottage near the coast – had just finished clearing away their breakfast meal when Huathe came to the door of the shelter.

'Fearn will take care of the child,' he commanded, and the young woman jumped to obey; Joanna had been in the process of washing Meggie's rosy bottom prior to dressing her, and Fearn took the cloth out of Joanna's hand and resumed the task.

Huathe was already setting off along the path marked with stones. Obediently Joanna fell into step behind him. They walked for a hundred or so paces and Joanna noticed that the path was getting narrower; the stone border had petered out and suddenly she had a weird sense of having stepped beyond the human realm and into some strange place that belonged solely to the woodland. To the trees, the flowers, the birds and the small, secretive animals whose presence was only detectable by tiny rustlings in the grass.

Perhaps some sort of reaction was common at this spot; for Huathe turned and gave her an encouraging smile. 'Not far now,' he said.

I don't mind how far it is, Joanna might have replied; this is like walking in paradise and I could happily remain here all day.

A movement caught her eye and she looked up to see a tree creeper searching for insects on the trunk of a pine tree. Then from further away, as if the bird knew how special this moment was for her and was celebrating it, she heard her first cuckoo of the year. Standing quite still, an entranced smile on her lips, she listened as the sound came closer.

Suddenly a pair of birds swooped towards her through the upper branches of the pine and the birch trees. She thought at first that they were sparrowhawks, for they seemed to carry their weight in their flattish heads and necks. She noticed that Huathe had also stopped and was standing a few paces further along the path; the birds, intent on their mating ritual, were oblivious to both of them. Then the male bird gave the unmistakable call: *Cuck-koo! Cuck-koo!*

Thrilled, she turned to Huathe, who was looking similarly delighted. 'We are blessed, Beith,' he said softly, 'for the cuckoo is a shy bird and it is rare for him to show himself.' Moving closer, he added, 'It is said among the country folk that in winter the cuckoo turns into a hawk, for he is never seen except in the spring and the summer.'

'Is he . . .' She hesitated, for the question seemed silly. But Huathe was looking at her with such kindness in his deep eyes that she decided it didn't matter. 'Is the cuckoo magic?'

Huathe laughed gently. 'No, Beith. I have had the luxury of time to observe the habits of birds and what I think is this:

some birds like a warmer or a colder winter than that common to these temperate lands. It is my conclusion that the cuckoo, in common with the swallow and the swift, flies away at the end of the summer to spend the cold half of the year in some warm place far to the south.'

'But how—' But how could a tiny bird fly so far? she wanted to demand; it seemed as silly as suggesting that cuckoos could magically turn themselves into hawks. Huathe, however, was her teacher and the man who ordered her days and it would not do to question his wisdom; she firmly closed her mouth.

They walked on. Huathe made a turn to his right and then they were climbing, the path winding this way and that as it ascended what appeared to be a low knoll set deep among the trees. Somewhere close at hand a chaffinch was singing, the distinctive three-note conclusion to its complicated trill sounding like *cross the stream!*

The sound of water was all around, rippling, bubbling and gurgling, always just out of sight through the trees and the undergrowth. Joanna peered into the dense green, trying to discover where the stream ran; she thought she saw a movement in the trees and, eyes darting back to the spot, she saw a flash of deeper green against the spring foliage and stared the more fixedly.

And Huathe gave a soft laugh and said, 'Do not try so hard, Beith! The fleeting glance obtains the best result.'

So there was someone – something – out there! Joanna's first reaction was excitement, and it was only after another spell of silent walking that she felt a tremor of fear.

Now they were deep in the forest and the path was little more than a faint animal track; one of so many similar ones that Joanna knew that, left alone here, she would never find her way out. The fledgling fear grew, threatening to overwhelm her. But then a cool voice said right inside her head, *Remember your initiation at the Rollright Stones. You were afraid then, too, but you used your logic and all was well.*

Yes! Oh, yes, she remembered that all right! She thought back to that extraordinary night and reminded herself how she had quashed her panic and used her common sense. I could do that here if I had to, she told herself firmly. And, walking on, raised her chin as if in answer to an unspoken challenge.

Huathe was moving more swiftly now and she broke into a trot to keep up with him. Under a broken branch, over an outcrop of stones, past the great bulge of a yew tree's thick foliage; they were still climbing and she was panting. Then a sudden sense of light as the forest canopy thinned: Huathe had stopped and, coming to stand beside him, she found herself looking at brilliant sunshine illuminating a wide glade right at the summit of the hill.

He did not speak but stood with a gentle smile on his face, allowing her to see for herself. And Joanna, already drugged with the very essence of spring, tried to take in everything at once and made herself dizzy in the attempt. Shaking her head, laughing, she tried again.

Gradually her eyes became accustomed to the dazzle of light on the amazing scene before her. Most of the trees had been cleared away, so that sentinel oaks stood in a protective circle around an all but bare hilltop; the exception was a lone oak under which there grew an ancient hawthorn that seemed to crouch like an old man huddled in upon himself. A long, thin white banner had been fastened to an upper branch. The hawthorn stood above a small cairn of granite rocks whose purpose she did not immediately discern.

Then she realised that the sound of water was much louder here. Leaping forward, she saw that the rise of the ground immediately in front of her had in fact concealed the stream that flowed out from the hillside, shallow across stones and as clear as light, running away down to her right, towards the valley below. Looking to her left, up to the very top of the hill, she saw now that the cairn marked the place where the water issued out of the earth. She glanced at Huathe and, at his nod of permission, she walked slowly up the stream to the cairn.

Beside the cairn, at the spot immediately above the sparkling spring, there was a huge, flat piece of granite, almost like a platform. It had an aura of power about it and she knew not to stand on it. Instead she fell to her knees and peered down into the hollow basin into which the spring flowed out of the hillside. The bed of the basin was pale, as if white powder had been spilt there, and at frequent intervals a small line of air bubbles would rise out of it and come up to the surface. It was quite hypnotic; Joanna wriggled round until she was lying on her stomach and, gazing into the water, she noticed that some of the flat stones on the stream bed had developing newts clinging to their smooth surfaces.

Presently Huathe spoke. 'This is the spring of Barenton,' he intoned, 'although some call it Merlin's Fountain.'

She knew he was going to speak again and so she did not answer. After a pause, he said, 'To us, this place is Nime, for that is the name of the goddess whose spirit is here. It is she who brings the Mother's gift of water from the Otherworld that is the source of life. Her presence blesses the water and the place and her power protects both.'

Nime, Joanna repeated to herself. Still she did not speak; there was something in the air – tension, anticipation – that told her not to.

'You have felt the power and the presence, Beith; I read this in you.' She nodded. 'I observed your glance at the stone' – he indicated the huge slab of granite – 'and I sense that you knew without being told that it is a force focus and not a place for the casual footstep.'

Joanna watched as he approached the stone platform and, after a low bow, knelt before it and put his hands on its glassy surface. Then he reached down into the basin and dipped his fingertips into the bright water, straightening up and allowing drops to fall on the granite.

It seemed to Joanna that a mist began to form immediately over the flat stone, as if the spring water were vaporising; the creamy mist swirled, forming itself into shapes that endured for the blink of an eye before dissipating and reforming as something else. Joanna thought she saw shadowy robed figures; a running horse; an arrow's flight; a sword. She felt a sort of pulse briefly beat through the warm air, as if thunder had exploded in the distance and its shock waves had reached her before its sound. Then, to complete the image, she heard a muffled thunderclap.

She whispered, 'What is it? What are you doing?'

Huathe smiled. 'Do not be alarmed; you are quite safe. People sometimes scare themselves here; for the unwary hear the rumours and the old tales and they come here to test them out. More than once we have had to treat foolhardy men who stamp on this sacred stone and then are terrified when the predicted response comes.'

'What happens?'

Huathe shrugged. 'Usually a storm, or what is perceived to be a storm.'

'And they – these people – they are injured?'

'Their minds are injured, for sometimes they imagine that lightning strikes them, or that it strikes trees which then fall upon them.'

'But . . .' She was struggling to understand. 'But these things don't really happen?'

Huathe was smiling again. 'Beith, there is so much you must learn. First, you have to open your mind to possibilities. Our great task is to search for the sublime, to delve into what is secret and arcane and, by so doing, achieve the uplifting that is our destiny.'

Reeling from his announcement, from the concept of opening a mind that she had never actually considered closed, she realised that he was speaking again; thankfully, for she was not sure how much more she could absorb, he had turned to matters which, in the light of her own experience, she felt better able to comprehend.

'We use the spring water to make our divination mirror,' Huathe was saying. 'The water is collected in a bowl of red granite. On clear nights, Moon's reflection in the still, dark water of the basin gives the illusion that she is drawn down to Earth and so we tell ourselves that she is temporarily within our reach.

'But,' he went on after a moment, 'the water has another purpose, and it is to do with this that you have been sent here.' He had moved away from the granite slab as he spoke and now stood beside her once more. Looking right into her eyes – into her soul, she thought, for she had no defence against his penetration and did not dare look away – he said, 'Beith, I know what you have done. You took life and an adjustment must be made.'

Adjustment. She did not know what he meant. 'I am to be punished?' She heard the shake in her voice.

'No, that would not be appropriate,' he said quickly, looking away from her and out across the glade, 'for to kill in self-defence or to protect those who cannot protect themselves is to us no crime. But because of your actions two men died, and your spirit carries the burden of that. The adjustment of which I speak involves recompense; in order to balance what has happened to you, you must save the lives of two people who are dying.'

'*Me!* I can't save life, I don't know how to!' Huathe, still serenely smiling, ignored her outburst. She forced herself to think sensibly. Save lives. Did that mean she was to treat the sick? 'It is true that I have a little herb lore,' she said tentatively, 'for I was well taught in my youth and have studied the matter more intensively in the course of the last two years. But I do not know nearly enough to save lives!'

'Not yet,' he remarked. 'And it is a good beginning, young Beith, to recognise one's ignorance.' He turned back to face her again. 'But you will learn,' he said in a tone that allowed no argument, 'and that is why you are here.'

Joanna stayed at Folle-Pensée throughout the spring and summer. It was a period of such intensive study and learning that at times she had to isolate herself from the community and, alone in the forest, try to order and make sense of the endless lore, the legends and stories, the whirling thoughts and inspirational possibilities that her teachers were instilling into her. She realised that, while people came and went from Folle-Pensée quite regularly, there remained a core of elders and teachers who were healers or instructors; sometimes, like Huathe, they were both. These elders lived in the relative comfort of the low granite cottages; for temporary residents such as Joanna, it was the shelter under the birch trees.

Not knowing how much she already knew, her teachers started at the beginning, telling her of the Goddess and the Earth that is her body; of the Earth's natural rhythms and how the people learned the Mother's lesson of how to position stones and mounds to maintain her body's balance. On a starry night at the end of April, Joanna joined a procession that wound its way down through the Broceliande on the long road south-westwards to the standing stones that marched in ranks on the headland above the sea. There, in the light of the stars, she stood waiting with her people, although she did not know what they waited for.

Then the Moon rose.

The first sight of the brilliant moonlight on the endless rows of huge stones, their shadows lengthening on the springy grass as if they were an advancing army, was something that Joanna never forgot. And when she heard the chanting begin – a sole voice joined by another, then another, then more and more until it seemed that the very Earth was singing – she thought her heart would break with joy.

As if that powerful experience had been the introduction, they taught her astrology and how to make a mental map of the night sky so that, when asked where to find the Little Bear, the Swan, Cassiopeia or the Heavenly Twins, she could instantly point in the right direction. They taught her to make the association between the moving pattern of the stars over her head and the turn of the seasons on Earth below and she understood then how the two were and had always been interdependent. She learned of the fundamental link between the heavens and the people, animals and plants of Earth, and she came to know instinctively how and why a person born in late January differed from one born in mid-August, and why crops must be planted and harvested only at certain times.

At the midsummer solstice she went with her people to gather at a long, ground-hugging structure made of great granite stones, arranged so that the doorway stones allowed but a low, dark entrance into the interior. They stood vigil through the short hours of darkness and then, as the Sun rose, his first rays shot like an arrow from the eastern horizon, over the hills and vales and straight into the entrance to the long barrow. The sexual imagery was obvious and, to Joanna's surprise, there was quite a lot of laughter and ribald joking. She asked her teachers later if this had not been disrespectful.

'Do *you* not laugh and joke after the sexual act, Beith?' they asked her. 'Does the Goddess-given ecstasy not make you joyful?'

'Er—' But the answer was complex and would have taken far too long, so Joanna did not give it.

They smiled, taking her reluctance as coyness. 'Do not be

shy,' an incredibly old woman said. 'And do not fear to join in the fun the next time you witness the God penetrate the Goddess and you feel their passion reflected in your own body!'

They taught her how to recognise, collect and prepare the magical drugs that give insight and, in a lucky few, open the window on the future and bestow the gift of prophecy. They watched over her as she drank down the draught that her own hands had prepared and they listened to her as, deep in her own inner world, she cried out and sobbed as the images formed, broke and formed again. She learned how to channel the power and use it for the benefit of others and, in time, dreams, trance and vision became some of her most valuable and potent tools.

She learned the long history of her people. Over four successive nights leading up to Lughnasadh, she sat with her people around a fire and they listened in utter silence to one of the great bards tell the story of how they came out of the East and the Great Mother showed them the vast river that winds through the lands like the blood in the Mother's own body. He told how she led them to the wonderfully rich and fertile area at the headwaters of three great rivers, giving them this precious piece of her body as a place in which they might settle and thrive so that, in time, their descendants grew numerous and confident and set out to spread themselves throughout the green lands. He described the journeys westwards and northwards and, because his gift of communication meant that he was aware how important it was to make a story personal for its audience, he finished by describing the very place in which they sat in the warmth of a summer night.

When she had learned all of that, at last they began on the long road that would make her a healer.

★

As the days shortened and the first leaves began to turn, a newcomer arrived in the settlement at Folle-Pensée. Joanna was preoccupied and barely noticed him; Huathe was teaching her the extraordinary concept that a person's body may be made ill because their mind is in distress, and she was undergoing another period of having her mind stretched to encompass something that she could hardly believe. Huathe had ordered her to spend the day with two of his patients, a woman whose grief for a stillborn baby had rendered her feeble-minded and mute and a youth who wanted them to amputate his arm as he feared it would pick up a sword and cut his parents to pieces. The impact of those two damaged minds had been harrowing and Joanna was exhausted when she returned to the shelter.

Fearn, who had remained there to greet her when she came in, gave her a hug and a mug containing a restorative infusion. 'Don't expect to grasp it all at once,' she murmured, and Joanna gave her a grateful smile. 'That's better!' Fearn said. 'Now, you sit there – here's Meggie, see, wanting a cuddle! – and I'll bring you something to eat. Then we're in for a treat because Reynard's here!'

At ten months, Meggie was a strong and active child, able to stand if she held on tight to someone's hand. As Fearn deposited her in Joanna's lap, the little girl turned to give her mother a smile.

You, my precious, smile like your father, Joanna thought. The resemblance was enhanced by Meggie's velvet brown eyes; if ever the two stood side by side, there would be no denying who had engendered *this* child . . .

Don't think about that, Joanna told herself. Think instead about this Reynard, whoever he might be, and why the fact of his having arrived is making Fearn so excited that she's just spilt the milk.

★

She never forgot Reynard, although his enduring place in her memory was more because of what came soon afterwards than for himself. Not that he was insignificant; nobody could have called him that. He was a man of indeterminable age who apparently lived alone in the wildwood and communicated with the animals; they said he was a shape shifter, one who was able to take on the spirit and essence of an animal and project it so that it walked the Earth and would sometimes act according to the man's wishes. He had a head of tangled russet-coloured hair and was heavily bearded and he wore a garment made of animal skins decorated with shells, feathers and small white teeth. His spirit animal, they said, was the fox; he wore its fur and his essence mixed with that of the fox.

Tired from her day's efforts, lulled by the warmth of the fire and the soft sounds of Meggie asleep in her arms, Joanna watched Reynard dancing and listened to his yelping song. In the firelight his image seemed to float close and then away again and, seen through the smoke, it really did appear that he changed from man to fox and back again.

But of course, she thought drowsily, he can't possibly do that . . .

On the night of the autumn equinox they told her that she must leave Meggie with Fearn and go off alone into the forest. She must find her way to the fountain of Nime. Naturally, they did not tell her why.

She had learned much in the six months since Huathe had first taken her deep in the forest to the spring and at first she was not afraid. She hummed as she strode along the tracks, aware of the forest life all around her but content in the knowledge that if she did no harm then no harm would be done to her.

Then she heard soft, stealthy movement away off to her right.

She remembered the faint green figure she had seen under the pines on that first visit.

She clutched the bear's claw that she wore around her neck and made herself stride on.

She reached the open glade, heartened by the happy sound of the stream. She gave a nod of greeting to the hawthorn bush – it looked even more like a crouching man in the moonlight – and went to kneel down so that she could put her fingers in the cold water of the spring. She resumed her humming.

Then he was standing beside her as if he had sprung out of nowhere. Without turning, she knew who he was; nobody on Earth smelled quite like he did. It was more than half a year since she had seen him, since he had summoned her at the great Imbolc festival, but as she leapt up and felt his warm, strong arms encircle her, it seemed as if she had been there, so close to him that she could feel his heart beating, all the time.

In that instant of reunion she remembered everything; how he had appeared to her simultaneously as bear and man, how her delight in him was in part because of the wildness of him, the feel of soft fur brushing against her naked flesh whose origin could equally well have been the soft skins in which they had lain or his own pelt.

But he was man, she knew that now, for they had coupled as man and woman and it had been an experience whose power had left her weak. Now he was here, she was in his arms once more and there was an inevitability about the meeting that told her it was destined; that there was a pattern to her life and he was a crucial part of it.

He kissed her, his hands under her tunic tender and warm on her bare skin. He did not hurry; it seemed that he would take all the time that was required to arouse her and make her ready for him. Entranced, enraptured, Joanna gave herself up to him and did not think to tell him that she had been more than ready from the moment he had touched her.

He led her across the glade and down a narrow track that led
to a bracken-roofed den lined with furs. Then he slipped her
tunic over her head and removed his own garments. Lying
down beside her, he touched the bear claw in its silver mount.
He smiled – she caught the glitter of white teeth – and then,
bending to kiss her, tip-tonguing his way from her neck down
over her breasts to her belly, his fingers on her, inside her,
slippery in her own moisture, slowly, slowly he entered her.

In the morning, just as before, she woke alone. Warmly
wrapped in furs that smelt of him, she lay on her back staring
up at the golden birch leaves high above. Soon – for she was
ravenously hungry – she sat up, dressed, tidied the den as best
she could and set off on the long walk back down to the
settlement.

9

Joanna's departure from Folle-Pensée came as suddenly and unexpectedly as her arrival; one morning in early October, when the clear sky appeared deep blue in contrast to the ochre and bronze of the autumn leaves, the order came that she was to prepare for her next journey and they would be leaving that evening.

Four of them left the Broceliande settlement as the sun went down: Huathe, Joanna, Meggie and a slim, lithe figure cloaked in dark grey who wore a deep hood concealing the head and face. They travelled through the woodland paths for a long time; Joanna could tell by the Moon that it was after midnight when they stopped, making their camp on the dry and dusty floor of a hollow crevice in an outcrop of rock. She had been watching the sky whenever the tree canopy allowed a clear sight and she knew that they had been walking north-westwards; wherever they were bound, it was not, therefore, to the beach where she had first landed in Armorica because that lay due north of Folle-Pensée. But there was no point in speculating; she would find out their destination soon enough.

They walked for all of the next day and the day after that. When Joanna became tired – for much of the time she was carrying Meggie and, at almost a year, she was no longer a lightweight – Huathe would take the child and let her ride on his shoulders. Their frequent but brief stops were usually taken when Meggie, fed up both with being carried in a sling and born aloft on Huathe's shoulders, clamoured too persistently to get down.

Their marching order did not vary: the hooded figure went first, maintaining a steady pace that allowed them to cover the ground quickly; then came Huathe; and Joanna brought up the rear. Late on the second day, Joanna sensed that they were near the water and as they reached the summit of a long, heather-covered incline, abruptly the huge expanse of the sea appeared before them, dark green and lit with diamonds in the fading light.

They made an awkward descent down a tortuous track that went steeply down the low cliff and emerged on to a narrow, rocky shore that faced out due north across the sea. Then Joanna was told to find a place out of the wind to feed her child and settle her for the night. 'We will come for you when we are ready,' Huathe said, 'but you must come alone.'

Once she might have protested that it was not safe to leave an infant sleeping alone under a cliff. Now she knew better. Although she did not know the identity of the hooded figure, she realised that he – possibly she – was one of the Great Ones and possessed even more power than Huathe. They would not allow any harm to come to Meggie.

And that, she thought with a sudden burst of confidence, is ignoring *my* power, for now I sense that I am fully competent to protect my daughter myself.

Soon they came for her. She was ready; Meggie lay warm, fed and deeply asleep in a cocoon of soft blankets inside Joanna's cloak. Joanna stood in her tunic and shift, barefoot on the sand, and felt no chill but instead a hot glow of anticipation.

She followed Huathe and the hooded figure along the shore to a place at the western end of the bay. The shoreline faced north-west and on the clear horizon Joanna thought she could make out the faint outlines of seven islands. A small fire had been lit and pieces of driftwood fuel had been set out beside it. A fur-lined cloak had been spread on the sand. Something was bubbling in a pot suspended over the fire on a simple tripod; curls of steam rose from the pot and a sharp scent mixed with something sweetish filled the air. The hooded figure leaned forward and, with a gloved hand, removed the pot from the fire, setting it in a hollow in the damp sand to cool. After a moment, the figure poured the liquid from the pot into a small pewter cup and offered the cup to Joanna. She said quietly, 'Am I to drink all of it?' and Huathe said 'Yes.'

The drug took hold very quickly.

She was aware of strong hands holding her arms, guiding her so that she lay down on the cloak. She was sufficiently conscious to mutter her thanks – already her legs had begun to give way beneath her – and then her soul seemed to fly out of her body away over the emerald sea . . .

She saw the seven islands but so swiftly that there was only time to count them. Then she flew on, over the waves that rose up to meet her and refresh her with their spray, on towards land. But it was no land that she knew, for it lay in the vast reaches of sea where the western ocean begins and, even as her eyes took in details, she realised that it existed not now, in her time, but in a time of the far past only reachable now in dream and in vision.

She flew over a shore of white sand and then inland, over a woodland where sunlight sparkled on hurrying streams and on the bright green of springtime. There were figures running and dancing beneath the trees and, flying low to look at them more closely, she saw that they were the Korrigan, the earlier race who were the first to come over the sea out of the west, bringing with them the most profound knowledge that was necessary for an understanding of the Earth.

Then she was floating over a city on a grassy plain, its towers flying proud banners that blew in the westerly wind.

The buildings were strange, delicate structures, in a style that she had never seen and that seemed too fragile, surely, to bear their own weight. They were made of pinkish stone and many had towers of pure white. Tall trees grew among the buildings and there were courtyards full of flowers where fountains played and the air was the colour of rainbows. There was a sense of vibrant colour, of a love of beauty that recognised it in nature and tried to emulate it in every man-made structure. There was song and laughter on the air, as if the people found life a constant delight.

She seemed to come to rest above a large building that must be a palace. It was situated above the sea so that, looking out through its many windows or from the numerous terraces, it would appear that you stood directly over the water and perhaps floated upon its surface. As if her eyes could travel independently of her body, she could see within the palace to where nine auburn-haired women dressed in white sat around a brazier in which blue and violet flames burned. The room where they sat was circular, its walls nothing but slim pillars through which the sound of the sea blew in on the scented air. The women were chanting softly and there was strong magic all around them.

Then the scene shifted and with a suddenness that was as shocking as the events themselves, Joanna saw a violating army come crashing through the palace. First came men in the garb of soldiers, then came the holy men with their shaven heads and their musty robes, holding wooden crosses in front of them as if they were swords. They came at the white-robed women like an advancing sea and drove them out of the pillared room, across the terrace and out over the dizzying gap beyond; it seemed to Joanna that the women turned into delicate, graceful white birds whose cry hung on the air like a lament.

Then the waters rose. High, higher, higher, and a deep voice chanted in a language that she did not understand. The soldiers and the holy men looked at first haughty, as if to say, we do not fear your magic! But their expressions became wary and then fearful; the waters were rising, rising, and from the city came sounds of masonry crashing down into the waves. The screams of the invaders mingled with the shrieks of the sea birds that wheeled and circled above.

Joanna made herself watch even when she would have shut her eyes against the dread sights. The soldiers and the holy men died, some bravely, trying to help their comrades; some as base cowards, scrambling over drowning men as they desperately tried to save their own skins.

All of them perished in the unforgiving seas.

When it was all over, there was nothing left on the surface of the water to show where there had once been land. But, listening carefully, Joanna thought she heard the doleful sound of a slowly tolling bell.

Then, without any sensation of travelling, she was somewhere else. It was a dark, sombre place, and the mood was sorrowful. Violence had been done; pain had been inflicted and there had been a death; the victim had been a great and important figure and both the death and the manner of it were greatly mourned. Joanna was looking down into a glade that was very familiar but, before she could latch on to that thought and identify the place, her mind was wrenched away. Now she saw a vast circle of white-robed figures moving slowly like a huge wheel, their heads bowed, small flames in their hands. They were chanting and, as the words translated in Joanna's head, she knew that it was a lament for the dead one. In the centre of the circle an enormous fire had been lit and as the flames scorched up into the sky, it seemed to Joanna that a figure rode upon them, a figure miraculously returned to youth who smiled and laughed and sang aloud for joy.

I know you! Joanna thought, you are—

But, again, her mind was torn away. And now, bizarrely, she was looking down at herself. She was dressed in a hooded red tunic decorated with rich embroidery and over it she wore a cloak in a sort of speckled wool, fastened at the neck with a gold pin. Her head was bare and her dark hair hung in a long, thick plait down her back. In her hand she held a short wooden stick, the end of which had been hollowed out so that a smoky brown crystal could be inserted. The crystal was roughly the length of her palm, cut to a flattened hexagon and with a pointed tip. She stood with her eyes closed, holding the wand over a bowl of clear water.

People were sobbing with pain, or perhaps fear; it seemed that they were calling out to her. Then suddenly Meggie was beside her; an older Meggie who stood confidently on her own two feet and, looking up at her mother, tried to speak. As Joanna stared at her vision self, she saw her daughter slowly begin to open her hand . . .

The transition back to the shore and the October night was brutal. Joanna lay on the sand, eyes tight shut, trying to control the dreadful dizziness that filled her head and her belly, putting her hands to her head to crush the terrible pain that seemed to be splitting her skull in two. The bile rose into her mouth and, raising herself up, she leaned over the sand and vomited.

There was a cool hand on her forehead, holding her while she heaved and convulsed. Then a voice said calmly, 'It is often thus the first time. You will never suffer as badly as this again.'

Small comfort, Joanna thought, as another spasm tore through her. She heard herself groan, then the same cool hand pressed her back so that she was once more lying on the cloak. Huathe appeared with a blanket, which he tucked around her; she was grateful for its warmth and tried to give him a smile of thanks. He muttered something about fetching her a restorative, and turned towards the fire.

Joanna stared up at the hooded figure. 'I know who you are,' she said, her throat sore from the vomiting.

The figure drew back the hood, revealing deep-set dark eyes in a face whose skin was so smooth and unlined that it belied the long, snow-white hair. She – for it was a woman – wore a pale robe under the dark cloak and around her throat was a silver lunula.

It was the Domina and, eight months ago, it had been she who initiated Joanna into the tribe. Now, looking down on Joanna with a kind smile, she said, 'Aye. I have been with you, child, for some time, for I am your *anam chara*. Your soul friend,' she translated. 'You have done well.'

'You were at Folle-Pensée?' I didn't see you, she wanted to add.

'I was in the forest. I stayed close to Nime's spring.'

'Yes.' It made sense, for the spring was the source of the power.

'You have just made your first soul journey,' the Domina went on, 'and, although I sense that I know what you saw, we wish you to tell us.'

Huathe had made her a hot drink, which he gave to her; she sipped at it and felt the restorative honey which he had melted into whatever herbal brew he had prepared course through her. The nausea had receded; she sat up and began to speak.

The vision was so fresh that she did not think she had omitted anything. As she spoke she saw the Domina and Huathe exchange occasional glances and once, when she described the death of the beloved figure in the dark wood, Huathe made as if to speak, but the Domina hushed him.

When Joanna had finished, the Domina briefly closed her eyes and raised her head, almost as if she were giving thanks. Then, dark eyes snapping open and drilling into Joanna's, she said, 'You are honoured. You have been granted a sight of the blessed land that was our first home here beyond the great sea, where the Korrigan settled and built their city of granite, marble and glass.'

'It's gone,' Joanna said, a sob in her voice. 'It slipped under the waves and they all drowned.'

'Not all,' the Domina corrected. 'Did you not hear the sea birds? The Korrigan flew away to safety as gulls; the Grac'h as terns.'

'The Grac'h?'

'We call them the fiery-haired ones; they were the high priestesses of the land.'

Joanna reached deep into her mind, for she was certain that she knew what the land had been called. The Domina waited calmly. Eventually Joanna said, 'It was Lyonesse.'

And the Domina said, 'It was. The land held true to the old ways and the men who brought the new faith could not abide that. They came with soldiers and would have slaughtered everyone in the land, down to the youngest baby. So the Grac'h called up the west wind and the waves blew in on the great sea that rose to their bidding. The land was lost to them, that loveliest and most serene of lands, but that was preferable to witnessing its rape and despoliation at the hands of the invader. The Korrigan flew south to the shores of Armorica and they discovered that, although this was no Lyonesse, it was a tolerable substitute.' The Domina sighed. 'But still, those of us who remember lament our first home.'

She must, Joanna decided, be speaking figuratively, perhaps of a folk memory that lived on in the people, kept alive by the bards' retelling of the old legend. Anything else was just impossible . . .

As if keen to move on, the Domina said, 'You also saw something else; the death whose wake you witnessed was that of one of our Great Ones.'

'Yes,' Joanna put in eagerly, 'and I really felt that, given a moment to think, I could have—'

'And you also saw a vision of your own future,' the Domina interrupted. 'This moment that you saw will come soon, for the time for you to take up your skill and your power is at hand.' Giving Joanna no chance to comment, she went on, 'We have prepared these things for you. Stand up and take off your tunic and shift.'

Joanna did as she was bidden. Standing naked on the sand, the Domina led her closer to the fire. Huathe came to stand beside her and he poured a clear liquid from a flask into a small cup of gold.

'Drink,' the Domina ordered.

Joanna obeyed. The liquid tasted clean and cool, and as the taste developed on her tongue an image of mossy stone around a lively stream came into her mind; she knew then that the water had come from Nime's spring. Then the Domina pushed her closer to the fire, so close that she feared the flames would singe the fine hair on her body and sear her bare flesh. Gritting her teeth, she forced herself to endure it.

The Domina's cry rang out into the night as she chanted a long string of words whose meaning Joanna could only guess at. It seemed to be a summons, and this was borne out when the Domina switched from whatever archaic tongue she had been using and cried, 'Hear our prayers, oh Great Ones of Lyonesse, and by the fire and by the water that must one day prevail, receive this woman Beith, who now takes on her new name in recognition of her adoption by her people.'

The fire was scorching now, burning Joanna's legs and thighs. Forcing herself not to move, the pain quickly became unbearable. Then, as if she had passed some test, the Domina gave an order to Huathe and he dragged her away from the fire, throwing the contents of a skin water bag over the front of her body. As the cold sea water doused the heat in her skin, she gave a cry that had in it more exhalation than pain.

And the Domina nodded, as if to say, well done.

Huathe repeated the sea water bathing several times and then he dried her with a soft cloth. The Domina reached into her pack and produced a clean white shift of fine linen, which Huathe dropped over Joanna's head. On top of that went the red embroidered tunic of Joanna's vision; in reality it was even more beautiful because, as well as feasting on it with her eyes, she could also touch the heavy gold embroidery and smell the sweet scent of new cloth. Over the tunic Huathe draped the speckled woollen cloak, fastening it with a gold pin in the shape of a stylised running horse. The cloak was heavy and warm and, at last, Joanna stopped shivering.

Finally the Domina gave her the short, thick stick. 'This is hawthorn,' she said, 'and hawthorn protects from both physical and psychic harm; it will protect you and also those upon whom you wield its power. The wood was gathered on the most auspicious day of the year and the wand has been prepared especially for you.' Pointing to the brownish-grey crystal embedded in the end of the stick, she continued, 'This is Caledonian quartz and it is sacred to us. Use it wisely, child.'

She put the wand into Joanna's outstretched hand. Not knowing what to expect, but anticipating something, Joanna was surprised to find that there was no jolt of energy, no force that made the hairs on her arms stand up. She might as easily have been holding a piece of driftwood.

She heard Huathe chuckle. 'Do not worry, Beith,' he said quietly, 'for when you need the power, it will be there.'

The ceremony was over. Huathe carefully poured sand on the fire, extinguishing it and then burying the embers so that every trace disappeared. The Domina fastened her pack, saying to Joanna, 'You may wear your finery for what remains of the night. Tomorrow, put it away and revert to anonymity.'

Joanna bowed her acceptance. Standing still barefoot on the sand, she wondered if it was permitted to put her boots on; the tide was coming in and the sand felt damp under her toes.

Huathe gave her a hug. 'Farewell, Beith,' he said. 'We shall meet again, but it may not be for many years.' He bent and kissed her, twice on each cheek, then, with a low reverence to the Domina, hastened away towards the cliff path. Joanna, who had by his action received the confirmation of what she already suspected – that she was leaving Armorica – looked expectantly at the Domina.

'Aye, child, you and your daughter are to sail this night back to Britain. The ship will be here soon. But, before you go, I would speak with you on a matter that has been kept from you.'

Several possibilities flashed through Joanna's mind. When the Domina spoke, it was concerning none of them. Instead she said, 'Have you not asked yourself why it is that you have been accepted into the tribe?'

Immediately Joanna was reminded of many small moments and incidents; of all the times that her new people had spoken of her as one of them; of the growing sense that they had all known about her long, long before she had been aware of them. She said, 'Yes. I have.'

'It is time,' the Domina said heavily, 'for you to be told.'

What she learned on the shore that night was such a shock that, when the small boat came grinding up the shingle to carry her and Meggie out to the ship that awaited them, Joanna could barely walk by herself and had to be helped by the two sailors. She felt weak and did not trust herself to take adequate care of Meggie, and the Domina entrusted the child to the sailor who was not engaged in rowing the boat. Joanna heard her daughter give a little cry of protest, but even that could not restore her. The Domina stood on the shore watching as the boat set off towards the ship; she might have been waving, but Joanna did not notice.

What she had just been told had removed, in a few words,

everything that she had believed herself to be. The fact of that former identity having been replaced by something far more interesting, and with many times the potential, she managed, for the time being anyway, totally to overlook . . .

The ship took her to a place the sailors called Ellan Vannin; the island, set in the seas between England and Ireland to the north of Mona's Isle, was to be her home until Imbolc. Still in a daze even after four days at sea, Joanna meekly followed the orders that anyone chanced to give her, going ashore into yet another new place and settling into what in fact seemed like better accommodation than she had enjoyed before. Sometimes she would hold on to the bear's claw on its chain around her neck, as if that alone had the power to reassure her that it was true, not a dream or the last fling of the wonder voyage she had taken on that Armorican beach.

In time she accepted the truth. As if they had been waiting for that moment, her new teachers set about the most intensive period of study that she had ever had, instilling into her that she had gifts but they had no virtue and no purpose if she did not learn to use them. Building on what she had learned at Folle-Pensée, they showed her how to make the soul journey into the heart and mind of another, how to seek out whatever malady might lie there and how to cure it. When Samhain came round, the combined effects of her mysterious studies and her exhaustion meant that she was very close to what lay the other side of the veil. Too close, in fact; her teachers, afraid that she would be tempted to raise the veil and venture beyond, would not let her attend the festival. 'Wait until next year,' they said kindly, seeing her bitter disappointment, 'next year you will be strong and the danger will be less.'

She was allowed – encouraged – to celebrate Meggie's first birthday on the last day of October. But on Samhain night they gave her a strong sedative and she slept, deeply and dreamlessly, into the month of November.

Yule passed. Joanna worked harder and harder, knowing, for all that she had not been told, that she would soon be leaving. In the New Year they sent her back to Mona's Isle, where she was received joyfully – and, it had to be said, with a certain amount of awe – by the friends she had made there. She celebrated Imbolc with her people there and then, a few days afterwards, the man with the gold earring came for her again and rowed her back to the mainland.

She knew what she had to do, for there had been so many hints that she had taken matters into her own hands and used her scrying bowl. As she trod the long road back to Hawkenlye Forest and her little hut, she was already building her mental strength for what lay ahead.

PART THREE

The War

IO

As Josse awoke in his quarters in the Vale on the morning following his visit to Gervase de Gifford, he went over their conversation. It had not amounted to much, but anything was better than allowing himself to think about the growing number of sick people who lay sweating and suffering not twenty paces from where he sat.

The welcome news that there were no cases of the foreign pestilence down in Tonbridge encouraged Josse to mutter fervent prayers of gratitude as he sipped at the hot herbal drink that Brother Saul had just brought him; Tonbridge lay on the river and its flat, marshy, mist-prone lands seemed to trap foul air. Many people living in and around the town suffered from the ague, and the disease was by no means limited to those who lived in the squalor of poverty. The consequences of this new peril let loose among such a weakened population did not bear thinking about.

Well, then I won't think about it, Josse decided. As long as sick folk come up here to Hawkenlye – which is, after all, the obvious place if they want help – then Tonbridge ought to be safe.

Brother Saul brought him a bowl of porridge. With a smile of thanks, Josse took it and, although he didn't feel much like eating, forced himself to finish it. Then he stood up, straightened his tunic and took his bowl and mug to wash them at the monks' trough. Saul hurried to take the utensils from him; although Josse protested, clearly Saul considered that washing up was no job for a knight.

Saul dried his hands on a piece of sacking and reported that morning's figures, which Josse had offered to pass on to the Abbess: the son and daughter-in-law in the party of five who had arrived the previous day were now very ill and unlikely to survive the day; the woman's sister was also feverish, although her child remained well. The crippled boy and the man who had arrived on the cart were also very poorly, but the woman who had brought them in had not sickened and was proving a great help to the nursing sisters.

Poor Sister Beata had developed an agonising headache but as yet showed no signs of developing a fever; two more nurses, Sister Anne and Sister Judith, had been ordered to report to the makeshift infirmary in the Vale.

There was one notable exception in Saul's report. Putting a hand on the man's arm, Josse said softly, 'And Brother Firmin?'

Saul's eyes filled with tears and he shook his head.

All in all, it was not very good tidings for Josse to bear to the Abbess.

Helewise had been waiting for Josse for some time when he finally arrived and as he gave her the news from the Vale, she was aware of exhibiting a degree of impatience, for which she quickly apologised.

'Please, think nothing of it, my lady,' he said courteously, 'I quite understand how you must feel.'

Oh, dear Josse, I don't think you do, she thought ruefully. Then, deciding that it would do no good to hedge around what she had to say, that, in fact, such tactics would probably annoy him and increase the chances of a refusal, she said, 'Sir Josse, you may have already been informed that yesterday Sister Tiphaine and Sister Euphemia made various attempts to harness the power of the Eye of Jerusalem in drinks and, for those too sick to swallow, in washes with which to bathe their wounds and their faces.'

He was watching her warily. 'Aye. Brother Saul told me.'

'Neither remedy had done any good by yesterday evening and, judging by your report, there have been no miraculous recoveries during the night.'

'No.' Now wariness had turned to something approaching hostility, as if he knew full well what was coming.

'Sir Josse, will you try?' Helewise implored. 'Will you take back the Eye and use it to save those poor, suffering souls under Sister Euphemia's care?'

He shook his head violently. 'My lady, you *know* what I think about that stone! Why do you persist in asking me to try to use it when you are fully aware that I fear it?'

'You fear giving it to your nieces!' she cried. 'It is not the same thing to try its power yourself!'

'I gave it away!' he shouted back. 'I gave it to you – you are now its rightful owner, you and the sisters!'

'But they have tried and failed! Oh, please, Josse, I'm begging you to help us!'

He glared at her but, as she watched, searching his angry face for any signs that he might yield, it seemed that his expression softened. 'Do you really think it will make a difference if the Eye is wielded by my hand?' he asked.

'I—' In truth, she had no idea. 'Possibly,' she said cautiously.

'Well, that's an honest answer,' he said wryly. 'Very well, my lady. I'll have a go.'

Together they went down to the Vale. Brother Augustus hurried to the shrine and fetched another flask of the holy water. Josse pushed up his sleeves and, taking the Eye of Jerusalem from Sister Tiphaine with such an expression of distaste that, had the situation not been so grave, Helewise might have laughed, he dipped it into the water. He held it there for some time. Then Sister Tiphaine said quietly, 'I reckon that'll do it, sir. If you have the touch, it'll have worked by now. If not . . . ' Tactfully she left the sentence unfinished.

Sister Anne was summoned and she disappeared into the shelter with the precious water.

They waited.

Later that morning, Sister Euphemia emerged from the temporary infirmary with blood on her apron and fatigue in her face. She located Josse, Helewise and Sister Tiphaine in the small shrine that housed the holy water spring. 'The two women who arrived yesterday morning are dead,' she said baldly. 'That's another motherless child to be taken care of,' she added, half to herself.

'The water did no good?' Josse asked. Helewise, observing his stricken face, felt a wave of compassion for him.

'No,' Sister Euphemia said. 'I'm sorry, Sir Josse. Looks like the Eye must have known you gave it away.'

'Oh,' he said lamely.

'We had to try, Sir Josse!' Helewise said, trying to rally him. 'We could not have known that—'

But Josse was not to be consoled. 'I am a coward and a fool,' he muttered, scowling, 'for we have in our very hands a jewel with the power to heal and by my actions I have rendered it useless.' He bowed, first to Helewise and then to the herbalist and the infirmarer, who stood close together with similar looks of concern on their faces. 'It is a heavy burden to bear,' Josse added. 'If you will excuse me, my lady' – he had turned back to Helewise – 'I shall take Horace out for a ride and think about how best I may make amends for my faults.'

Before she could say a word, he was off, hurrying away off up the path back to the Abbey.

The three nuns watched him until he was just a small, anonymous figure climbing up the steep path; the very way he was moving spoke of dejection and failure. Then Sister Euphemia said quietly, 'Oh, dear.'

Helewise had been thinking hard, arguing with her conscience. She came to a decision.

As the infirmarer announced wearily that she must be getting back to her patients, Helewise lightly touched the arm of the herbalist. 'Sister Tiphaine,' she said, 'walk with me, please.' To her distress her voice was not quite steady. She took a breath and tried again. 'I would speak with you on a private matter,' she continued, very softly, 'and we shall take the path beside the pond and continue until there is no danger of our being overheard.'

Sister Tiphaine's eyes widened but, disciplined nun that she was, she bowed to her superior, muttered, 'Of course, my lady,' and, as Helewise strode away, fell into step behind her.

Helewise continued along the path until she reached the place where it began to curve around the end of the pond. Then, beneath the skeletal branches of a copse of winter-bare birch trees, she turned and faced the herbalist.

'Sister Tiphaine,' she began – she had been rehearsing what she would say as she walked – 'you may or may not be aware that there is a prophecy concerning the Eye of Jerusalem, which was revealed to Sir Josse when the jewel came into his hands.'

'Indeed, my lady?' The herbalist's face remained blank; if she was aware of any such thing, it appeared that she was not going to admit it to her Abbess.

Helewise sniffed. 'Indeed,' she repeated. 'The Eye was presented to Josse's father by some foreign prince in Outremer in gratitude for Sir Geoffroi having saved the man's little son. It was lost – stolen, in fact – but in due course it found its way back to its rightful owner, who, Sir Geoffroi having died, was Sir Josse. At the time the Eye was presented to Sir Josse, it was predicted that one day it would go to a female descendant of Sir Josse's who would have the power to bring the stone alive and awaken its full powers, which are apparently considerable and extend far beyond lowering fevers and testing for poison.'

'Oh, aye, that they do,' muttered the herbalist.

But Helewise, intent on what she was saying, barely registered the remark.

'Now Sir Josse has no wife and no child,' she continued, 'and when he heard these words he was alarmed, because he thought, quite reasonably, that the man who spoke them was referring to one of his nieces; he has four brothers, Sister, and between them they have three little daughters. Or is it four?' She frowned, trying to remember what Josse had told her. 'No matter. Nieces there are, and Sir Josse greatly feared laying this extraordinary and frightening burden on to any one of them.'

'He was right to be wary,' observed Sister Tiphaine. 'Such a thing should not fall into the wrong hands. For one thing, it would remain inert unless whoever holds it knows what she's about.'

'Quite, quite,' said Helewise. Again, her preoccupation with the delicate matter she was trying to raise meant that she paid less than full attention to her herbalist's comment, which, considering it revealed that Sister Tiphaine appeared to know more than a nun ought to about pagan power objects, was perhaps just as well.

'Sister,' Helewise said boldly, 'I am going to describe a sequence of events to you that may or may not actually have happened. Two years ago, in the February of that year, Sir Josse met a young woman who was fleeing from – well, never mind what she was fleeing from. The relevant fact is that she – her name was Joanna de Courtenay – hid in the Great Forest close by Hawkenlye, where she and Sir Josse met and . . .' Oh, but this was difficult! Agonising, Helewise thought, supposing I am wrong and have been wrong all along? If so, I shall be making accusations that damage the good names of two innocent people!

But there was something in Sister Tiphaine's wary expression that suggested Helewise was not wrong at all . . .

Heartened, she continued. 'Let us imagine for a moment that Sir Josse and Joanna de Courtenay became lovers and that she conceived a child. That child would have been born some time in the autumn of that year, and so now he or she would be about sixteen months old.'

She paused to see if Sister Tiphaine would comment. The herbalist remained silent.

'Sister, if indeed a child has been born to Joanna de Courtenay, and if Sir Josse is that child's father, and if the child is a girl, then do you not see what it will mean?'

'I do, my lady,' the herbalist said quietly. '*If* those events really happened, then the descendant spoken of in the prophecy could be alive now.'

Helewise could not help but notice the heavy emphasis on *if*.

'Sister Tiphaine,' she said, after a pause, 'it is said of you that you keep a foot in the pagan past and I admit that I have always considered there to be something – er – slightly *strange* about you.' A brief flash of humour crossed the herbalist's impassive face, there and gone before Helewise could properly register it. 'However, you are a dutiful and obedient nun, a skilled herbalist, wise in the lore of healing and, in general, an asset to our community.'

'Thank you, my lady.'

'For this reason I have permitted a certain leeway over your comings and goings that I would not tolerate in another sister.' Now Helewise fixed the herbalist with a glare. 'In particular, I speak of your links with the forest people. Oh, it's no use denying that they exist, Sister, for I am convinced that they do.'

'I was not going to deny them, my lady,' the herbalist said tranquilly. 'I learned much of what I know from the forest people and I have never found any malice or evil among them.'

'They are pagans, Sister, and you are a professed nun and vowed servant of Our Lord Jesus Christ and his holy father,' Helewise reminded her.

'Aye, and right glad I am to serve him,' Sister Tiphaine said. 'But—'

She bit back what she had been about to say, instead bowing her head and, with an air of humility, waited for whatever her Abbess might say next.

But Helewise did not speak. Into her head, where she had heard it before, a calm voice said, *All gods are one god and behind them is the truth.*

Who *are* you? Helewise cried mutely. Won't you tell me?

But, as before, there was no answer.

After a moment, she addressed Sister Tiphaine again. 'I am not asking you to speak now,' she said, pleased to find that her voice held its usual authoritative tone, 'I am simply asking you to consider what I have said and to think how best to act so as to benefit the greatest number of people.'

Sister Tiphaine nodded slowly. 'A gem of power wielded in the destined hand would be useful just now, my lady, even if the hand were but that of a small child,' she said. 'There's no denying it.'

'Exactly!' Helewise said eagerly. 'You and Sister Euphemia have tried, Sir Josse has tried, but none of you have met with success. People are dying, people who could perhaps be saved.'

Again the herbalist nodded. 'Aye, my lady. I am aware of that.' She paused, deep eyes looking away down the Vale and back towards the small collection of buildings. After some time she returned her gaze to Helewise. 'Have I your leave to go into the forest, my lady Abbess?' she asked.

Why ask me this time? You do not usually bother, Helewise thought, but she bit back the remark. 'You have,' she replied.

Sister Tiphaine gave her a low reverence. 'Thank you. I will return as soon as I can.'

With that she was off, pacing away along the track, her very movements suggesting that, had she not been a nun clad in the habit of obedience and decorum, she might well have broken into a run.

Helewise watched her go. With you, Tiphaine, she said silently, goes our hope.

Then she sighed and, slowly and reluctantly, followed in the herbalist's footsteps back to the infirmary in the Vale.

Josse rode hard for a few miles and then, drawing rein at the top of a low hill to the north-west of the Abbey, sat for some time looking out at the view. Before him the valley of the Weald stretched from west to east; behind him to the south rose the vast, mysterious forest. After a while, becoming slightly uneasy at having the dark woods at his back, he turned Horace and stared out over the trees.

He was thinking, so hard that his head ached, about what had caused a secret killer to cross to England, and what could be so sensitive about his mission that the two men who might have witnessed him boarding or leaving the ship that brought him across the Channel had had to be silenced.

It *had* to be connected to King Richard's release and his imminent return to England! But just how, Josse was at a loss to see.

He realised that he was growing cold; it would do neither him nor Horace any good for the sweat of exertion to chill them so, with an explosive oath that did a little to express his frustration, he turned the big horse and set out back to Hawkenlye.

He reached the Abbey in the mid-afternoon and Sister Martha greeted him at the gate. 'You've had a hard ride, Sir Josse,' she observed, looking at Horace with a critical eye, 'and the old boy's all lathered.' She patted Horace's neck and he whinnied in recognition. 'Leave him to me and I'll give him a good rub-down.' Glancing up and meeting Josse's eyes, she added quietly, 'I'll be glad of something to do. Evil times, Sir Josse; evil times.'

Josse slid off Horace's back and handed the reins to Sister Martha. 'Aye, that they are,' he agreed heavily. 'Thank you, Sister.'

He was on the point of setting out back down to the Vale when he heard a voice calling his name. Turning, he saw the porteress, Sister Ursel, hurrying towards him. It was only then that he realised she had not been at her usual post, in the little lodge by the gate, when he rode in.

He walked back to meet her; she was coming from the direction of the Abbess's room at the far end of the cloister. 'I thought you might have been with the Abbess Helewise,' Sister Ursel panted, 'but you weren't and she's not in her room either. She's probably down in the Vale' – Sister Ursel nodded as if in confirmation of her own deduction – 'although I pray to the dear God above that she keeps herself out of harm's way. There's poor old Brother Firmin sick, and now poor Sister Beata's got the fever, they say, and Sister Euphemia's got her hands full even with the two extra who have gone down to help.'

'Aye, it's a bad time all right,' Josse agreed. Before Sister Ursel could continue her recitation of woes, he put in gently, 'You were looking for me, Sister. How may I help?'

She smiled at him. 'Ah, there's the kind soul that you are, Sir Josse. I always say so. It's never a surprise to *me* that so many folks come here after you, wanting some of your precious time!'

'Has someone been here today asking for me?' It sounded like it.

'Oh, yes!' She paused and then, amending the affirmation, added, 'Well, not asking for you exactly, although you came to mind the moment she said why she was here.'

'I see.' He was not at all sure that he did.

But Sister Ursel was hurrying ahead with her tale. 'It was – oh, let me see, was it after Sext or after Nones? Nones, I'm sure of it; it wasn't all that long ago. Anyway, I was returning to my post at the gate – one of the lay brothers relieves me when I go into church for the Offices, Sir Josse, although of course not always the same one, and then he, whoever he is, returns to his duties when I get back.' She stopped. 'Where was I?'

'Returning to the gate after Nones,' he prompted.

'Aye, aye, that's right. There was someone waiting with the lay brother – it was young Brother Paul; you probably don't know him, he's new, see – and Paul had told them to wait till I got back from church. He didn't really know the usual form so really he did the right thing, telling her to wait for me.'

'The visitor was a woman?'

'Aye, a young woman, maybe twenty-two, twenty-three. Pretty as a picture.'

For a moment Josse's heart leapt.

'She was fair,' the porteress continued, dashing his hopes, for the woman he had in mind was dark, 'with neatly braided hair under a close-fitting cap. She had blue eyes and a worried expression and her garments were good quality, not cheap. Nice gloves, fur-lined at the wrist – squirrel, I think – and she wore a deeply hooded cloak which she only drew back when she was safe inside the gate. It's my belief' – Sister Ursel dropped her voice and leaned close to Josse – 'that she was afraid. That she knew someone was after her and didn't want to be identified.'

Josse reflected that Sister Ursel, for all her verbosity, had a sharp pair of eyes. 'And this young woman was asking for me?'

'Not by name. She said she had been given to understand that people came here to the Abbey with all sorts of problems and difficulties that get sorted out for them here and she hoped someone might do the same for her, and so of course *I* thought that you, Sir Josse, might be able to help her.'

'Is she still here?' Josse asked urgently; he had the sudden irrational but very strong feeling that this mystery woman, whoever she was, could be important . . .

'No, she's gone,' Sister Ursel said. 'I told her to warm herself in my little room while I tried to find you; I keep a bit of a fire in there, Sir Josse, and the Abbess Helewise turns a blind eye because it's cold as the tomb in the winter. Anyway, she accepted right gladly and I left her warming her cold hands. I looked for you in the Vale and I was gone longer that I intended because, what with them working so hard to keep the healthy away from the sick, it wasn't easy finding someone to ask whether you were about. When I got back here she'd gone. I went to the Abbess's room to see if she knew where you were so I could tell you about the woman, but she wasn't there. Still, you're here now and I've told you!' Sister Ursel beamed her relief.

'Was the young woman riding or walking?' Josse asked; if the latter, then, provided he guessed right as to in which direction the young woman had set off, he might be able to fetch Horace and catch her up.

But: 'She was riding, on a pretty grey mare,' Sister Ursel said. 'Tied her up to the post there.' She nodded to a small pile of horse droppings.

'I see.' Josse frowned. 'You say that the young woman seemed afraid, Sister; is it possible, do you think, that while she waited in your little room, something happened that made her feel threatened?'

'Like whoever's following her turning up outside on the road?' Sister Ursel said. 'I can't say, Sir Josse. I didn't see anybody, but then,' she added shrewdly, 'a man who sets himself to trail someone isn't going to make a song and a dance about it, is he?'

'No,' Josse agreed. But, he thought, if the woman thought she had spotted her pursuer, then surely the last thing she would do was to mount her mare and leave the safety of the Abbey.

It was a mystery. No, he corrected himself, it was *another* mystery.

He gave Sister Ursel a smile. 'Thank you, Sister, for your detailed report,' he said. Then, almost as an afterthought, he added, 'I don't suppose this young woman said who she was and exactly what it was she wanted help with?'

'Well, it's odd, what with her being so secretive and that, but she did,' Sister Ursel replied. 'Perhaps she thought it was safe, what with me being a nun.'

'And you have the sort of face that people trust, Sister,' Josse said, lavish with his praise in the excited anticipation of having a couple of questions adequately answered at last. 'Well?'

'Her name,' Sister Ursel said, frowning with concentration, 'was Sabin de Retz.' She spoke the name with care. 'She came here looking for the same person you've been enquiring after.'

'And who,' Josse said, strongly suspecting but hardly daring to hope his suspicion was right, 'might that be?'

'Why, the young man that was slain in our Vale!' Sister Ursel exclaimed. 'She's come here searching for Nicol Romley!'

11

Josse had to wait until late in the day to speak to the Abbess concerning the visit of Sabin de Retz and her puzzling mission; the Abbess spent most of the afternoon and evening down in the Vale, where Josse did not think it appropriate to disturb her. It was not until the community were leaving the Abbey church after Compline that Josse finally caught up with the Abbess.

She looked exhausted.

It suddenly occurred to Josse that surely there were better things he could do to take from her some of the huge burden she was carrying than to race off chasing a mysterious stranger hunting for a dead man. But swiftly he changed his mind: Nicol Romley had been suffering from the foreign pestilence, even though it had not been the cause of his death. Therefore anything connected with him might be important in the crucial work of containing the outbreak of the disease.

He fell into step beside the Abbess as she walked slowly back to her room. 'What news from the Vale?' he asked.

She shrugged. 'Little that you would wish to hear, Sir Josse. The old man brought in by his daughter fails before our eyes, despite her devotion. She refuses to leave his side and tends him herself.' The Abbess frowned. 'I cannot understand why she shows no sign of the sickness, for, according to Sister Euphemia, she breathes in his very air and her hands are soaked in his blood.'

'I too have wondered at the apparent invulnerability of some people to the pestilence,' Josse agreed. 'I'm told that some members of the Hastings maidservant's family did not suffer so much as a headache, whereas others of the household sickened and died within a matter of days. My lady, do you think—'

'Sir Josse,' the Abbess interrupted, 'I am sorry, but I am too tired to think.'

'Of course you are!' He was instantly solicitous. 'May I fetch a restorative for you? Some wine?'

'No, thank you.' Briefly she touched his arm. 'I have one or two matters to attend to and then I shall go to my bed.'

Josse, appreciating that he ought not to detain her, quickly told her about Sabin de Retz. 'I've worked out,' he said, concluding an admirably succinct version of the tale, 'that probably the only person who could have told the young woman that Nicol Romley was coming here was the lad's master, Adam Morton.'

'You reason well, Sir Josse, as usual,' the Abbess put in.

'I thank you, my lady, although in truth the link was not difficult to make. So you see, I need to return to Newenden and speak to Adam Morton again to see if he can tell me anything more about Sabin de Retz and why she wanted to find Nicol Romley.'

'Back on the road, then, first thing tomorrow?' she suggested. 'Sir Josse, it is many miles that you've covered these past days.'

'Aye, but sometimes in times of trouble it's easier on those who have a definite job to do.'

'Easier than waiting and watching helplessly while they die?' she said bitterly. 'Oh, yes, Sir Josse, you are the lucky one, for indeed it is.'

There was a short and, on Josse's part, uncomfortable silence.

Then she put out her hand to touch his and said, 'Forgive me, old friend.'

'Nothing to forgive,' he muttered gruffly.

They walked on, both deep in their own thoughts. At the door to her room she turned and said, 'Sir Josse, may I ask a favour of you?'

'Anything!' he cried. 'Whatever you like!'

She managed a brief smile. 'It is nothing *that* great,' she said. 'It is merely to ask if you would take Brother Augustus with you tomorrow.'

'Young Gussie? Of course; nothing would give me more pleasure than to have his company on the road.'

She made a face. 'He is not himself, Sir Josse, for he is sorely grieved over Brother Firmin. Firmin has been like a beloved grandfather to Augustus and the boy will not accept that he is dying.'

'It is true, then?' Josse pictured the kind old face and he felt like weeping. 'There is no hope for Brother Firmin?'

'There is always hope,' she said swiftly, 'but Brother Firmin moves further along the road that takes him away from us with each hour that passes. He barely speaks and indeed he sleeps most of the time, waking only to drink some of his precious holy water.'

'It has saved many lives before,' Josse said stoutly. 'Let us pray that the miracle will happen for dear old Firmin.'

'Amen,' the Abbess said fervently. Then, with a courageous lift of her chin that went straight to Josse's heart, she bade him goodnight and disappeared into her room.

Josse and Brother Augustus were on the road early the next morning. Augustus did indeed seem very downcast and it was not long before he let out all his pain and grief to Josse.

'I keep asking if I can nurse him,' he said, close to tears, 'but they won't let me and I feel so *guilty* not being beside him. It's just the infirmarer and her nursing nuns that are allowed into that temporary ward they've made in the Vale and they tell me

I must obey their orders and keep away from him. But, Sir Josse, I can't bear it, I want him to know how much I love him and that I'd do anything to make him well again!'

Bearing in mind what the Abbess had told him, Josse chose his words carefully; it seemed kinder to prepare Augustus for the worst than to give him any false hopes.

'Gus,' he began, 'for one thing, you're a lay brother and you have to obey those in authority over you; you've no choice. So you mustn't feel guilty that you can't be with Brother Firmin.'

'I keep him supplied with holy water from the spring,' Augustus butted in, 'at least I can do that for him.'

'Brother Firmin would no doubt say that's the best service you could render him,' Josse said. Then, gently: 'Gussie, you say that you'd do anything to keep him alive, but it's not for us to choose the time of a man's death.'

'It's up to God, aye, I know, and Brother Firmin's an old man; so they all keep telling me,' Augustus said wearily. 'If he could only have a little bit longer, Sir Josse! Just a little while!'

How many times, Josse wondered sadly, had that cry gone up at the bedside of a beloved person on the point of death! But then he thought – and the thought brought a sort of comfort – well, aren't those people the lucky ones, to die knowing they are loved and will be sorely missed?

He was about to say as much to Augustus when the young man spoke. 'I've promised God I'll take my vows and become a monk if he lets Brother Firmin live,' he said.

Josse's first thought was, oh, *no*, Gus! In the years that he had known the lad, he had always considered that Augustus had more to offer the world outside the Abbey than within it and he would never have been surprised, on returning to Hawkenlye, to be told that Augustus had put aside his lay brother's robe and gone.

'I am not sure, Gussie,' he said carefully, 'that God really wants monks who enter the religious life as part of a bargain.

Are you quite sure it's what you want? What's right for you and for God?'

There was a long silence. Then Augustus said miserably, 'No, Sir Josse. I'm not sure at all.'

'Speak to God, then,' Josse said. 'Tell him of your doubts.'

'But if I withdraw my offer then Brother Firmin will die!' wailed Augustus.

'He may well die anyway,' Josse said. 'But whether he lives or dies, I do not believe it will have anything to do with your offer, Gus. I don't think God works that way.'

Augustus turned reddened eyes to look at him. 'Don't you?'

'No,' Josse said firmly. 'Tell you what, Gus – we'll ride along without talking for a while and you have a bit of a prayer. Tell God how you're feeling, how much you want to save Brother Firmin but how you're not sure that offering to become a monk is the right thing for you after all.'

'But how can we pray?' Augustus looked worried. 'We're not in church.'

Josse gave a shout of laughter. 'Sorry, lad, but I couldn't help it,' he said; Augustus was looking horrified. 'You don't have to be in church to pray, Gus. If you're sincere, which you are, and if you put your heart into your prayers, which I know you will, then I reckon God can hear you wherever you are.'

Augustus eyed him doubtfully for a few moments. Then he closed his eyes and Josse heard him muttering under his breath. Resigning himself to a long period of silence, Josse clicked his tongue to Horace and steered the big horse in front of Augustus, mounted on the Abbey cob; it would not help the poor lad if his horse decided to wander off the track and into danger while Gus had his eyes shut, and the cob was more likely to keep to the path with Horace leading the way.

Quite a long time later, with Augustus still praying, they rode into Newenden.

★

Josse had been noticing that whenever they passed through any inhabited areas, from villages and hamlets down to lonely farms or solitary hovels, those who dwelt there dashed inside and slammed their doors. This road, he told himself, is the route of the pestilence: it went from Hastings to Newenden and from Newenden to Hawkenlye. No wonder the people barricade themselves in against passers-by; they are terrified of infection.

Newenden was deserted. Augustus, open-eyed now and looking considerably more cheerful, remarked on the lack of people.

Josse told him why the place was empty.

'Oh, aye, of course.' The boy nodded. 'Will this apothecary we've come to see open up and talk to us?'

Josse had been wondering the same thing. 'I hope so,' he grunted.

He rode along the street to the apothecary's house. Dismounting, he handed Horace's reins to Augustus and banged on Adam Morton's door.

There was no answer and so he banged again, more loudly, this time calling out, 'Master Morton, I would speak with you! It is Josse d'Acquin and I have ridden from Hawkenlye Abbey.'

Even as he spoke the words he realised his mistake: Adam Morton would no longer be the only man in Newenden to know there was pestilence at Hawkenlye, even though he had probably been the first.

But then there was a sound from the other side of the oak door and Adam Morton's voice reached Josse, muffled but audible. 'What do you want now?' he demanded. 'I will no longer open this door to you, Sir Josse, so it's no use your thumping on it; you'll only serve to put dents in it.'

'I understand,' Josse shouted back. 'I do not ask admittance, Master Morton; only information.' It was embarrassing, holding a conversation at such a volume that the whole street could hear; it was also, given the delicacy of the question to which he had come to seek an answer, potentially dangerous.

Perhaps Adam Morton's good sense got the better of him; there was a long pause, then he said, 'Go along to the wall that divides my herb garden from the street. Mount your horse and you will be able to see over it; I shall go into my garden and stand on my bench.'

Josse did as he was told. Augustus, watching, raised his eyebrows and Josse made a grimace. 'Better than nothing,' he remarked.

Presently there came sounds of a bench being dragged across the ground and then Adam Morton's face appeared over the top of the wall. He held a piece of spotless white linen up to his nose and mouth and Josse caught the scent of lavender oil. 'Don't you come too close!' he warned Josse, 'and you, lad' – he waved a finger at Augustus – 'you stay over there! Now,' he said, turning back to Josse, 'what is this information you want?' He added something under his breath, something to the effect of *as if I didn't know*.

'I believe that you sent someone to Hawkenlye Abbey,' Josse said, speaking as quietly as the distance between him and Adam Morton allowed. 'A young woman named Sabin de Retz, who came to you looking for news of Nicol Romley.'

The apothecary gave a weary sigh. 'Yes, I did,' he admitted.

'You did not think to tell her that he was dead?' Josse hissed.

'Ah, but when she came to see me I did not know!' Adam Morton protested.

Stunned, Josse said, 'But—' Then: 'So you mean she visited you before I came here with Gervase de Gifford? Yet you didn't think to tell me she was also looking for Nicol?'

'I don't see why I should have told you,' the apothecary said somewhat stiffly. 'And *obviously* she came before your first visit; I should hardly have sent such a lovely young woman chasing after a man I knew to be dead.'

'Yet you knew he was sick,' Josse reminded him.

'He might have recovered!'

Aye, Josse thought, that he might, had not some unknown hand struck the poor young man down.

And, as that thought brought him right back to the reason for this visit, he said, 'Did Sabin de Retz tell you why she needed to see Nicol?'

Adam Morton appeared to be thinking. Then he said, 'She said she had come from France. She met Nicol in Troyes and something happened there that she would not tell me. I gathered from her manner that it was something that had frightened her, for she went quite pale when she spoke of it. There had been danger and she had escaped. She knew Nicol was bound for Boulogne, where he would take ship for Hastings and then travel back here to Newenden, and she followed him. She told me that she *must* see him, that it was a matter of life and death.'

'And so you sent her after him to Hawkenlye,' Josse said, half to himself. 'Yet it was not until yesterday that she came to the Abbey looking for him. I was not there,' he explained to the apothecary, 'and when I returned, there was no sign of her.'

'Yes, she appeared furtive when she was here,' Morton agreed.

'With good reason, perhaps,' Josse suggested.

'Maybe, maybe.'

'I am wondering,' Josse said, 'why it took Sabin de Retz the best part of a week to travel from Newenden to Hawkenlye.'

The apothecary reached up to smooth the long white hair beneath the spotless cap. He looked away, first across his herb garden and then beyond Josse to the road. Then, almost disinterestedly, he said, 'I have no idea.'

'Thank you for that,' Josse muttered ironically. Then, as an

earlier thought returned to him, he said, 'I should still like to know why you did not tell me on either of my previous visits that you had sent Sabin de Retz to Hawkenlye.'

'I am an apothecary,' Morton snapped. 'In my profession there are many secrets and a man grows used to speaking only when he must.'

There seemed, Josse thought, no suitable reply to that. 'Is the young woman staying here in the town?' he asked.

'I do not think so,' Adam Morton replied. 'She was mounted on a grey mare and the horse looked as if it had been ridden hard.'

'She went from Hastings to Newenden, then on to Hawkenlye,' Josse said slowly, thinking aloud, 'and, given the present climate of fear, she'd have found precious little in the way of hospitality for a traveller in between the three locations. So,' he looked up and met the apothecary's eyes, 'where is she?'

The apothecary gave an apologetic shrug. 'Again, Sir Josse . . .'

'You have no idea,' Josse finished for him. 'Thank you for your time, Master Morton.' He turned Horace and, with a nod to Augustus, set off back down the street.

'Where are you going?' Adam Morton called after them.

Josse spun round in the saddle. 'We're going to look for her!'

Somebody else had left Hawkenlye Abbey even earlier that morning, slipping out secretively before it was light and when the majority of the community were still asleep. Sister Tiphaine had wrapped herself in her thick cloak, exchanged her sandals for the stout sabots she used for gardening and set off into the forest.

She had not enjoyed the previous day's conversation with the Abbess at all. While it was true that she had contacts with the forest people – far stronger and more regular contacts than

Tiphaine hoped anyone at Hawkenlye was aware – she also had an overriding duty to the Abbey and its Abbess. It had been hard – and strangely painful – to stand mutely listening to the Abbess's speculations concerning the outcome of the brief liaison between Sir Josse and Joanna and make no comment. But then the secret was not Tiphaine's to tell . . .

Of course, the Abbess had been absolutely right. Joanna had born a child to Sir Josse, and a girl child at that. In addition, given what Tiphaine knew about Joanna – and the child – it was highly likely that both mother and daughter had power in their very blood, although since little Meggie was only fifteen months old, nobody would yet have put her to the test.

A magical jewel, Tiphaine thought as she strode along the faint forest tracks, which were so familiar to her that she barely needed to look where she was going. What might such a precious and powerful thing do in the hand of Joanna or her child! Why, lives could be saved, even that of the old fusspot Firmin, who always looked askance at Tiphaine as if searching for her horns and tail!

No.

Tiphaine made herself arrest that line of thought, for it was far in the future, if indeed it was to happen at all. First she must find a way of approaching Joanna, then she must find the words with which to phrase her request, neither of which tasks she had very much confidence of easily achieving.

She knew the location of Joanna's hut and, indeed, the secret forest paths that she now trod took her quite close to it. She had been there once, on the night that Joanna bore Josse's child; she and her old friend from the forest people had helped the young mother bring Meggie into the world, and Lora had taken the baby outside into the cold October night and briefly placed her naked body on to the Earth so that the Mother would know her own. Lora had prophesied that night that Meggie would be one of the Great Ones of her people, and apparently the same had been said by others during the months of Meggie's short life.

Knowing the location of Joanna's dwelling by no means meant that Tiphaine could simply stroll up, knock on the door and ask admisssion, for Joanna had grown greatly in power over the past year and Tiphaine did not dare approach unannounced, uninvited and alone. Before she could seek out Joanna, she knew she must first find an intermediary. Which was why, as the sun rose on to another cold and bright February day, she was making her way to the oak grove deep in the forest that was her usual meeting place with Lora.

Time passed.

By mid-morning, there was still no sign of Lora and Tiphaine was beginning to wonder if she ought after all to go on to Joanna's hut. There was no guarantee that Lora would come; the forest people might be miles and miles away and, even if word had somehow reached Lora that Tiphaine was looking for her, sheer distance could well mean that Lora would not appear in the glade today. And it certainly was not acceptable to keep Abbess Helewise waiting when her request and her need were so very urgent.

The low midday sun of winter was shining down into the glade when a slim, supple figure clad in soft grey stepped out from behind the concealing trunk of a huge oak tree. Her silvery eyes held the knowledge of ages and her long hair was white, yet the smooth skin of her tanned face had barely a wrinkle and she moved like a dancer. Coming forward into the sunshine, she smiled as she called out Tiphaine's name.

Tiphaine rose hastily to her feet from the log on which she had been sitting and the two women embraced. 'You were asleep,' Lora said.

'I was not!' Tiphaine protested. 'I was closing my eyes against the sun's glare.'

'Ah, yes,' Lora said, 'that February glare.'

'I need to see Joanna,' Tiphaine said, ignoring the mild jibe. 'There's sickness at the Abbey. I am not sick,' she hastened to reassure Lora.

'I know that,' Lora replied calmly. 'I should not be here standing so close to you if you were.'

'They've got this jewel that they've been trying to use to make people better,' Tiphaine continued, 'but it's not working. It's a family treasure of Josse's' – it was odd, she thought fleetingly, how worldly titles had no meaning here when she was among the forest people – 'and they reckon there's some old prophecy that says the stone will only be truly effective when it's in the hand of a female of Josse's kin.'

Lora had been nodding as if this was no news to her, although she did not interrupt but allowed Tiphaine to finish. 'So they need Joanna's child, do they?' she said thoughtfully. 'They would think it appropriate to allow a fifteen-month-old infant to try out her power?'

'They do not know for sure that Joanna *has* a child,' Tiphaine protested, aware both that she was evading the issue and that it had not gone unnoticed.

'The Abbess knows,' Lora said.

'Aye, I reckon she does. But she has never breathed a word to – to anyone else, even though they're such close friends.'

'She has not told Josse, you mean.'

'Aye.'

Tiphaine waited. Lora was one of the venerated elders here in this forest domain and it did not do to hurry her. Since any chance of Tiphaine's getting to see Joanna rested entirely with the woman standing before her, the herbalist tried to control her impatience by silently reciting a list of the Healing Herbs . . .

'You can stop that,' Lora said. 'You are distracting me.'

'Sorry.' Tiphaine had known Lora far too long to be surprised at her ability to overhear another's thoughts.

Finally Lora spoke. 'I have no quarrel with the Abbess,' she announced, 'for our impression of her is that she has a good heart and, although she suffers from a sense of her own importance, she uses her position more to help others than to inflate her pride.'

'She—' Tiphaine began, but made herself stop.

'And similarly I can find no fault with her wish to use an object of power to save life, even though it is clear that she cannot have the first understanding of what this stone is. Therefore I will agree to take you to Joanna.'

'Thank you, Lora,' Tiphaine said humbly.

But Lora had not finished. 'I say only that I will take you to her,' she warned. 'You may then tell Joanna what you have told me, but I caution you not to put any pressure on her.' She lowered her voice and added, 'She has been to our sacred places and she has learned a very great deal. She is not the woman you once knew, Tiphaine.'

A shiver of fear went through the herbalist. 'I will do as you command, Lora,' she whispered. 'I sense already that Joanna has come into her power, for even from some distance away, I could sense her presence in her hut.'

Lora nodded. 'Aye. She is back there, with the child, after a year's absence. She is busy strengthening her defences.'

Tiphaine nodded. She knew without being told that the defences were not on the physical level; no wonder, she thought, she had sensed Joanna's power.

I am afraid of what lies before me, she realised as she trod in Lora's footsteps across the clearing and out between the trees. *If it were left to me, I should turn tail and flee back to the safety of the Abbey, to the arms of a gentler god than the force they bow before out here in the woods.*

But it was not up to Tiphaine.

Squaring her shoulders, praying both to the old god and the new for their protection, she bent down beneath the tangled undergrowth to follow Lora into the mouth of the hidden path that led to Joanna's hut.

12

Josse and Augustus found no trace of Sabin de Retz on the journey back to Hawkenlye. That was not to say, as Augustus remarked, that she was not there, hidden away in some house where, out of charity, they had taken her in before the dread threat of the pestilence became common knowledge.

It was possible, Josse agreed, although from his knowledge of how gossip travelled in country districts – it was as unstoppable as rats in a hay barn – he privately considered it unlikely. Had the young woman in fact found sanctuary somewhere along the road, then he reckoned that one of the handful of people who had reluctantly opened their doors a crack to speak to him would have known about it. And, with no reason to keep it secret, they would have told him all about her, probably adding all sorts of highly colourful and unlikely speculative details for good measure.

Deep in the country, he mused as they approached Hawkenlye, it was so rare for anything unusual to happen that, when it did, people habitually made the very most of it.

'D'you reckon she's putting up in Tonbridge, then, Sir Josse?' Augustus said, coming to ride alongside him as the track broadened; they were only a few miles from the Abbey now and soon would pass the turning that led down to the town.

Josse glanced at him, pleased to note that a day in the fresh air and away from his anxieties had put colour in the lad's face. 'She may be,' he agreed, 'although if she is and has been enquiring after Nicol Romley, then I imagine news of that would have reached Gervase de Gifford and he would have told us.'

'He keeps his eyes and ears open, that one,' Augustus remarked solemnly. Lowering his voice to a whisper, he added, 'They do say he has spies everywhere.'

'Do they?' Josse hid a smile, amused at the concept of an innocent young lay brother such as Augustus knowing all about the sophisticated professional practices of the sheriff of Tonbridge.

'Oh, aye,' Augustus was saying, 'we talk to lots of folks from down in the town when they come up to the Vale for the water and for Sister Tiphaine's simples. They suffer terribly from the rheum down there, you know, Sir Josse – it's all that water and marshland so close to where they live. It's said you can't tell a sheriff's man from an innocent traveller putting in at Goody Anne's for a mug of ale and a piece of pie, so well do they blend in with the company.'

'How so?' Josse was curious, and also cross with himself for his patronising attitude; just because a boy chose to live in an Abbey did not mean he had cut himself off from all contact with the rest of the world.

'Because the sheriff recruits men and then tells them not to reveal that they work for him,' Augustus said. 'That way folks enjoying a drink at the end of a hard day's work speak freely and it all gets back to the sheriff.' Shaking his head with a frown, he added, 'I couldn't do that. Pretend to be friendly just so as to make a man talk, then sift out the important details and run to tell the sheriff.' His intent eyes met Josse's. 'Could you, sir?'

'I—' Yes, I could, would be the honest answer but somehow he felt it would diminish him in Gus's eyes. 'Well, it would depend on the circumstances,' he said evasively.

Augustus nodded. 'I dare say there's times in the sort of

world you move in when such things are necessary,' he said gravely.

The sort of world I move in, Josse echoed to himself.

The trouble was that sometimes he was no longer sure what that world was . . .

Jerking his thoughts back to the present, he reminded himself that he had a job to do. As they approached the Tonbridge road, he said, 'Gus, I'm going to ride down to the town right now to see if anyone has seen Sabin.'

'Want me to come with you, Sir Josse?'

'No, thank you. But I should be grateful if you would ride on to the Abbey and tell the Abbess where I am and that I shall report back to her on my return.'

'I'll do that,' Augustus said. 'Good luck, sir.'

The tavern was almost empty when Josse arrived and he was served with his mug of ale almost immediately. Goody Anne came hurrying in, apparently as pressed as ever, and, spotting Josse, immediately put a hand to the spotless cap covering her hair, straightened her voluminous apron and came over to the fire to speak to him.

'Thought you'd found yourself another woman and abandoned me,' she greeted him cheerfully. 'How are you, Sir Josse?'

'Well, thank you. And you, Goody Anne?'

The humour left her face and she sighed. 'I am well, too, thank God,' she said, 'but business is dreadful. It's these rumours of sickness up at Hawkenlye.' Staring at him, suddenly she went ashen and took two very large paces back. 'You've come from there?' she whispered.

'Aye, but do not fear, for they know how to keep the sick well away from the healthy.'

She did not look reassured. Keeping her distance, she said, 'No offence, Sir Josse, and it's not like me to turn away custom, especially now when things are so bad and when I'm that glad to see your friendly face, but would you be so kind as to finish your ale and leave?'

His initial hurt feelings quickly subsided as he studied her expression; her request clearly distressed her more than it did him. 'Of course,' he said. 'I understand, and it was thoughtless of me to have come, my connection with the Abbey being common knowledge.'

Goody Anne nodded. 'Knew you'd be reasonable, a fine man like you,' she muttered. Then, as an afterthought, 'Why *did* you come? They serve a good mug of ale up at the Abbey, so I've always been told, so you're not here just for my brew.'

'No. I'm looking for someone. A young woman, well dressed, mounted on a grey mare. She arrived in Hastings, went to Newenden and then came to seek me up at the Abbey, only—'

But Goody Anne's pallor was back. 'She followed the plague route, then,' she whispered. 'Hastings, Newenden, Hawkenlye.'

Josse had imagined this to be a secret known to few. He might have known better. 'You have had no such guests here at the inn?' he asked, already knowing what her response would be.

'No.' Goody Anne shook her head. 'I've had no travellers putting up here with me in a week or more, Sir Josse. Folks are frightened and they stay within their own walls as much as they can.'

'Is there anywhere else in the town that this young woman might be staying?' he persisted.

Goody Anne thought for a moment. Then she said firmly, 'No. I reckon not. I'd have heard about her if she were here.'

Josse finished his ale. 'Will you let me know if she comes?' he asked. 'Her name is Sabin de Retz.'

'If she comes, I'll let you know.' Goody Anne had already

picked up his empty mug and was moving away towards the scullery. 'If,' she added, with a trace of her smile, 'I can find anyone brave enough to ride up to Hawkenlye and seek you out.'

Josse rode next to Gervase de Gifford's house on the edge of the town. De Gifford was relaxing before a blazing fire and just about to eat; he persuaded Josse to join him. Between mouthfuls of roast fowl with garlic sauce, Josse told the sheriff about the mysterious woman and her quest to find Nicol Romley, and how he and Augustus had gone to speak to Adam Morton.

'. . . but now she's disappeared,' he concluded. 'No sign of her in Newenden or on the road, and Goody Anne says she's not staying here in the town.'

De Gifford poured more beer into Josse's mug, nodding. 'I imagine Goody Anne is right,' he said. 'The young woman came from Hastings, you said, so could she have returned there?'

Josse sighed at the prospect of yet another couple of days in the saddle. 'I suppose so,' he said miserably. 'Yet surely, if she is intent on finding out what happened to Nicol Romley, she would stay near to the place where he died?'

'Does she know he's dead?' de Gifford asked.

'She—' Josse stopped. It was a good question and, he realised, one to which the answer might well be *no*. Adam Morton hadn't told her, for when he encountered her Nicol was, as far as Morton knew, still alive. And surely Sister Ursel would have had more tact and kindness than to blurt out news of Nicol's death the moment someone came asking for him.

'She may not,' he admitted.

'The trail has led her to Hawkenlye,' de Gifford said, 'and to you. Wherever she is, I would guess that she is not far away for, until she has found you and learned news of the man she seeks, she will need to return there.'

'I can't just sit and wait for her to come back!' Josse protested.

De Gifford smiled. 'Unless you can find out where she's hiding, you may have to.' The smile left his face and he said quietly, 'If you find this Sabin de Retz, Josse, persuade her, if you can, to see me.' Before Josse could comment, de Gifford added, 'Amid all our other concerns, let us not forget that I have poor Nicol Romley's murderer to find and to bring to justice.'

It was fully dark by the time Josse got back to the Abbey. De Gifford had pressed him to stay for the night but Josse was anxious to speak to the Abbess. Hoping there would still be a light shining through the gap under her door, he walked as quietly as he could along the cloister.

She opened the door as he put up a hand to knock. 'I thought you would not retire before we had spoken,' she said by way of greeting. 'Come in, Sir Josse, and warm yourself.'

He did as she said, removing his heavy gauntlets and stretching out his ice-cold hands to the small brazier that stood in one corner of the little room. Without turning round, once more he gave a report of his day's findings.

She heard him out in silence and made no comment even when he had finished. Turning, he said, 'My lady?' but even as he spoke, it occurred to him that all but the final piece of news she would have already heard from Augustus.

Perhaps that explained her distracted look . . .

She raised her head, met his eyes and said, 'I am sorry, Sir Josse, I *was* listening but—' She broke off with a small shrug, as if explaining herself were beyond her.

'You've a great deal on your mind, my lady,' he said kindly, 'and, in truth, there is little in what I have just said to keep the attention.' She made to speak but he went on, 'Any new cases of the sickness?'

'Sister Judith has a fever,' she said dully. 'And Sister Beata is very unwell with the bowel flux.'

'I regret deeply that I have no power to use the Eye of Jerusalem,' he said. 'If only—'

'Sir Josse, what if—' she began, but instantly closed her mouth on whatever speculation she was about to make.

'What if?' he prompted her. 'Please, my lady, share your thought with me.'

But she shook her head. 'It is late,' she said, 'and I am weary beyond imagination, as indeed you must be too.' She managed a faint smile. 'Let us speak in the morning, Sir Josse.'

He watched her but she would not look at him. With unease stirring deep within him, he bowed and left the room.

She might be sufficiently exhausted to sleep, he thought a long time afterwards. I thought I was, too.

But there was something wrong, something she could not bring herself to tell him. Knowing her as well as he did, it had been a surprise to see an expression on her face that he had never seen before.

When she had started to ask him something, only to stop again almost instantly, she had looked almost . . . He thought hard for the right word.

She had looked ashamed.

Helewise had been asleep but it had been a brief surrendering to her fatigue and had only lasted a few hours. Now she lay wide awake, demons racing around her head.

I have begun on a course of action that will bring Josse face to face with something that will change his life, she thought miserably. I have done this for a very good reason and, when he finds out, he will understand that I had to do everything within my power to save the lives of the sick who have come here for help.

He may well understand, the thought continued. But will he ever forgive me?

And I have sent Sister Tiphaine into danger, she went on remorselessly, determined to face up to the full horror of her actions. She went into the forest – or so I conclude, for she has not been seen in the Abbey all day – and she has not come back.

Oh, supposing something had happened to her! Supposing night had come upon her when she was alone out there, lost in that terrible place, and even now she was lying injured, with wolves circling and those strange forest people threatening her with death for having trespassed in their lands!

Sister Tiphaine is in no danger from the forest people, the sensible part of Helewise's mind told her firmly. She has regular contact with them and knows their ways better than you do; she will be fully aware what she can and cannot do out in the forest and she is probably tucked up quite safely somewhere. The only reason for her continuing absence is probably that she has not yet fulfilled her mission.

It was a comforting thought but Helewise soon came up with something else to worry about.

Her mission. Yes, Sister Tiphaine's mission.

And, unfortunately for Helewise, that brought her straight back to Josse.

She lay awake, restless and very anxious, for what remained of the night.

In the morning Josse made it his first task to seek out Sister Ursel.

'The young woman who came here looking for Nicol Romley,' he began, after greeting her and exchanging a few remarks about the weather, which was still cold and clear.

'Sabin de Retz,' Sister Ursel said promptly.

'Aye. Sister' – he paused, wondering how to phrase his question without giving offence – 'Sister, when she asked after him, obviously the name was familiar to you and you knew to whom she referred, but—'

'I didn't tell her he was dead, if that's what you're asking,' Sister Ursel interrupted, not looking the least offended. 'I knew what his name was, of course – you can't keep a thing like that a secret in a community such as Hawkenlye – and I recognised it when she spoke it. But it wasn't my place to break the news to the poor lass, Sir Josse, especially not when she'd just asked to speak to you. I knew you'd be able to tell her far more about the whole sorry business than I could,' she added confidently.

I don't know that I could have done, Josse thought ruefully. 'I see,' he said.

'Anyway,' Sister Ursel concluded, 'standing by the gate is no place to receive bad news, eh, Sir Josse?'

Smiling, pleased with himself for having so accurately guessed what Sister Ursel would say, he agreed that it was not. He left the porteress with strict instructions to inform him the instant Sabin de Retz returned – *if* she returned – and was just trying to decide whether now was the moment to speak to the Abbess and demand to know what was the matter with her – apart from a murder on her doorstep and a ward full of desperately sick people, he thought ruefully – when someone called out his name.

Turning, he saw Brother Augustus running towards him.

'Good morning, Gussie,' Josse greeted him. A sudden chill caught at him; was Augustus racing to bring bad news? 'How is Brother Firmin?'

Augustus stopped, panting, and said, 'He is still holding out, Sir Josse. I have been praying since I awoke and they tell me Brother Firmin is praying too.'

'When – if the moment comes, Gus,' Josse said gently, 'then surely he will soon be with God in heaven.'

Augustus looked faintly surprised that Josse might even be

thinking anything to the contrary. Then, with a shake of his head as if to drive out that thought and proceed to another, he said, 'It's not about him that I've come looking for you. It's about the young woman.'

'Sabin de Retz?' As if there could be any other young woman.

'Aye.' Augustus sounded impatient, as if he too thought the interjection unnecessary. 'Sir Josse, when I wasn't praying for Brother Firmin I've been thinking about where she might be. Like we were saying yesterday, it's unlikely anyone's taken her in, what with the sickness and that, and I'd guess you found no trace of her in Tonbridge for the same reason.'

'You guess right,' Josse agreed.

'Well, there's one sort of place where they never turn people away even if the whole county falls ill,' Augustus pressed on eagerly. Then, when Josse didn't instantly reply, he cried, 'Places like Hawkenlye! Religious foundations!'

God's boots, but the lad was right! 'Well done, Gussie,' Josse said, clapping him enthusiastically on the shoulder. 'Even now she could be joining the community at their prayers in . . .' He realised he had no idea where the nearest religious house was. 'Er, where might she be, d'you think, Gus?'

Augustus smiled. 'There's West Abbey,' he began, 'that's north of here and they're Benedictine nuns, only the place burned down a few years ago and I don't know if they've rebuilt their guest quarters. There's the canons down at Otham, but they're in the middle of plans to move their foundation somewhere more suitable and I doubt they've much accommodation for guests either. There's St Martin's at Battle and then there's . . .'

But Josse had remembered something. A year ago, when word had first come of King Richard's capture and imprisonment, Queen Eleanor, beside herself with anxiety, had sent two trusted abbots out to Speyer to see the king and report back to her. One abbot came from . . . where was it? Boxley, aye, that was it, and wasn't Boxley up near Rochester? The other envoy was the abbot of Pont Robert, or Robertsbridge, as the people called it. And Robertsbridge was only some fifteen miles south of Hawkenlye.

'Robertsbridge!' he cried.

Augustus shot him a glance. 'I was just going to say Robertsbridge.'

'What do we know of the place?' Josse demanded eagerly.

Augustus had a think and then said, 'It's run by the White Monks and they're farmers and foresters. The Abbey's tucked away in the forest, like all Cistercian houses, because the monks aren't allowed near towns.'

'Would they accommodate a young woman like Sabin de Retz?'

Augustus shrugged. 'I can't say for certain, but the Cistercians are known for their charity and their care of the poor.'

'It doesn't sound as if Sabin is poor,' Josse said, half to himself, thinking of the grey mare and the fur-lined gloves.

'Maybe the old White Monks wouldn't be above letting her stay anyway but rattling the poor box under her nose,' Augustus said shrewdly.

Josse grinned. 'Very possibly,' he agreed. 'Is it a good road to Robertsbridge, Gus?'

'Reckon so, Sir Josse. It's the Hastings road nearly all the way.' Returning Josse's smile, he said, 'Want me to ask leave to go with you?'

'Aye, do that, lad. I'll go and tap on the Abbess Helewise's door and explain where we're going.'

He found the Abbess sitting behind her table. She seemed to have plenty to do, judging by the rolls of parchment spread out in front of her and the stylus in its horn of ink, but Josse had the distinct impression that, immediately before he went in, she had been staring into space. The look of anxiety on her face barely diminished as she greeted him.

'Sister Beata is dead,' she said.

It had been expected, Josse well knew, but nevertheless the news hit him like a fist in the stomach. 'I am sorry,' he said quietly. 'She was a loving and a lovable woman.'

'She was,' the Abbess agreed. Raising dull eyes briefly to meet his before she looked away again, she said, 'What is it, Sir Josse? As you see, I am busy.'

What is the matter with her? he wondered yet again. The death of Sister Beata was hard to accept, aye, but normally under such circumstances the Abbess would surely have derived comfort from talking over her grief and pain with Josse. And here she was, hinting that the sooner he said what he had to say and got himself out of her presence, the better she would like it.

Coolly he said, 'Brother Augustus has come up with the bright suggestion that Sabin de Retz is probably lodging in a religious house. He and I are off down to Robertsbridge, it being the nearest one to us, to see if we can find her.'

'I see,' the Abbess said neutrally.

He waited, but it did not appear that she was going to say any more. 'I'll come and find you when we return.' He realised he had sounded curt but just at that moment he didn't care.

He spun round and strode out of the room, closing the door rather forcefully behind him. He thought he heard her cry out his name but when he paused to see if she would call again, there was nothing but silence.

He hurried on to the stables, where he found that Augustus had prepared the horses and, wrapped warmly in his cloak, was already mounted on the Abbey cob. Trying to put the Abbess out of his mind, Josse got up on to Horace's broad back and led the way out through the gate and away south-eastwards.

★

Helewise sat, miserable and alone, in her room. She knew she must get up and set about the preparations for Sister Beata's interment but she had no heart for the task. She knew too how the death of one of their own was going to affect an Abbey full of people already stretched beyond the limit and that somehow she must find the words to rally the community, remind them that God's purpose is often unclear and exhort them to go on giving of their very best without expecting any immediate reward.

She had little heart for that, either.

Sickness, misery, death and grief. Am I, she cried in silent agony, expected to be immune from distress? Sister Beata is dead, Sister Judith is very ill and Brother Firmin is at death's door, and there is no time for me to lament, to weep, to ask God why this pestilence has come to us.

And above all that – as if it were not enough – she was expecting at any moment to receive word that Sister Tiphaine had returned. Trying to control her turbulent, panicky thoughts, Helewise realised that she did not know which of the two possible outcomes she was hoping for: that Tiphaine would return without Joanna, thereby losing any chance the Abbey nursing nuns might have had of employing the Eye of Jerusalem; or that the herbalist would bring Joanna back with her and that Helewise would have to find a way of breaking the news to Josse, when he got back, that the woman he had loved and lost was within the Abbey precincts.

Neither outcome, Helewise's miserable thoughts concluded, would happen if Tiphaine were lost or hurt within the mighty forest . . .

Not expecting any great measure of success, she pulled a parchment towards her, picked up her stylus and listlessly set herself to work.

13

Josse and Brother Augustus made swift time on the journey down to Robertsbridge. The road was indeed good and there were relatively few places where potholes and cracks meant slowing down to pick a careful path.

Augustus must have asked directions – perhaps he already knew the way, for before coming to Hawkenlye his young life had been spent travelling on England's roads – and as they approached the place he was able to lead Josse along increasingly narrow paths and tracks until, deep in the forest and with the gentle slope of a hill behind it, they came to Robertsbridge Abbey.

Josse was not sure what he had been expecting; in the back of his mind he had had a vague picture of a smaller and more isolated Hawkenlye. As soon as the settlement known as Robertsbridge Abbey came into view, however, he realised that his mental image was quite wrong: Robertsbridge was nothing like Hawkenlye and, had it not been for the rough wooden cross affixed to one of the larger buildings, it could, from a distance, have been mistaken for a primitive peasant hamlet.

As they rode closer, Josse could make out a plan. The monks had hacked away trees, shrubs and undergrowth from the edges of what appeared to have been a pre-existing open space in deep woodland. Judging from the position of the sun, the monks had utilised the low hill for protection from the easterly winds, for the settlement was built to the west of it.

Their foundation consisted of a wide central cloister surrounded by cells on the west side and gardens on the east,
the latter tucked under the lee of the hill and exposed to the
south to gain maximum sunshine. The communal buildings
were small and built of roughly shaped wooden planks infilled
with wattle and daub. A stream winding round the base of the
hill had been diverted so that little channels ran through the
vegetable and herb gardens; presumably the site had been
selected because of proximity to the stream.

To the right of the monks' buildings and some two hundred
paces along a track leading into the forest, Josse could just
make out the outlines of another small group of dwellings;
probably stables, farm buildings and workshops. They would
be invisible from the abbey, he realised, once the trees and
bushes were in leaf.

Perhaps that was the idea.

A low wooden fence with a gate, at present standing open,
surrounded the monks' buildings; the fence would not have
deterred a determined intruder and Josse guessed that it was
probably intended to keep out livestock or the wild animals of
the forest.

He led the way through the open gate. All was still and quiet
– the monks must either be at prayer or out somewhere
supervising the work on their lands – but nevertheless he felt
quite sure that he was being watched.

He and Augustus drew rein just inside the gate and Josse
called out, 'Halloa the Abbey! We have come from Hawkenlye
and would have speech with you!'

For a moment nothing happened; Josse thought he
caught a snatch of whispered conversation but decided
that it was probably his imagination, stimulated by the
susurration of the wind in the bare branches of the trees.
Then out of a long, low building to the left, roofed with
thatch and totally unadorned, a man appeared. He was

clad in a simple white habit of coarse wool tied at the waist with a length of rope.

He walked over to Josse, staring up at him out of bright, round eyes that reminded Josse of those of an inquisitive bird. He said, 'I am Stephen. What do you wish to speak to me about?' As Josse hesitated, he added, 'Please, dismount, and your companion too.' The shiny brown eyes turned to Augustus and Stephen gave the lad a nod of greeting.

'I am Josse d'Acquin,' Josse said, sliding down from Horace's back, 'and this is Brother Augustus of Hawkenlye.'

'Good day to you both,' Stephen said. Then, with a sudden radiant smile, 'Welcome! I will see to your horses and then we shall take food and drink together; simple fare, I fear, but what we have you may freely share.'

Waving away Josse's thanks, Stephen took the horses' reins and led the animals in the direction of the track branching off towards the buildings in the forest; he called out, 'Bruno! Come and take these horses and tend to them!' A boyish figure dressed in brown appeared from behind the church where, to judge by the way he was brushing earth from his hands, he had been engaged in some gardening task. He gave Stephen a reverential bow, then took the horses and hastened off with them down the track, making a quiet sound in his throat that sounded remarkably like a horse's soft whinny.

Stephen gazed after him, shaking his head. 'Poor Bruno is short of wits,' he said very softly, although the lad was too far away by now to have heard even a voice speaking at normal pitch. 'He is dumb and cannot talk to his fellow man, but God has compensated by bestowing upon the boy the ability to communicate with animals and, if it does not sound too strange, with plants.'

'Plants?' Josse and Augustus said together.

Stephen smiled. 'Aye. Bruno's vegetables, herbs and flowers put those grown by the rest of us to shame. He treats his plants as if they were little creatures and we cannot but conclude that it is the boy's very breath that encourages such extraordinary growth.' Shaking his head at the vagaries of the natural world, Stephen led the way into the long, low building from which he had earlier emerged.

Josse saw that it was a very rudimentary refectory. The long tables were of plain wood and the benches either side of them so narrow that being seated on them must have been like sitting on top of a fence rail. The candlesticks were simply made, and of undecorated iron. Stephen had called out as he entered the room and in response another white-robed monk now appeared bearing a wooden tray on which were a pottery flagon, two tankards and some hunks of what looked like rather coarse bread.

'Small beer is our usual beverage,' Stephen said, filling the tankards. 'And I fear the bread may be dry to your taste for we do not use animal fat.'

Josse, who had taken a mouthful of bread and was now trying to summon sufficient saliva to chew it, had to agree, but good manners made him say, as soon as the bread was under control, 'We are grateful for your hospitality, Stephen, and the victuals are most welcome.'

Stephen nodded in satisfaction. He watched Josse and Augustus eat and drink and, when they had finished, he said, 'You have ridden some distance to speak to us here. Now that you are refreshed, will you explain why?'

Josse had been rehearsing what he would say; monks and nuns were not, in his experience, people to waste time with unnecessary words and so he tried to be brief. 'A young woman came asking for help at Hawkenlye Abbey,' he said. 'Her name is Sabin de Retz and she was in fact looking for a friend. She came to Hawkenlye because she had been told he had gone there. We – Augustus and I – rode to Newenden, the town where the young man, Nicol Romley, lived, and we discovered that Sabin had also been there asking for him. It was there that she was told he had gone to Hawkenlye.'

Josse had the distinct sense that he was making the explanation more complicated than it need be and was fleetingly surprised to see that Stephen was nodding his understanding. 'Did she not speak to you at the Abbey?' he asked.

'No, for I was not there,' Josse replied, 'and, indeed, since she had not heard of me, she could not have asked for me by name. She did not find Nicol Romley either,' he added. 'In fact, Nicol is dead.'

'Dead!' The monk's eyes widened dramatically. 'Dear me!'

'Ever since I learned that Sabin de Retz was looking for Nicol,' Josse continued, 'Augustus and I have been trying to find her. She's not staying in Newenden nor, as far as we can ascertain, anywhere along the road to Hawkenlye, and it appears she's not in Tonbridge either.' Glancing at Augustus, he said, 'Brother Augustus here had the bright idea that she might be enjoying the hospitality of a monastic house and, yours being the obvious choice, we have come here to ask you if you know of her or have had any word of her.'

There was quite a long pause. Then Stephen said, 'She is not here, Sir Josse.'

Josse's heart sank. It was not until he heard Stephen's denial that he realised how much he had been banking on finding her here. 'And—' He swallowed and tried again. 'You do not even recognise the name? She's young, as I say, well-dressed, apparently, and mounted on a good mare.'

Stephen gave a shrug. Cursing monks for their habits of economy of speech, Josse turned away before Stephen could read his expression; it was not, he thought fairly, the monk's fault that he could not provide the happy solution that Josse so badly wanted.

Stephen's voice broke the uncomfortable silence. 'You say that the young man is dead,' he said. 'Forgive my curiosity –

very little happens in our daily life here, Sir Josse, and we enjoy the occasional scrap of news of the outside world – but how did he die?'

Josse studied the monk's face. He wore a bland smile but there was a certain avidity in the round eyes, as if he were hungry for a good gossip and a few gory details. 'Nicol Romley was suffering from a pestilence that we believe was brought across from the continent,' he said, speaking more curtly than was polite. 'But he didn't die of the sickness; someone struck him over the head and rolled his body into the lake in Hawkenlye Vale.'

Stephen had gone white.

Josse said, after a moment, 'Do not fear contagion from Augustus and me, for the nuns and monks of Hawkenlye have arranged matters so that the sick and the healthy are kept well apart.'

Again, Stephen seemed to weigh his words before speaking. Then he said, 'I thank you, Sir Josse, for the reassurance.'

Eyes on those of the monk's, Josse had the sudden quaint thought that Stephen's intent stare meant he was trying to convey something about which he would not speak. Perhaps he wants to know more about the foreign pestilence, Josse thought, but fears to ask in case Gus and I condemn him for his morbid curiosity. 'The disease takes the form of a high fever with a deadly looseness of the bowels that leaches every drop of fluid from the body,' he began, but Stephen put up a silencing hand.

'I pray to the merciful one above that I shall not need to know the symptoms,' he said. 'We shall include the sick of Hawkenlye in our prayers.'

'Thank you,' Josse said gruffly.

'Well,' Stephen said after a moment, 'if there's nothing else, I will send Bruno for your horses and see you on your way.' With a beaming smile, he edged Josse towards the door. 'We live a life of hard work, you know, and these lands that we wrested back from the wild need our constant vigilance to keep them productive.'

'We would not keep you from your work,' Josse said. 'It was good of you to spare the time to see us and I apologise for troubling you.'

'Oh, think nothing of it!' said the monk brightly. 'Bruno! *Bruno!* Leave your digging and fetch the horses – our visitors are going now.'

'Now why,' Josse said to Augustus as they emerged from the track on to the main road up from Hastings and could ride side by side, 'do I have the impression that Brother Stephen was eager to see the back of us? Can he have truly been in that much of a hurry to return to whatever he was doing when we arrived?'

Augustus frowned. 'It's odd he should speak of working hard on the land,' he said slowly.

'Why? I understood that to be the way of the Cistercians, to carve out a clearing deep in the forest and cultivate it? I thought their rule involved less hours praying in chapel and more out working the land.'

'It does,' Augustus agreed. 'Or, rather, it did, until the White Monks discovered that, as any farmer could have told them, working the land thoroughly and well doesn't really leave *any* time for saying your prayers, at least not when the prayers are of any length.'

'So how do they manage?'

'They invented the system of lay brethren,' Augustus said. 'That boy Bruno, he was dressed in brown instead of the white that Stephen wears. Well, he'll be a lay brother.'

Josse frowned. 'But we have lay brothers at Hawkenlye, although you wear black like the monks.'

'Aye, but the Cistercians had them first,' Augustus said with a grin. 'Reckon whoever set about making sure that the system at Hawkenlye Abbey worked all right wasn't above pinching a good idea from another order.'

Josse smiled in response. Then, recalling where the conversation had begun, he said, 'So what you're saying is that it's odd for Stephen to say he's got to get back to manual work because it won't be the likes of him who carries out the farming and forestry tasks?'

'Aye,' Gus agreed. 'If he wanted an excuse to see us on our way, it seems to me he ought to have come up with something more convincing.'

An excuse to see us on our way. Aye, Josse thought as, the road smoothing out in front of them, they kicked their horses to a canter. Aye, that's just how I saw it.

And as they covered the miles back to Hawkenlye, he tried – with a singular lack of success – to work out why Stephen had wanted them gone. By the time the Abbey came into view, all that he had managed to come up with was that Stephen had not been as convinced by Josse's reassurances concerning the sickness as he claimed to be.

Back at Robertsbridge, as soon as Josse and Augustus had ridden off down the track, Stephen had raced to climb the hill behind the Abbey. He knew from long experience that, on a clear day, it allowed someone standing at its summit a good view of the place where the track to Robertsbridge Abbey joined the main road coming up from the coast; he wanted to make quite sure that his visitors had gone.

He waited for some time, stamping his bare feet in their rough sandals against the cold, hard ground and, as the sweat of exertion cooled, wrapping his arms round himself in a vain attempt to stop the shivering. Then at last the two horsemen came into view; the young monk was leading, the big knight following. As Stephen watched, a smile of relief on his face, the pair emerged on to the road and their pace increased. He watched until they were out of sight and then turned and hurried back down to the Abbey.

He turned left instead of right at the foot of the hill and ran along the track to the buildings hidden in the forest.

She was waiting for him.

'Have they gone?' Her accent was strong but he could understand her if she spoke slowly.

'Aye. I waited until they broke into a canter to be sure. They're hurrying back to Hawkenlye now.'

'They will not return here?'

'I do not think so.'

'What did they say about Nicol?' she demanded urgently. Her face was pale and her wide blue eyes showed her fear but she was still beautiful, even to an avowed monk who ought not to notice such things.

Stephen took a step closer to her and placed a gentle hand on her arm. 'He did not die of the sickness,' he said. 'That knight – he is Sir Josse d'Acquin – says he was struck down by an unknown assailant.'

Sabin gasped. 'It is just as I feared!' she cried. 'They tried before in Troyes and now they have followed us to England. Nicol would not accept that we were in danger and so would not agree to take care, and now he has paid the price for his – his *insouciance* and he is dead. Oh, dear God, he's been *murdered*!' She gave a sob that seemed to come up from the very heart of her.

'You are safe here,' Stephen reassured her, 'we are so deeply buried in the forest that nobody can find us unless they know the way.'

'That Sir Josse found you,' she pointed out coldly.

'Aye, but he had a lad with him who's a monk and probably knows all about us,' Stephen replied.

She drew her heavy cloak more firmly round her, pulling the

hood up over the neat white cap that covered her fair hair. Turning to Stephen, she gave a very small smile and said, 'I apologise for my rudeness. It is not right to speak in this manner when you and the other monks have been so kind to us during the week and more that we have imposed ourselves upon you.'

Stephen spread his hands, palms upwards. 'It is what we are here for, to help those in need,' he said simply. Then: 'How is he?'

Sabin shrugged. 'Restless. He was not in his room when I went to find him earlier and I was worried that he had somehow found out that the knight and the young monk from Hawkenlye had come here.'

'He was not in the Abbey buildings when they arrived,' Stephen said quickly.

Sabin smiled again, more generously now, and a dimple winked in her pale cheek. 'He was,' she corrected him. 'He'd gone to beg some ingredients from your herbalist and he heard the horses. He hid in that little room just inside the gate and watched.'

Stephen sighed; Sabin's old grandfather was becoming quite unpredictable. But then, the monk reminded himself, the poor old boy had been through a lot recently and probably spent much of his waking hours afraid of another attempt on his life. 'Has he returned to the guest quarters?' he asked.

'Yes,' Sabin replied. 'Now that he has the necessary ingredients to finish whatever remedy he was in the process of making up, he will be quite happy. For the time being,' she added, looking anxious again.

'Sabin,' Stephen began cautiously, 'I do not in truth believe that the knight represents any threat to you or your grandfather. He seemed to me to be a good man, sincere in his wish to find you and, I would surmise, in so doing discover who killed poor Nicol and why.'

Sabin stared at him, blue eyes intent. 'Perhaps,' she said softly. 'But what if you are wrong? Somebody tried to kill Grandfather and me in Troyes by setting fire to the lodging house where we were staying. Now somebody – perhaps the same man – has pursued us to England and he has slain Nicol. I followed poor Nicol to Newenden in order to insist that he take the danger seriously but I arrived too late; they told me he had gone to Hawkenlye. I would have followed him there straight away but for Grandfather; I had to return here to Robertsbridge because he was still so sick from the smoke that he breathed in and the pains in his chest that followed. When finally I went to Hawkenlye, almost a week later, still in pursuit of Nicol and also to try to find if anyone at the Abbey could help me, it was to overhear that he was already in his grave.' Her face working with emotion, she said, 'And now we find out that he did not die of the pestilence but was struck down by an assailant! Stephen, I dare not trust *anybody*, even your knight!'

Stephen gave a faint shrug. 'Then you had better stay here,' he said, with a note of resignation that did not go unnoticed.

'Where else should I go?' Sabin asked, spreading her hands wide in appeal. 'Should I return to Hawkenlye, dragging Grandfather with me, for us to suffer the same fate as Nicol?'

'Perhaps you would not,' Stephen said. 'If you could but persuade yourself that Sir Josse d'Acquin is no threat but in fact your protector, then might returning to the place where Nicol was slain be the first step in bringing his killer to justice? There is much that you could tell the knight that would help in that worthy aim, is there not? We could arrange an escort for you to ensure your safety on the journey; have no fear on that score.'

She stared at him for some moments. Then she said, 'Grandfather overheard you talking to the knight, Stephen. He left the little gate room and crouched just outside the door of the refectory and he didn't miss a single word.' Her expression chilling until the blue eyes were icy, she went on, 'Just when, I wonder, were you going to confirm to me what, from my visit, I already suspected: that the sickness that drove Nicol to seek help is now rife at Hawkenlye Abbey?'

14

Sister Tiphaine and Lora had spent the night in the forest, in a compact shelter deep in its heart that the forest people occasionally used when in the vicinity. Despite the cold, Lora had contrived to make the shelter quite comfortable; she lit a small fire, prepared warm food and a hot drink and, when it was time for sleep, provided Tiphaine with a woollen cover that kept the herbalist as cosy as she usually was in her own bed back at Hawkenlye.

There had been no sign of Joanna at her hut when they went looking for her that morning. Lora had found the place without any difficulty and it was clear to both women that somebody – almost certainly Joanna – had recently been there for the dead bracken had been cut away from the clearing in which the hut was situated and the patch of earth where Joanna grew her herbs and her vegetables had been weeded and dug over ready for the spring planting. The hut itself was, Tiphaine had noticed, quite hard to spot, even when you knew quite well where it was. The undergrowth had advanced around the base of its walls and the branch of a birch tree bent low over its roof, in a gesture that was almost protective. Standing with her hands on her hips at Tiphaine's side, Lora had observed that Joanna had learned a lot since she had first fled to hide in the Great Forest; when Tiphaine queried the remark, Lora turned to her with a wry expression and said, 'She's learned how to disguise her habitation so well that even I had to look twice.'

They had waited for the rest of that day. When it grew dark – and much colder – Lora had announced that they'd give it up for the day and try again tomorrow.

Now tomorrow had come.

As the two women strode through the forest, Tiphaine wondered if Joanna would be there this time when they reached the clearing. It was a strange thought, and one undoubtedly brought on by the unusual experience of sleeping out beneath the stars and the trees, but the herbalist realised that she would not be surprised at all to find that, this morning, Joanna had managed to make her hut totally invisible.

They approached the clearing and automatically slowed their fast pace. Tiphaine sensed that even Lora felt a little cowed by the force that seemed to emanate from the hut, and Lora was one of the elders of the forest people and a powerful woman herself.

Lora turned to Tiphaine with a grimace. 'She knows we're here,' she said quietly. 'Best go up to her openly; no sense skulking in the undergrowth.'

Tiphaine fell into step behind her and they strode across the clearing until they stood before Joanna's door.

'Joanna,' Lora called, 'we need to speak to you.'

No answer.

Lora raised her hand and tapped on the stout wood of the door. 'Joanna!' she said a little louder.

Still no answer.

Then she was standing right behind them, so close that Sister Tiphaine's veil brushed against Joanna's arm as the herbalist spun round.

Lora said somewhat caustically, 'Very clever, my girl. Demonstrating your skill, is that it?'

Joanna did not speak for a moment. She stood quite still, dark eyes studying first Lora, then Tiphaine. Then she said, 'I knew you were looking for me, Lora, and that there was another with you. Until now, I did not know the identity of the other.'

Then, with a sudden wide smile, she opened her arms and embraced the herbalist, then turned to Lora and gave her a quick bow. 'Lora, I am glad to see you. And you, Tiphaine,' she added in a murmur, 'helped me when Meggie was born. I do not know why you have come' – she had turned back to Lora – 'but you are welcome. Come in.'

Stepping forward, she unlatched the door of the hut and led them inside. Tiphaine remembered the night of Meggie's birth too and she noticed that the hut seemed little changed since that day. Joanna had clearly been busy since her return, for the place was spotless and smelled pleasingly of lavender; the pile of ashes in the small central hearth had been brushed up within its ring of stones, and kindling and small logs were laid ready for the day's fire. The iron pot that stood ready beside the hearth was black with age and long use but it had recently received a good scrubbing. The beaten earth floor had been swept and the planking shelves on the far wall were dust-free, their contents neatly arranged. The steps up to the sleeping platform were in good repair and there was now a slim barrier bar on the side not protected by the wall of the hut; a low rail along the open side of the platform had also been added. On the platform were a straw mattress and several woollen blankets; among the blankets sat a very pretty child.

Tiphaine stared at the little girl whom she had helped bring into the world and the little girl stared right back, her well-shaped mouth breaking into a tentative, friendly smile. The child had smooth dark hair and her eyes were brown, although of a lighter shade than her mother's; it was almost, thought the herbalist, as if the child had gold light in her eyes.

And those eyes quite definitely reminded Tiphaine of those of somebody else; somebody whom she knew quite well. In fact, the more she stared, the more she could see Josse in the child's face. As if Joanna read her thought, she came up to stand beside the herbalist; 'It's the smile,' she said softly and Meggie, obliging child that she was, instantly turned her shy smile into a beaming grin, laughing down at her mother and Tiphaine. Then, after a tense moment, Joanna whispered, 'Does he know?'

Tiphaine shook her head.

'Does anybody at Hawkenlye know?'

'The Abbess Helewise guesses, although I have not confirmed that she guesses aright.'

'I see.'

Tiphaine could feel Joanna's faint distress; it felt as if someone were rubbing the fine hairs on her skin in the wrong direction. It occurred to the herbalist that if Joanna could provoke such a reaction when surely no more than mildly disturbed, what might she do when really angry?

I think, Tiphaine decided, that I prefer not to dwell on that.

Lora was standing in the doorway and now she called to Tiphaine to attract her attention. 'You have something you wish to tell Joanna here, do you not?' she said.

'Er . . .' Suddenly it did not seem such a good idea.

'Go on,' Lora said relentlessly.

Joanna was looking enquiringly at Tiphaine. 'What is it?' she demanded. The anxiety in her eyes suggested she thought it might be to do with Josse and it was Tiphaine's instant need to reassure her that Josse was quite safe that gave her the courage to speak.

'There is a bad sickness at Hawkenlye,' she began, and swiftly went on to tell Joanna what she had yesterday told Lora; unlike Lora, however, it seemed that Joanna had had no idea that the foreign pestilence had struck.

'But the nuns are healers, are they not?' she said when Tiphaine paused for breath. 'You too, Tiphaine, have fine skills that will help the sick. Why have you come to me?'

This was the tricky bit; Tiphaine summoned her courage and told Joanna about the Eye of Jerusalem, how it was said to operate and the identity of its rightful owner.

Finally her words stumbled to an end, to be followed by a very long silence. Then Joanna said, 'This prediction that you speak of says that a female of Josse's blood will be the stone's most powerful master and you have come here asking that I present myself at the Abbey with my daughter and put the jewel into her hands.' Joanna's eyes, hard as rock, fixed on Tiphaine. 'My daughter,' she said icily, 'is but sixteen months old.'

'Aye, I know,' Tiphaine said evenly, retaining her composure with an effort. Sensing Joanna's anger, she knew better than to try to explain herself.

'And what if my child falls ill herself with this pestilence that you would have her treat in others?' The sarcasm was bitter.

'I don't know about *treat*,' Tiphaine said, evading the main issue, 'I'd imagined it'd be more a question of Meggie's being the hand that held the Eye and dipped it in the water.'

'So you would not actually insist that she nurses the dying?' Joanna said, one eyebrow raised in an expression of contempt.

'Well, no.' Tiphaine forced herself to meet Joanna's eyes. 'Like you say, she's too little for that.'

'She's too little to have anything to do with magic stones and objects of power!' Joanna shouted.

But Lora said, 'That is not necessarily true, Joanna. You know her heritage; can you truly say that, once past babyhood, any age in such a child may be deemed too young?'

'I can! I do!' Joanna's distress was growing.

Lora went on pressing her. 'But is that not because you are still battling to accept what you have recently been told of that heritage, which naturally is also yours?' Her dictatorial tone softening, she said, 'I know what the Domina said to you as you were leaving Armorica, Joanna.'

Now Joanna looked . . . haunted, Tiphaine thought, watching the young woman with pity. 'Did you know?' Joanna whispered to Lora.

'Aye.'

'Did everyone know?'

'No, only the elders.'

'Why didn't they tell me before?' Joanna pleaded. 'It's hard, so hard, to find out *now*!'

Tiphaine began to understand.

'We felt it better for you not to be told until the time was right,' Lora said. 'Until it was plain that you were ready for this other life that you have chosen.'

'But I did not begin this life until it was too late!' There were tears in Joanna's eyes. 'She died too soon, and I never knew, never had the chance to feel her arms around me in the full knowledge of what she really was to me! And now she's gone and I can never tell her how much I loved her!'

Lora stepped forward and, perhaps with the desire to be some sort of a substitute, put her arms around Joanna's slim body. 'There, child,' she said gently, 'there.' One graceful hand smoothed Joanna's hair. 'Now you've been told before that she's not really gone, haven't you?'

Joanna raised her head from Lora's shoulder, a slight frown on her face. 'Yes. The Domina said hadn't I felt her presence, and I realised that I had. I still do; I hear her voice in my head and sometimes I feel that if I can just turn my head quickly enough, there she'll be.'

'Well, then.' Lora resumed her stroking. 'You had to wait till you were able to sense her, see. If you'd been told too soon your reaction might have been different. Back in your old life, it might have displeased you to know the truth.'

'No!' Joanna's protest was instant and quite definite. 'I always loved her, far, far more than the woman I knew as my mother.'

'Perhaps,' Lora murmured. 'Anyway, we're not here to discuss the rights and wrongs of all that. The important thing now is that you have the gifts bestowed on you through your blood, and these gifts have been passed on to your daughter here. Now we must add to them this precious jewel of Josse's – no, Joanna, don't recoil from the mention of it; don't you know better than to reject an object of power when it presents itself? – and we also should take into account what Meggie may have inherited from the other half of her ancestry; from her father.'

Joanna gave a short laugh. 'Don't go telling me Josse has magic power because I simply won't believe you.'

'Then you'd better think again,' Lora said tartly, 'and not be so swift to pass judgement.'

Joanna muttered an apology. Then, with a kind of affectionate humour still evident in her expression, she said, 'I did not detect power in him. Please explain to me, Lora, how it was that I missed it.'

'That's more like it.' Lora gave a curt nod. 'Well, happen you're right in a way, because he doesn't know his own forebears, or at least not the particular one who is relevant to our present concerns. His mother's family came from the Downland and, six generations back, one of them was a woman who tended the sacred fire up at the place they now call Caburn.'

'She was one of the elders?' Joanna asked.

'She was one of the Great Ones.'

Joanna slowly shook her head. 'That's the name they keep associating with my daughter,' she said. 'Meggie, they say, will be one of the Great Ones.' Her eyes pleading with Lora as if she hoped to be contradicted, she whispered, 'You said the very same thing yourself.'

'Aye, I remember.' Lora sighed. 'It's a heavy burden for a child not much over a year but, Joanna, she's a very special child and you couldn't stop this thing that has come to her even if you wanted to; she *will be* the person she is destined to be. She'll develop the strength to deal with it, don't you worry.' Releasing Joanna from her embrace, Lora turned to Meggie, who had been watching the proceedings with interested eyes. 'Well now, child of the ancient line, bearer of the pure blood-line of the people, what do you reckon, eh?' She took one of Meggie's small hands and the child smiled at her.

Lora studied the little face for a while. Then she said, 'The child is like her father, as we can all see. But she's also like you, Joanna, and even more like her grandmother.' Then, turning to Tiphaine, finally Lora confirmed it: 'Do you see it?' she asked, smiling. 'Can you see what I see in Meggie's sweet face?'

'I only met her but once,' Tiphaine said, 'and that was a very long time ago, in my life before I entered the Abbey. But, aye, I see it too.'

Joanna had moved away and was standing staring out through the half-open door into the clearing beyond. Tiphaine and Lora exchanged a glance; it was clear to both of them that Joanna was thinking about what they had asked her to do, for her very stance emanated tension and worry.

Neither of the older women spoke. Meggie returned to the plaything that had been entertaining her before the visitors arrived – it was a small sack stuffed with sheep's wool and cleverly fashioned into the shape of a little doll, with black eyes and a smiling red mouth – and there came the faint sounds of her quietly chatting in nonsense language to herself.

They waited.

After what seemed a very long time, Joanna turned and said, 'I will not do it.'

Tiphaine felt herself sag with disappointment.

Lora said evenly, 'Will you tell us why not?'

'Yes. For one thing, there is no guarantee that this Eye of Jerusalem is the power object they claim it to be. What, then, if

I take Meggie to Hawkenlye only to have her fall sick with a fatal illness which I cannot cure? I will not take the risk of losing my child!' The last words were spoken in a very quiet whisper but their force still reached the child sitting on the platform, who gave a little whimper.

'What if we brought the Eye and the water out to the forest?' Tiphaine suggested. 'Would you agree to let the child wield the stone far away from any danger of infection?'

'I—' Joanna frowned, as if she had to think hard to find an acceptable way of rejecting this most reasonable request. Then, apparently deciding that nothing but the truth would do before Lora, who would know if she lied, she said, 'It's Josse. You, Tiphaine, have just told me that he does not know about Meggie. I have made my life without him; he, presumably, manages quite well without me.' She glanced up at her beautiful child and her expression softened. 'And he cannot miss that little person if he is not aware of her existence. No,' she said, more firmly. 'I will not undo all that I have achieved over the past two years. I am sorry, but that is my final answer.'

Tiphaine was about to plead, to describe the suffering of the sick and see if that would melt Joanna's resolve, but Lora gave her a dig in the ribs and she shut her mouth.

Lora said calmly, 'Very well, Joanna. Thank you for agreeing to speak to us; we shall leave you to your solitude now.'

'I—' Whatever Joanna was about to say, she changed her mind. 'Farewell, Lora, Tiphaine.'

As the two older women passed her by and left the hut, she gave them both a curt bow and then closed the door behind them.

'Could we not have tried to persuade her?' Tiphaine said crossly as they hurried away along the winding forest tracks. 'People are dying, Lora, and she could help!'

'It is Joanna's decision,' Lora said firmly, 'and that's an end to it.'

Watching her face, Tiphaine wondered why, when she seemed to be resigned to failure, Lora should look quite cheerful about it . . .

Back at Hawkenlye that evening, Josse and Augustus were the first to return. Josse went straight to the Abbess to report that they did not find Sabin de Retz at Robertsbridge but that he and Gus both had the distinct impression that the monk to whom they spoke was eager to see the back of them.

'The Cistercians are renowned for their love of solitude,' the Abbess remarked. 'Could this monk's demeanour have been simply the desire of a man who has become accustomed to his own company to be free of outsiders?'

'Perhaps,' Josse agreed. 'Only Gussie pointed out that Stephen – that was the monk's name – excusing himself by saying he had to get back to work was odd since the White Monks have lay brothers for the hard labour.'

'There is work in a monastery apart from tilling the fields and digging,' the Abbess said, indicating her heavily loaded table. 'Possibly this Stephen was behind in his accounts?'

Josse sighed heavily; he was far too tired to rack his brains to find the words to explain the subtle sense that both he and Gus had felt that Stephen was being economical with the truth. 'No doubt you are right, my lady,' he said, rather more tetchily than he had intended; the Abbess, he noticed, gave a faint smile. 'But what of matters here?' he asked, hastening to change the subject. 'How fare the infirmarer's patients in the Vale?'

Now it was the Abbess who sighed. Putting her hands up to rub at her eyes, she said, 'More sick people arrived this morning; five very ill and three with fever but sufficiently well to help their relatives. Two are dying; for another two there is little hope. And a man came stumbling into the Vale not long ago; he is a thatcher and lives in a hamlet under the eaves of the forest some five miles from here. He is sick but ignores his own symptoms out of anxiety for his twelve-year old son; that boy too, according to Sister Euphemia, will be lucky to see the morning.'

'I see.' Josse's faint optimism that there would be no more new cases said a brief farewell and melted away. 'How is Sister Judith?'

'She is holding on.'

Josse hesitated. 'Brother Firmin?'

The Abbess closed her eyes, as if in a brief prayer. 'He, too, is still with us.'

Observing her face, Josse said gently, 'There is still hope, my lady.'

'Hope for what?' she snapped back. 'Nearly a dozen dead and the accommodation in the Vale filled to overflowing with feverish, pain-racked, vomiting people who void their bowels as fast as the nursing nuns and monks can pour the liquid into them! It is a nightmare down there, Sir Josse; a vision of hell, complete with sounds, stenches and suffering that must be making the devil dance with glee!'

She paused, panting, and he waited. Then, calming herself, she said more quietly, 'I am sorry. You know these things as well as I do and I should not have shouted at you.'

'Shout away, my lady, if it helps,' he said kindly.

She was looking at him with an odd expression in her eyes, and he remembered how strange she had seemed before he had left to go to Robertsbridge. Puzzled, he was about to ask her outright what was the matter when she spoke; her words serving only to increase his mystification, she said, 'Oh, Sir Josse, do not be generous with me; I do not deserve it.'

'My lady, I—'

But she was not going to allow him to speak. Standing up, she said, 'I must seek out Sister Tiphaine, for there is a matter I wish to discuss with her. Sir Josse, I will not keep you any longer from your well-earned rest; off you go to the Vale where, I am quite sure, Brother Saul will be able to find you something hot to eat.'

Reckoning that he had rarely received such a clear dismissal, Josse opened the door for her and stood back to allow her to precede him out into the cloister. He watched her stride away in the direction of the herbalist's hut, then spun round and hurried away to the rear gate of the Abbey and the path down to the Vale.

I would do anything in my power to help you, you stubborn woman, he thought angrily. But if you prefer to keep me shut out, then you render me helpless and I am happy to leave you to it.

But as his anger faded he knew that *happy* was completely the wrong word.

Helewise had no idea whether in fact Sister Tiphaine had yet returned from the forest; she had used a visit to the herbalist as an excuse to see Josse on his way. As the hours had passed she had been feeling increasingly guilty about the events she had set in motion and having him standing right in front of her being *kind* to her had been more than she could bear.

She hastened past the Great West Door of the Abbey church, hurried on by the sinister, windowless walls of the leper house and turned right along the far perimeter of the Abbey, pacing along the path to the herbalist's garden and hut.

There was a light showing under the hut's closed door; it looked as if Sister Tiphaine were back. Opening the door, Helewise stepped into the warm, scented air of the little room and immediately Sister Tiphaine bent in a low reverence.

'My lady Abbess, I would have come to find you straight away following my return,' she said after the customary exchange of greetings, 'but I saw Sir Josse approaching your room and deemed it best not to see you when he was in your presence.'

'Quite right, Sister.' Trying to keep the eagerness out of her voice, she said, 'Now, what news?'

Sister Tiphaine's very expression seemed to speak of her failure; straight away she said, 'It's no good, I'm afraid, my lady; she won't agree to it.'

Oh, dear God, no!

But it was not the role of abbesses to appear before their nuns distraught and hopeless; rallying, Helewise said, 'I see. Now, Sister, will you please tell me the full story?'

'She's back,' Tiphaine said shortly. 'Joanna, I mean. She's been away learning skills from the Great Ones of her people and now she's formidable.'

A shiver went down Helewise's back. 'You mean – is she dangerous?'

Sister Tiphaine gave a brief snort that could have been laughter. 'I'm sure she could be, my lady, but that was not what I meant. She's been in training as a healer.'

'A healer.' Helewise stored that away for future thought. 'And there is a child, isn't there?'

Tiphaine gave her a thoughtful look. 'You already knew that, my lady, did you not?'

Yes, was the truthful answer. But Helewise said somewhat stiffly, 'It was but idle speculation.'

Tiphaine looked as if she was not fooled for a moment. But there was nothing but the usual respect in her tone when she spoke. 'The child is a little girl, some sixteen months old. She is dark haired and has eyes that dance with light. She seems to have a sweet disposition and she is very pretty.'

'She is the child of Sir Josse?' Helewise just had to have it confirmed.

'Aye, my lady.' *But you knew that too* hung unspoken in the air.

'She is— Does she resemble her father?'

'Oh, aye. There would be no doubt in the mind of anyone who had seen both father and child that Meggie is his.'

'Meggie,' Helewise repeated softly. 'A pretty name for a pretty child.'

'Aye, my lady.' The herbalist stood silent, eyes cast down, waiting for her Abbess to speak.

Which, eventually, she did. 'Was any reason given for Joanna's refusal to bring Meggie here to Hawkenlye?'

'She fears the sickness, not for herself but for the little one. We suggested that she need bring the child no nearer than the forest fringe, where we could take water and the Eye to her, but Joanna's real reason for staying well away from Hawkenlye is because of him.'

We, Helewise noted. Tiphaine had not been alone when she approached Joanna, then. Letting that pass, she said, 'Because of Sir Josse, you mean.' Yes, she could well understand why Joanna would not wish to open old wounds, either her own or Josse's, and a part of her was dancing with delight at the young woman's forbearance.

But Joanna keeping Meggie away would not help the Hawkenlye sick, she told herself firmly. Then, swallowing her pride because she was fairly sure what the answer would be, she asked tentatively, 'Would it make any difference if I spoke to Joanna?'

'None whatsoever, my lady,' Sister Tiphaine said promptly. 'I am sorry to speak so bluntly.'

'It's all right, Sister; I asked the question and I wanted an honest answer.'

There was a short silence and then Sister Tiphaine said, 'Are there many sick now?'

And there was nothing for Helewise to say but, 'Oh, yes, Sister, I'm afraid there are.'

15

That night, sleep was in short supply for many people. The very sick at Hawkenlye were not so much asleep as in varying states of unconsciousness and coma; some, indeed, stood shadow-like at the gates of death and some passed through. Those who tended them – and of these there was a steadily increasing number – grabbed short cat naps when they could.

The Abbess Helewise knew that there was small chance of her being able to relax sufficiently to fall asleep and so she worked until after midnight, battling her fear into submission by a relentless attack on the all but illegible accounts submitted by the incompetent whose duty it was to keep the Abbey informed of affairs on its lands over to the north of the Weald. The diversionary tactic was only partly successful; she managed to complete the task but, having done so, found that her anxieties returned all the more forcefully for having been briefly banished from her mind.

In the Vale, Josse tried and failed to block his ears from the sound of the sick and the dying. Eventually giving it up as a bad job, he got up from his blanket and his thin straw mattress, made his way out of the shelter and found Brother Saul, busy carrying an endless supply of holy water from the spring in the shrine to the waiting hands of a weary Sister Caliste. She took the full vessels inside the makeshift infirmary for the hard-working nursing nuns and monks – so many of them there now selflessly caring for the sick! – to give to those patients still able to drink. With no word but just a brief understanding smile, Saul indicated a pile of empty vessels and Josse fell into step beside him; for what was left of the night, the two carried water side by side.

In the forest, Joanna lay fighting with her conscience. She had already used her minor weapons: what has the world ever done for me that now I should risk the person I love most to help its people? Why, in particular, should I be made to feel obliged to an Abbey full of nuns and monks when the worst of my sufferings were brought about by the dirty mind of a priest working on and encouraging the sexual perversions of my elderly and long-dead husband? Strange, she thought in a brief moment of total honesty, how those arguments did not seem to carry the weight they once had . . .

She had moved swiftly on to more persuasive arguments. Oh, it was all very well for Lora and Tiphaine to say that Meggie need go nowhere near the Abbey and that there would be no danger of her becoming sick, but how did they know? How could they possibly be sure, when diseases such as this one that they described seemed to have a life and a volition all of their own? And, even given that Meggie's safety was totally, unquestionably assured, there was still Josse.

He would not hold back because of the pain of seeing *you* again, she thought, with as much conviction as if he himself were standing before her and in her presence had been asked and answered. He would reason that his pain and yours ought to be seen in their proper place, and that place was well behind the possibility that some joint action of his and hers might ease the agony – even perhaps save the lives – of many people who were otherwise doomed to a particularly horrible death.

'I cannot do it!' she wailed softly to herself. 'I have left the world of the Outlanders behind me. This is my place now, mine and Meggie's, and here is where I must remain.'

When the stars began to fade ahead of the dawn, at last she slept. But it was to dream that the Bear Man was with her, holding her in strong arms as she wept, and somehow – for he did not use spoken words – imparting the message that there was a purpose to everything and that included the claw that he had given her and the healing powers that she now possessed.

It was only a dream. On waking, she told herself that over and over again; he was far away, she knew he was, and so it was strange that, in the mud on the bank of the stream that ran close by her hut, she should find the marks of huge, claw-tipped paws.

In the dense forest around the isolated settlement at Roberts-bridge, poachers crept beneath the trees searching the monks' land for anything edible. One of them was a trembling lad not much more than ten out on his first hunt and forced into the excursion because his father was sick, his brother was in hiding from the law and his mother and three little siblings were slowly starving. He was spooked into an evasive leap and a suppressed scream by a movement in the shadows; seconds later a large, pregnant sow boar broke cover and ran off into the night, twigs and low branches snapping with loud cracks marking her progress. The lad received a cuff round the ear for his carelessness and went home empty handed.

The sow's panicky rush through the undergrowth was, however, heard by someone other than the poachers; she took a track that went close by the monks' settlement and even closer to the rough guest accommodation, where yet another person lay sleepless. For him, however, it was a fairly routine state, for he was very old and did not need much sleep.

The noise of the boar made hope of even an hour or two's light slumber towards dawn quite out of the question, for the old man misunderstood the innocent sounds of the boar's headlong flight and ascribed them to a very different cause. He lay in a cold sweat of terror for some time after the boar had gone, waiting almost without breathing for the creak of the door, the knife at his throat or – terror of terrors – the first hint of smoke like that which had come that last dreadful time.

When dawn came and he was still miraculously alive, he roused his companion and announced that they were leaving immediately. In answer to the puzzled questions – why? What is the rush? Where should we go? – he simply said, 'He's found us.'

And then there were no more questions; only a fast-growing fear that soon overtook his own. The pair were packed up ready to go within moments and as soon as Stephen could be persuaded to provide an escort – which, given Stephen's urgent wish to be rid of his guests, for which he would subsequently do grave penance, took even less time – they were on their way and riding off along the road that led north-westwards.

He was losing control.

The sensation was unfamiliar for one such as he, who was meticulous both in the planning and the execution of a mission. He had not experienced failure in all the years he had been operating and it was this reputation for total reliability which, he believed, had caught the eye of the powerful man who had commanded the present task.

But things were going wrong.

For the first time in his professional life, he was indecisive and he was quietly, smoulderingly angry, for the indecision came about purely because his master kept changing his mind. Well, to be fair, he had changed it once: he had outlined the mission – and how well the man recalled that moment when his employer had announced the target! – and the man had considered the proposal, agreed that he would do it and, after the usual careful planning stage, had set off to accomplish it. Everything had gone smoothly; he had located his quarry, finalised the details of how the deed would be done and, even more important, how he would ensure a clean escape afterwards, and he had been poised to strike.

At the very last moment, the messenger had arrived to tell him to withdraw: the employer was in receipt of new intelligence and no longer wanted the mission to be carried out.

And then, purely because the man's softly spoken fury had for a moment got the better of him, everything had started to go wrong. He always worked alone and the very presence of the messenger had disturbed him, making him act out of character. That must have been it, he told himself yet again, for what else could explain his breaking of his self-imposed rule of total silence until an operation was over? But the messenger had been there right in front of him, white-faced with the pain resulting from his own stupid clumsiness, cowering because he could plainly see the effect that the new instructions he had just relayed had had and, knowing the man's profession and reputation, understandably terrified. The man had used the trembling messenger as a whipping boy and, for one self-indulgent moment, said, quietly but viciously, exactly what he thought about employers who changed their minds at the very last second.

It should have been all right and he ought to have got away with it. He and the messenger were in an out-of-the-way place where surely it was highly unlikely for them to have been overheard. But overheard they were: as the man had finished his brief but articulate rant, an emotion-charged silence ensued and into this silence came a small sound.

Anyone lacking the man's long experience of survival against the odds and his talent for self-preservation might have dismissed the little noise as rats in the drains or mice in the stone walls. But the man's acutely developed sense of hearing picked up the sound, checked it against like sounds stored in his memory and located the source. It was a very particular noise and the man knew exactly who had made it: nobody else coughed quite like that.

And that moment had led to this endless pursuit that had resulted in two deaths and would probably soon lead to two more.

Sitting on his horse in the forest clearing above the Hastings to London road and watching the five-strong party emerge from the track and set out northwards, the man wondered yet again why the pair of them had suddenly decided to run. They knew he was after them, he was quite sure of that, and he had begun to think that, if they persisted in demanding sanctuary at Robertsbridge, he was never going to get at them; this morning's move was a surprise. He had almost missed the departure. They must have been up at dawn to have been on the road so early and it was pure luck that the man's sleep had been restless that night, so that he was at his observation post some time sooner than he had been for the past few days.

Again he went through the possible reasons for the pair's sudden move. This time he started further back, with the intention of trying to discover if there were some salient fact that he had left out of his considerations.

He had followed the pair to Troyes, where they had made the acquaintance of the apprentice lad. The man was quite sure they'd told him what had happened, what the old man had overheard; why else would the lad suddenly start looking over his shoulder, acting like a bodyguard, hardly letting the pair out of his sight and going about with his hand on his sword? The lad had been trying to impress the girl; of that the man was quite sure. Not that she'd have been very impressed if the man had chosen to make his attack in the open, for he would have made short work of the apprentice *and* his sword and dispatched him with the ruthless speed of a heavy boot crushing a cockroach.

But it was not the man's way to attack in the open; he had

got rid of the old man and the girl by firing their lodging house and then, still under cover of night, he had gone after the apprentice. He ought to have cornered him and seen to him that same night but the lad must have found a very good hiding place; the man had not been able to find him.

If he had only succeeded in finishing the business and curtailing the dangerous secret there and then in Troyes! It would have been a simple matter to go on to Paris, claim his payment and proceed on his way, putting the whole affair out of his mind. But he had been foiled again, this time by sheer bad luck: the old man ate a bad oyster at supper and, when the lodging house had gone up in flames, he had been alternately kneeling before and squatting over the privy in the yard voiding his system and the girl had been tending him.

The man was not to discover this until much later.

Although several other people were killed in the blaze, both the old boy and the girl had escaped unharmed. But, thinking them dead, he had hastened to pick up the apprentice's trail and had followed him up to Boulogne. Somewhere along the road the lad must have become aware that he was being followed, for he had displayed all the symptoms of increasing fear. So close had the man been upon his trail that the man was quite sure the apprentice had not revealed his dangerous knowledge to anybody; there simply had been no occasion for such a sharing of confidences. In Boulogne the lad had met up with a merchant and on board the ship that they took for England, on to which the man had stealthily crept after them, the two had soon put their heads together. The man knew exactly what had been the main topic of conversation for, concealed in the dark shadows, he heard the lad speak. Eager to impress his wealthier and more sophisticated companion, the apprentice had carefully looked around him to make sure that none of the crew could overhear and then spilled out the full tale.

The man followed the merchant and the apprentice ashore in England and as soon as he could he killed them. The merchant he smothered with his own pillow – an easy death, that one, for the merchant had been weak with fever – and then he had set out to find the apprentice. The lad almost got away for, just as the man was about to make his move, the apprentice set off on his master's horse and made his slow way to Hawkenlye Abbey. But there again the man's luck was in, for the lad reached the Abbey on a very cold day just as the light was fading. Nobody had been about and it had been a simple matter to strike down the lad and roll his body into the pond.

That should have been that. The four people who knew what the man's sensitive mission had been were dead and the secret had died with them.

Then, as the man had set off back to the coast to pick up a boat back to France, he had seen what at first sight he had thought must be a couple of ghosts. In deep countryside outside Hastings, following his usual practice when out in the wild of drawing off the road and concealing himself when he heard riders approaching, he had watched with increasing disbelief as the old man and the girl rode up from the port towards him. There was no time then to ask himself what they were doing in England or, indeed, how it came to be that they were still alive. In that urgent moment he calculated swiftly and, deciding that it would be best to slay them there and then, he had been about to pounce.

Then an ox cart had come crawling along the road from Hastings, in the direction from which the old man and the girl had come, accompanied by three horsemen and a troupe of peasants. The old man and the girl had paused to rest at the top of a rise and the group had caught up with them. With a quiet curse, the man had withdrawn deeper under the trees; unless he was prepared to kill the lot of them, attacking the old man and the girl here was just going to create yet more problems.

He followed them and watched from a safe distance as they rode for a few miles with the ox cart party and then turned off at the track for the abbey at Robertsbridge, where they were given lodgings. A few days later he trailed the girl as, escorted by a couple of burly monks, she rode to Newenden to ask after the apprentice, and he was sure she must also have made a similar excursion to Hawkenlye; there was a day where he had not been able to find her and he guessed that was where she had gone. She would probably know by now that the apprentice lad was dead, unless his body were still under the ice in the dark heart of the pond.

There had never been an opportunity to attack her and, indeed, killing her would only have achieved half the task, for there remained the old man, and *he* had the good sense not to leave the settlement at Robertsbridge.

And there matters had stood, the girl making occasional forays on to the tracks and the roads, always accompanied and therefore unassailable, and the old man all but camping out under Robertsbridge's altar.

Until now . . .

He waited until the group of riders were almost out of sight – a monk led the way, followed by the old man and the girl, with a pair of monks bringing up the rear – and then he nudged a knee into his horse's side and, moving with his usual stealth, set out after them.

'Are those structures also part of Hawkenlye Abbey?'

Sabin de Retz's accented words managed to sound authoritative and faintly dismissive, as if the sight of the Abbey buildings down in the Vale was somehow a disappointment.

It was not the case; she was driven by her need to sound calm and confident, which was not easy when her heart was thumping with fear. This place, she had been thinking as the journey proceeded relentlessly to its destination, this place where we're going, which I saw but briefly before and where I'm bringing Grandfather, is the place where poor Nicol was struck down. Not only that, but it's now foul with disease and we approach it at our peril.

The monk in the lead – his name was Brother Basil and he was broad in the shoulders and his heavy-featured face showed the scars of some violent past left behind when he entered Robertsbridge – turned at her words. 'Aye, lady,' he acknowledged. 'The main foundation's up there on the rise. Down in the valley' – he indicated with a jerk of his head – 'is where they discovered the spring with the precious healing water.'

Sabin stared down into the Vale. Two distant black-clad figures were carrying a long, slim shape wrapped in a sacking shroud into what had to be an improvised burial ground, where there were a number of obviously recent graves, scars of brown earth on the frosty ground; she bit back the remark that the holy waters didn't seem to be making much headway against the pestilence.

'Why have we stopped?' Her grandfather's voice was quer-ulous, tinged with the very edge of complaint; knowing him as she did, for she had lived with him all her life and he had been training her as his assistant for the last fifteen years or more, she realised that the moment was ripe for some encourage-ment.

'We are discussing what is the best option now that we are here, Grandfather,' she improvised, casting a quick glance at Brother Basil in apology for the small lie.

'Didn't you say we must search out that knight who came asking for us down at Robertsbridge?' Benoît de Retz said tetchily. 'Isn't that why we've come all this way on a bitter morning? Surely the *best option*' – he mocked her words – 'is to ride right up to the Abbey gates and demand to see him!'

Sabin hesitated. Her grandfather knew about the sickness at

Hawkenlye – it had been he who had confirmed it to her, having overheard the knight Sir Josse tell Stephen – but he could not see what she was now looking at, and the sight of the new graves and the body being carried to the graveyard brought the severity of the danger home to her far more forcefully than mere words had done. Benoît would undoubtedly have refused to leave Robertsbridge, she reflected, had he somehow had a preview of the scene now before them. It had crossed Sabin's mind that she could leave him there in relative safety while she went alone up to Hawkenlye to search for Sir Josse, but every instinct had argued against it. Her grandfather had cared for her diligently, if not especially tenderly, ever since her parents had died when she was three. Now that he was old, feeble and all but blind, it was her turn to look after him. It had been different when she had made the earlier journeys to Newenden and to Hawkenlye alone, for then he had been too sick to travel and she had had no alternative. Now that he was once more well, leaving him for what might be quite a long time in the care of strangers was just not a choice.

Making up her mind, she said bluntly, 'There is very much sickness at Hawkenlye. The situation is worse than we thought. We can see the monks burying a body even as we sit here.'

Benoît gasped, crossed himself and muttered a hasty prayer. 'We cannot risk going any nearer! To do so would be folly!'

We could help. Sabin bit back the exclamation. You, Grandfather, she thought, are renowned far and wide for your skills, not a few of which you have passed on to me. But: 'Very well,' she said instead. With a jerk of her head to Brother Basil, she asked, 'Where else might we put up hereabouts? Is there a town nearby?'

'Aye. Just down the hill there.' He pointed back along the

track to where another road led off down the slope of the hillside. 'Tonbridge is but a short ride and there's an inn.'

He appeared to know the area quite well so she ventured another question. She was thinking that, if this Sir Josse d'Acquin had indeed returned to Hawkenlye Abbey and thus rendered himself out of bounds, as it were, to anybody who had not already risked an encounter with the sickness, then she would need to find someone else to talk to about the death of Nicol. 'Is there a—' She was not sure what the right word would be. 'Will I be able to find a man of law down in this town?'

'A sheriff?' Brother Basil shrugged. 'Probably. There's a big castle there and not a few wealthy folks, and where there's money there's usually rules to protect it and that means a man of law.' He risked a very small smile as he used the words that she had done.

'Then, please, Brother Basil, if you will,' she said courteously, 'increase our indebtedness to you by escorting us on to Tonbridge.'

Brother Basil looked at her for a moment, then, with a nod to the two monks sitting shivering on their mules to the rear of Benoît, he nodded and kicked his sandalled feet into his horse's sides.

And, quite a short time afterwards, the three monks had left their two charges safely ensconced in the inn at Tonbridge and were on their way back to Robertsbridge. Meanwhile Sabin, bemused and trying hard to understand everything that was said to her, had been met by an effusive Goody Anne delighted to have even two customers in these terrible times. Anne had led Sabin and Benoît along to her best guest chamber, sent for hot water and hot drinks, told them to make themselves comfortable and to come along to warm themselves by the fire as soon as they were ready, where she would cook them up something to take the chill out of their bones.

'Where are we?' came Benoît's plaintive voice. 'Is that woman a nun?'

'No, Grandfather,' Sabin said, lapsing with relief into her own language. 'I told you, we couldn't go to the Abbey at Hawkenlye because there's sickness there. We're in a town nearby called—' No; she had forgotten. 'Well, never mind what it's called. But it's big enough to have a castle and a sheriff, so as soon as we've eaten whatever that kind woman is going to prepare for us, I'll say I want to speak to the sheriff and see if he can tell us anything about Nicol's death.'

'He didn't die of the sickness,' Benoît said mournfully. 'That knight on the big horse said he'd been murdered. I heard him! Someone struck Nicol over the head and rolled him into a pond.'

'I know, Grandfather,' Sabin said gently, wishing in passing that there was some way to stop his unfortunate habit of creeping about and listening to conversations that were none of his business. But then, she could understand well enough why he did it. A man in his profession – he had once been at the very top of it, one might say – became accustomed to being important. How wretched it must be, she thought, to grow old, to develop shakes in those hands that were once so precise, to lose the keen eyesight that was so vital to one whose work involved such delicacy and accuracy. It is simply, she concluded with a sigh, that he does not wish to be shunted aside and ignored; his sly habit of hiding himself away and picking up fragments of other people's private conversations is his way of keeping himself at the hub of what goes on around him. And those keen ears of his – she had noticed that Benoît's hearing seemed to have improved as his eyesight failed – ensure that he picks up more than is good for him.

Far, far more . . .

She studied him. He still looked half perished with cold; the tip of his nose had a large dewdrop about to fall from it and automatically she reached for a linen handkerchief, handing it to him. The handkerchief was spotlessly clean, as indeed was almost all of their personal linen; the enforced idleness at Robertsbridge had at least given her the opportunity to catch up with her domestic duties.

In addition to appearing to be cold, Benoît also looked miserable, confused, weary and hungry; his brow was creased in a pathetic frown and his lean cheeks seemed to be caving in on themselves. Well, hunger at least we can do something about, she thought, rousing herself to a smile. Taking hold of his thin arm, she said brightly, 'Come on, dear Grandfather. That nice woman promised to prepare a meal for us – remember? – so let's hurry off and see if English cooking is really as terrible as they claim.'

Her show of optimism must have convinced him. As they made their slow and careful way along to the main room – Benoît was confident enough on home ground, where he knew every room, hallway, corridor and little hidden passage, but everywhere else he trod with the nervous care of a man walking on glass – he was already cheering up. 'Maybe,' he said hopefully, 'she'll cook beef. They say the English are good at beef.'

Agreeing that it might be a possibility, Sabin led him into the tavern's tap room, sat him down by the huge fire and, her own stomach growling in anticipation, sought out Goody Anne to ask her to bring their supper.

He was tired, hungry and cold.

He had followed them to Hawkenlye, waited in hiding as they had stopped for some sort of discussion, then had to back hurriedly deeper into the undergrowth on the skirts of the Great Forest as suddenly they had turned and ridden back towards him. He had thought for a puzzled moment that they were going to ride off back to Robertsbridge, but then they had turned off the road on to another that went away downhill in a roughly north-north-westerly direction. He had known the direction because the wind was coming from the north and for an uncomfortable time that seemed to go on for ever they had all been riding straight into it. The three monks had left the woman and the old man at an inn and then ridden away.

The man had waited for a while to see if either of his quarry might emerge again, but they did not. The light was fading fast and he had still to find somewhere to spend the hours of cold darkness; there was no point in watching the inn any longer that night, he decided, and soon he had quietly slipped out of his hiding place and set off out of town.

He had to get rid of them, he told himself. They still carried the secret and he could not allow them to live. But is there in truth any point in killing them? he wondered dismally. They have been with the monks at Robertsbridge, now they are presumably settling down for a convivial evening in a tap room full of people – he was not to know that Sabin and Benoît were Goody Anne's only guests that night – and so how many more people are now privy to what should never have been over-heard?

Where, he wondered, depression seeping insidiously through him like an ague, where will it all end?

No! It was no use thinking like that. It will end, he told himself firmly, when the old man and the young woman are safely dead and no longer a threat. Then he could leave this damp, foggy, cold and unwelcoming island, head back across the Channel, find his master in Paris, receive his fee and lose himself somewhere in the vast heart of France.

But he won't pay up, he thought lugubriously. He'll wriggle out of it and I'll be left with nothing to show for all of this effort but a few more deaths on my conscience.

He could find no consolation to help him out of his misery. Riding on down the desolate and overgrown track that he had found and that seemed to lead to marshes, he looked around half-heartedly for some sort of shelter. He came to a wild bramble hedge and, beyond it, the slowly decaying shape of what had once been a dwelling. Thinking that even that was better than nothing, the man dismounted, kicked open the door, eyed the dank and dark interior and then, with a nod, went out again to see to his horse and set about finding some firewood.

Later, when he had eaten from his meagre and fast-dwindling supplies of dried meat strips and the hard heel of a loaf, he tried to get comfortable in his thick cloak and his blanket. He slept – he did not know for how long – and then woke to find that the fire had died down and he was shivering violently. He stoked the fire, wrapped himself up again and went back to sleep, to dream that he was back at the Troyes lodging house trying to dash into the raging fire because he had left his pack behind the door . . . Waking, he found he was sweating, his skin hot, burning.

He rolled over on to his back, pushing back the blanket and feeling the relief of the cold night air on his face and his neck.

He realised that his head was aching.

16

At Hawkenlye, it was becoming increasingly difficult for even the most optimistic souls to believe that the outbreak was under control. Twenty-three people lay sick and, in some cases, dying in the infirmary in the Vale. Sister Beata had been joined in death by a young monk called Roger and a little novice nun whom nobody knew very well because she always kept her head down and never spoke unless she really had to. Sister Judith was still very ill. Brother Firmin, who had serenely given himself up to death, appeared to be a little better.

Sister Euphemia, despite the best efforts of her senior nurses, continued to bear on her broad shoulders the full responsibility for the sick. This was due neither to vanity nor an overwhelming sense of her own importance; it was simply that she appeared to have a God-given gift for healing and she refused to set it aside. It was as if, when face to face with someone who had decided that death was just around the corner, the infirmarer possessed a penetrating voice that, even if it did not always call the dying one back, at least gave the patient the opportunity to see if there was an alternative. Sister Euphemia possessed hands which, once laid upon the forehead of a feverish man or woman, instilled relief and a new confidence; more than one recovering patient was heard to observe that it was the big sister in charge who'd made them better; 'She told me I weren't so sick as I'd feared,' one woman said, 'and, once she'd got a few mugs o' that cold water into me, reckon I started to believe her.'

Sister Caliste could see that the infirmarer was on her knees with exhaustion. She pleaded with her superior to rest, to retire to her bed and catch up on her sleep, but Sister Euphemia insisted that the occasional short spell napping on a screened-off cot at the far end of the temporary infirmary was all that she needed. Such spells were, however, not very restful at all since, as Sister Caliste well knew, the infirmarer's acute ears picked up even the faintest sounds of distress, at which she would be up and out of the little recess the moment she had straightened her veil. And sounds of distress were all too common in that place of suffering.

Finally Sister Caliste, hating herself for the disloyalty, went to the Abbess. Entering in response to the Abbess's quiet 'Come in', and bowing low, she said, even before she had straightened up, 'My lady Abbess, I am sorry to disturb you but I must report that Sister Euphemia urgently needs a respite from her labours and—' She stopped herself before she could add 'and flatly refuses to take it.'

But the Abbess knew her infirmarer of old. As Sister Caliste straightened up, she found the calm grey eyes watching her. 'And I imagine,' the Abbess said, 'that, despite the repeated pleas of all her nursing nuns, she will not rest?'

'No,' agreed Sister Caliste.

The Abbess was silent for some moments. Then she said, 'Sister, assess for me, if you would, the strength of the nursing staff.'

Sister Caliste paused, ordering her thoughts. Then she said, 'Sister Tiphaine is the most respected, after Sister Euphemia. Although her skill is primarily in the preparation of herbal remedies, she has a wealth of experience and people believe in her. We've lost Sister Beata, of course, and she is sorely missed, and Sister Judith is still sick. Sister Clare has joined us, and Sister Anne, as well as Sister Emanuel, whose particular touch with the elderly is most useful. Then we have a number of other sisters, as well as two monks, who tend the patients when their other duties allow.'

The Abbess was still regarding her. 'You have left someone out,' she observed.

Sister Caliste frowned. 'Have I, my lady? I am sorry, I—' But then, blushing, she realised what the Abbess meant.

'Sister, I have in mind to organise three teams of nurses,' the Abbess said after a moment. 'If you are willing, I propose that you lead one, and that Sister Tiphaine and Sister Emanuel lead the others. Each of you will select a senior nursing nun as your second in command, and Sister Euphemia will be in overall control. I will ask for volunteers and, provided our nuns and monks respond as I hope and pray they will, we will aim at teams of perhaps as many as six. I am right in saying, am I not, that the nursing duties required amount more to sheer hard work than to any particular skill?'

'You are, my lady,' Sister Caliste agreed, 'for indeed it is in the main a matter of making the patients drink, of getting them to take their draughts of the remedies and of bathing them when they are feverish, washing the sheets and cleaning them up when they've – er – of cleaning them.'

'Quite so,' murmured the Abbess. 'What do you think, then, Sister? Would this plan persuade Sister Euphemia that it was permissible for her to take a day off and sleep?'

Sister Caliste smiled. 'I believe it might, my lady, were it you who proposed it.'

The Abbess answered her smile. Rising to her feet, she said, 'Then let us waste no more time.'

Sister Caliste waited outside the Vale infirmary while the Abbess went in and summoned Sister Euphemia. The two

senior nuns soon emerged and walked a short way off down
the path that led to the lake. The two veiled heads were close
together; the Abbess and the infirmarer were obviously deep in
conversation. Sister Caliste took the opportunity to slide down
onto a bench beside the infirmary door and close her eyes for a
precious few moments . . .

'There is no need to repeat yourself,' Helewise said, restraining her impatience with difficulty, 'I heard you the first three
times, Euphemia.' The infirmarer made to speak but Helewise
held up her hand. 'If you continue to work all day and all night,
soon you will be exhausted, nature will take over and you will
collapse, whether you wish it or not. Then where should the
rest of us be? We can work according to your instructions, my
very dear Sister, but if you have driven yourself to unconsciousness, where will you be when we need your advice?'

'I—' the infirmarer began.

'This is an order, Sister,' Helewise said gently. 'Out of my
great respect for you and bearing in mind our long friendship,
I am reluctant to remind you of our relative positions here.
But, nevertheless, in this case I am so doing.'

Sister Euphemia stared at her. The infirmarer's eyes were
ringed with dark circles, the eyelids swollen from fatigue.
'What must I do?' she asked.

Helewise's heart almost failed her. But, summoning her
resolve, she said firmly, 'You are to go to bed and you are to
stay there until tomorrow morning. In the dormitory, mind; I
don't mean that cot of yours at the end of the Vale infirmary.'

'But it's the middle of the morning!' Sister Euphemia
protested. 'Nuns don't go to bed in the middle of the day!'

'They do if they are worn out from hard work and their
Abbess demands it,' Helewise replied coolly. 'Now, go to the
refectory, tell Sister Basilia that I have ordered that you be
given whatever you wish to eat and drink, then go and sleep.'

All at once Sister Euphemia's resistance fell away. It was the word *sleep*, Helewise decided, watching her with compassion; hearing it, the infirmarer's eyes had all but closed and she swayed on her feet.

'Go on,' Helewise urged.

Sister Euphemia made one last effort. 'You are quite sure that these rotas of yours will work properly?'

'Oh, yes,' said Helewise serenely.

'Hm.' The infirmarer took a step up the path towards the Abbey. Then another.

'Off you go,' Helewise prompted.

And then Sister Euphemia obeyed. Without a backward glance, she strode away up the path and was soon attacking the slope that led up to the rear gate.

Helewise watched her. As she did so, she slowly rolled up her wide sleeves, baring her strong hands and forearms. Then she returned to the Vale infirmary, gently tugged at Sister Caliste's sleeve to wake her up and led the way inside.

'I shall call for volunteers later today,' she said quietly. 'In the meantime, find me an apron, please, Sister Caliste, and instruct me in what I must do.'

Sister Caliste's mouth fell open. '*You*, my lady?'

'Yes,' Helewise agreed. 'If you are agreeable, Sister, I would be honoured to be a member of your nursing team.'

She hid her amusement as, with a number of expressions flitting across her lovely face, Sister Caliste hurried to obey. Shortly afterwards, with her veil pinned back so that it did not fall forward as she bent over patients, a large white apron enveloping her from shoulders to shins and her rolled-up sleeves tied securely, Helewise followed Sister Caliste down the long room and was introduced to the full horrors of the foreign pestilence.

★

Word spread around the community well before Helewise made her announcement. By the time the request for volunteer nurses was read out, nuns, monks and lay brothers in all areas of the Abbey's work had asked themselves whether they had the courage to answer the summons. They all knew the risk: lurid descriptions of some of the more ghastly deaths were circulating and nobody was in any doubt that nurses could become sick just like everyone else did.

Helewise had asked that anyone willing to join the nursing team was to present her- or himself in front of the Abbey church after Sext. Emerging from the church after the community had left – she had stayed behind to send up a brief private prayer that her scheme would work – the sight that met her astonished eyes was all but unbelievable.

With the exception of those whose duties were all-consuming, everyone in the Hawkenlye community was there; the open space in front of the church was so crowded that they stood shoulder to shoulder. Right at the back, tall between Brother Saul and Brother Augustus, stood Josse.

Helewise made to speak but her voice broke. Clearing her throat, she tried again. 'Thank you,' she said. 'Bless you all. We—' But emotion was rising in her too powerfully for her to contain it; Sister Caliste, reading the situation, hurried to her side and whispered, 'My lady? May I help?'

Helewise smiled, briefly touching the younger nun's hand. 'Stand beside me, please,' she whispered. 'Summon Sister Tiphaine and Sister Emanuel, if you would.'

While the three nuns walked across to stand beside her, Helewise took the time to compose herself. Then, her voice pitched strongly to carry to the back of the crowd, she outlined the new arrangements. When she had finished – she would leave it to her three team leaders to arrange the details – she said, 'We will strive together, with God's help, to do all that we can to defeat this evil that has come to us. We shall be as one, an instrument for good in our heavenly father's hands. We will support each other and our own wishes will be put aside. We shall not let this thing get the better of us!' Sensing the mood change as, with the light of battle in their eyes, people took up the idea of a fight, she cried, 'We shall not be defeated!'

And from the ranks of nuns, monks and lay brothers before her, a great cheer went up.

The euphoria carried the community through the rest of the day. Those who were the first to take on new nursing duties were sorely in need of it for, as Helewise had discovered earlier, the brutal realities of caring for people suffering from this particular disease were not for the squeamish.

Sister Caliste's team were to work until Vespers, after which Sister Tiphaine's team would take over. Helewise spent the first part of her afternoon giving sips of the herbalist's febrifuge to some of the recovering patients. Then, quite sure that Sister Caliste was saving her from the more arduous duties, she asked to be put to something else. After a short debate with her conscience – she was quite sure her Abbess would go on asking until she got what she wanted – Sister Caliste nodded meekly and said, 'One of the dying requires a wash and a change of linen, my lady. If you would please follow me?'

Helewise had only herself to blame; summoning all her strength, she ordered herself not to let her revulsion show. The patient was a woman of about forty and could not have been in good health even before the sickness struck, for her emaciated body was covered in suppurating sores and there were the clear signs of lice infestation in the hair of her head and body. Her eyes were closed, the lids gummed with some sort of foul residue, and her toothless jaws seemed to have fallen in upon themselves. As if aware of her superior's struggle and wishing to help, Sister Caliste drew her attention by saying very softly,

'We do not know her name, my lady, for she was far gone when she was brought here. We have observed that those already weak succumb the fastest.'

Helewise was horrified in case the dying woman should hear. 'Sister, should we speak in this way before her?' she whispered back.

Sister Caliste paused in her washing of the woman's thighs and buttocks to stare up at the deadly white face. Reaching out to touch the sunken cheek with a gentle hand, she said, 'I do not think she can hear, my lady.'

That touch, and indeed her own reaction, somehow made the task easier for Helewise; it was as if the combination of the two things turned the dying woman from a filthy, stinking body back into a human being. Confidence surged through her; taking the wash cloth from Sister Caliste, she said, 'I will finish cleaning her and making her comfortable, Sister. When I have finished, I will come to find you to be given my next task.'

Sister Caliste nodded and left. Then Helewise, all disgust gone, went back to her patient. Keeping her voice low, she began to talk to her. 'There, I'll just finish washing you down there – oh, but that looks sore! Perhaps I can find something to soothe the poor skin – and then I can roll you back on to a clean sheet . . . Now that's better, isn't it? Nice and cool on your hot skin. We'll have a new piece of cloth and I'll sponge your face . . . and smooth out your hair. Then when we've finished, I'll tuck you up and leave you in peace.'

It was probably her imagination, Helewise told herself, but she almost thought that, just for an instant, the dying woman's mouth twitched into a smile.

Helewise's last task before her team was relieved was to tend the thatcher and his young son who had been brought in the previous day. Contrary to Sister Euphemia's prediction, the boy was still alive, although very sick and with a fever so high that he seemed to be on fire. The father had not moved from his son's bedside and Helewise was hoping to persuade him to have some rest.

She walked over to the cot where the boy lay and at her approach the father got to his feet.

'Please, sit down.' Helewise said. 'You too are sick, are you not?'

The man resumed his place at his son's head. 'I thought I was yesterday,' he admitted, 'but today the fever's gone and so has the headache.' He managed a weak grin. 'Reckon I must be tougher than I look.'

Helewise studied him. He was of average height, fair haired, dark eyed, and appeared to have a wiry strength that might indeed imply a resilient constitution. 'You are a thatcher, are you not?' she asked.

'Aye, Sister. Name's Catt. This is my son Pip.' He stroked the boy's sweat-darkened hair back from his pale face.

'How old is he?'

'Twelve.'

'And have you other children?'

'No, lady. His mother, she died when Pip's little sister was born, and the baby died too.' He sighed, then tried to smile. 'Pip and me, we're all each other has got, if you take my meaning.'

'I do.' She went to sit on the opposite side of the boy's narrow bed, studying his features. 'He has a look of you,' she said.

'D'you think so?' Catt seemed pleased. 'Me, I always see his mother in him, but I expect that's only natural. We see what we want to see, and I miss her.'

'Yes, I understand, and I'm sure you're right,' she agreed. She reached out to touch the boy's hot forehead. 'I'll fetch some cool water and we can bathe him,' she said, getting to her feet. She hurried to the long table where the lay brothers – and

Josse – ensured that there was always a plentiful supply of spring water, clean cloths and freshly washed out containers. She was in luck for someone had just delivered a full jar of lavender oil; its fresh and invigorating fragrance cut clean through the assorted stenches of illness and seemed to bring with it a vision of sunshine, a thread of bright purple light running through the sombre dimness of the Vale ward. She poured water into a bowl, added several drops of lavender oil and, selecting a cloth, returned to the thatcher and his boy.

She squeezed out the cloth and carefully sponged the lad's brow and cheeks. At first the cold made him frown but quickly his face cleared and he seemed to relax. The thatcher, watching closely, sighed softly.

'Look at that! You've got the touch, Sister,' he said. 'But then I expect you've been at it a long time.'

'At what?'

'Nursing.' Catt chuckled. 'There now, you're that tired, you've forgotten your own profession!'

She smiled with him. He was clearly unaware who she was, and it would have been both unnecessary and rather unkind to get on her high horse and tell him. Anyway, she was not at all sure that *she* knew who she was just then; it was suddenly much more important to be a nurse than an Abbess.

After some time of silent sponging, Helewise removed the cloth to wring it out. The thatcher put his hand on his son's forehead. 'It may be my imagination, Sister,' he said tentatively, 'but it seems to me he's not quite so hot.'

She felt the boy's skin. 'Perhaps,' she said. 'Although it is probably just the effect of the cold water.'

'It's holy water,' Catt said knowingly. 'It works miracles, they do say.'

'It can do,' she agreed. Then, for her cautious response had clearly affected him, she said, 'Shall we see if he'll take a drink? The water is also effective when drunk, you know.'

'Aye, I know. You stay there, Sister' – he pushed her back when she made to get up – 'I'll fetch the water.'

The boy managed to drink half a cup of water. Then he turned his face away.

Helewise knew she must leave the pair and get on with her next task, although her instinct was to stay; she was quite sure that the lad was approaching some sort of crisis. But the new system had been her idea and she would undermine others' obedience to it if she ignored it herself.

She got up quietly. 'I must go,' she said to Catt. 'We change shifts at Vespers and, although I wish I could return, it will be another nun who comes back later.'

He grinned up at her. 'That Abbess keeps you on your toes, I warrant,' he said. 'Bit of a tyrant, is she?'

Helewise smiled. 'Just a bit.'

Then, with a nod, she turned and left.

She ate a swift supper after Vespers and went to her room to do some work. But she could not concentrate; the image of the boy's pale face kept getting between her eyes and the parchment. Finally she gave up and, having forced herself to complete the present task and leaving everything neat and tidy (for she had the strong suspicion that she would not be sitting at her table again for some time to come) she left her room and firmly closed the door behind her.

She made her way across the cloister and through the rear gate, hurrying down the path to the Vale. There was considerably more activity down here that there had been up at the Abbey; hardly surprising, since everyone not presently on duty nursing the sick, including herself, was meant to be up there resting quietly ready for the next shift, whereas here in the Vale was where the battle was being fought.

As she approached the door of the Vale infirmary, Josse appeared at her side.

'You are disobeying your own rules, my lady,' he said softly. 'You should be asleep.'

'So should you,' she whispered back, but so glad, in that moment of closeness, that he was not.

'I'm about to go to my bed,' he admitted, stifling a huge yawn. 'It's been a long day.' He eyed her curiously, as if something about her puzzled him.

'What is it?' she demanded.

'Hm? Oh, nothing. Nothing.' And with a low bow, he turned and hurried away to the monks' shelter where she knew he had made his sleeping place.

She stared after him for a moment. She felt that she might understand his perplexity; she was aware that she had been acting oddly towards him, her guilty conscience bothered as it was by the approach to Joanna that she had ordered. Well, that appeared to have come to precisely nothing; for better or for worse, Joanna had refused to have anything to do with the Eye of Jerusalem, with the sick people in the Vale and with Hawkenlye in general. Of course it was a great pity – who could say what might have been achieved with the help of the magic jewel wielded by the rightful hand? – but that was that and there was no use moaning about it.

With that particular weight lifted from her, Helewise felt distinctly lighter. And Josse, bless him, had picked it up . . .

No wonder the poor man had looked bemused.

Smiling, shaking her head, Helewise went into the ward.

Head lowered so that her face was hidden by her coif – she did not want the nuns on duty to see her – she made straight for the thatcher and his boy. Catt was dozing, resting his face on his hand as he sat awkwardly on his son's bed. The boy's face was scarlet.

She hurried forward, and put her hand on the burning forehead. Her movement woke the thatcher; with a start, he looked up at her. 'What is it?'

'He is very hot,' she said. 'I will fetch water.'

She repeated her actions of earlier in the day. This time the boy's brow almost sent steam from the damp cloth, so high was his fever.

Helewise realised that she was on her knees. The thatcher dropped down beside her, eyes closed, hands pressed together; he seemed to think that she was praying, and it occurred to her that this was a very good idea. The lad was on the very precipice of death and only God could save him now.

Helewise began to pray softly, almost under her breath, and she heard Catt murmur the responses. They prayed for some time. Then she got to her feet and stood looking down at the boy.

The thatcher said, his voice cracking with emotion, 'If you save him, Sister, I'll make sure that your Abbey has the finest roofs in all the country.'

Helewise was about to tell him that few of the Abbey buildings were thatched but something stopped her. 'His life is in God's hands,' she said gently. 'We have prayed and done all that we can; now we must wait.'

They waited.

Time passed. Helewise fetched two more bowls of cold water. The boy writhed under the sheet soaked in his own sweat, fighting for air, and it seemed to her that his efforts became a little more difficult with each labouring, gasped intake of breath. Then suddenly he seemed to stiffen as if his muscles had locked and his back arched, lifting his narrow chest up off the bed.

Helewise prepared the words that she would say. It is God's will, even though we cannot understand his great purpose. The child is innocent and will surely spend minimal time in purgatory, especially if we all pray as hard as we can for his soul. One day the two of you will be reunited in heaven, with your wife and the baby girl too.

All of which, in the face of the thatcher's vast grief, would be next to useless.

The boy gave a long groan. His father fell like a stone to the lad's side, crying his name and muttering incoherently, calling out to the boy not to leave him.

The lad opened his eyes, tried to sit up, gave a stifled cry of pain, then dropped back and lay still.

Helewise knelt beside the thatcher, her hand already searching for his; if nothing else, at least she could show him that she was there with him, aware of his terrible agony and ready to help him through it.

'He is out of his pain now,' she began, 'he—'

But that was not right. Could not be right, for, her eyes on the boy, she saw that he was breathing, softly and deeply.

Darting up, she put her hands to him, on his forehead, on his chest. The heat was gone and the sweat had cooled on his skin. The tension had left the young face, replaced by the natural look of utter relaxation.

Pip was fast asleep.

Helewise felt joy surge through her and in that sublime moment sent her thanks up to the God who had understood a father's desperation and answered his prayer. She put her hands on the thatcher's shaking shoulders – he had buried his face in his hands to weep – and, bending down to speak in his ear, she said, 'Get up, Catt, and have a look.'

'I don't want to—' he began, but then something in her tone must have penetrated his grief, for he removed his hands, looked up at her and then, obeying her command, stood up and stared down at his son.

A sound broke from him, a sound of such unique quality that Helewise never heard the like again. Then the thatcher lowered himself on to his son's bed and, with the infinitely tender touch of a mother intent on not waking her baby, he picked up one of the boy's hands and pressed it to his face. Weeping still, but now from relief, he whispered, 'Pip, oh, my Pip.'

Helewise, tears in her own eyes, crept away.

17

In the morning a young monk sought out Josse and announced that a messenger had come to speak to him. On being asked who the messenger had come from and where he was, the lad said he didn't know and outside the main gate.

Having fleshed out the admirably brief response, Josse wiped his hands – he was still engaged in the water-carrying task – and made his way up to the front gate of the Abbey. The messenger had the good sense to stand a short distance off – probably, Josse reflected, everybody in the county now knew that there was sickness at Hawkenlye – but nevertheless Josse recognised him. He was one of Gervase de Gifford's men and his name . . . Josse struggled to recall . . . was Matt.

'Good day to you, Matt,' he called out.

Matt nodded. 'Good day, Sir Josse. I won't come closer, if it's all the same to you.'

'No, please don't. What can I do for you?'

'Not for me. It's the sheriff as wants to see you,' Matt replied.

'Very well. I will make my way down to Tonbridge as soon as possible.'

'Not the town,' Matt said. 'He says to meet at the top of Castle Hill. Safer.'

Matt had always been a man of few words, Josse remembered. 'I admire his sense,' he said. 'I'll set out for Castle Hill as soon as I get my horse saddled.'

Matt nodded again. 'I'll fetch Sheriff, then.' Without another word, he turned his horse and rode off.

It was not long before Josse too was setting out from the Abbey along the track towards the turning down to Tonbridge. He was intensely curious as to why de Gifford wanted to see him. So great had been his involvement in the monumental struggle going on at Hawkenlye that he had had to remind himself of what had happened last time he and the sheriff had been together. For a moment, he was struck by the triviality of those earlier preoccupations; set against the huge shadow of the foreign pestilence, they seemed to be of little significance.

But a young man died, he reminded himself; Nicol Romley was struck down right there in our Vale. And the merchant in Hastings – Martin Kelsey – he was dead, too. No; those matters were far from trivial, and Josse knew he owed de Gifford all the help he could give him.

Gervase was waiting for him at the place where the track bent down across the face of the hill towards Tonbridge. He held up a hand as Josse approached; like Matt, he wanted to keep distance between himself and Josse.

'I will come no nearer, don't worry,' Josse called out.

'How stand things at the Abbey?' de Gifford asked.

Josse shook his head. 'More than twenty sick; many dead or near it.'

'I see.' De Gifford bowed his head for a moment. Then, raising his eyes, he said, 'I have news for you.'

'Concerning Nicol Romley?'

'Yes. Somebody has been asking about him.'

'Who?'

'I do not know her true identity, although I can guess it. She is lodged with Goody Anne, where she gave her name as Matilda Hedley. However, not only does Anne report that the young lady speaks with an accent; Anne also heard her addressing the old man who is with her in what Anne described as some peculiar foreign tongue. She – Goody Anne – is now in an agony of indecision because, although she's very pleased to have the business, she suspects that her two guests have come over from France and she's terrified they may have brought the pestilence.'

Josse found that he was not all that affected by two people who might at some future date succumb to the sickness when he had recent first-hand experience of the poor souls who already had. He shrugged. 'It is possible.' Then, returning to the main concern: 'You think that the foreign tongue suggests this woman is Sabin de Retz?'

'Undoubtedly,' de Gifford confirmed. 'She asked to speak to the sheriff and I went to see her. She did not give any name to me, true or false; she merely asked if it was true that Nicol Romley had been murdered. I said it was and she asked for the details, which I gave her.'

'How did she react?'

'She already knew he was dead, Josse, so there was no sudden outpouring of grief. However, I glean from her demeanour that she was fond of the lad. Very fond, I should say.' He sniffed.

Josse was thinking. 'Gervase, she did not know of Nicol's death until she reached England. Her mission here was, I suggest, to find him and warn him that he was in danger, only she was too late. His killer had already arrived, found the poor lad and murdered him. Also,' he added excitedly, struck by another fact, 'she gave her real name to Sister Ursel at Hawkenlye yet she is now travelling under an alias, which suggests to me that something has happened – such as discovering that Nicol has been murdered – to make her sufficiently afraid to disguise her identity.'

'Yes, you are right,' de Gifford said. 'There would be no

point in a mission to warn someone if one knew they were already beyond help. But, knowing he is dead, why should she come here, unless perhaps she has such feelings for him that she would see his killer brought to justice?' He frowned, as if the thought displeased him. Then he said abruptly, 'Who told her Nicol was dead?'

'Not Adam Morton, for when he sent Sabin on to Hawkenlye, he thought Nicol was still alive, although sick. Not Sister Ursel, for I have asked the sister and she confirmed that she did not think it appropriate to speak of such a thing while standing at the Abbey gate.' Josse frowned, thinking hard. Then he said, 'My guess is that she was at Robertsbridge, although she had persuaded the monk who received Gus and me there not to tell anyone. Perhaps she overheard me tell Stephen – the monk – that Nicol had been murdered. Perhaps Stephen told her.'

'So she comes up here to the very vicinity of the lad's death, when it is clear that she fears for her own safety? A brave woman, Josse, thus to put herself at risk.'

'What was the alternative?' Josse countered. 'To remain in hiding at Robertsbridge for the rest of her days?'

De Gifford lifted an eloquent shoulder. 'Better than being dead.'

'Only just,' Josse muttered. Then something occurred to him. 'You said she's travelling with an old man?'

'Yes. He's blind and quite feeble, and she appears to care for him very tenderly.'

'And yet she has brought him into danger with her, if we are right in our assumption that there *is* danger for her here from this mystery murderer?'

'Oh, there's danger, be in no doubt, Josse.' De Gifford gazed at Josse, his expression grave. 'She has given me to understand that there is some dread secret at the heart of all this and somebody – perhaps more than one person – is fighting very hard to suppress it. Sabin knows what it is, although she has not admitted that. Nicol Romley and Martin Kelsey were killed to keep the secret, and now we can be certain that the murderer is after Sabin and probably the old blind man too.'

'She will not open her heart to you?'

De Gifford's expression softened. 'She's terrified, Josse. She's an intelligent and intuitive woman and I would imagine that she usually judges friend from foe with little effort. But now she's scared of her very shadow and no longer trusts anyone.'

Even the handsome sheriff of Tonbridge, who is already not a little affected by her, Josse thought. 'What should we do?' he asked.

De Gifford smiled. 'I rather hoped that you and I could speak to her together. I could fetch her from the inn, we could ride a safe distance from the town and from overly interested ears and eyes, and we could meet you out in the open.'

'How would that help?

De Gifford's smile deepened. 'You have a reputation for honesty, Josse. When Sabin asked Goody Anne how to find me, Anne told her quite bluntly that if she was in any sort of trouble then she should seek out Josse d'Acquin, who was probably to be found up at the Abbey.'

Josse felt embarrassed and tried to disguise it with a curt question: 'How do you know that?'

'One of my men was in the tavern and heard the conversation.' De Gifford waved a hand as if brushing that aside. 'What do you say, Josse? Will the honest man come to talk to the lost and frightened woman?'

'Of course I will. Name the place, and I shall be there.'

De Gifford's house was at the end of a road leading out of Tonbridge, far enough past the dwelling places and the hovels of the town for the sheriff to breathe clean air with the tang of the river and the countryside on it. The place that he suggested for the meeting was half a mile or so beyond his house, on a slight rise above the river where two tracks intersected. Arriving there first, Josse had to admire the choice; there was a stand of winter-bare oak trees with a thick undergrowth of bramble, holly and hazel to screen them from curious eyes, but they would have the advantage of being able to watch the tracks to see if anyone approached. Even if the killer was about and managed to follow Sabin out here, Josse thought, the man would hardly make a move against her when she had both de Gifford and Josse with her.

He waited.

Then, on the track leading out of the town, he saw two figures approaching. One was de Gifford – Josse recognised the horse before the rider – and the other . . . he narrowed his eyes to make out the details – was a woman on a white horse. He remembered Sister Ursel's description of a fair-haired, blue-eyed woman well dressed in a heavy, hooded cloak with good gloves, who rode 'a pretty grey mare'.

He dismounted, tethered Horace and walked to the side of the track to greet her.

She was a very striking woman. She was dressed in good-quality but plain garments, which suggested to Josse that she was more concerned with comfort and practicality than fashion. The fair hair was tightly braided and in the main modestly concealed by a cap of stiff white linen. Seeing him as she and de Gifford rode up, she dismounted, handed her mare's reins to de Gifford and strode towards Josse.

'I am Sabin de Retz,' she announced from a few paces off, 'and you are Sir Josse d'Acquin.'

'Yes, that is my name.' He answered her in French; de Gifford, an educated man, would understand the language of the nobility even though he habitually used the common speech.

But it was in the latter language – heavily accented – in which she had first hailed him that she replied: 'I am not French and it is not my mother tongue.'

'You should keep your distance, my lady,' he warned, 'for I have of late been at Hawkenlye Vale, where—'

'I know what is happening at Hawkenlye Vale,' she interrupted, coming closer – he picked up a faint scent from her, one that, after a moment, he identified – 'for I have seen both the dead and the fresh graves. I am not afraid and I will not insult you, Sir Josse, by standing off from you with a look of terror in my eyes, for it is how I am regarded here and I know how it affects the soul to be treated as a leper.'

'You are courageous, lady,' Josse murmured.

She gave a bitter laugh. 'Am I?'

De Gifford had also dismounted and had tethered his and Sabin's horses next to Horace. Now he came to stand beside Sabin.

She glanced at him. 'You too brave the shunned, Sheriff?' she asked.

De Gifford met her eyes. 'I would not be shown up as a coward,' he said simply. 'There remains only one alternative.'

Josse said, aware of breaking an almost tangible thread of tension between de Gifford and Sabin, 'I do not believe I present a danger, for I have been at the Vale for some days now and yet I remain well.'

'Do not tempt the fates!' de Gifford warned.

Sabin emitted a sound that sounded like *pouff* and was clearly expressive of scorn. 'The fates have nothing to do with it,' she said baldly. 'The spread of sickness follows a set pattern; we have but to discover what that pattern is.'

'But—' de Gifford began.

Josse interrupted; they were not here to discuss such incomprehensible scientific mysteries. 'You followed Nicol Romley from Troyes to England because you had to tell him that his life was in danger,' he said bluntly to Sabin. 'You went to see his former master, the Newenden apothecary Adam Morton, who said the lad had ridden over to Hawkenlye Abbey because he was unwell. It was some days before you managed to pursue him on to Hawkenlye, but when you did so you did not find him there either. You needed a place of safety in which to stay while you went on with your search and you settled on Robertsbridge Abbey, where you convinced the monk Stephen to lie if anyone came asking for you. You learned that Nicol has been murdered and then you decided to brave whatever danger pursues you and come up to the place where he was killed to discover what you can of how he died, why he was killed and who killed him.'

'I know the reason why he was killed,' Sabin said softly. 'That, Sir Josse, is the one thing I can be sure of.' But before Josse could ask what that reason was, she went on, 'You are right in essence. We met Nicol—'

'*We?*' put in de Gifford.

'Grandfather and I.'

'The old man who is with you at the inn?'

She sighed. 'Of course. His name is Benoît de Retz, the father of my late father. He and I were at the market in Troyes, where we had gone to buy – to buy things that were needed in our work. There we met Nicol and, since he was a lonely young man in a strange town, we befriended him. We shared a meal one night and we drank too much of the excellent wine they serve there. Grandfather wanted to impress Nicol and, his tongue loosened by the wine, he told Nicol something that should never have been told. Somebody was following Grandfather and me – someone who was aware that we possessed this dangerous knowledge – and, observing our friendship with Nicol, must have assumed, quite rightly, that the secret had been passed on to a third party. This someone set fire to our lodging house and it was only through chance that, other than some unpleasant symptoms resulting from breathing in the smoke, Grandfather and I were not harmed. The man who was after us must have believed us to be dead – which was not unreasonable since the lodging house was burned to the ground and they pulled out several bodies – and I guess that he set off after Nicol, the other person who knew the secret, to silence him too. When Grandfather was sufficiently recovered to travel, we too followed Nicol, but our intention was to warn him of the danger he was in.' She hesitated. 'Well, to speak honestly, it was also in my mind that Nicol would protect us.'

'You were not able to find him in Troyes to seek his help and to give him the warning?' de Gifford asked. Josse, who had been wondering the same thing, nodded.

'I searched for him, naturally, as soon as I had found somebody to look after Grandfather. But I could not find him.'

'Perhaps, seeing the burning lodging house where he knew you to be staying, he guessed that he too might be about to be attacked and made a run for it?' de Gifford suggested.

'No.' Sabin spoke the denial as if there could be no shade of doubt. Then, with a slight frown, 'Well, perhaps. But Nicol would not have deserted me – us, that is. He must have been in hiding somewhere . . . I do not know. But, seeing what he believed to be Grandfather's and my fate, who can blame him for fleeing Troyes?'

I could, Josse thought, and, from the look on his face, so could de Gifford. Both of us might have taken the time to see if we could help you and the old grandfather, or at least to confirm that you were really dead, before we turned tail and ran.

'So you followed Nicol to Boulogne, and then across the Channel to Hastings?' de Gifford was prompting.

'Yes. He'd said that he would sail home via those places

because his home was in Newenden, and there was quite a good road to the town from the port. My search for him was as Sir Josse suggested, with the exception that it was at Hawkenlye that I found out Nicol was dead.' She paused, eyes downcast, as if affected by the memory of that moment. 'I heard some people talking and they spoke of the dead young man found in the Vale; they even spoke his name, so I was left in no doubt. I thought that he must have died from the sickness, for I already knew that he had gone to the Abbey in the hope of being cured. Although, even then, I experienced a sudden intensifying of my dread, almost as if I knew in my heart what had really happened. For sure, I knew that Grandfather and I must remain in hiding, and I hastened back to Robertsbridge and reminded Stephen that, if anyone came asking, he had never heard of Sabin and Benôit de Retz and they certainly were not secreted away in the guest house of his Abbey.'

'So what persuaded you to break cover?' Josse asked.

'You,' she said simply. 'You came to Robertsbridge and Grandfather, who is in the habit of listening at doors, windows and keyholes, heard you tell Stephen that Nicol was murdered. I then had two options: to take Grandfather back home and hope that our particular fate' – she glanced at de Gifford – 'never finds us, or to come out of hiding and find out the identity of the man who killed Nicol and have him hanged. Since the man undoubtedly knows who we are and where we live and work, the chance of his failing to find us is negligible. That left only the other option. So here I am.'

'You say you would see the killer hanged,' de Gifford said, 'but I must tell you, my lady, that here in England we do not tolerate summary justice. The man would have to be tried and found guilty before such a punishment was imposed.'

'Naturally,' Sabin said with a touch of impatience. 'But I would tell them that the man killed Nicol.'

'You have proof?' de Gifford asked.

'Yes. No. Proof would be found,' she finished grandly.

'How do you propose that we find this man, when you implied just now that you do not know who he is?' Josse said.

Sabin turned her clear blue eyes to him. 'He will come after Grandfather and me and you will catch him and arrest him,' she said, as if explaining to one whose reasoning was particularly slow.

De Gifford gave a short bark of laughter. 'Indeed? We put the pair of you in some nice, obvious spot and wait for this man to attack, then pounce on him and throw him into gaol?'

'Yes.'

'*No*, my lady,' de Gifford said very firmly. 'I would never put you at such risk.'

'Then what do you suggest?' she said angrily. 'Grandfather and I will die unless this man is stopped, for he will not give up until our lips are sealed by death.'

'What is this secret that must not be told?' Josse asked. 'We have surmised that the man who murdered Nicol and who seeks you and your grandfather has come to England on some secret and deadly mission, and I guess that somehow you and Nicol have discovered what it is.' She turned to him as he spoke and he saw a strange expression fleetingly flash in her eyes; he must have been wrong, but he thought it looked like relief. 'Will you not reveal the truth to us?' he pleaded.

She kept her eyes on him. 'No,' she said, with a small smile. 'If I were to do so, then you too would be in danger.'

De Gifford gave a snort of disbelief. 'You surely do not think that this man will go on killing until everyone to whom you could possibly have unburdened yourself is dead!' he exclaimed.

'No, I do not think that,' Sabin agreed. 'He knows, I believe, that we are aware that we should never speak of what we know.

It was, as I said, only the wine that led to Grandfather revealing the secret to Nicol.'

Something had dawned on Josse. 'The killer went to Troyes to murder you and your grandfather,' he said slowly. 'He followed you there from your home, wherever that is, where you came by the secret. Why did you go to Troyes? Why select that town in particular as a hiding place?'

'We had a good excuse to go there,' Sabin said, 'for there is a wider choice of wares available there than anywhere else in northern France and there were, as I have explained, par-ticular ingredients – particular purchases that we wished to make. Our – the person whom we serve accepted that we must make the journey but we knew that, for her own good reasons, she would tell nobody else where we were bound. We hoped that the killer would not find out our destination and I do not see how he could have done; it is likely that he had a simple stroke of luck and spoke to someone who had seen us on the road. From then, I imagine it was quite easy to follow our trail; the combination of an old, blind man on a fat bay and a woman on a grey is not a common one.'

Josse was working hard, trying to store away the fragments of information which, despite her clear intention to the contrary, Sabin was unwittingly giving away. He heard de Gifford ask her a question – something about what work she and her grand-father did – and he heard Sabin politely refuse to tell him.

Josse, however, thought that he already knew.

Sabin had given him other clues, too, including one small fact that nagged away at him because it chimed with some-thing that he had picked up recently; a piece of court gossip, he had thought, although now, faced with the enigma of Sabin de Retz, he was beginning to wonder.

De Gifford was suggesting that they return to their respec-tive dwellings. 'We can gain nothing from standing out here in the cold,' he said, 'and I have decided upon a course of action.'

'What is it?' Sabin asked.

'Aye?' Josse spoke at the same time.

De Gifford looked from one to the other. 'It is, in a way, a variation of the plan that the lady proposed.' He gave a small bow in Sabin's direction. 'I suggest that you and your grand-father move into my own house, where I have servants to care for you and where I can arrange an armed guard to protect you. Having ensured your safety and my staff's silence, I will then spread false word that you are still lodging at the tavern and wait—'

'Wait for him to set fire to that too?' Josse broke in, angry at the way in which de Gifford appeared to be disregarding the safety of the tavern and everyone within it. 'That will please Goody Anne!'

'I will protect the tavern,' de Gifford said calmly. 'This man, whoever he is, will not find it an easy matter to approach the Tonbridge inn and fire it; not with my men waiting for him.'

'Hm.' Josse was far from convinced. He was about to offer his own services when he remembered that he already had a mission up at Hawkenlye. The thought prompted the realisa-tion that he had already been gone far too long; the endless water-carrying would be that much more arduous for the monks and lay brothers without him. 'I must be away,' he said. Meeting de Gifford's eyes, he added, 'You will keep me informed if—?'

'I will,' de Gifford assured him.

He and Sabin mounted their horses and Josse collected Horace and did the same. Then they rode back towards the town, Josse saying farewell as they passed de Gifford's house – where the sheriff was going to lodge Sabin before riding on to fetch her grandfather and her few possessions from the tavern – and heading on up towards Castle Hill and Hawkenlye.

De Gifford's plan, such as it was, seemed to Josse to be full of flaws, not the least of which was that it was hardly fair to put

Goody Anne's tavern – her livelihood – at such risk in the slim hope of the killer turning up there to murder two people who were not even within.

There had to be something better.

Reaching the summit of the hill, Josse went over what he had deduced about Sabin de Retz and her grandfather. He would seek out the Abbess, he decided; he would put the facts before her and then the two of them would put their heads together, as they had done so many times in the past, and see if they couldn't come up with something that would help them guess what secret the old man and the young woman were keeping, why it was so dangerous, the identity of the killer and the place where he was hiding out.

It was a tall order and, he thought with a rueful smile, a virtually impossible task. But then he and the Abbess had achieved the impossible before.

And, besides, he could not think of anything he wanted to do more than to sit with her in her little room, talking, puzzling, watching the intelligent grey eyes and the light that entered her face when she thought she had found a possible solution.

I'll present myself for water duty for the rest of the morning, he told himself, then I'll go and seek her out.

With that happy prospect in mind, he put his heels to Horace's sides and, on flat ground now, cantered off along the track that led to the Abbey.

PART FOUR

The Last Battle

18

The sickness came upon her so swiftly that she barely had time to realise how unwell she felt before she slipped into a feverish sleep that was more like unconsciousness.

She had been feeling a deep ache in all her bones when she went to bed the previous night but, exhausted by her role in the first spells of nursing duty under the new roster system, had ascribed the discomfort to fatigue. Rising in the morning, it had taken her longer than usual to perform the tasks that daily repetition over the years had made all but automatic; for one frightening moment, she had forgotten how to pin her veil.

She managed to get through Prime and, later, Tierce, although she was almost sure she had briefly slept during the latter and added to her prayers a hurried request that nobody had noticed her lapse. The idea of eating revolted her; she did not even feel up to going near the refectory in case some odour of food should waft out, at which she was quite sure she would have vomited.

Then it was time to return to the Vale infirmary for the next spell of duty. Her head ached violently, with a sharp-edged pain behind the eyes that seemed to be sawing off the top of her skull. She felt hot, had begun to sweat and then was suddenly cold, shivering as the clammy dampness held her like an icy shroud. Her skin felt tender to the touch; even the pressure of her garments hurt.

They were discussing the importance of making sure that recovering patients ate, even if, as often happened, this meant that whoever was nursing the patient had to sit beside them and spoon the thin but nourishing soup into their mouths.

Soup. Mouth.

Her own mouth filled with water and, making a dash for the door, she ran along the outer wall of the ward and, rounding a corner, threw up on to the frosty grass. When she had finished – her body convulsed into several acutely painful, dry retches after her stomach had emptied itself – she felt so weak that her legs would not hold her up. Her back against the wall of the Vale infirmary, she slumped down to the ground.

Where, she was not sure how long afterwards, they found her.

She was in bed at the very end of the long ward where she was meant to be caring for others. Somebody had removed her habit and she wore just her high-necked undergown. Her head was bare – she put up a shaky hand to feel her short hair – and she seemed to be lying on a thick lump of folded linen . . . Yes. She had seen that done for others. It was in order that, when the flux of the bowels began, the soiled linen could be removed and replaced without disturbing the patient and remaking the whole bed.

I have the sickness, then, she thought.

Tears filled her eyes and she felt their course down her hot face.

So much that I wanted still to do with my life. So many things not yet said that need to be said. So many . . .

Her mind slipped away. Losing the thought, she lapsed into unconsciousness.

In the forest, Joanna woke from a compelling dream. The details were already fading as she struggled up from the depths of sleep but she was left with a most vivid impression that somebody had been talking to her, taking her to task: a voice had sounded inside her head, telling her something – no, reminding her of something of which she was already aware – and, if she concentrated hard, she felt she could almost hear it again.

Because of your actions two men died and your spirit carries the burden. The adjustment involves recompense . . . in order to balance what has happened to you, you must save the lives of two people who are dying.

She closed her eyes and instantly the bright day at Nime's fountain appeared in her mind. She allowed herself the luxury of staying with the vision for a few precious, strengthening moments, then she opened her eyes and banished it back to the deep recesses of her mind.

She got down from the sleeping platform – it was early yet and Meggie was still fast asleep – and quietly crossed the floor of her hut and opened the door. It was cold and still outside. March weather, she thought absently. Hard and frosty, with new life beginning but too deep down, as yet, for most eyes to see the signs.

She strolled around the carefully tended clearing in front of the hut. Her mind was bursting, teeming with possibilities; she stilled her thoughts as she had been trained to do and, standing quite still under the oak tree that marked the northern boundary of her patch of earth, closed her eyes and listened.

After some time – she had no idea how long she had stood there, although the rising sun was making long shadows in the clearing by the time they had finished with her – she returned to herself.

It was strange, she mused as, back in the hut, she set about making up the fire and preparing food and drink for Meggie's and her breakfast. Strange because she had thought, when they told her she was to be a healer and then straight away taught her how disorder in the mind produces sickness in the body, that she was to continue to learn the sort of healing that was done at Folle-Pensée. Indeed, since she had been back in the Great Forest she had gone on thinking deeply about everything she had been told; if – or, she had thought, probably *when* – the call came, she wanted to be sure she was ready.

But now she had to face up to the possibility that she had been sent back here to the Hawkenlye Forest for a very different reason. She could no longer see it as mere accident that her return coincided with a major outbreak of a fatal disease. Neither could she ignore – much as she wanted to – that it was not only herself but Meggie too who carried the powerful blood of an ancient line of healers in her veins.

They – she and her daughter – could do so much good.

And that was without this jewel of Josse's that they'd told her about . . .

'What should we do, little Meggie?' she asked her daughter, busy stuffing a quarter of an apple into her mouth. Meggie chewed on the apple for a moment, then gave Joanna a dazzling smile and said, 'Bink.'

'Drink, please,' Joanna corrected automatically, blowing on the contents of Meggie's cup in case it was still too hot.

I know what we must do, Joanna thought, watching her precious child finish her drink, burp and then scratch her bottom. They have taught me, they have told me who I am and explained that Meggie has our people's great power in her ancestry on both sides. But, when Lora and Tiphaine came to ask for my help, I refused it.

Yet again she went over her justification. The night's potent dream seemed to have changed her in some way; she could no longer fool herself that the refusal had stemmed primarily out of fear for Meggie's safety, for there would be no danger of infection if the child went no nearer than the forest fringes to do whatever it was they wanted her to.

And as for the other reason – could she bear to see Josse

again? Could he bear to see her? Perhaps she could explain Meggie away as the child of another forest woman, temporarily in her care?

No. Unless Josse had suddenly lost the use of his eyes, that would never work.

The tumult of her thoughts had risen to a crescendo. Through them a voice spoke, a familiar, beloved voice which now occupied the very centre of Joanna and all that she was. Even as she sensed him enter her mind, already she was clutching at the claw that he had given her. He said, quietly but with utter authority, *Do what you must do, for all other considerations are subordinate to that.*

After that, there was no need to think about it any more.

Josse had been frustrated the evening before in his desire to discuss with the Abbess the whole matter of Sabin de Retz and the mysterious, lethal secret that threatened both the young woman's life and that of her grandfather. Returning to Hawkenlye from Tonbridge, Josse had sought her out in her little room, only to be told that she was taking a turn at nursing down in the Vale. His informant – it was Sister Basilia – noticed his frown.

'She'll be all right,' she said bracingly. 'And, having got so many volunteers, she's not going to leave it to everyone else and not join in the nursing duties herself, is she?'

'No, I suppose not.' Of course she wasn't; she knew as well as he did that it was always a sound decision to lead by example. But, sound or not, the fact remained that she had put herself in the danger zone.

'She'll be back up here later,' Sister Basilia said as she hurried away. Everyone, he thought glumly, was in a hurry these days. 'You'll be able to see her then!'

He had waited, but she did not return. He gave up soon after Compline; he must have missed her, he guessed, and no doubt, not knowing he wanted to talk to her, she had gone early to bed.

Ah, well. He would just have to restrain his impatience until morning.

But the morning made its own demands on him. Returning to the Vale for water duties, he discovered that Brother Augustus had taken a bad fall inside the shrine, slipping on the steep stone steps that led down to the spring in its rocky basin. Gus had not broken any bones, Sister Caliste had announced after examining him, but he was already coming out in an enormous bruise that extended from the small of his back, right across his left buttock and down as far as the back of his left knee. He was very sore and stiff, shaking from the shock and the pain.

Relieved of water-carrying, Gus was sent to Sister Tiphaine to learn how to put together the ingredients for her convalescents' remedy. Standing at her workbench finely chopping dried leaves and plant stems was about all he was good for that day.

Meanwhile Brother Erse, the carpenter, had set about building a wooden handrail to run the length of the shrine steps. The constant carriage of water up them had made them sopping wet and the stone was as slippery as ice. Seeing him struggling with a large piece of timber, Josse offered his help. For the rest of the morning the two worked together within the shrine and by the time the community was summoned to Sext, the new rail was almost finished.

The Abbess would be in the Vale infirmary after the office; Josse was aware that her hours of duty were from Sext to Vespers. Well, he would keep an eye out for her and if he failed to get a chance to speak to her, he would be waiting outside the Vale infirmary when she finished her duties in the evening.

With a sigh he went back to smoothing down the new handrail.

Sister Tiphaine was deeply worried and her heart was heavy. She was privy to a confidence and she knew that one did not break faith lightly. But her co-conspirator was out of her reach and it was up to her to make the decision.

She stayed on in the Abbey church after Sext, praying for guidance. Then she left the church and slipped round to her little hut, but she had forgotten about Brother Augustus, diligently chopping dried herbs and managing to give her a cheery grin despite the considerable pain he must be suffering; Tiphaine had seen the bruises, having rubbed in the first application of salve for the poor lad.

She needed a place where she could be alone, for she had to speak to the other, older powers that she still held in almost the same awe as the new God; leaving Gus to his chopping, she hurried away down the path, out through the front gate and up the faint track that led to the forest.

She did not go far. She did not need to, for even from eight or ten paces away she felt the force of the forest reach out to her. She stopped, stood quite still and silently voiced her problem.

In time, the answer came.

It was the same one that she thought she had heard in the Abbey church. Her mind quite made up, she hastened back to the Abbey, crossed it and left by the rear gate. In the Vale, she quickly located Sister Caliste and, with a peremptory tug at her sleeve, took her outside to where they could speak privately.

Sister Caliste's bleak expression and red-rimmed eyes mirrored the anxiety and misery that Tiphaine felt; indeed, that everyone felt who knew.

'Any change?' Tiphaine asked gruffly. Sister Caliste shook

her head. 'Sister, there is something we could do. *Must* do, in fact; it may be the only hope.'

'What is it?' Sister Caliste asked wearily. 'We have tried everything, Tiphaine; we may just have to accept that there are some of them whom we just cannot save.'

'We must not give up yet!' Tiphaine said urgently. 'Listen.'

Briefly she told Sister Caliste about Joanna. And about Meggie; Sister Caliste's eyes widened at the mention of Joanna's daughter, and Tiphaine, who believed the child's paternity to be a well-guarded secret known among the Abbey community to only herself and the Abbess, could imagine Caliste's surprise. But there was no time for that now. She hurried on to explain about the Eye of Jerusalem and the prophetic words of the strange man who had said there would come a female of Josse's line whose hand would wield the stone with the greatest force of all time.

Caliste looked shocked. 'You are saying that this little girl is Sir Josse's child?' she whispered.

'Aye. Did you not guess as much just now when first I spoke of her?'

'No, oh, no.' Caliste smiled. 'My response then was amazement, for I was not aware that the ancient line to which Joanna belongs has been extended to a new generation. But *Josse!*' She shook her head.

'He has no idea,' Tiphaine said.

'Oh, have no fear – I shall not tell him.'

Tiphaine was watching the younger nun with a considering expression. 'You know about Joanna's heritage, don't you?'

'Yes.'

'But then you're a child of the forest people yourself, young Caliste. Sometimes I forget, seeing you in your habit and with your nun's serenity apparent in your every move and expression, where you came from.'

Caliste smiled again. 'So do I. But my roots are still out

there.' She lifted her eyes to look at the dark mass of the great forest up on top of the rise behind the Abbey.

'We must make a fresh approach to her,' Tiphaine said, following Caliste's line of sight. 'I know where she is. Will you come with me?'

'Back into the forest?' Caliste turned to her, wariness in her eyes. 'I don't know. It would feel very strange to experience the tug of my own past.'

'It may tug but you will be more than capable of dealing with it,' Tiphaine told her firmly. 'Now, make up your mind, Caliste; if you're not prepared to take the risk, I'll go on my own.'

'I'll go with you,' Caliste announced. 'Come on!'

The two nuns took a discreet path around the outside of the Abbey walls, branching off to slip across the open ground and creep in under the trees. Caliste felt the power, just as Tiphaine did; she had been born to the Forest People, her birth the product of the most solemn ceremony by which the continuity of the pure bloodline of one of the central families was ensured. But Caliste had been a twin; her sister, identical to her in every way, had been born first and Caliste had been left on the doorstep of the poor but loving family who had brought her up. Caliste had been one of Hawkenlye Abbey's youngest nuns and not for a moment had she ever regretted her decision to enter the community.

Now she was back where she began . . .

Tiphaine reached out and gave her hand a squeeze. 'Don't be afraid.'

'I'm not – well, I am, but it's more that I feel I'm being watched. Scrutinised, in fact.'

Tiphaine chuckled. 'That's because you are, child.'

The herbalist led the way, unerringly following the right path. They had covered about half the distance to their

destination when quite suddenly, with absolutely no warning
of their approach, two silent figures appeared before them, one
standing a little behind the other.

Both Tiphaine and Caliste recognised the foremost figure
and, as one, they dropped to their knees before her. The
Domina reached out her hands, first to Tiphaine – 'Welcome;
it is good to see you again' – and then, a tender expression
flooding the ageless face, to Caliste. She raised the young
woman to her feet and then took her in her arms, whispering in
her ear, 'And welcome, too, to you, beloved granddaughter.'

Caliste, memories rising irrepressibly, found that she was
weeping.

Then Lora – for she it was who attended the Domina –
stepped forward and gently reminded her honoured elder that
their purpose was urgent. The Domina released Caliste,
turned and, with Lora at her side, led the small procession
on to Joanna's clearing.

A strange sensation was waxing in Tiphaine. She was well
aware of the strength of Joanna's earlier refusal to give her
help – she had witnessed it, after all – but somehow that did
not seem to count any more. Fight as she might to suppress the
feeling, she could not; and the sensation was optimism.

The Domina entered the clearing before Joanna's hut, Lora
a pace to the rear and the two Hawkenlye nuns behind her.
Caliste, Tiphaine observed, was very pale; this return to her
birthplace and her own people must, Tiphaine realised, be
traumatic. She moved closer to the girl and Caliste, sensing
her presence and probably also her compassionate concern,
turned and gave her a very sweet smile. 'Don't worry; I am all
right,' she whispered.

'Good girl,' Tiphaine whispered back.

They came to a stop behind the two forest women. Then the
Domina called out, in a voice that was pitched low but

somehow, like the call of a bird, carried pure and clear, 'Beith, come out.'

Beith. Birch, Tiphaine thought. That must be Joanna's name within the tribe. The deep honour of being included in one of the forest people's mysteries – their secret identity known only to a precious few – affected her profoundly and she bowed her head.

But then there came a succession of small sounds as Joanna opened her door and stepped out. Eyes blinking open, Tiphaine stared at her.

She looked quite different; in no way was she the everyday Joanna whom Tiphaine knew and had last seen. She wore a hooded red tunic, heavily embroidered with rich gold, and over it a widely flaring cloak made of some sort of speckled wool. It was fastened with a golden pin like running horse. Her long dark hair was braided, the plaits hanging down over her shoulders and reaching well below her breasts. The leather sandals on her feet were beautifully made and their clasps were of gold. A leather satchel hung from her shoulder and in her hand she held a rod of wood – it would be hawthorn, Tiphaine thought – in whose tip had been inserted a brownish crystal.

She stood quite still now, staring out at them with dark, unfathomable eyes. She has indeed come into her power, Tiphaine thought humbly, and, almost without her own voli-tion, she gave a deep and respectful bow.

Then there was the sound of a child's laughter; Meggie had come out after her mother and was expressing her delight at seeing Lora, whom she knew and loved. The sweet sound broke whatever spell was on the clearing and Tiphaine let out a sigh of relief.

'Beith, we come as four women from two different worlds with the same request,' the Domina said. But before she could go on, Joanna spoke.

She went on her knees before the Domina, the wide skirts of

her cloak flowing gracefully around her, and, head down, she said, 'Forgive me, but I know what you would ask of me. I have already decided that I must do what you want.'

The Domina paused, then said, 'Another has spoken to you.'

'Yes,' Joanna agreed. She raised her eyes and an unreadable exchange of glances flashed between her and the Domina.

'It is well,' the Domina breathed. 'Beith, you know now what is required of you and of your own free will you have accepted the task. This is so?'

'It is,' Joanna said firmly.

The Domina held out her hand and helped Joanna to her feet. 'Then,' she said, casting her eyes around the small group, 'let us be on our way.'

They stopped when they reached the outer fringes of the forest. Hawkenlye Abbey lay before them; Joanna would not take Meggie any closer.

Tiphaine and Caliste hastened away, Caliste running down the slope and along the path that ran outside the walls, racing to fetch a vessel of the holy spring water; Tiphaine to fetch the Eye of Jerusalem from its hiding place in the Abbess's room. While they were gone, Lora sat down on a fallen branch and kept Meggie entertained; the Domina stood still and silent as a statue.

Joanna, her mind turned inward as she summoned all her reserves of concentration and power for the task ahead, stared out over the Abbey to the Vale in the distance. She felt for the bear's claw on its silver chain beneath her tunic and, extracting it through the neck of the garment, held it tight in her right hand.

The waiting continued.

Tiphaine returned first. She looked up at the Domina, who gave a nod, and then she held out to Joanna the wrapped object that she held in her hand.

Joanna took it, slowly unfolding the soft leather until the object was laid bare. She lifted the stone up by the chain from which it hung and the Eye of Jerusalem blinked in the soft grey daylight.

She felt the power surging inside it and the shock of it almost made her drop it. She took her eyes off the huge sapphire for an instant and looked at the Domina, who gave a brief nod. Then she returned her mind to the stone, giving herself up to it while it continued with the painful and quite lengthy task of revealing to Joanna just what it was and what it could do.

She had been in the trance state. When she came out of it, it was to find herself sitting on the grass leaning against an oak tree, the Eye of Jerusalem in her lap and Meggie standing anxiously beside her. Caliste had returned; she had brought two stone jugs full of water.

'Now, Beith, do what you must do,' commanded the Domina.

This was the moment that Joanna had dreaded. Now that she had held the Eye and felt its incredible power, she was even more reluctant to let Meggie touch the precious thing. The Domina, of course, picked up her fear.

'The child will be what she is born to be, as I have told you before,' she intoned. 'You cannot prevent this, Beith. Give her the Eye and show her what to do.'

Joanna got up and then knelt down beside Meggie, the jars of water before them. She picked up the stone by its chain and said, trying to keep her voice level and to speak in her normal tones, 'Hold the lovely stone, Meggie. Look! See how the blue jewel flashes as it catches the light?'

But Meggie was no ordinary child, to be beguiled by a pretty plaything. Something in her blood recognised an object of power and at first she was afraid and drew back. Joanna said no more but merely knelt there slowly swinging the stone to and fro. And, in the end, curiosity overcame fear and Meggie took the chain from her mother's hand and held aloft the Eye of Jerusalem.

There was magic in the air. Tiphaine sensed it; Caliste, who had thought to have put all that behind her when she entered Hawkenlye, felt it too and shivered in dread. Lora squared her shoulders, almost as if she felt the forces swirling around as a physical assault.

The Domina stood unmoving, watching.

Joanna gently touched Meggie's wrist, careful to avoid the Eye or its chain, and guided the child's hand until it was right over the first jar of water. 'Dip the stone into the water, Meggie,' she said softly.

There was a brief hesitation – the mere blink of an eye – and then Meggie obeyed.

Tiphaine watched.

At first nothing happened.

Then a very faint wisp of steam, or perhaps smoke, rose up from the still surface of the water. The liquid went cloudy and, before Tiphaine's bewitched eyes, pictures seemed to come and go within the milky swirls. Then the water cleared again.

Meggie still held the Eye submerged in the water. Just as Tiphaine was starting to think that it was over, that whatever magic the jewel had worked was now complete, something else happened.

The water began to shine.

As if a minuscule fragment of a bright star had fallen into it – or perhaps was reflected in it – for the space of a few heartbeats the water emitted a brilliant light. It faded, quite slowly, but when it had gone the water had changed; it was purer, clearer and brighter.

It will work, Tiphaine thought jubilantly. Whatever power is in the stone, whichever god has put it there for mankind's use, it has had the right effect.

The others were quietly rejoicing, too; nobody spoke, but then they did not need to. Joanna, a smile of pure relief on her face, was encouraging Meggie to dip the Eye into the second jug and, as the same miracle happened, Meggie began to laugh. Lora and the Domina stood a little apart; their eyes were fixed on Meggie and Lora made a quiet remark to the Domina, who suddenly smiled.

Caliste looked as if she were in a dream.

Tiphaine went over to her and gave her a hug; it was not something that nuns habitually did to one another but so unusual and strange were the circumstances that Caliste did not seem to notice. She returned the hug and Tiphaine discovered that the girl was trembling.

'It's all right, child,' Tiphaine murmured. 'It's done. Now you and I will take the water down to the Vale infirmary and we shall see what we shall see when we try it out on those most in need of it.'

Caliste raised her eyes to stare at Tiphaine. 'It *will* work, won't it?'

'Oh, yes, it'll work.' Tiphaine gave her a last, bracing squeeze, then turned to bow to the Domina. And to Joanna, still sitting on the ground and looking dazed.

'May we return with more water?' Tiphaine asked her humbly.

'Of course,' Joanna replied. 'We shall be here.'

Tiphaine nodded. Then she and Caliste each picked up a jug and hurried off, as fast as they could without risking spilling any water, back to the Vale infirmary.

As they strode along, Tiphaine was trying to work out how she would phrase her announcement; how she would tell senior nuns such as Sister Emanuel and, indeed, Sister Euphemia, who was expected back on duty later in the day, that somehow she had come upon a special type of sacred water that might just do the trick.

That might, when all else had failed, bring the dying back from the brink. The dying who now included, and had done since that morning, the Abbess Helewise.

19

It was not until quite late in the day that Josse finally realised just who was the latest victim of the foreign pestilence.

He had been busy as Brother Erse's temporary apprentice carpenter until well into the early afternoon – they'd had trouble fitting the top stanchion of the new handrail, there being nothing but virgin rock to which to fix it – and, by the time Josse was free to seek out the Abbess, he knew that she would already be on duty in the Vale infirmary. Although many nuns, monks and lay brothers were now on the nursing rosters and actively involved at close quarters with the sick, still the rule applied that nobody who was not nursing went anywhere near them. And it was thought that Josse, although he would have taken his turn if asked, was better engaged using his strength elsewhere.

Such as the endless task of water-carrying, which resumed at full capacity once Brother Erse finally announced himself satisfied with his brand-new safety measures.

As soon as Josse took the first load of full vessels over to the door of the infirmary ward, he realised that somebody important to the community was very ill. The faces of the nurses gave that away. And Sister Euphemia, back on duty after sleeping eighteen hours with only a couple of breaks to eat, could be heard from several paces away giving strings of orders to everybody working with her.

It was clear that somebody was close to death; in the late afternoon, Father Gilbert was sent for.

Josse wondered how the Abbess would feel, watching some poor soul that the nuns had not managed to save as he or she slipped away. Well, if whoever it was were sufficiently conscious to appreciate that she stood at their bedside, he told himself comfortingly, then what better farewell could they have to this earth?

He decided it must be dear old Brother Firmin who was dying. It was sad – the old monk had a kind and gentle spirit and a simple, loving heart – but then he was old, so perhaps it was merely that his time had come to be called back to God.

Trudging to and fro between the shrine and the infirmary ward, Josse kept a vision of the old boy in his mind's eye and wished him well.

Early in the evening, when the short day had already begun to darken, Josse saw Sister Tiphaine and Sister Caliste returning to the Vale infirmary. He probably would not have noticed two more arrivals amid all the comings and goings, except for the fact that the two nuns were moving so quickly that they were all but running.

He was not the only one to notice the unusual flurry of their arrival; several of the monks and lay brothers on the chain of water carriers also stopped and stared.

Josse put down his buckets and followed the two nuns to the doorway of the ward and would have gone inside after them but for the looming figure of Sister Euphemia. Josse had just had the time to observe the quizzical, half-impatient look she gave to the pair and overhear her demand to know where they'd been all afternoon when, spotting him, the infirmarer gave him a quick, compassionate glance that he totally failed to understand and then politely but firmly shooed him away and closed the door.

★

Inside the Vale infirmary, Sister Tiphaine had taken Sister Euphemia aside to tell her that she and Sister Caliste had brought a new draught that they had good reason to believe might well prove to be efficacious in the worst cases of the sickness. The infirmarer looked dubious; remembering how often in the past the two of them had all but fallen out over the relative merits of herbal concoctions versus good, painstaking nursing care, Tiphaine said gently, 'Try it, Euphemia. Just try it. We shall soon see what it can or cannot do.'

The infirmarer scowled and was about to make a caustic comment when suddenly it dawned on her what this strange new remedy might be. She guessed that Sister Tiphaine had been having another try at using the Eye of Jerusalem; while she admired the herbalist's optimism – she did indeed seem to believe that this time the results might be different – Euphemia saw no reason why the Eye should now work when it had so dismally failed to do so before.

But, on the other hand, they had to do *something* . . .

Sister Euphemia knew that, in fairness, she should treat her most badly off patients strictly in the order in which she came to them along the ward. But, with a quick and silent prayer for forgiveness, instead she went straight to the bed that stood apart in its curtained recess at the far end of the room. She remained closeted within for some time. Then she emerged, caught Sister Tiphaine's eye and said, 'We'd better try it on some of the others.'

'Did it not make any difference?' Tiphaine whispered as they proceeded to the next in line, an old man who was by now all but incapable of swallowing.

'No,' Sister Euphemia said shortly. 'But she is far away from us now. I fear that nothing can reach her any more.'

Stifling her grief, Sister Tiphaine watched as the infirmarer began to administer small drops of the water to the old man.

★

The two jugs were soon emptied; Sister Caliste had been working her way from the opposite end of the ward and she and the infirmarer – with Sister Tiphaine at her shoulder – met in the middle.

'I don't know what you think you've got here,' Sister Euphemia began in a cross whisper, glaring at the two nuns – acute disappointment had made her good nature temporarily quite desert her – 'but it doesn't seem to be doing any good whatsoever.'

But Sister Caliste had her eyes on a young woman who was lying just inside the door and who had been the first person she had treated. 'Wait,' she murmured. 'Just wait . . .'

Tiphaine and Euphemia, noticing where she was looking, also turned their attention to the young woman. As they watched, she opened her eyes and struggled to raise her head. The three nuns hastened over to her. She was still sweaty and hot but her skin had lost the burn of high fever; the rash that had mottled her chest and face seemed to have faded from dark red to pink and little scabs were forming on the open lesions.

The woman's eyes were wide with fear. 'I was in the lane,' she muttered, 'calling for the children . . .'

'You are at Hawkenlye,' Sister Caliste said gently, sitting down on the edge of the bed and taking the woman's hand. 'You have been very unwell but now you are going to get better.'

'Am I?' The woman frowned. 'It doesn't feel like it. Oh, I *ache*! All over!' Then, panic crossing her face, she cried, 'Where are my children?'

'Hush, hush,' Caliste soothed her. 'They are here, but in a different room. They too were sick but both are recovering.'

The woman looked as if she could hardly believe what had happened. 'We're not dead? Not dying?'

'No.' Sister Caliste smiled at her. 'You will be very weak for some time, I fear, but eventually you will be able to go home again.'

The woman's eyes closed. 'Very well, Sister. Whatever you say.' The she gave a huge yawn and went to sleep.

The pattern was repeated in several of the patients for whom Sister Euphemia had all but given up hope. Afterwards, with the luxury of time to consider, she often asked herself whether that mysterious draught really had anything to do with their recovery or whether it was simply that the illness had run its course and at last left their racked bodies. As with all plagues, she reflected, there were always some who were stronger than the rest and who better withstood the ravages of the disease.

Rational thinking was all very well, however; the other part of Sister Euphemia, the one which *knew* that she had observed not one but several miracles, put logic right out of mind and prompted her to go down on her knees and thank God for his mercy.

The Abbess Helewise did not respond to the miracle draught. She lay quite still, her body voided, so deeply unconscious that, when they tried to offer her water of any sort, it just rolled into her partly open lips and dribbled out again. The danger of some of it going down her inert throat and choking her was, Sister Euphemia decreed, too dangerous and so they had to stop. Sister Caliste, who had begged to be allowed to nurse her, had to content herself with bathing the Abbess's face and forehead with a cloth wrung out in the draught.

They had clipped her already short hair closer to her head in the hope of thus lowering her alarmingly high fever and now Caliste repeatedly put the damp cloth on to the short, springy curls. She all but forgot that this woman was Abbess of Hawkenlye; deadly white face, red-gold hair darkened with sweat and water, eyes closed and already appearing to have sunk back into the skull, she could have been any woman brought in for the Hawkenlye nuns to care for.

Except, Caliste thought, tears in her eyes, I don't necessarily love any of the others as I love her.

Gently she removed the cloth – it was quite hot in her hands – wrung it out yet again and replaced it on the Abbess's forehead.

Tiphaine made another visit to the forest fringes. Without Caliste, she carried back both full vessels herself. When they were empty, she found a handcart and this time made the trip with three times as many jugs.

Eventually, of course, someone asked her what she was doing; with a shrug, as if it was not that important, she muttered something about a preparation she had made up in her little hut. The explanation was accepted and soon everyone was aware that the herbalist had come up with something that really seemed to work.

Tiphaine knew that she could not go on taking the credit. But all that, she decided, ignoring her aching back as she pushed the handcart back up the track towards the Abbey for the third time, would just have to wait.

Josse sat outside the Vale infirmary waiting for the Abbess to come off duty. It was the hour for Vespers and he thought he might accompany her up to the Abbey church, attend the office with her and then persuade her to go along to her room so that he could tell her all about Sabin de Retz, her grandfather and his own musings as to what might lie behind the mystery.

He waited.

She did not come.

Finally Sister Euphemia came out. She took Josse's hand and led him a short way off along the path that bordered the lake. Then she halted, turned and looked him in the eyes.

'Sir Josse, the Abbess Helewise has the sickness.'

There was an instant in which his whole soul rejected the news. Then, as it began to sink in, he felt a vast wail of grief well up inside him. No, oh, no!

He contained it. His voice harsh with emotion, he said gruffly, 'Will she live?'

'I do not know,' the infirmarer said steadily, 'although I fear the worst.'

'Why did you not tell me sooner?'

'We hoped – *I* hoped – to avoid it and save you this pain,' she confessed. 'I went on believing that she would suddenly take a turn for the better. But . . .' She held out empty hands, palms uppermost, in a hopeless gesture.

'What can we do?' He began pacing to and fro. 'We must fetch the Eye from the Abbess's room!' he cried. 'We've tried it once, I realise that, but perhaps—'

'Sister Tiphaine has already done that,' the infirmarer told him.

'And?'

She hesitated. 'In some cases, the dying appear to have been brought back.'

He knew the rest without her having to say it. 'But not the Abbess.'

'No. Dear Sir Josse, no.'

'Should I have another try?'

Knowing how he loathed the Eye and everything to do with it, Sister Euphemia realised what the offer must have cost him. 'I fear it would not help, for she is beyond swallowing any of the water.'

His eyes wild, he tore at his hair and then shouted, '*What*, then? Do we just let her die?'

And Sister Euphemia said, very quietly, 'I have just sent for Father Gilbert again.'

★

Much later that night, when in almost every place except for Hawkenlye Abbey all activity had ceased for the night and the world was deeply asleep, a dark shape crept from its lair out on the marshy land beside the river and made a quiet, unseen way into the town.

He had felt sick earlier and the headache had developed until the very daylight had been like a flaming, searing torch held up to his eyes. He had slept on the rotten straw-filled mattress that he found in the corner of the hovel, wrapping himself in his thick cloak and pulling the filthy sacking up to his neck when the shivering began. He had slept and, on waking, felt a little better. He found kindling and firewood and got a small, hot blaze going in the hearth in its circle of stones. Then he had prepared a hot drink and made himself eat – sparingly – from his dwindling supplies. The drink had, he reflected, probably done him more good than the food, for he carried a variety of remedies in his pack and this one had been sold to him by a stallholder in Paris who swore it would ease the worst headache and stop an incipient fever dead in his tracks.

Perhaps – the man gave a brief, grim smile – the stallholder had not after all used the word *dead*.

But the drug was strong – he thought he detected the bitterness of opium – and his depression of earlier in the day quickly gave way to an uplifting sense of elation.

Now, setting out on the faint track that led back along the river to Tonbridge, the man felt new energy coursing through him, a firm new resolve to finish the job and get out. He had packed up his belongings and fastened his pack behind his horse's saddle, then worked hard for a short time to ensure that he had left no sign of his brief occupation of the hovel for others to find and question. He would leave his horse hidden nearby, he thought, slip into the house, do what he must do and then, before anybody had realised what had happened, be on his way south to the coast and home.

Where was home? He asked himself the question as he trudged along, waiting until the path was more clearly defined before he mounted; it would be folly to risk his horse putting a foot into some hidden hole in the rough ground and pulling up lame. Home . . .

He had been born in a small town in Normandy, the product of a liaison between the daughter of a tanner and a man who had been a soldier under old Geoffrey Plantagenet, Henry II's father, but who had lost his right hand and, no more use as a fighting man, spent the remainder of his life haunting inns, taverns, tap rooms . . . anywhere, in fact, where someone would sell – even better, buy – him a drink. He had the patter down to a fine art and the hideous stump that was the end of his right arm evoked sympathy and revulsion in equal parts; people often stood him a mug of small beer or of thin, sharp wine purely to make him cover it up again.

This unlikely couple remained together for the duration of the woman's pregnancy and for a further five or six years, when the foul odours of the tannery finally got the better of the one-handed soldier and he took off in the middle of the night, never to be seen in his home town again.

Surprisingly, he took his little son with him. The boy – he had been christened Gilles – had shown a precocious intelligence and a talent for mimicry and it was quite possible that the father saw the lad as a likely source of income. A spot of entertainment, a clever little trick that amused men halfway to drunkenness and made them laugh, and the *sous* would roll in.

Gilles soon found out how to talk himself out of trouble; in his father's habitual haunts, not every broken man wanted female company for the fumble in the straw after the lamps were extinguished, and young Gilles grew up handsome of face and slim of body. As he entered adolescence he added fighting skills to his repertoire. He killed his first victim at the

age of fourteen, a man unwise enough to corner him and hold
a knife to his throat until he gave up his purse. Gilles had got
his own knife unsheathed and into the man's heart before the
assailant had even finished his hoarsely whispered demands.

His father died when he was fifteen. Not that the demise of
his parent made much difference to Gilles, for by then his
father had sunk deep into alcoholism and barely recognised his
son except when, as he often did, he tried to touch him for
money. Gilles was already planning his own future and without the burden of his father – it was strange but, for all the old
man's faults, Gilles had loved him in a way and had never
managed to persuade himself to abandon him – he was now
free to pursue the path he had set. He knew of a certain local
lord who, engaged in a quarrel with a neighbour, was in need
of mercenary soldiers to support his cause. The lord laughed
at Gilles when he presented himself as a potential fighting
man, for he was still slightly built and had the face of an angel.
But the graceful young body was strong as steel: Gilles,
undeterred, drew his sword and showed the lord what he
could do with it. He was engaged on the spot.

But Gilles did not intend to be a rank-and-file soldier all his
life. The local lord was but the first step on the ladder that
would win for Gilles the life he wanted and he used his position
in that household ruthlessly, advancing his own cause to
anyone with the slightest influence in higher circles who
was prepared to listen to him. Within a year he was working
for a minor duke; within five he had been engaged by a
particularly aggressive bishop who needed the discreet removal of a persistent but prominent troublemaker. That
murder was the first of the efficient and totally clandestine
killings which were to become the trademark – although a bare
handful of people knew it – of Gilles de Vaudreuil.

The rumour of an efficient and highly professional killer
spread quietly and steadily through the ranks of Norman,

Angevin and Plantagenet aristocratic circles; it was quite amazing, Gilles often thought, just how many rich, ruthless and influential men with their eyes firmly set on some personal goal required the disappearance of somebody else in order to achieve their ambition. As Gilles's experience grew, so did the fee that he demanded; such was his reputation that they always paid him what he asked. By the time he was thirty he had lodged a small fortune safely away with the Knights Templar; their discretion was as assured as his own and he knew his money was safe. One day, he told himself, one day when I grow tired of killing, I shall return to that pretty little river deep in the hills of Normandy, buy myself a modest manor and some land and live a life of ease and comfort until I die.

This present mission had come as no great surprise. When his current paymaster had sent for him, Gilles had guessed that the target victim must be one of two men, both of whom stood between this master and where he wanted to go. One target Gilles dismissed as unlikely; the man was just too famous, especially now, and the attention currently surrounding him and his entourage and following every move that he made would make it very difficult, although not out of the question, to kill him. But when Gilles's new master asked him if he thought it possible to kill the other person, who in fact turned out to be the intended victim, Gilles had already begun to consider ways and means. 'Oh, yes, Sire,' he had calmly replied. 'It is not only possible but achievable.'

He had been hired – for a huge fee – and then he had disappeared. He had made his way to the abode of his victim, paid for one or two pieces of information, then sat patiently and simply used his eyes for a few days until he had completed his observations and his arrangements were in place. Then he had climbed a wall erroneously believed to be unscalable, crossed a stable yard as silently as a shadow and been on the very point of slipping through a doorway to the private, secret passage that led to the heart of his victim's quarters when the unthinkable had happened. Someone had caught up with him and, barely able to speak for the pressure of Gilles's hand at his throat, forced out the message that the mission was off.

In the terrible rush of emotions that surged through him as the adrenalin ebbed away, one thing annoyed Gilles perhaps even more than his master's last-minute cancellation of the job: the fact that the messenger had been able to pick up his trail and follow him right to the very door of the secret passage. When the two men were once more outside the castle walls – Gilles had been required to half-carry the messenger, who had sprained his ankle in getting over the wall – Gilles had demanded how the young man had achieved it. The fellow had said with a shy grin that, unable to find Gilles, he had instead hidden away to watch the one place where he reckoned Gilles could achieve access to the victim.

The fact that another man seemed to possess his own abilities, which he had hitherto regarded as unique, shook Gilles de Vaudreuil to the core.

And this unwelcome realisation was, although he had not yet fully admitted it to himself, the prime reason why his thoughts were suddenly turning more and more to that dream house in Normandy.

He had reached the town. Dismounting, he led his horse along the road that led to the sheriff's house. The secret was out that the girl and the old man were now lodged there; Gilles had observed the sheriff fetch the old man from the tavern and, even had he missed that, the talk in the tap room had been of the pretty young 'un and the old granddaddy under protection at Sheriff's house.

He took to the rough ground on the left as he passed the last of the town's dilapidated and stinking dwellings. He walked on for a quarter of a mile or so, and the sheriff's house loomed up as a dark bulk on his right, on the other side of the track. He walked on, wraith-quiet; he had bound the metal parts of his horse's bridle and stirrups so that the horse too moved all but silently. When he was some distance past the house, he tethered his horse to a tree, checked that his dagger, fine garrotte rope and short stabbing sword were in their accustomed places, and then crept back the way he had come.

He saw the four men outside the sheriff's house almost immediately. Clearly they were not used to mounting an invisible guard; two of them were actually talking to each other, albeit in whispers. Nobody could have told them, Gilles thought, that the sibilant, whispered *s* sound carried further than virtually any other on a still, cold night. He began to feel almost sorry for the sheriff if these men were the best he could find, for they were evidently bored and cold and, as Gilles watched, patiently waiting his moment, the other two moved from the side of the house and came to join the whispering pair. One of them said something, all four chuckled and then the man who had spoken drew something from under his cloak. It was a flask of some liquid – probably alcohol, which gave the temporary illusion of warmth – and Gilles observed all four men take turns at swigging from it.

They seemed in no hurry to separate and return to their own posts; two, indeed, were now leaning comfortably against the wooden posts either side of the entrance to the courtyard. Gilles simply crept round the side of the house, keeping his distance, and climbed the courtyard wall. He dropped down inside and approached the house from the side, where it was totally unguarded. Then, in the shadows of the house, he tiptoed round to the door. The guards stood in the gateway, all four of them huddled together, but now the flask was on its third round and they had forgotten all about guard duty.

The stab of pain hit him as he slipped the heavy blade of his short sword in the narrow gap between the door and the lintel, with the intention of easing up the latch that fastened it from the inside. So acute was the headache that for an instant he could think of nothing else. It passed as quickly as it had come; swiftly he returned to the task and soon the door gave before him. He opened it the merest crack, slipped inside and closed it again, although, thinking ahead to his escape, he lowered the latch only as far as was necessary to hold the door shut.

It was Gilles's misfortune that the shaft of pain had hit when it did. Had his full concentration been on the task in hand, it might have occurred to him to wonder why the heavy bolts at the top and bottom of the door had not been shot. But, on the other hand, the hall was dark – the only light was from the embers of the fire – and not every door had bolts as well as a stout latch.

Lord, but it was cold! The dying embers gave out no heat, at least, none that he could feel, and he was shivering violently, his teeth chattering. Making himself ignore the fast-growing discomfort, he crept across the floor, feeling the icy cold of the stone penetrating the rushes that covered it. His soft boots made no sound. He could make out an archway in the opposite wall and, approaching it, he saw some steps leading upwards. He climbed them, his breath steady; he was quite calm. At the top of the short stair there was a doorway and another low arch; where, Gilles wondered, was the sheriff? Orientating himself, he recalled in which direction the front of the house was; would the largest chamber be there or at the rear? Standing stone-still, ears alert for any sound, he peered into the shadows and, after a moment, realised that a pair of boots stood outside the door to his left, the one beyond the archway.

The boots were scuffed and stained with the mud of travel. They appeared to be quite large; surely too large for a woman?

Then either the sheriff or the old man – probably both – were to be found in that direction.

Killing two together was naturally more difficult than one alone, especially when that one was a woman. Making up his mind, Gilles quietly opened the door before him and slid into the room beyond.

At first he thought that there must be a fire in the room, for he was assailed with a sudden surge of heat throughout his entire body. Blackness overwhelmed his sight and he was suddenly blind; he felt as if a knife had been thrust into his forehead above his left eye. Nausea rose up from the pit of his stomach; taking a deep breath, he swallowed it down.

Get on with it!

By the moonlight coming through the high window he made out the dark shape of a bed, on it the outline of a body. He could smell a faint scent – lavender. Yes, that would be her, for she must surely use the plant so often that its fragrance must have penetrated all her garments. There was the suggestion of white on the pillow; a woman's small night cap, he thought, modestly covering her fair hair. Yes, she was a neat, clean woman; just the sort to maintain her personal standards even as she slept. On a bench under the window was spread a cloak. Hers.

Knife or garrotte? Or should he simply smother her with her pillow, as he had done the merchant in his bed in Hastings? But the merchant had been feeble with illness; she, as far as he knew, was strong, fit and healthy.

He drew the garrotte out of its place in the pouch on his belt. Running his hands along the fine rope, he felt for the toggle of wood that he used to wind the rope tight. Yes, there it was, just as it should be.

He crept closer to the bed.

The heat scored through him again as if someone had doused him in boiling water. He let out a small moan as pain swelled in his joints. Was this, a part of him wondered, what it felt like to be torn limb from limb? The black shapes spread across his eyes again and suddenly he was weak, so terribly weak; his legs gave out and he sank to his knees.

The nausea was back, undeniable now, and, trying to make as little noise as possible, he retched and a pool of foul liquid splattered on to the rushes on the floor.

The thought came to him quite unexpectedly that he was probably going to die.

I shall kill her first, he decided. Struggling up, he stepped closer to the bed. Then he thought, why should I? There is little point if I am not to be paid. *Will* he pay me, though, even yet, if I kill her and the old man, or will he say that the necessity to ensure their silence was my own fault for having allowed them to uncover the secret in the first place?

He shook his head. Sick, in agony, fever raging through him and with the urgent need to void his bowels, his brain did not seem to be working and he could no longer think it all through with his usual cold rationality.

She is young and she has a bright future, he mused. I think – yes, I think that I shall spare her.

Smiling at the pleasure that his own magnanimity was giving him, he turned and tiptoed back towards the doorway. In the bed, the body-shaped hump beneath the bedclothes did not move.

As the pestilence took him, Gilles de Vaudreuil fell down the steps.

At the bottom of which Gervase de Gifford was waiting for him.

20

Gervase de Gifford, thrilled because his trap had worked and he had the killer in his hands, at first did not take in just how sick the man was.

Summoning the four guards from the courtyard, he gave orders for his prisoner to be manacled and chained to the heavy iron ring set in the wall. The guards took the drooping form of the dark-clad stranger and dragged him away.

De Gifford went straight to the small door leading off the passage between his hall and the kitchen area. It opened on to steps down to the undercroft and was covered by a heavy woollen hanging; a wicked draught came up from the dank cellar below in all but the warmest weather. De Gifford took out a key, inserted it in the lock and turned it. He opened the stout door and called out, 'We have him. It is safe to come up now.'

Sabin and Benoît de Retz, the latter shivering inside his cloak and blanket and complaining steadily and vociferously not quite far enough under his breath, came up the short flight of steps and emerged into the passage. Sabin was holding the old man's hand, guiding his footsteps where necessary. De Gifford noticed in passing that she had a cobweb in her hair and a dark, smutty smudge on her cheek but, in his eyes, neither did anything to mar her beauty.

'Your ruse worked?' she said quietly. 'He thought the straw sack was me and—' She paused, swallowed and managed to continue, '—and he attacked?'

De Gifford frowned. 'He entered the chamber and approached the bed, yes, for I watched from the top of the stairs. But, my lady, I cannot say that he attacked the shape that he surely believed to be you, for in truth he did not.'

Benoît gave a snort of impatience. 'He must have guessed that it was not Sabin asleep in the bed!' he exclaimed.

De Gifford considered this. 'No,' he said eventually, 'I do not think that is the answer.'

'And why not?' Benoît demanded.

'Because of his demeanour,' de Gifford replied. 'Had he seen through the trick and realised that his intent had been foiled, then I should have thought he would be furious. He might have thrown back the bed covers to make sure, then possibly thrust a knife into the sack to vent his anger. I am sorry, my lady.' He had noticed Sabin's shudder of horror. Hastening on, he said, 'In fact he did not even have a close look in the bed. He simply stood staring down at the shape lying in it, then, after some time, turned and quietly stepped away. I had scarce enough time to race back down the stairs before he came out of the chamber, slid down the steps and collapsed at my feet.'

'He fell?' Benoît asked.

'I believe so,' de Gifford agreed. 'I think he must have injured himself in some way in falling for, when he felt me grab at him, instead of resisting he seemed to sink into my arms.'

'I should like to see him,' Sabin announced.

De Gifford looked at her. 'Is that wise?' he asked. 'He is a violent man and—'

'He tried to kill Grandfather and me in Troyes,' she flashed back. 'It is almost certain that he came here tonight to achieve the task in which he previously failed. Would *you* not want to look your killer in the face, given the chance?'

'My lady, I am responsible for your safety,' de Gifford insisted. 'I do not think that—'

Benoît chuckled. 'You're wasting your breath, sheriff,' he said. 'Once Sabin has made up her mind on something, she's like a terrier with a rat.'

De Gifford and Sabin stood eye to eye. Hers were steely blue and hard with resolve. 'Well, I suppose it is perfectly safe now that he is in chains,' he murmured.

Sabin smiled at him and the change in her was startling. 'Thank you,' she breathed. Then, sweeping up her long skirts, she strode off down the passage, across the hall and out into the courtyard. De Gifford quickly set off after her but a plaintive cry from Benoît – 'Oi! Just you come back and help me! I'm blind, you know!' – called him back.

By the time he and the old man reached the courtyard, the four guards were standing a few paces off, all looking slightly shamefaced, and Sabin was on her knees beside the huddled form of the prisoner.

Before de Gifford could say a word she turned, glared up at him and said, 'This man is very sick! He has a dangerously high fever and he is in agony. You must remove the shackles and take him somewhere where he can be cared for properly.'

'But—' de Gifford began.

Again, Benoît interrupted him. 'What a short memory, sheriff,' he observed. 'What was I just telling you? This man might have been set on killing us as we slept but he's sick and my granddaughter is a born healer. She will not stand aside and see someone suffer, even one such as he.'

Cursing her for her stubbornness, de Gifford thought hard. If the prisoner was truly that sick, then to throw him in gaol would likely finish him off. And, the fair-minded Gervase told himself, there is as yet no real evidence that he has committed any crime. *Somebody* tried to kill Sabin and Benoît in the Troyes lodging house – unless the fire was in fact no more than an accident, which is quite possible given the normal urban overcrowding and people's inherent carelessness with fires and torches and the like – and *somebody* killed both the Hastings merchant and Nicol Romley. This man came here tonight and I believe that his intention was to curtail the spread of this dangerous secret by silencing Sabin and her grandfather. Yet, when he had the chance to attack the body in the bed, he did not.

In short, he concluded, as yet I cannot prove that my prisoner has done anything worse than to break into my house. If that is the sum of his crimes, then I have no business signing his death warrant by refusing him healing care.

'Very well,' he said curtly. 'Prepare a cart,' he ordered, turning to the guards, 'wrap the prisoner warmly and put him on it. We'll take him up to Hawkenlye.'

'Should we chain him?' one of the guards asked.

De Gifford glanced at Sabin. Then, answering the guard, he said, 'Manacle one wrist and fasten the end of the chain to the cart.'

Sabin rewarded him with another dazzling smile.

When the small procession was ready to set out, Sabin presented herself at de Gifford's side. 'I shall fetch my mare,' she said, 'and accompany you.'

But this time – for he had guessed she would want to go up to Hawkenlye with him – he was ready with an answer.

Taking hold of her gloved hands, he looked down into her eyes and said, 'Please, lady, no. For one thing, your grandfather is chilled and miserable and surely needs your attentions. For another, we shall wait only to deliver our prisoner into the hands of those who will tend him. I will leave two of my men on guard and then I shall come straight back.' Improvising but guessing he had it right, he added, 'They do not allow anyone into the infirmary unless there is no choice so you would not be able to stay with him. And I shall leave instructions that I am to be informed the moment he is capable of talking to me. Believe me, I am almost as anxious as you to hear what account he will give of himself.'

Her eyes steady on his, she said, 'May I come with you then, when you question him?' Sorrow crossing her face, she whispered, 'I do need to know about Nicol, you see. I have to – that is, until I know what became of him, his memory keeps me from proceeding with my life.'

'I understand,' he said gently, although he was not entirely sure that he did. 'You have my word, lady. When – or perhaps if – I am able to ask the man to explain himself, I shall do my utmost to make sure you are with me.'

She bowed. 'Thank you.' Then she disengaged her hand, stepped back and walked back into the house.

It was long after midnight; the dead hours of the night that hold sway before dawn.

The Abbess had all but slipped away.

Earlier – some time late the previous evening – Father Gilbert had stood over her pleading with God to forgive her her sins and explaining that she would of course have confessed them and humbly asked for his indulgence, only she could not speak.

Now Josse sat alone on a bench outside the Vale infirmary. He had begged and begged to be allowed to see her – 'You let Father Gilbert in!' he had shouted at the infirmarer – but Sister Euphemia was adamant and would not break her rule, even for him. Especially for him, she had thought, for when the Abbess goes, we shall have need of his strength while we learn how to manage without her.

The moon had come up and the night was bright. All was quiet.

It seemed to Josse, half out of his mind with mental fatigue, physical exhaustion and grief, that he was aware of her soul hovering somewhere near. Turning his head as if trying to catch some faint essence of her through eyes or ears, it seemed to him that he felt her light touch on his shoulder.

He spun round so fast that he felt dizzy.

Sister Tiphaine stood over him. She said, 'Sir Josse, there is something that I must tell you.'

'She's dead?' He could hardly get the words out.

'No, but death is very close.' Tiphaine sat down beside him. 'You are aware of this new draught that we have been giving to the patients?'

'Aye, and you've been using the Eye of Jerusalem to prepare it. I already know, Sister, and you're welcome to the jewel. It's done *her* no good,' he added bitterly.

'No,' Tiphaine agreed, 'although you may be pleased to know that after drinking it, several others have been brought back from the brink.'

Josse supposed he should be glad for those others but, try as he might, he could not manage the charity. As if she knew this and shared his thought, Tiphaine reached out and took his hand. 'I know,' she murmured.

After a time she said, 'It was not in fact our use of the Eye that I wished to discuss with you.'

'No? What else, then?' He could not imagine – and didn't much care – but it was only polite to ask.

Tiphaine took a breath, then said, 'Sister Caliste and I have had some help this time in our use of the stone. We have been into the forest and fetched Joanna.'

Joanna.

Amid the swirling emotions of that endless night, here was yet one more.

'And precisely why are you telling me this, Sister?' His voice emerged sounding far angrier than he intended. 'Sorry,' he muttered.

She squeezed his hand. 'I am telling you because she has become a very powerful healer. I wondered what you might think if I suggested we – you and I – went to find her and asked her if she would come to see what she could do for our lady Abbess.'

At first Josse could find no words with which to reply. Then he said, 'Is she willing?'

'I have not yet put the question to her,' Tiphaine replied. Then, with a small smile: 'I thought the request might have more chance if it were you that made it.'

Josse managed an even smaller smile in response. 'Let's go,' he said, getting to his feet.

He found that, as he and Sister Tiphaine approached the forest fringes, he was holding his breath.

'Do you know where she is?' he said in a very audible whisper to the herbalist. 'Will we be able to find her hut in the darkness?'

Sister Tiphaine did not reply. Half turning, Josse saw that she had stopped a few paces behind him so that, beneath the first great oaks of the forest, he stood alone.

He seemed to know what was required. His heart hammering, he strode on.

There was a narrow clearing some dozen paces within the forest where the undergrowth was thin and where low hazel trees were interspersed with holly. As Josse stepped into it she emerged right in front of him. In the moonlight shining down on the clearing, he could see her quite plainly.

He stared at her.

She was Joanna, of course she was. But oh, how she had changed!

He stood and drank her in, from the glossy brown hair above the high forehead to the feet in their gold-clasped sandals. The wide folds of the cloak that she wore disguised her body but he had the overriding sense that she looked . . . stronger, was the only way to describe it.

Her face had a new serenity that enhanced her strange beauty. The eyes, dark under the arching brows, were fixed on his and, as he stared at her, she gave him a smile.

'Hello, Josse.'

'Joanna, you look—' He shrugged, grinning. 'I can't begin to describe it.'

'Don't worry,' she said kindly, 'I think I know what you are trying to say.'

'What's happened to you?' he burst out. 'Where have you been and what have you been doing? Tiphaine says you're a great healer now?' He could not prevent the remark turning into a question; he wondered if she knew how much hung upon her answer.

She was silent for a moment. Then she said, 'It is true that healing is my destiny and I have already put my feet upon the long path that will allow my powers to emerge.' Observing his puzzled look, she laughed softly. 'Josse, I apologise – in short, the answer is, yes, I am a healer. Of sorts.'

'You have been taught by – er – by your own people?'

'My own people,' she repeated, half under her breath. Then, again picking up that he was not following her, said, 'Yes, that's right. I have been far afield, Josse, and I have seen sights that have frightened, inspired and greatly affected me.'

He wanted more than anything to ask if she was prepared to try to help heal the Abbess, but somehow it did not seem diplomatic, on seeing a former lover for the first time in two years, to ask almost immediately if she would go with him to help another woman.

But the other woman is the Abbess, he told himself firmly. He opened his mouth to speak but Joanna got in first.

'Of course I will come, Josse,' she said.

He glanced back at Sister Tiphaine; the herbalist was no more that a vague dark shadow, some distance away. 'Has she already asked you, then?' he demanded. 'She said not, she—'

'No, Tiphaine has not spoken. I read it in your mind, dear Josse.'

'You – is *that* the sort of thing they've been teaching you?' Even to his own ears, he sounded like a shocked and prissy old woman.

Now she was laughing and, despite everything, he found himself joining in. It was impossible not to: she carried a joy in her that was irresistible. 'Anyone could pick up what pre-occupies you at the moment,' she told him, 'especially one who was aware of your deep love of the Abbess Helewise.'

'I don't—' he began. But why deny it when it was true? Saying the first thing that came into his head, he asked, 'Do you mind?'

'That you love her? Josse, why should I?' Joanna sounded genuinely puzzled.

Trying to set aside the bewildering swirl of emotions that the brief exchange had sparked off, Josse spun round, said, 'Let's be away to her, then,' and stomped off out of the forest.

He was quite sure that he heard Joanna's soft laughter behind him.

Marching along behind Josse's broad shape – Sister Tiphaine was trotting at his side – Joanna tried to overcome her surprise at what the reunion with him had done to her. Ever since she had realised that the meeting was inevitable – Tiphaine had told her that the Abbess was dying and she had known Josse would come, sooner or later – she had been dreading it.

Now, most of her mind already thinking ahead and seeking out the Abbess's spirit in order to try to call her back, Joanna reflected briefly that, while she had known she still loved him, she had never expected the surge of sheer happiness that his appearance in the clearing had given her.

But it was no time to think of herself or of him; she had a job to do and she knew it was going to be a tough one. Sending out a fleeting thought to Meggie – the child had been taken home to the hut by Lora, who would look after her until Joanna returned, whenever that might be – she turned her thoughts to what lay ahead.

They must have realised that she worked alone. The large nun with the kind eyes showed her to the recess at the end of the ward and then, with the curtain pulled behind her, it was just the Abbess and Joanna.

Joanna studied the statue-still figure lying on the narrow cot, taking in the visual signs. The prospect of bringing this woman back from where she now was seemed all but impossible; the Abbess was burning hot, deadly pale and the infrequent, shallow little breaths barely lifted the chest beneath the white sheet.

Joanna stood quite still and closed her eyes. She concentrated on her breathing, turning her full attention to each deep intake and outlet of air. She felt them come to her almost instantly, as if they knew her need and were just waiting for the chance to join her.

You are a channel, they had told her. *You do not heal; healing is bestowed through you. It is we who heal.* Who are *we?* she had asked. *We are the collective spirit of the people. We are the consciousness that was ancient even when the first stones were set up; the consciousness that awoke and greeted the first day. We are always here for those who seek us with the right mind; you have but to learn what that mind is and how to achieve it.*

Joanna had spent a year doing just that. She was a rank beginner, she well knew it; a green sapling among mature, majestic oaks, birch and beech. She had undergone the exacting, alarming and sometimes downright painful initiations; she had experienced her first spirit journey. She had the supreme soul friend in the Domina and this was, Joanna was well aware, an important factor in having achieved the progress she had managed.

Now, standing in the recess where the Abbess lay dying, Joanna drew on all that she had been taught and sent out a silent cry to the spirits clustering around her to help her find the swiftly receding soul and try to bring it back.

She did not know how long she stood there; time as a phenomenon of the earth ceased once she had entered the trance state and walked with the spirits. Presently she saw that she was in a little hollow beside a stream; it was a lovely place, bright and shining with spring greenery and with the scent of growing things on the soft air. Helewise sat before her on a narrow strip of sandy shore that formed a beach by fast-rushing, shallow water.

Joanna sat down beside her.

'Helewise,' she said after a while, 'you are on the brink of passing from this world on to another.'

'Yes.' Helewise sounded dazed. 'I guessed that might be the case.'

'Are you sure that you truly wish to go?' Joanna kept her voice low, hypnotic; nothing in that dream-like place was loud or discordant.

Helewise considered. 'I thought I saw Ivo waiting for me,' she murmured. 'This is where he and I first met. Where, not very long afterwards, my first son was conceived.' She laughed, a sound of such happy remembered joy that it touched Joanna's heart.

'Will you go on to him now?' she asked.

Helewise hesitated. 'I – a part of me is so tired and in such distress that I long to lie in his arms again and find my comfort in him, as once I did.'

'But?' Joanna prompted. She knew there was a but; there usually was.

'But I feel that my road in this earth—' She stopped, turning puzzled eyes to Joanna. '*Are* we still within this earth?'

Joanna smiled. 'Our bodies certainly are. As for our spirits . . .' She shrugged.

Helewise appeared to accept that. 'My road on earth goes on,' she said simply. 'I can see it sometimes if I try *not* to look, if you see what I mean.'

'I do,' Joanna assured her. 'What is on your road? Can you see?'

Helewise broke into a lovely smile. 'Oh, very many things! My son and his wife are there . . . my grandson Timus . . . Oh! And a baby girl too and she's called Little Helewise! Isn't that delightful? And . . . yes, there's my younger son and his skin is so deeply tanned – whatever has he been doing? There is a look about him that I . . . And there's— *Oh!*' The last vision, whatever it was, affected her very much.

'What is it?'

But Helewise turned to her, still with that happy smile, and said, 'I will not tell you, if you don't mind.'

Joanna could have been mistaken but she thought there was a slight emphasis on *you*; as if Helewise were saying, anyone else I might tell, but not you.

'What is your decision?' Joanna asked. 'Will you go on or will you let me help you return?'

For a long time Helewise did not speak. She sat there smiling, face turned up to the sun so that brightness shone on her, *from* her; as if some wonderful, blessed light beamed down and she felt its power and its benevolence.

Eventually she said simply, 'I would like to go back, please.'

Joanna swayed on her feet as the healing force of her people surged through her and out through her hands, extended over the Abbess, and into the dying body. The power came in waves; one at the start was so strong that she felt as if a great jolt had flowed through her, jerking her like a puppet dancing on its strings.

She heard them; sometimes she thought she could see them. They chanted – quietly, hypnotically, continuously – and they wore white. In their hands they held rods tipped with quartz that looked very like her own. But the mighty strength that came pulsing out from them was as far removed from anything she had yet achieved as a puddle is from an ocean.

Humbly, more aware than ever in her life of her smallness and her unimportance, Joanna stood and let them use her until they were done.

Much later – or was it only a matter of moments? – Joanna opened her eyes. Something had woken her; listening, she heard quiet sounds from the ward beyond the curtain – booted feet on the floor; the sound of a cot being dragged across the stone; hushed voices – and she wondered absently whether yet another victim had just been brought in.

She was bone weary, so exhausted that she could barely stand. The agonising headache that followed trance work was just beginning; like the distant sound of a hammer on an anvil, the thumping pain was faint as yet, although it carried within it the full menace of what it would soon become.

Instantly aware of her patient, she fell to her knees beside the still, pale figure in the bed, reaching out her hand to touch the one that lay like a marble sculpture on the bedcovers.

The Abbess was breathing deeply. She was relaxed and her fever had gone down.

Joanna felt a painfully dry sob break from her. Pressing her face into the bed, she suppressed it. Then, looking up at the Abbess's face, she whispered, 'I think you chose right, Helewise. Welcome back.'

Then she got to her feet and, trying to straighten her back and walk like the woman of her people that she was, she pushed the curtain aside and walked out into the ward. The big nun stepped forward, her terrible anxiety evident in the very way she stood, straining forward, and the pain in her eyes shot out to Joanna as if she had loosed an arrow into her heart.

'She is a little better,' Joanna whispered. The pounding in her head was growing to a cacophony of agony. Gasping as she tried to control it, she reached into her leather satchel and extracted a small flask. It contained water in which Meggie had held the Eye; the jewel had had a longer contact with this particular water and Joanna hoped that it was correspondingly more potent. 'Give her some of this as soon as she is able to swallow,' she told the big nun. 'I think – I am sure – it will help.'

The nun was watching her with the professional eyes of another healer and Joanna knew she could read the pain. 'You poor soul,' the nun said gently. 'Would you like to lie down awhile, dear? You look exhausted.'

Joanna managed a smile. 'No, I would rather return to my own place.'

'Want me to find someone to go with you and see you safely home?'

It was a kind offer but one that Joanna knew she must instantly reject, for the most likely candidate for the task was Josse and she really could not cope with Josse right now. 'I shall be perfectly all right alone. Thank you,' she added.

The nun caught her sleeve. 'Will you come back and see how she does?'

Joanna tried to think what it would mean if she said yes but the pain and the deadly fatigue were interfering with her mind. She said yes anyway.

The big nun still had not finished with her. 'There's another patient just been brought in,' she said quietly, nodding to a cot quite close to the curtained recess where the Abbess lay. 'He's near death and—'

'I'm very sorry but I can't do any more now,' Joanna whispered.

'I was not going to ask you to!' the nun said. 'Dear child, you've done more than enough already.' Dear child. The sweet words touched Joanna's heart. 'I was just going to ask,' the nun was saying, 'whether we could spare him some drops of this.' She held up the flask that Joanna had just given her.

'Of course. Give it to him with my blessing.' Even to herself, Joanna's voice was sounding distant. If I remain here any longer, she thought, I'll lose my last chance of getting back to the hut before I collapse.

With what she hoped was a dignified bow to the nun, she straightened her back, lifted her chin, strode out of the long ward and set off on the path that would take her home.

21

Josse watched Joanna climb the path that led up to the Abbey. Her dark figure moved fast as, leaving the track, she strode off around the outside of the Abbey walls and disappeared from sight. Following her in his mind's eye, he saw her hurry across the open ground and, finally reaching the safety of the trees, melt into the shadows of the Great Forest.

He was not sure whether or not she had noticed him standing there outside the Vale infirmary door as she hurried past. She had been staring straight in front of her, eyes narrowed as if fixed on some difficult goal that she might or might not achieve. He had so much wanted to reach out to her but there had been something about her – almost as if she wore invisible armour – that had stopped him.

So he had let her go.

Firmly putting her out of his mind, he turned and stepped inside the ward. Sister Euphemia was already hurrying towards him; she held a small flask in her hand and she was smiling.

'You already know, don't you?' she said softly, taking him by the arm and leading him back outside again, where they sat down side by side on his bench.

Josse smiled. 'Aye. I felt – oh, I don't know.' He scratched his head vigorously as if it might stir up his brains. 'I had all but given up and then suddenly I had this picture of her with light on her face and she looked so happy, so beautiful—' He broke off, not sure if he trusted his voice enough to continue.

'Our prayers have been answered,' Sister Euphemia said. 'Her fever's come down and she's asleep. She's still very ill,' she added warningly, 'and we shall have to take very good care of her.'

Josse looked at her anxiously. 'But she won't – she's not going to die?'

'No, Josse,' Euphemia said gently. 'I don't think she is.'

Soon afterwards she stood up and announced she must be getting back to her patients. With the awful fear gone, Josse realised how tired he was; yawning, he stumbled away to his corner in the monks' shelter, threw himself down fully dressed, huddled into his blankets and was soon soundly and dreamlessly asleep.

They did what they could for the man in the bed next to the Abbess's recess. They washed him, bathed his hot face and tried to make him take some sips of the special water from Joanna's flask. Sister Emanuel, who had the task of removing and folding his garments, found a small, wrapped parcel of some herbal mixture in the purse on his belt; Sister Euphemia thought it contained opium and, since the parcel only appeared to contain a small portion of what it had once held, they deduced that he had been dosing himself with it and decided that it could surely do no harm to give him the remainder. He was very close to death; anything was worth a try.

By morning, he had regained consciousness. Of a sort: the drug must have been strong, for he seemed to be in some waking dream that was indistinguishable from reality. But the spell of lucidity did not last long and presently he slipped back into a coma.

Two days later, the infirmarer, Sister Tiphaine and Sister Caliste got their heads together for a brief discussion. There had been a total of forty-six cases of the foreign pestilence at

Hawkenlye, out of which twenty-nine had died not counting poor murdered Nicol – and sixteen had recovered. Within the Hawkenlye community, they had lost dear Sister Beata, the young monk called Roger and the quiet little novice; another nun who worked in the laundry had become ill but recovered. A dozen recovering patients still lay weak and querulous in the Vale infirmary, where there was also the Abbess Helewise, slightly stronger now, and the man brought in on the night she almost died. He alone was still giving grave cause for concern for his fever remained high and he only emerged from his deep coma on rare and very brief occasions. Whenever he did so he was given water from Joanna's flask.

Since the night of his arrival, there had been no new cases of the sickness. The nuns hardly dared think it, let alone say it, but each was just starting to hope that the disease might just have run its course.

Inside the ward, Brother Firmin – who had recovered sufficiently to get up for an hour or so each day – went to sit by the unknown man's bed. Waiting patiently until the man opened his eyes, he said, in the manner of one speaking to the deaf, 'DO – YOU – KNOW – WHERE – YOU – ARE?'

The man gave a wry smile. 'Not in heaven,' he muttered.

Brother Firmin was faintly shocked. 'Oh, dear, no!' he said, wondering if he had just heard a blasphemy. Deciding that, if he had, then it was forgivable under the circumstances, he said, 'You are at Hawkenlye Abbey, in the temporary infirmary that we have set up down in our Vale, where the holy water spring is situated, and our nursing nuns are doing their utmost to help you get better.'

Before he had finished his little speech, the man had closed his eyes and wearily turned away. Firmin put out a tentative hand. 'Are you in pain, friend?' he asked. 'Is there anything that I can do for you?'

The man opened his eyes again. 'I am dying,' he said baldly.

'Oh, you must not say that!' Firmin told him. 'There is always hope, and God is merciful.'

The man's eyes fixed on to Firmin's in a stare so intense and blank that Firmin shrank back. 'Is he?' the man demanded. 'Is there mercy even for one such as me?'

'There is mercy for everyone,' Firmin assured him. Then, made nervous by what he read in the man's eyes, 'Would you like me to send for a priest?'

After a long pause, the man nodded. Then, as Brother Firmin made to call out to one of the nuns to fetch Father Gilbert, he caught the old monk's sleeve. With an attempt at a smile, he said, 'Better find one with time on his hands, Brother, for I have much to confess.'

The infirmarer had decided that she could no longer put up with Josse's constant demands to be allowed in to see the Abbess. Almost sure now that the danger of infection was past, she put her head out through the doorway of the Vale ward, saw him in his usual place on the bench and told him he could come in. She did add, 'But you can only stay with her for a few moments'; however, he had already leapt to his feet and rushed in past her and she was quite sure he could not have heard.

Josse made himself walk slowly down the long ward. For over a week he had been imagining what was going on here and now he could see the aftermath with his own eyes. The floor was still damp from the latest scrubbing – Sister Euphemia's nursing nuns had to be very thorough about scrubbing – but nevertheless, behind the aroma of lavender there was a lurking sickroom stench. Certain dark stains that refused to yield to the hot water and the brisk brush bore witness to where patients had uncontrollably voided liquids from the orifices of their weak, feverish bodies. Unoccupied cots had been stacked in a corner, stripped bare of their palliasses and of the covers. The remaining handful of patients were grouped around the middle of one side of the ward. One or two managed to give Josse a friendly smile as he passed by. All of them looked pale and frighteningly fragile.

He passed the mystery man, who lay asleep; Josse was aware that Gervase de Gifford was waiting to question him and had undertaken the duty of informing the sheriff when the man was up to it. Trying to summon up righteous indignation – the man had probably killed Nicol and the Hastings merchant! – Josse's resolve was undermined by pity.

He had a fair idea of what to expect when at last he twitched aside the curtains around the Abbess's bed and stared down at her.

She was propped up on pillows and clad in a spotless white gown fastened chastely around the neck. Its sleeves extended to the wrist and her hands, emerging out of the smooth linen, lay folded upon the bedcovers. Her head was bare but for a simple white cap, beneath which he could see her reddish hair in short, soft curls. Her face was pale and her skin had a dryish look, as if any extreme expression might crack it clean open. Her eyes looked huge and were circled with dark rings.

On seeing him, she risked everything and gave him a wide smile. 'Dear Sir Josse,' she said, and he noticed that her voice was weak and shaky, 'how good it is to see you.'

He knelt on the floor beside her bed. 'My lady Abbess, I feared that this moment would never come.'

'But it has,' she answered. He felt her hand on his head – such a tiny, feeble touch! – and, raising his face, he looked up at her.

'She came for me,' the Abbess whispered. 'I was on my way and she appeared at my side and asked me if I was sure I was ready to go. I saw – oh, I saw many things.' She was studying him intently, something that he could not identify burning in the grey eyes. She was silent for a moment, then said, 'What I saw ahead was so beautiful, Josse, that I could easily have slipped away and I am quite sure that I would have been happy. But I know now that it is not yet my time to go.' Her smile was back. 'So I came back.'

He did not know what to say; either he must find the words to say all that was in his heart or else only the briefest response would do. Faced with the yawningly huge task of the former, he settled for the latter. He said gruffly, 'I'm glad.'

And he heard a sound he had thought never to hear again: she began to laugh.

All too soon the curtain twitched back and Sister Euphemia appeared. 'It's very good to hear you laugh, my lady, but that's enough for now. Sir Josse!' She gave him a stern look.

He raised the Abbess's hand to his lips to give it a swift kiss and then, getting up, winked at her and followed the infirmarer out of the recess, letting the curtain fall behind him. Sister Euphemia, having assured herself that he had obeyed her and left the Abbess to rest, gave a nod and then hurried away up the ward to attend to a patient calling for water.

Josse walked slowly after her. He glanced again at the stranger as he passed and noticed that the man was twisting from side to side in the bed, one hand reaching out as if in supplication. Going over to him, Josse said quietly, 'What ails you?'

The wavering hand appeared to have purpose in it; looking in the direction in which it pointed, Josse saw a jar on the floor. 'Is this what you want?' he asked, picking it up and holding it where the man could see it.

'Yes!'

Josse was unaccustomed to nursing but he had on occasion been nursed by others. Folding back the bedclothes, he raised the man's gown, pushed the jar down between his thighs and helped him position himself so that the meagre stream of urine went in the right place. The small effort brought the man out in a sweat and Josse felt the fever burning in his skin; removing the jar, he helped him to settle back again and pulled the covers over him. He carried the jar outside, took it over to the privy and emptied it, then rinsed it and took it back to the man's bedside.

The man's eyes were open and he was studying Josse.

'I never thought,' he said, 'to have my piss pot emptied by a knight. I thank you, whoever you are.'

'Josse d'Acquin,' Josse replied.

'Acquin.'

'You have heard of it?'

'No. Is it in France?'

'Aye.'

'Yet here you are in an abbey in England.'

'My family lands are at Acquin. My own manor is here.'

'You hold your land from the King?'

'Aye.'

'You are a King's man?'

'Aye.' Josse wondered if it was right to go on answering the abrupt questions; might it not be better for the man to rest? But then he seemed agitated, as if he were working up to something important.

The man was watching him closely. 'A King's man,' he repeated softly. 'The King that is or the King that shall be, I wonder?'

'King Richard!' Josse exclaimed angrily. 'Beware of treason, sir, to speak of a future king while the present one yet lives and reigns!'

The man waved his hand as if treason held no fears for him. Then, looking down the ward, he said, 'They have promised to find a priest for me, Sir Josse, for I have much that I wish to confess before God and I stand face to face. There is no sign of the man as yet, so may I ask a favour of you?'

Feeling that he could hardly refuse, Josse said, 'Aye.'

The man's face twitched into a brief smile. Then he said, 'Hear my tale, sir knight, and tell me, if you will, what you think this priest will say to me, for I would know for how long I must do penance for my many sins.'

It was a strange thing to say. Intrigued, Josse said, 'Tell me the tale, then, for I have no pressing duty.'

'Very well.' The man shut his eyes tightly for a moment, his lips moved, perhaps in prayer, then without any warning preamble he said, 'I have killed many men. Some I slew in battle, engaged as I was in the squabbles of lordlings and counts. But I have also killed thirty-two men and two women in the role of hired assassin. I am good at my job, Sir Josse; they used to say that I was the best.' A puzzled frown creased his white face. 'I could not kill her, though. I stared down at the bed and I thought, what is the point? If she has revealed the secret, then I am too late; if not, then why should she not live? I am tired; I have had enough of death and there is too much blood on my hands.'

There was a silence.

Stunned, Josse brought to mind the matter that had been obsessing him before the Abbess fell ill and everything else was obliterated. He knew how this man had come to be arrested; had been told by Gervase de Gifford of the trap set and sprung, of the sick man extracted from it and brought up to Hawkenlye. 'You broke into Gervase de Gifford's house with the intention of murdering Sabin de Retz and her grandfather,' he said sternly. 'Before that you killed Martin Kelsey in his sickbed in Hastings and you struck down Nicol Romley here in the Vale.'

'Those deeds I admit,' the man said. 'But I was not going to kill Sabin; I just told you that.'

'You say you are a paid assassin,' Josse pressed on, 'and we have surmised that you came to England on a killing mission.'

The man smiled wryly at that but did not speak. 'I would say that Sabin learned who it was that you were going after and, becoming friendly with Nicol Romley when the two met at the market in Troyes, she confided in him what she knew. You learned that your secret was out and you tried to kill Sabin by firing the lodging house. Then you set out after Nicol to stop his mouth too, but by the time you caught up with him he was already travelling with Martin Kelsey who, for all you knew, had now also been told the identity of the man you were setting out to kill.' A new thought occurred to Josse and, excited, he leaned forward and said, 'You had to kill all of them in case they warned your intended victim! That's it, isn't it?'

'I am sorry,' the man said courteously, 'but I must correct you on one or two points. First, I was not coming to England to fulfil my mission; the victim, as you call him, is not in this land. So, although I hate to dampen your ardour, I must tell you that it was not to prevent them issuing a warning that I killed the apprentice lad and the merchant. It was, as you earlier suggested, with the intention of keeping the matter secret.'

'*What* matter?' Josse almost wailed the question.

The man smiled; he seemed to be enjoying the game. 'See if you can guess, Sir Josse. Think of what you have already worked out.'

With an effort, Josse thought back to the evening three days ago – only three days! God's boots, but it felt like a lifetime – when he had hurried back to Hawkenlye to tell the Abbess his thoughts on Sabin and Benoît de Retz. Recalling his impressions, he said, 'I was summoned by Gervase de Gifford to speak with Sabin. I was aware that she was careful to give little away but I noticed a few interesting things. One, when I spoke to her in French she said it was not her native tongue. I listened carefully after that and it occurred to me that she is a Breton.' If he had expected confirmation from the man, it was not forthcoming. 'Then I noticed a faint scent on her which I recognised, for I have smelt it on others who habitually work with herbs. Added to the fact that she spoke of visiting the fair at Troyes for purchases needed in her work, I guessed that she is an apothecary, for I know that Troyes market is an excellent source for the rare and the exotic. Later in our conversation she said that she had to buy particular ingredients in order to treat her employer. Here again, I made a guess, and this time it was indeed an outrageous one.'

'What was it?' The man sounded amused, indulgent.

'I am probably wide of the mark.'

'Never mind! Let me hear your outrageous guess.'

Josse went over the small clues that had seemed to point in the same single direction. 'I would say that Sabin and her grandfather are the private apothecaries of some rich man, for she at least, whom I have seen, I know to dress in plain but costly garments of fine quality. In addition, she rides a good mare. She has, or perhaps I should say they have, rare skills that have earned them their employer's respect and indulgence, for he was willing to have them ride off to Troyes to fetch whatever it was they claimed to require. I would further surmise' – here he was on shakier ground, for he was basing this guess on the flimsy foundation of a piece of gossip picked up some months ago when on the fringes of court circles – 'that the master who pays so much to have Sabin and her grandfather's discreet and expert care suffers from a disease of which he is ashamed. I was told,' he lowered his voice to a whisper, 'that Philip of France has syphilis and my guess is that Sabin and her grandfather have the care of him.'

To his dismay, the man burst out laughing. After a moment, he controlled himself. 'I am sorry, Sir Josse, for my laughter. You reason so well, right up to the last, and my amusement was simply because, in the matter of the French king, I fear you have been listening to barrack-room gossip. He is, I am sure, as free of the shameful disease that you ascribe to him as the good infirmarer over there.'

'Oh.'

'But in all other respects, I believe I underestimated you,' the man said. 'Sabin and her grandfather are indeed Bretons and they practise the profession of apothecary, as you say, in the employ of a wealthy and important patron. My mission was to kill a member of this patron's household and I was on the point of making my strike when my master called me off. By an ill stroke, Benoît heard the exchange between my master's messenger and myself; the old man may be blind, Sir Josse, but he has keen ears and misses little. He must have overheard the identity of the person I had been sent to kill and it would not take a genius to work out from that the man it was who had sent me and who wanted the victim dead, and why they wanted it. Benoît had therefore to be stopped, for if the secret were to get out, then my master would have had me killed instead; be in no doubt of that. But before I could apprehend the old man, he and his daughter disappeared, and it was some time before I knew where they had gone. I tried and failed to kill them in Troyes, by which time they had also revealed the secret to Nicol Romley, who, or so I feared, passed it on to Martin Kelsey. Two of the potential leaks have been stopped for good; two now remain.'

'Yet when you thought Sabin lay defenceless before you, you stayed your hand.'

'Yes.' The man sighed. 'As I said, I have had enough.'

'Will you not tell me the secret?' Josse said after a moment.

The man stared at him for some time. Then he said, 'No. I do not think I will.'

He closed his eyes. The exertion of the conversation had brought him out in a sweat, and his deadly white face was beaded over the forehead and across the upper lip. Two hot spots of red burned in his cheeks.

'Will you take a drink?' Josse asked softly.

The man's eyes opened. 'No,' he said with a smile, 'for it has already done its work for me. To take any more will possibly bring about the wrong outcome.'

Josse was about to ask him what he meant – although in truth he had a fairly good idea already – but the man had turned his face away.

Later that morning, Father Gilbert arrived and, so they said, sat with the stranger for a long time. Not long after he left, the man slipped into a deep coma from which he was not to emerge.

PART FIVE
Victory

22

In the morning Josse rode down to Tonbridge to Gervase de Gifford's house to tell him that his prisoner was dead. He also explained that, the previous day, the man had told Josse that he was a hired killer; also that Sabin and Benoît de Retz had somehow learned the identity of his prominent victim, that he had killed both Nicol Romley and Martin Kelsey and that he had tried to murder Sabin and her grandfather, all in the interests of keeping the secret safe.

It seemed to Josse, however, watching the younger man's reaction, that he was almost glad of the news; deciding that he knew de Gifford well enough by now to query this, he did so.

De Gifford ran a hand across his smooth hair and for a moment his suave manner deserted him and he looked almost bashful.

'The lady – Sabin de Retz – will, I think, be relieved that the man is not to come to trial and hang,' he said. 'I saw her with my prisoner, Josse, and her pity for his abject state overrode her hunger for revenge.'

'But he killed her young man and tried to burn her and her old grandfather alive as they slept!' Josse protested.

'Nicol Romley was not her young man,' de Gifford said rather too promptly. 'She said he – er – that is, I am given to understand it was just a fleeting attraction.'

Appreciating which way that particular wind blew, Josse forbore to remark that this fleeting attraction had been strong enough to make Sabin travel all the way to England with her blind and elderly grandfather in tow in order to warn Nicol that he was in danger. 'I see,' he said instead.

'She will be relieved that the matter is over,' de Gifford was saying. 'Now she'll be able to put the sad episode behind her and she'll – that is, she can return to her normal life.'

'Aye,' Josse agreed absently. He was thinking. Then he said, 'Gervase, what is her normal life? Now that this man who threatened to kill her to keep her silent is dead, is there any chance that she will tell us what all this has been about?'

De Gifford regarded him for some moments. Then he said, 'I will invite her to come down – she is in the upper chamber with the old man. Let's ask her.'

When de Gifford escorted Sabin and the old grandfather into his hall, Josse guessed by the young woman's face that de Gifford had already told her the most important piece of news. Her face had lost the look of strain and she looked arrestingly handsome. She met Josse's eyes, gave him a quick smile and then busied herself helping her grandfather to sit down on a bench close to the hearth. Moving over to help her – the old man wanted the heavy bench moved closer to the welcome blaze – Josse said quietly in her ear, 'Ever the healer, lady, thinking of the welfare and comfort of others.'

'How did you know?' she hissed.

'I guessed that you are an apothecary; yesterday I had it confirmed.'

Straightening up, she said, with a touch of haughtiness, 'It may be an unusual profession for a woman, but nevertheless I am proud of what I do.'

'With justification, my lady.'

She stared at him as if searching his face for sincerity. Apparently finding it, she smiled. 'Thank you.'

De Gifford invited her to sit down beside her grandfather. Then he said, 'Sabin, now that the man who wanted you dead is no more a threat to you, will you tell us exactly why he wanted to kill you? We know it was to ensure that a secret was kept; could you, do you think, enlighten us as to what that secret was?'

She looked at de Gifford, briefly at Josse, then had a short, muttered conversation with her grandfather. 'I do not know that I can,' she said eventually, 'for it is a secret about which, did you know what it concerned, both of you would, I am certain, urge the utmost discretion.'

Josse spoke up. 'My lady, I have surmised from what little I already know that this business into which you have stumbled involves some very well-known, important and influential people, although I am not aware of their identities. Would it reassure you if I were to tell you that I am reasonably well accustomed to such circles and that, if you could see your way to unburdening yourself, you would have my solemn oath that what you tell me will go no further?'

She met his eyes and he read in hers a great need to reveal the story. Looking across to de Gifford, she said, 'Would you undertake that, if I do tell you, you too will not mention a syllable of it beyond these four walls?'

'I will, my lady,' de Gifford said. 'On that I give you my word.'

She turned back to her grandfather; he seemed to be encouraging her to go ahead. Finally, after a brief closing of her eyes – perhaps, Josse thought, she was praying – she began.

'Very well. I do in truth feel that I shall die if I don't tell you!' She managed a brief laugh that did little to ease her evident tension. 'Grandfather is a renowned apothecary and I am his apprentice.'

'An apprentice who does the majority of the work nowadays,' the old man put in, reaching for and patting her hand.

Sabin smiled. 'I do not mind. I love what I do and I am

proud to carry on the work of the de Retz clan. We live in Nantes,' she went on, 'where, over the years, Grandfather's renown has earned him quite a long list of wealthy clients who know he is the very best and are prepared to pay him for his skill. We treat the poor as well,' she assured her listeners, 'for Grandfather always says that healing is a gift and that we should not reserve our help only for those who can pay the most.' With a glance at the old man sitting nodding in agreement beside her, she added, 'Sometimes we charge the rich a little more than is strictly fair, but it is purely in order that we may treat those who come with empty pockets.'

'The rich can always afford it,' Benoît remarked.

'Word spreads when someone is very good at their job,' Sabin went on, 'as it was in Grandfather's case. A person who is of the highest importance in Nantes suspected the onset of certain symptoms and, because of the status of this person, they needed to find an apothecary who was both highly skilled and totally discreet. Grandfather's name was mentioned to this person and we – Grandfather and I – were summoned for a consultation.'

'When was this?' Josse asked.

'Oh – a year ago. Perhaps a little less.'

'I see.' Then you, Sabin, Josse was thinking, would have been the dominant party in the de Retz partnership, for even then, surely your old grandfather's blindness would have made diagnosis less certain.

'I examined the patient,' Sabin was saying, 'and as I did so I told Grandfather what I found. We then moved apart to speak privately together, after which we had to announce to our patient what we believed the sickness to be. Our patient was horror-struck and barely took in the measures that we proposed to keep the disease at bay.'

'You could not cure it?' de Gifford asked.

She turned to him. 'There is no cure for this particular

sickness. Our patient was in the very early stages and the symptoms were as yet mild. There was some stiffness and paralysis, some unsightly, knobbly patches on the skin. Because of the person's position, discretion was vital and Grandfather and I were sworn to secrecy. We needed to make frequent visits, especially when the treatment first started, and so a private access was arranged for us from the stable yard, up a little-used stair and along a short passage directly into the quarters inhabited by our patient. When Grandfather or I were expected, the door at the top of the stair would be unbarred so that we could slip inside without attracting attention.'

'Is this the secret that men were killed for?' de Gifford demanded; he was, Josse observed, growing impatient.

Sabin shot him an affectionate look. 'No, Gervase. Be patient; I am approaching it.' Then, pausing to take a breath, she continued. 'The victim that your dead prisoner was paid to kill lived in the same place as our patient. The assassin was clever and painstaking and he discovered what people who pass by it every single day overlooked: the entrance to the passage that leads up into the very heart of the castle, and that Grandfather and I use when we treat our patient. He made his careful plans and then the night came that he had selected to make his strike.

'But something else had happened two days previously, far away on the other side of the continent; something that removed at a stroke the reason for the murder that the assassin had been paid to do. The messenger reached him at the very last moment, when he was already about to enter the secret passage. The message was given and the assassin gave vent to his fury, cursing his master and damning him for changing his mind and calling off a perfectly good plan over which the assassin had spent so long in painstaking preparations.

'Grandfather was on his way out of the castle following a

visit to our patient and, hearing someone approach the stable entrance to the secret passage, had quickly hidden. He heard every word. Now my dear Grandfather' – she bestowed a tender look upon the old man – 'is normally adept at moving quietly and not alerting people's attention to his presence – blindness has made his hearing very sensitive, you see, and he dislikes a lot of noise, even noise that he makes himself.'

'The killer heard him?' de Gifford put in.

'Yes, yes, he heard me,' Benoît said crossly. 'I do wish you would not speak about me as if I were not here! His ears must have been as sharp as mine, for I swear that I was silent as a mouse as I stood there in terror listening to them speak of the murder that had been about to take place.'

'I expect you gave that little throat-clearing cough, Grandfather,' Sabin said gently. 'It is something of a habit of yours and, indeed, I believe that you scarcely are aware that you do it.'

'I *do not* have a little cough!' Benoît exclaimed, which seemed to prove his granddaughter's point.

'So the assassin not only knew he had been overheard but also by whom,' Josse said reflectively.

'Exactly,' Sabin confirmed. 'As soon as Grandfather came home and told me, the first thing I asked was, did they know you were there? He said no, he didn't think so, but we could not take the risk. I went straight back to our patient and made up some tale about having to set out straight away for some ingredients required in the treatment and I said we'd have to go far afield. Our patient agreed – well, I phrased it so that there was no choice – and that night Grandfather and I set out.'

'Why did you go to Troyes?' Josse asked.

'It is a town we visit quite frequently for the purchase of supplies,' Sabin replied. 'We have friends there – or rather, we *had*.'

'Did they perish in the lodging house fire?' Josse asked sympathetically.

'They did.' Sabin's tone was curt, as if she were warning Josse away from matters that caused her pain.

'And in Troyes you met Nicol Romley,' de Gifford said, 'and, afraid and far from home, you confided in him and told him of your peril.'

'It was not quite like that,' Sabin began.

But Benoît interrupted. 'No, it was me, silly old fool that I am.' He was holding Sabin's hand tightly. 'I had too much wine, my friends, and when Sabin brought Nicol to the tavern where we were eating our supper, I wanted to impress her young companion with our importance – he couldn't be allowed to think that we were just nobodies!' He shook his head sadly. 'I let my tongue run away with me and I told him why Sabin and I had left the comfort and safety of our home and were forced to act like fugitives.'

'He *was* impressed, Grandfather,' Sabin said kindly. 'You did at least achieve what you set out to do.'

'It is no consolation whatsoever, Sabin, as well you know,' he replied. 'Because of me and my blabbermouth, Nicol was killed, as was the poor merchant with whom he travelled back to England. Sabin and I have been forced to travel miles and miles, then cross the narrow seas and travel some more, and the dear Lord alone knows when we shall be able to go home again!'

'It may be safe to go home some time soon,' Sabin said softly. 'The assassin is dead.'

'Who is your patient?' Josse asked. 'I believe I have already guessed, my lady, but I wish you would tell us.'

She turned to him. 'She is the Duchess Constance of Brittany,' she said simply. 'She is in the early stages of leprosy.'

De Gifford gave a gasp, quickly suppressed, and Josse would have had a similar reaction but for the fact that he had already worked out the disease, if not the victim; he had remembered how, when he had first met Sabin, she had been distressed at being shunned as a possible carrier of the foreign pestilence. He recalled her exact words: *I know how it affects the soul to be treated as a leper.*

He had thought, even then, that the passion with which she spoke suggested that the pain came from personal experience. Now, guessing that she had great affection for her mistress, he knew he was right. Fear of how people would react if her shameful secret were to come out must make the Duchess Constance's life a veritable misery.

'I believe,' he said slowly, 'that I am now able to name the assassin's victim.' She was watching him steadily. 'I believe that he is young Arthur of Brittany, Constance's son.'

Sabin let out a short gasp. 'You are right, Sir Josse.' Then she slumped, dropped her face into her hands, and through them muttered, 'So now you know.'

De Gifford was looking puzzled. 'Arthur of Brittany,' he said slowly, 'is the posthumous child of Geoffrey, younger brother of our King Richard.'

'More relevant is that he has been named by Richard as his heir,' Josse said. His mind flying to put the puzzle together, he raced on, speaking fast. 'All the time that Richard was a captive of Duke Leopold, only Arthur stood between the throne and the man who wants it with such hunger.'

'Prince John,' breathed de Gifford.

'Aye, Prince John. They say he has been plotting with Philip of France to keep King Richard imprisoned, if not for ever then at least until the two of them have mustered the power to complete their overrunning of Richard's continental territories and are strong and powerful enough to fight anyone who tries to wrest them back. It is in Philip's interest to have his ally John on the Plantagenet throne – Philip has no wish to see Arthur there. The Bretons are not, never have been and never will be friends of the French.'

'So while Richard was out of the way – an arrangement that John has tried to make permanent – the only man between John and the throne is Arthur of Brittany?' de Gifford demanded.

'He is not a man,' Sabin put in reprovingly. 'He is but six years old.'

'The assassin would have killed a child?' De Gifford's furious incredulity showed what he thought of that.

'That is what paid killers do,' Josse said.

'But why did the assassin's master – Prince John – call him off?'

Josse had been thinking about that. 'I believe that I know,' he said, 'or, at least, that I can give a likely reason. King Richard was originally to be released on the seventeenth of January; that was the date set back in October of last year. But later it was postponed – nobody seems to know why, although many suspect that it was because Prince John and the French king put in a higher bid.'

De Gifford looked horrified. 'Then – good God, if they had succeeded, then that vast ransom that we have raised and that has caused such terrible hardship would have been all for nothing!'

'Aye,' Josse agreed, 'I do not suppose for a moment that anybody would have got their money back. But it did not happen, Gervase; our Richard has not been wasting his time while in captivity and it is ever a policy of his to befriend those who might subsequently be useful to him. He made allies of some of the empire's influential princes and it is said that it was they who persuaded Duke Leopold that it was not fitting to sell a king as if he were a side of bacon being bargained over by two old women in the market place.'

'So—' De Gifford was clearly concentrating hard. 'So the English bid was accepted?'

'I am sure it must have been,' Josse agreed. 'For the fact that

King Richard was about to be or had just been released was
surely what prompted Prince John to reverse his order to the
assassin. There is, after all, little point in having Arthur of
Brittany killed while King Richard is on the throne; with
Arthur gone, the King would simply name another heir,
and whoever he was, he still would not be Prince John.'

There was silence in the hall. Josse, greatly relieved at having
the matter exposed and thoroughly discussed, was reflecting
on the ways of kings and princes, which did not seem to take
the same account of basic right and wrong as those of ordinary
people, when Sabin's quiet voice broke across his reverie.

'What will happen to Arthur,' she said, 'when King Richard
dies?'

Nobody broke the silence; not one of us, Josse thought,
wants to think about that.

Josse was out in the courtyard preparing to set off back up to
the Abbey when he heard the sound of light footsteps. Turning, he saw Sabin hurrying towards him.

'My lady?' he said courteously.

'I came to thank you, Sir Josse, for all that you have done for
Grandfather and me,' she said breathlessly.

Nonplussed, for he couldn't think of very much that he *had*
done, Josse muttered a brief acknowledgement.

But thanks, it became clear, had not been her main motive
in following him outside. Looking up into his eyes, she said,
'Do *you* think it is safe for us to return home to Nantes?'

Her emphasis on *you* making him wonder if someone else
had suggested it wasn't, he said carefully, 'It would seem that
the threat has been removed with the death of the assassin, my
lady. There is the messenger, I know, who also knew the
secret, but we do not know that he was aware even of being
overheard, never mind by whom. The killer, I would wager,
surely would not share that knowledge with a mere messenger,

and I do not think that removal of witnesses would even occur to the man. And you have your poor patient to consider, as well as the rest of the good people of Nantes who have reason to be grateful for a first-rate apothecary.'

'Grandfather and I could work here in England, and there are other apothecaries in Nantes,' she said. He thought she sounded wistful. 'Tonbridge seems to be a nice town.'

And it has a very handsome and eligible sheriff, he thought. 'You could,' he agreed, 'and aye, Tonbridge is pleasant enough. What does your grandfather think?'

'He's tired, Sir Josse,' she said. 'He needs a long rest.'

'Then, since you seem to be asking for my opinion' – he grinned at her and her answering smile confirmed it – 'my advice is that you postpone making a decision until your grandfather is ready to travel. In the meantime . . .' He decided it was best to leave that up to her to decide; he was quite sure she would think of something.

Now her smile was radiant. 'Oh, what good advice,' she said softly. 'Thank you; I shall take it.'

With a swirl of her skirts she was off, running lightly back to the steps that led up into Gervase de Gifford's hall. Where, Josse was quite sure, the sheriff would greet her announcement that she and her grandfather would like to stay on for a while with a delight that he would find quite difficult to conceal.

'Oh, Horace,' Josse said to his horse as they rode out on to the track and he spurred him to a trot, 'what it is to be young and in love!'

His mood quickly sobered as he put the town behind him and headed for Hawkenlye Abbey. He was due to visit the Abbess and, for perhaps the first time, there was something – a very major something – that he knew he must not tell her. It was a very small reason to be grateful that she was still not herself, for the terrifying sickness had left its mark on her, as on all its victims, and she seemed to have but a hazy memory of events that happened immediately before she was taken ill.

She had remembered about Nicol Romley and vaguely recalled something about a dead merchant in Hastings; Josse had explained briefly that the killer had been apprehended and was now dead, and, most unusually for her, she had accepted this without demanding more details.

That alone – her almost total lack of curiosity – told him how unwell she had been and still was. He prayed for her whenever he thought of her, which was many times each day, and one of his chief requests was that her wonderfully agile and enquiring mind had not deserted her for ever.

Time would tell.

At least she was still alive; that, he thought as Horace climbed to the top of Castle Hill and, from long habit and without being prompted, broke into a canter, was probably quite enough for now.

23

When Josse rode down into the Vale an astonishing sight met his eyes. The monks and lay brothers were laying into the temporary infirmary with mallets, hammers, sticks and even their bare hands and already one wall was no more than a great heap of plaster and splintered wood.

Tethering Horace at a safe distance, Josse approached the work gang. Brother Saul, noticing him, gave him a grin and said, 'We're ordered to pull it down and burn it, Sir Josse. The infirmarer says it's the only way; she's had us scrubbing the floors again and again but still the smell hangs on, and when we tried to wash down the walls, quite a lot of the daub came away.' Leaning closer, he whispered, 'There were all manner of insects and small rodents in that wattle and daub, you know; it fair turned some of the younger brethren's stomachs, I don't mind telling you.'

'Not yours, Saul, I'll warrant,' Josse said, slapping him on the shoulder. 'So there's going to be a bonfire later?'

'Aye,' Saul said happily, eyes sparkling like a lad's at the prospect. 'We've only a few convalescents here now and they've been safely moved up to the main infirmary. Sister Euphemia, she's arranged a curtained-off area for them.' He leaned closer to Josse. 'The Abbess was taken up there this morning,' he confided.

'She was strong enough to be moved?' The sudden sharp anxiety took him by surprise.

'Oh, yes,' Saul said, looking at him kindly. 'She wouldn't

have been moved otherwise, don't you worry. Four of us carried her well wrapped-up on a litter, Sir Josse, and she was that light, it fair amazed me!'

Josse found that he was temporarily unable to speak, so he merely nodded.

Saul, who obviously sensed his emotion, tactfully picked up the conversation. 'Now you may well be wondering just what we're going to do without this here old place.' He waved a mallet in the direction of the fast-disappearing shelter. Josse, who had actually been wondering nothing of the sort, smiled. 'Well, there was a thatcher came in with his son,' Saul was explaining, 'and he thought – everybody thought – that the lad would surely die. But he was saved, Sir Josse! The lady Abbess, she tended the boy herself and knelt there by his bedside with his poor desperate father, and God heard her prayers and the lad got better!'

'It was indeed a miracle, Saul,' Josse said solemnly.

'The thatcher – his name's Catt, and that's him over there up on the roof hacking away at the supporting beams – well, Catt, he promised the Abbess that if God spared Pip – that's his boy – then he'd put new roofs on any of the Abbey buildings as needed them. Since our roofs are in good repair' – there was a note of pride in Saul's voice, quite justified since he it was who did most of the repairing – 'Catt said that instead he'd build us a new shelter. He says it'll be the best shelter we've ever seen, although as young Gussie pointed out, since most of us have only got the old one to judge by that's not saying a lot.' Saul chuckled.

'A good man, this Catt, so to honour his undertaking,' Josse remarked.

'Oh, aye, he's that all right.' Catt, it was clear, had impressed Brother Saul. 'Pip's up in the infirmary with the other convalescents, being as how he's still very weak, and until he's well enough to get up, Catt's going to get some of us to work with him.' Saul looked down at his sandals. 'Thought I'd offer to help,' he said bashfully. 'Got some thanks of my own to give.'

Josse knew exactly what he meant.

He found the Abbess in a bed at the end of the infirmary. He thought she looked a little better; there was a very small amount of colour in her face. He went to sit beside her on the stool that Sister Euphemia had supplied for people visiting the infirmary's most important patient.

'Hello, Sir Josse,' the Abbess said faintly. 'What have you been up to?'

There was no need to mention the visit to Tonbridge and what he had found out unless she specifically asked. She must put all her energy into getting strong and it would not help her to fret about problematic situations that were now over and done with. 'I've just come from the Vale,' he said with perfect truthfulness. 'They're getting on well with demolishing the old shelter.'

'Good,' she said.

'That fellow Catt is working like three men. No doubt he can't wait to start on the new building.'

'No doubt,' she echoed.

'The Abbey will gain something from this terrible episode, won't it? The new shelter, I mean; it's bound to be a great improvement on the old one.'

'Oh, yes.'

I am tiring her, he realised. So, making himself as comfortable as he could, he patted her hand and then contented himself with sitting quietly at her side.

Presently she went to sleep.

The infirmarer came to check on her after a while. Josse discreetly moved out of the recess and quite soon Sister Euphemia came along the room to find him.

'She is doing well, isn't she?'

The infirmarer smiled. 'She's not doing too badly, Sir Josse. She's just very, very weak and even speaking a few words tires her out.'

'That's what I thought.'

'Yes, and it was considerate of you to sit there quietly, not making her talk to you. Even though she seemed to be asleep, she may well have been aware that you were there.'

'I will be able to talk to her properly again, though, won't I?' The question burst from him before he could stop it and he was ashamed of himself; he sounded like a child frightened by the dark pleading for reassurance.

But the infirmarer understood. Taking hold of his hand, she squeezed it and simply said, 'Yes.'

He went up to the Abbey church for Nones to pray with the community. They gave thanks, in simple but very affecting terms, for the cessation of the pestilence, for the recovering patients and, in particular, for their beloved Abbess's life. Leaving the great building afterwards, Josse thought suddenly that somebody ought to go and thank Joanna.

I will, he decided.

He left the Abbey by the main gate, crossed the open ground between the track and the forest and was soon following the track that he knew led to her hut. He was not very confident of finding his way – it was a long time since he had been there – but he knew he must try. After several false trails, suddenly he had the impression that someone was guiding his steps for, every time there was a choice of tracks, he unerringly took one or another. And he seemed to know he was going in the right direction.

Soon he came to the clearing that he remembered. There was the small patch of neatly tended earth where she grew vegetables and herbs. Over there, carefully kept apart, was the special place for the plants which, touched or nibbled at by the unwary, would have effects that, far from curing the hurts and ills of animals or humans, would actually do the reverse.

The hut stood over to one side and it was quite difficult to make out; it was as if it had been deliberately camouflaged to keep it secret from curious eyes. He found that he could see it better if he did not look straight at it but observed it out of the corner of his eye.

Just as he was pondering on this strange fact he heard voices. A woman's voice, then a child's happy laugh. The last was such a happy, musical sound and it put him in mind of something . . . or someone . . .

Then, as if she had felt his presence, the door of the hut opened just enough to allow Joanna to emerge. She closed it carefully behind her and walked slowly across the clearing until she stood before Josse.

So many things flashed through his mind. But he had come for just one reason. 'Thank you, Joanna,' he said, 'for saving the Abbess Helewise's life.'

Joanna watched him steadily for some time. Then she said, 'She was not ready to go on.'

'Perhaps not, but she'd have gone, ready or not, had you not intervened. Your skill saved her, and—'

'Not my skill alone,' Joanna interrupted. She paused as if trying to decide whether or not to speak. Then she said, 'Your magic jewel played its part.'

Completely taken aback, he said, 'You used the Eye of Jerusalem?' Somehow he had not expected that.

'Yes. Tiphaine told me that some of the nuns had tried and so had you. They – I imagine they thought it was worthwhile allowing me to have a go.'

'With success,' he said.

'It is an object of power,' she said simply. 'Very old, extremely potent.'

'I was told that one day a female of my blood would use it and be the first person to extract its full potential,' he said. 'That was why I gave it to the Abbess; I was afraid to put such an alarming burden on the girl children of my brothers.'

'It is not an alarming burden in the right hands,' she said calmly. 'It is likely that your instant reaction to keep it well away from your nieces means that theirs are not the right hands.'

'No, there's no magic in my family!' He spoke lightly, trying to alleviate the growing gravity that he sensed in the mood between them.

'There is, Josse.' Her voice was low, strangely compelling. 'You have an ancestor, a forebear of your mother's, whom we recognise as one of our Great Ones.'

'I—' Astounded, he did not know what to say. 'I am not sure that I want to know about her,' he muttered.

She shrugged. 'That is your choice.' But the smile around the corners of her mouth suggested that she was well aware that he did; was avid, in fact, for details, although he was never going to admit it.

He tore his mind away from his own bloodline. 'You are a Great One now, Joanna,' he said.

'No!' Quickly qualifying the denial, she said, 'I have only just begun, Josse.'

'But I can feel the power in you.'

'Oh, the power is there, although we are taught that we are but channels through which it passes to do its work. That is certainly the way with such healing skills as I possess.'

'They sufficed for the Abbess,' Josse said.

Joanna was watching him and he saw a question in her eyes. Abruptly she spoke. 'They – Josse, I had been given to understand that there would be two people for me to heal at Hawkenlye and the night I sat with the Abbess Helewise, I left some of the especially potent water for one of the nursing nuns to give to a man lying in a bed near to the Abbess's. I – well, I wondered if you could tell me what happened to him?'

'He died, Joanna,' Josse said softly.

Her face fell. 'Oh. I see.' Now she was frowning, clearly puzzled.

'But I think you did save him, for all that,' Josse went on.

'What do you mean?'

'Joanna, he had a great deal on his conscience. Your healing talent gave him the precious time to make his peace so that he died shriven of his sins. So, in a way, although you did not heal him in this life, you gave him hope in the next.' She did not speak, merely sat hanging her head. 'Or do your people not believe in the promise of eternal life?'

Now she looked up at him and she was smiling faintly. 'Oh, yes, Josse. In our own way we certainly do.' She nodded slowly. 'Thank you for that. Now I think I understand.'

There was silence for several moments. Then, as if she were bracing herself to raise some other matter, a flash of emotion crossed her impassive face and she said, 'Josse, they told me something while I was away on my travels. Do you remember what I told you about my parents?'

'Er – you told me very little. Your father was a son of a minor branch of the de Courtenay family. Your mother, you said, was rather weak and not in the best of health.'

Joanna smiled. 'That sums the poor soul up very well.' Then: 'She wasn't my mother.'

'Your people told you that? But how on earth did they know?'

'They knew about me long before I was aware of them. My parents wanted children, as most married couples do, and my elder brother was born sickly and he died in infancy.'

'Aye, you told me that.'

'They tried time after time for another baby but without success. Then they had the idea that my father might beget a

child on someone else and bring him or her up as their own.
There was a woman they knew whom they admired and
trusted. Although mature, she was still of childbearing age
and she was fit, strong and intelligent. They approached her.'

'Was she not insulted, to have friends ask her such a thing?'

'No, Josse. She wasn't exactly a friend; she worked for my
mother's uncle and his wife.'

'The people who left you the manor house in the woods?'

'Yes.'

He was beginning to understand. 'Go on.'

'The woman was one of ours; one of the best, or so they tell
me. She had foreseen the approach from my father; she had
foreseen my birth and what I would become. She *made* him
have the idea, Josse, because she knew it all had to happen so
that – so that I would be born. My father lay with her just once
and I was conceived. When I was born the people whom I
believed to be my parents took me in, although the woman was
always there to keep an eye on me. She was my wet nurse and
she remained a very important part of my life all through my
childhood.'

She paused, eyes looking out across the clearing to the
pond, now rimmed with a thin fringe of ice. 'She died for me,
Josse. Here in this very place, she was tortured to make her
reveal my whereabouts but she would not tell. Then her head
was pushed under the water and she drowned.'

Then Joanna was in his arms, the sweet sensation accompanied by the bitterness of her dry sobs. Smoothing the
braided hair, he said, 'I know, my love, I know. I saw her.'

She pulled away from him, staring up into his face. 'You –
yes! Of course you did!'

'She was brave and she very obviously loved you very
much,' he said, trying to comfort her.

'I just wish,' Joanna cried, 'that I had known she was my
mother!'

'*She* knew,' he said.

'Yes. *Yes.*' Joanna was standing apart from him again, brushing away her tears. Giving him a brave attempt at a smile, she said, 'To have Mag Hobson as my mother was very special and being her daughter remains true, I know, even thought I was not aware of it until very recently.' She took a shaking breath. Then: 'Josse, because I know what it feels like not to know that someone very wonderful is one's parent, there's something I must show you.'

She grabbed his hand and strode away towards the hut, marching fast as if she had to act quickly before she changed her mind. She opened the door wide, then gave Josse a nudge and said, 'Go in.'

He stepped cautiously into the hut. It was quite dark inside; it was only afternoon and as yet, no candle flame had been lit to brighten the corners of the little room and the small fire had died down to golden embers.

On the floor by the hearth sat a child. Dark-haired, very pretty, she was playing with a little figure made of sticks that was dressed in miniature garments made of sacking and wool. She looked up at Josse and he saw his father's eyes gazing up at him with a most interested expression from under the thick, glossy hair.

He knew then why the sound of this child's laughter had been familiar; the little girl laughed as musically as her grand-mother had done.

'She's mine?' His voice was all but inaudible.

'Yes.'

'You did not think to tell me you carried my child?'

'Josse, I – no.'

'But you—'

'Kneel down beside her,' she whispered. 'Make friends with her. Her name's Meggie.'

Josse crouched, knelt and finally sat on the clean-swept floor of the hut. He stared at his daughter and her dark eyes did not look away. 'Hello, Meggie,' he said gently. 'What have you got there?'

Trustingly she held out her stick doll. 'She's very pretty,' he said. 'What is she called?'

'Ba'ee,' the child said promptly.

'Baby? Oh, I see. Your little baby.'

'Ba'ee,' the child agreed. She put the doll into Josse's large hands and he jiggled it up and down as if to soothe it to sleep. Then he pretended to drop it, catching it at the last minute with a great show of relief and his daughter laughed in delight. Taking the stick doll back again, she thumped its head on the floor a couple of times then gave it back to Josse, who kissed the stuffed head better.

Meggie seemed to like that. She clambered on to Josse's legs, clutched at a fold of his tunic to lever herself up and, when she could reach his face, gave him a kiss just like the one he had given the doll.

Very slowly he put his arms around her. She snuggled against him as if she had known him all her life.

For the remainder of the day, until it was time for Meggie's bedtime, Josse and his daughter were not parted for a single moment. He let her lead him outside, where she showed him how she could leap across the stepping stones that allowed Joanna to cross the little stream without getting her feet wet. Meggie made Josse do it and then he watched her while she did it another eleven times. Then she showed him her favourite places in her small domain, all the while babbling away in her own infant language in which Josse recognised about one word in ten.

Joanna came to stand beside him as he watched Meggie throwing stones into the shallow, rushing water of the stream. 'She will be talking fluently soon,' she said.

'She's doing that now.'

Joanna smiled. 'I meant that soon she'll be talking comprehensibly.'

'I rather like the nonsense.'

There was a rather awkward pause. 'Josse,' Joanna began, 'I should explain—'

But Meggie needed her father's help to lift a heavy stone and, with a haste born out of relief, for he was not yet ready to talk to Joanna in any depth, Josse hurried to assist.

Later Joanna made a simple supper for the child and she ate it sitting on Josse's lap, with him spooning the thick soup into her mouth. Joanna watched indulgently; Meggie was quite capable of feeding herself if one did not object to quite a lot of mess. Then Josse washed the child's face and hands in water that had been warmed a little over the fire and Joanna stripped the child down to her shift for bed.

Josse tucked her up in the covers that were neatly folded on top of the sleeping platform's straw mattress. Meggie put her thumb in her mouth and around it she said, 'Sto'y.'

'*Story?*' Josse echoed, as if it were the most outlandish request in the world. Meggie laughed.

'Once-upon-a-time-there-was-a-little-girl-called-Meggie-and-she-went-to-sleep-the-end,' Josse said very quickly.

Meggie laughed again, although Josse thought it was more at his sudden burst of rapid speech than because she understood what he had said. 'Sto'y,' she repeated firmly.

So he began again.

'There was once a man called Geoffroi,' he said softly, 'and he went a very long way away to fight in a great battle in a foreign land. There he saved the life of a little princeling and as a reward the boy's grandfather gave him a very precious jewel. This jewel was deep blue, like the summer sky at the end of the day, and it was set in a very old coin that was made of solid gold . . .'

He heard Joanna give a faint gasp from where she was sitting on the floor behind him. Smiling to himself, he proceeded to tell his daughter the old family tale that his own father used to tell him of the Eye of Jerusalem and how it came into the family. For she is my family, he thought as the tale wound to its conclusion; she is as much the grandchild of my parents as those beloved nephews and nieces in Acquin.

Meggie had been drowsy even when she was put to bed and she was already asleep when Josse kissed her goodnight and returned to sit down beside Joanna.

'I don't think she heard the end of the story,' he said softly. 'Not that she'd have understood the part she did hear.'

'Oh, I shouldn't be so sure,' Joanna replied. 'But, with your permission, I'll tell her the story again, many times. It is important that she knows it.'

'Because the Eye is her inheritance,' he said. 'Aye. I had worked that out for myself.' It was not the only thing he had worked out; between the shock of being presented with his daughter and the opportunity to talk about it, he had had time for a great deal of thinking.

There was a pause, heavy with unspoken things.

Then Joanna said, 'It was Meggie who held the Eye into the water.'

'I thought it might have been.'

As if she felt the need to defend herself, Joanna hurried on, 'They'd asked me before, Josse, and I refused. Even when they told me about the prophecy and I knew it must mean Meggie, I wouldn't let her do it. I was afraid for her safety, with a fatal sickness affecting the Abbey and those within it. But beyond that, I was afraid of seeing you again.'

She paused as if to allow him space to comment, but he was not ready yet. 'Go on.'

'It wasn't that I didn't want to see you; it was that I felt I'd managed to make my life without you and I guessed you had done the same. Seeing each other would only open old wounds.'

'And has it?'

She turned her eyes to his. Her eyes were much darker than her daughter's – almost black in the dim light – and he felt a surge of unexpected pleasure at this confirmation that Meggie's eyes were indeed like his father's and not like Joanna's. There will always be something of the d'Acquins in her, he thought, whatever her life brings to her.

But then Joanna said very quietly, 'Of course it has.'

Hastening away from treacherous ground, Josse said, 'I asked you earlier why you did not tell me that you were pregnant with her but now I think I know. Joanna, you do not want to live the life that I lead, do you? Even if I promised you all the freedom you needed, you were not born to be somebody's wife.'

She reached out and took his hand, pressing it to her face. 'No, Josse. I know now what I was born for and it isn't that. But don't let that fact make you think I do not love you for, in my way, I certainly do. Meggie was conceived in love and now, seeing you again, I realise that love is still there.'

Was it in him too? He watched her, head bent over his hand, and the answer soon came. 'As is mine for you,' he said gently. 'What, then, are we to do?'

She straightened up and edged closer to him and he put his arms round her. 'I may not want to share your life as your wife,' she said tentatively – perhaps, he thought with a wry smile, she's just realised that I haven't in fact asked her to marry me; not recently, anyway – 'but that doesn't mean I never want to see you again.'

'I'm glad. I should not like to think that this was the last time.'

'Apart from our feelings for each other, there's Meggie,' she went on. 'She has a father as well as a mother and it is your right, if you so choose, to influence her upbringing.'

'I don't know.' Josse frowned. 'What am I and what have I to offer her, against the world you now occupy? You've just told me you're the daughter of one of your people's most powerful women and that your birth, and presumably Meggie's, were foreseen because the child was somehow predicted.'

'That is how I understand it, yes.'

'Then, Joanna, what influence can a man like me have on such a one as she?'

'Do not underrate yourself, Josse. If Meggie's birth was foreseen, then what happened between us that led to her conception was also part of the prediction.'

It was a shock. His mind instinctively tried to reject the thought that his role in the advent of this wonder child had been preordained. He was about to ask *why me?* but, deciding it would sound too like an invitation for her to list his virtues – and *that* would be a short list – he didn't.

It was all too much to take in.

As if she realised this – which would not surprise him as she seemed to pick up virtually everything else – she said, 'Josse, there's no doubt that Meggie has some special touch. The Eye changed the water instantly and we all saw it. And the charged water did seem to possess a unique healing power.'

'The Abbess is doing well,' he said, aware that his thoughts had gone off at a tangent. 'But then the water was only the second form of treatment; you had already brought her back.'

'You asked me to save her life,' Joanna said gently. 'I could not refuse. Not only for her sake – and I know full well she is a good woman – but also for yours. Josse, you would be lost without her.'

'I did nearly lose her,' he mused. For a dangerous moment he allowed himself to imagine life without her. He'd have gone back to New Winnowlands, probably returned to Hawkenlye now and again, but with the Abbess in her grave every inch of the place would have been nothing but an agonising reminder that she was no longer there.

The cumulative emotional shocks of the recent past seemed to gather themselves together and rush at him. He felt Joanna's compassion wrap around him like a warm, soft blanket. It was the easiest thing in the world to drop his head into her lap and weep.

Later, lying side by side beneath the covers up on the sleeping platform, he said, 'Joanna, this is what I suggest. I will return to my life at New Winnowlands' – such as it is, he almost added – 'and you, naturally, will pursue the path that has been set for you, developing your healing skills and guiding Meggie's steps along her own destined path. I trust you to protect her and do your best for her; I do not think you would allow any harm to come to her.'

'I won't,' Joanna said quickly.

'With your permission, I will visit you here from time to time. If you are away or do not want to see me, then I'm quite sure you will find a way to ensure that I do not find you.'

It sounded hard and she must have thought so too. 'I would only do that if there were some pressing reason,' she replied. 'There are certain times of the year when we—'

'Don't tell me,' he said swiftly. He did not think he could bear to know the details of this strange other life that Joanna lived and into which his only child had been born.

'Very well.' She hesitated. 'It is – beneficial, Josse. The power is frightening sometimes but nobody is made to handle it before they are ready.'

'A sixteen-month-old child may wield a magical healing stone, however.'

It was unkind and he immediately regretted it. But she said evenly, 'Meggie is a special case.' Then, quickly: 'But you have my word that I will never allow her to do anything that I believe to be beyond her.'

And with that, he realised, he would have to be satisfied.

They lay in each other's arms. He very much wanted to make love to her – of course he did – but his child lay beside him and it did not seem right. Eventually he slept.

He left her early in the morning while Meggie was still asleep. Quickly, with no words of farewell and no turning back. He hurried through the forest, just waking to the first light of the new day, and was back at the Abbey in time for Prime.

Then he went straight to the infirmary and took his seat on the stool by the Abbess's bed. She was asleep but that was where he needed to be.

When she's better I'll tell her, he resolved. I'll tell her that when we were first thrown together, Joanna and I were lovers and that she conceived my child. I'll describe Meggie to her and I'll tell her how beautiful my daughter is. I might even tell her that it was Meggie's strange power that made the Eye of Jerusalem work as it was intended to.

He watched the Abbess's sleeping face. With only the simple cap in place of her coif and veil, she looked like any other woman and it was sometimes quite difficult to recall that she was far from being that.

Joanna.

Helewise.

Meggie.

On the other hand, he thought with a grin, maybe I won't tell her anything at all.

POSTSCRIPT

Hawkenlye Abbey 27th March 1194

The King was back.

News came quite quickly to the Abbey because Josse had been involved in the triumphal receptions prepared for Richard at Rochester and Canterbury, culminating in the state entry into London on 23rd March.

Knowing that everyone within and on the fringes of the Hawkenlye community would be avid to know the latest news, Josse made sure to make frequent return visits to the Abbey. The King, he reported, looked fit and well; Queen Eleanor looked happy but very tired. Along every mile of the King's progression from Sandwich, where his party had landed on 12th March, people lined the streets and cheered; it was a fine display of wholehearted welcome for a returning monarch.

But, as Josse confided in the Abbess, now sitting up in bed and quite clearly desperate to be allowed up, the joyful celebratory mood had not in truth come about spontaneously. It had been a major part of Josse's job – and that of his companions also summoned to assist in the arrangements for the homecoming – to whip up a bit of enthusiasm in a cynical population among whom the prevailing mood was resentment at the terrible privations forced upon them by the ransom demands.

However, a king was a king and a magnificient, colourful spectacle had its own way of raising the spirits. Cheering was apparently even more infectious than the foreign pestilence that had so recently devastated Hawkenlye and, in the end, Josse was quite sure that King Richard must have believed his people were overjoyed to see him back and reckoned the unbelievably high price they had had to pay for him was money well spent.

On the night of 23rd March, Josse arrived at the Abbey with incredible news. The King and his mother were to embark on a round of visits to abbeys where there would be services of appreciation for Richard's safe return and where the King would take the opportunity of thanking the religious communities that had prayed so hard for his delivery. He was to visit St Albans, Bury St Edmunds and . . . Hawkenlye.

Josse had half-feared to deliver the announcement since he was worried by what such anxious excitement would do to the convalescent Abbess. But he had reckoned without her calm confidence; on expressing the careful sentiment that she must be sure not to overtire herself, she said, 'Sir Josse, Hawkenlye Abbey has entertained royalty before. Queen Eleanor has been a frequent visitor and, as I am quite sure you will recall, Prince John also stayed with us not so many years ago. We shall do our best to make the King welcome and that will have to suffice.'

Her recent close brush with death, he reflected ruefully, seemed to have increased her serenity; as the day of the visit approached, he wished he had her steely nerves.

The morning of 27th March dawned bright and dry. The Abbey looked as if every inch had been scrubbed, buffed and polished. The new building in the Vale was completed just in time; Catt had done a magnificent job. It was a long, low building, simply but stoutly made, and Catt had been meticulous in the details so that the room was well insulated and would be practical and easy to keep clean. He had finished it off with straw thatch; the roof was a joy to behold.

Many of those who had been cured of the sickness either remained at or came back to the Abbey to attend the great service of thanksgiving. The King might not know they'd had a narrow escape, they reasoned, and he might be under the impression that the thanks were for his release. But it didn't matter, the people reasoned, because *they* knew and – much more importantly – so did God that they were really giving thanks for their own deliverance.

Some families had been torn apart by the sickness, but, as compensation, in some cases new families had been formed. A strong young woman who had brought in and lost her father adopted an orphaned child and a crippled boy. A young merchant took pity on a widowed bride and promised to take care of her. When Waldo was eventually able to take his little brother and his baby niece back home to the house in Hastings, Catt had undertaken to make sure the children got safely home. And Catt himself appeared to cast rather a lot of glances in the direction of the strong young woman . . .

Nobody, it seemed, would be able to forget the brush with death; those who survived would perhaps find life the sweeter for having come close to losing it.

The arrival of the King was a moment that none who witnessed it ever forgot. He was magnificently dressed in white trimmed with scarlet and rode a fine black horse. Queen Eleanor, veiled against the dust of the roads, wore a dark cloak over a gown as golden as summer sunshine. Mother and son alike glittered with fine jewels; it was as if the King were stating plainly that he might have suffered the ignominy of imprisonment but look, everyone, here he was as strong, splendid, regal and rich as ever.

The thanksgiving service went on for a long time. Josse

stood in his place among the King's men watching the Abbess in an agony of anxiety; she had only got out of bed two days ago and he was so afraid that today would prove too much for her. But Sister Euphemia stood on one side of her and Sister Tiphaine the other; they could be trusted, he told himself, not to let harm come to her.

The service was followed by a feast, modest in comparison to what the King must surely be used to but, as the Abbess had calmly said, the best that the community could offer. The King seemed satisfied; he was as usual, Josse observed, too busy talking to pay much attention to his food but he did seem to enjoy the wine.

The King and Queen Eleanor were escorted down to the Vale to look at the new building. The King exclaimed on the magnificent thatched roof and Catt was commanded to step forward as the craftsman who had made it. Watching him, Josse was struck with the dignity of the man; not in the least overawed, he answered the King's questions briefly and politely with no hint of nerves.

He's rightly proud of his work, Josse thought. And probably Catt, like the Abbess, had been too deeply affected by the recent past to be unduly discommoded by the presence of royalty.

And I bet, Josse concluded, that King Richard can't lay thatch to save his life . . .

The wonderful day came to an end; the royal party rode off to seek out their night's lodgings down in Tonbridge Castle and peace descended.

Josse would be leaving too the next morning; he was part of the escort that would see the King and Queen Eleanor safely up to Nottingham, where they were to hold a meeting of the Great Council.

'Will you come back and tell us what transpires?' the Abbess asked as he took his leave of her in the morning.

'Aye, that I will,' he agreed. 'Although I do think, my lady, that I should first pay a visit to New Winnowlands; I have been absent for a long time.'

'Of course,' she agreed. 'Just as long as I know that you won't desert us, Sir Josse.'

Oh, I won't do that, he thought as he rode away. Not now I know that *every* piece of my heart is now held captive here.

Turning his thoughts to the exalted company in which he would spend the next few days, he kicked Horace and cantered off on the road to Tonbridge.

There is no historical evidence to suggest that John sent an assassin to kill Arthur of Brittany in the early months of 1194 although, since Richard had nominated Arthur as his heir, John must certainly have viewed the boy as an obstacle between himself and the throne that would otherwise be his if Richard were to be prevented from regaining his liberty.

However, Arthur continued to be a provocation to John after the latter was crowned king. He made a botched attempt to wrest John's territories in western France from him, during which he committed the impertinent folly of trying to hold his grandmother Eleanor hostage in the castle of Mirebeau, in Anjou, and use her for bartering purposes. In the devastatingly efficient revenge assault on Mirebeau, Eleanor was released unharmed and taken away to safety; Arthur was captured. John's magnates recommended maiming the young man, who was now about fifteen years old, in such a way that he was 'deprived of his eyes and genitals' and thus rendered unfit to beget any offspring who might follow him into treachery. Although this monstrous suggestion was not carried out, Arthur did not reappear and rumours began to circulate that he was dead.

Arthur's true fate is not recorded. One tale – which achieved widespread credibility at the time – was that in Rouen at Easter 1203 John got drunk and, his frustration finally getting the better of him, killed Arthur with his own hands and, having weighted the body with a stone, slung it into the Seine.

Whether or not this version is accurate, it remains true that Arthur was never seen again after Easter 1203. It was widely believed to be tantamount to suicide to mention the lad's name, especially in the same breath as that of the king, which pretty much speaks for itself.